NEW ESSAYS ON CANADIAN THEATRE
VOLUME SIX

PERFORMING INDIGENEITY

NEW ESSAYS ON CANADIAN THEATRE
VOLUME SIX

PERFORMING INDIGENEITY
EDITED BY YVETTE NOLAN AND RIC KNOWLES

PLAYWRIGHTS CANADA PRESS
TORONTO

Performing Indigeneity © 2016 by Yvette Nolan and Ric Knowles
All essays herein are copyright © 2016 by their respective authors

First edition: May 2016
Printed and bound in Canada by Marquis Book Printing, Montreal

PLAYWRIGHTS
CANADA PRESS

Playwrights Canada Press
202-269 Richmond Street West, Toronto, ON M5V 1X1
416.703.0013 :: info@playwrightscanada.com :: playwrightscanada.com

Cover photos of Muriel Miguel and of PJ Prudat and Derek Garza © Nir Bareket
Cover design by Leon Aureus

LIBRARY AND ARCHIVES CANADA CATALOGUING IN PUBLICATION
Performing indigeneity / edited by Yvette Nolan and Ric Knowles. -- First edition.

(New essays on Canadian theatre ; v. 6)
Includes bibliographical references and index.
ISBN 978-1-77091-537-4 (paperback)

     1. Canadian drama--Native authors--History and criticism. 2. Native peoples in
literature. 3. Native theater--Canada. I. Nolan, Yvette, editor II. Knowles, Ric, 1950-,
editor III. Series: New essays on Canadian theatre; v. 6

PS8089.5.I6P37 2016   C812.009'897   C2016-900223-3

We acknowledge the financial support of the Canada Council for the Arts, the Ontario
Arts Council (OAC), the Ontario Media Development Corporation, and the Government
of Canada through the Canada Book Fund for our publishing activities.

Canada Council Conseil des arts
for the Arts   du Canada

ONTARIO ARTS COUNCIL
CONSEIL DES ARTS DE L'ONTARIO

an Ontario government agency
un organisme du gouvernement de l'Ontario

Ontario

Ontario Media Development
Corporation

To
Philip and Christine

CONTENTS

GENERAL EDITOR'S PREFACE
by Ric Knowles   V

ACKNOWLEDGEMENTS   IX

FYRST, AN INTRODUCTION
by Yvette Nolan   1

WELCOMING SOVEREIGNTY
by Dylan Robinson   5

SOVEREIGN PROCLAMATIONS OF THE TWENTY-FIRST CENTURY:
SCRIPTING SURVIVANCE THROUGH THE LANGUAGE OF SOFT POWER
by Jill Carter   33

KIPPMOOJIKEWIN: THE THINGS WE CARRY WITH US
by Marrie Mumford   66

THE SEARCH FOR SPIRITUAL TRANSFORMATION IN CONTEMPORARY
THEATRE PRACTICE
by Jani Lauzon   87

ON THE TRAIL OF NATIVE THEATRE
by Carol Greyeyes   98

SAINTS AND STRANGERS: A RAPPROCHEMENT FOR INDIGENOUS
PERFORMANCE
by Michael Greyeyes   114

ARTHOME
by Tara Beagan   124

THANKSGIVING
    by Falen Johnson   131

BRINGING FORTH THE SACRED, SPEAKING FOR THE SPIRITS: A BRIEF BRAID
    by Andréa Ledding   136

SPINE OF THE MOTHER: MOVING MOUNTAINS . . . CREATING DANCE
    by Starr Muranko   147

A COMEDIC HISTORY OF ABORIGINAL PROPORTIONS
    by Drew Hayden Taylor   158

NATIVE EARTH PERFORMING ARTS'S DEATH OF A CHIEF:
UNEARTHING SHAKESPEARE'S JULIUS CAESAR
    by Jason Woodman Simmonds   167

"THAT'S WHO THE STORIES ARE ABOUT": CREE WAYS OF KNOWING IN
KENT MONKMAN'S MISS CHIEF: JUSTICE OF THE PIECE
    by June Scudeler   197

(RE)ANIMATING THE (UN)DEAD
    by Michelle La Flamme   214

TRICKSTERS AND CREATURES AND GHOSTS, HO-LEE!
INTIMATIONS/IMITATIONS OF THE SACRED
    by Daniel David Moses   246

#MYRECONCILIATIONINCLUDES . . . JUST DANCE!
    by David Geary   263

SHE BEGINS TO MOVE
    by Michelle Olson   271

WORKS CITED   285
NOTES ON CONTRIBUTORS   299
INDEX   309

GENERAL EDITOR'S PREFACE
RIC KNOWLES

New Essays on Canadian Theatre (NECT) is a book series designed to complement and replace the series Critical Perspectives on Canadian Theatre in English (CPCTE), which published its last three of twenty-one volumes in 2011. CPCTE was primarily a reprint series, with each volume designed to represent the critical history since the 1970s of a particular topic within the broader field of Canadian theatre studies. Most volumes, however, also included essays specially commissioned to fill gaps in the coverage of their respective topics and to bring the books up to the moment. These new essays, some of them scholarly prize winners, were often among the volumes' most powerful, approaching the field and the discipline from important new perspectives, regularly from those of minoritized and other under-represented communities.

NECT consists entirely of newly commissioned essays, and the volumes themselves are designed to fill what I perceive to be gaps in the critical record, often, once again, taking new approaches, often, again, from minoritized and under-represented perspectives, and in almost every case introducing topics that have not received book-length coverage. NECT volume topics may range as broadly as did those of CPCTE, from the work of an individual playwright to that of a whole community, however defined, and they are designed at once to follow, lead, and instantiate new and emerging developments in the field. Volume editors and their contributors are scholars, artists, and artist-scholars who are doing some of the most exciting and innovative work in Canadian theatre and Canadian theatre studies.

Like those published in CPCTE but more systematically, NECT volumes complement the catalogues of Canada's major drama publishers: each volume serves as a companion piece either to an already existing anthology or to one published contemporaneously with it, often by the editors of the NECT volumes themselves. As a package, NECT and their companion volumes serve as ideal introductions to a field, or indeed as ready-made reading lists for Canadian theatre courses in these topic areas.

But generating new materials and entirely new fields of study takes time, and while CPCTE published at the heady pace of three volumes per year, the production of NECT is more leisurely with, initially at least, only one volume launched each spring, beginning in 2011. The first of these was *Asian Canadian Theatre*, edited by Nina Lee Aquino and myself and designed to ride the tide of a flurry of activity in the first decade of the twenty-first century among Asian Canadian theatre artists. It complements Nina Lee Aquino's two-volume anthology *Love + Relasianships*, published by Playwrights Canada Press in 2009. The second, *New Canadian Realisms*, edited by Roberta Barker and Kim Solga, dealt with a wholesale revisioning of realism in Canada, and was published alongside the companion anthology *New Canadian Realisms: Eight Plays*, also edited by Barker and Solga. The third, *Latina/o Canadian Theatre and Performance*, together with its companion anthology *Fronteras Vivientes: Eight Latina/o Canadian Plays*, both edited by Natalie Alvarez, launched an exciting and vibrant new sub-field within the disciplines of Canadian Theatre Studies and Latina/o Studies more broadly. The fourth, *Theatres of Affect*, with its companion six-play anthology *Once More, With Feeling*, both edited by Erin Hurley, introduced to Canadian theatre scholarship and teaching the rich approach to theatre that is involved in taking feeling seriously. The fifth volume, edited by Richie Wilcox, aimed to correct the egregious neglect within scholarship of the much anthologized and widely produced work of Daniel MacIvor.

It is enormously satisfying that so many of these volumes have been recognized with awards for their editors, contributors, or both; a sign, I believe, of the tremendous health of a field of study that is still young.

The current volume, the final in the series under my general editorship, returns to the subject of the first volume of the CPCTE series, *Aboriginal Drama and Theatre*, edited by Rob Appleford, and appropriately comes full circle in its focus on *Performing Indigeneity.* Co-edited and introduced by Yvette Nolan (Algonquin), it features an all-Indigenous list of contributors and complements Playwrights Canada Press's two-volume anthology *Staging Coyote's Dream.*

It has been exciting for me to see the development of Canadian theatre criticism since its inception as an academic discipline in the mid-1970s, when the first academic courses on the subject were offered and the first journals founded, together with the then Association for Canadian Theatre History (now the Canadian Association for Theatre Research)—the first and only scholarly association to specialize in Canadian theatre. It was also very satisfying to serve as founder and general editor for the CPCTE series that tracked that development and made some of its key writings widely available and key critical histories and genealogies visible. I am equally excited by the contributions that have been made by the NECT series, and look forward to it flourishing under the editorship of Roberta Barker.

ACKNOWLEDGEMENTS

The editors would like to acknowledge the unfailing support and patience of Annie Gibson and Blake Sproule at Playwrights Canada Press and the patience and persistence of all of the contributors in meeting our deadlines, answering our questions, and dealing with our editorial intrusions into their lives. And we would like to thank our ever-supportive partners, Philip Adams and Christine Bold, to whom this book is dedicated.

FYRST, AN INTRODUCTION
YVETTE NOLAN

"First" is a complicated word, a complicated idea. The etymological origins of the word is the Old English *fyrst*, which means "foremost." First and foremost: it evokes visions of prizes, of champions, of competitions and races. It implies that this thing is best, because of its position as first. "First" is somewhat problematic in terms of Indigenous world views, where we work in circle, where humility demands that none of us is more important than the others, not more important than the fish or the birds or the animals or the water or the trees. Who can be first in a circle?

This book is something of a first, in that all the writers who have contributed are Indigenous scholars, artists, and academics. There have been collections before about Indigenous theatre—Rob Appleford's 2005 *Aboriginal Drama and Theatre* in the Critical Perspectives on Canadian Theatre in English series has been cited for a decade—but as far as we can tell, this is the first volume of newly commissioned pieces about Indigenous performance in which all of the writers are Indigenous.

The writers who have contributed to this collection hail from what the government currently calls First Nations, although they themselves identify as Cree, as Mohawk, Creek, Ntlakapamux, Stó:lō, and many other nations. Several of the contributors' roots reach back to the First Nations; they identify as Métis, the long-time companion in the catchment term of Aboriginal, or the current phrase in usage, "First Nations, Inuit, and Métis."

We invited scholars to contribute essays on some aspect of Indigenous performance, artists to contribute statements on whatever they felt was important to them as theatre creators. As with any good Indigenous assembly, the members were free to speak about what they wished, and we were gifted with the opportunity to listen. As with any good assembly of like-minded members, themes and observations often dovetail and echo each other. So it was with this assembly; as the chapters started arriving we began to see certain themes emerging.

One of the recurring themes is training, which many authors addressed in their pieces, some overtly, some less directly. Michael Greyeyes writes about the need for a training institution that serves Indigenous performance companies that have emerged in the last decade. Jani Lauzon unwittingly bolsters Michael's argument, tracing her own path and tracking how she acquired training, creating a practice that is assembled from the teachings of everyone from an early ballet teacher to a Japanese artist to an Odawa Elder to the women of Spiderwoman Theater.

Sometimes training is addressed more incidentally. Marrie Mumford's chronicle of her journey from Redcliff, Alberta, to Nozhem First Peoples Performance Space at Trent University is also a chronicle of training, touching on Brandeis University, Morris Carnovsky, Native Earth Performing Arts, Tomson Highway. Similarly, Carol Greyeyes's "On the Trail of Native Theatre" is both a reflection of her own path and an acknowledgement of how she acquired training over the decades, going from training at the University of Saskatchewan to heading up, some thirty years later, the Aboriginal Theatre Program, called *wîchêhtowin*, in the Department of Drama at the same university.

Many of the artists in these pages articulate a connection between the work they do and their cultural identities. Falen Johnson finds her way to ceremony through her work in the theatre, coming the long way round to her culture, even though she grew up in her community on Six Nations. Andréa Ledding sorts through the entrails of identity as a Métis artist, proud of all her roots—"Irish, Scandinavian, Michif (Métis), French, Haudenosaunee (Mohawk), Nehiyaw (Cree)"—but consistently identified as Métis "because in this world you can only be one thing." Drew Hayden Taylor writes about how and why he has committed much of his career to "exploring, celebrating, and sharing the Aboriginal sense of humour."

Until now, there has been little writing by Indigenous writers about the history of Indigenous theatre in this country. Some of that history is documented in these pages, a collateral benefit.

If you stand back and look at the pieces, you can see how they weave together. Certain names appear over and over: Tomson Highway and *The Rez Sisters*; James Buller, who is largely credited with the beginning of a Native theatre in this country; Maria Campbell and the play she created with Linda Griffiths, *Jessica*; René Highway; Larry Lewis. The writing of these chapters is one way of making manifest kippmoojikewin, the things we carry with us, as noted by Marrie Mumford citing Leanne Simpson, one way of honouring our teachers and our artistic ancestors.

Not surprisingly, the training of Indigenous artists and the development of Indigenous theatre seem to go hand in hand; the artists accumulate the skills and tools and they want to apply them to the creation of work, which in turn leads to a body of work, which leads to the establishment of institutions, such as Native Earth Performing Arts, De-ba-jeh-mu-jig Theatre (now Debajehmujig Storytellers), the Centre for Indigenous Theatre.

Another theme running through these chapters is that of claiming—or reclaiming—space, literal and metaphoric. Jason Woodman Simmonds looks at how the Native Earth adaptation of *Julius Caesar* claimed both territory, produced as it was at the National Arts Centre, and conceptual space, occupied by William Shakespeare. June Scudeler suggests that Kent Monkman's Miss Chief Eagle Testickle is reclaiming space on a much grander scale, using her exhaustive knowledge to expose "colonial restrictions on Indigenous identity," reaffirm Indigenous rights, and at the same time welcome everyone—Indigenous and non-Indigenous—into the circle. And Dylan Robinson challenges the reader to consider how the performance of welcoming gestures strengthen or undermine the sovereignty of the Indigenous people on whose territory we stand.

Tara Beagan articulates how her company ARTICLE 11 uses the *United Nations Declaration on the Rights of Indigenous Peoples* to claim space in which to create a home where she and her colleagues can work. And in the most profound way, Michelle La Flamme creates space where the dead can live again, in her examination of Marie Clements's play *The Unnatural and Accidental Women*.

As we grow as a performance community, we look outward as well as in. Starr Muranko talks about her transnational collaboration with South American artists, tracing the Spine of the Mother. David Geary, part of our transindigenous whānau, speaks from his position as a Māori theatre artist now living in Canada about what he sees and what we share. Daniel David Moses traces the sacred and the numinous in a dozen plays from the Indigenous body of work, illuminating a path both behind us and leading forward.

These writings are infused with love. Jill Carter addresses the love head on in her "Sovereign Proclamations of the Twenty-First Century: Scripting Survivance through the Language of Soft Power," clocking the artists who reclaim and rejuvenate through soft power. Michelle Olson speaks lovingly of the moment in the theatre when the lights go down and "the memories in our blood and bones sit with the audience and stand with the performer." But love shimmers and shines throughout these essays, manifesting in different ways: love of our stories; love of our artistic ancestors, naming them and honouring them and their teachings; love of being gathered to experience something together.

This book may be a first in one way or another, but of course these voices were already speaking out in the world, in theatres and galleries and institutions, in their work and in their practices. That we were able to gather them together in this assembly is a testament to the wealth and generosity of the Indigenous thinkers and practitioners currently working in the performance world. We are gratified that so many of them accepted our invitation into the assembly. As with any good Indigenous assembly, we are gifted with the opportunity to listen to what each participant has to say. First will always be first, but we hope that it is not the only. It is our hope that this book is just a beginning, a way of inviting more voices into the conversation.

WELCOMING SOVEREIGNTY
DYLAN ROBINSON

sq̓eq̓íptset íkw̓elò, kwexáls sq̓eq̓ó, xwélmexw qe xwelítem.
ts̓áts̓eltsel xwoyíwel tel sqwálewel kw̓els me xwe̓í sq̓ó talhlúwep íkw̓elò.

All writing is addressed to specific and general audiences. This essay, situated as it is in a series on Canadian theatre, will be read by theatre artists and scholars working in theatre and performance studies, as well as those working in Indigenous arts and Indigenous studies. You may be reading this as an Indigenous theatre artist, as a settler artist, or as xwelítem. You may be reading as a member of an audience unnamed, or yet to be named. My opening epigraph is both for you, and also not for you. It is written for an audience yet to come, for future generations of fluent Halq̓emeylem readers and speakers, of which there are currently few.

This essay's aim is to examine the degree to which Indigenous sovereignty is constituted through gestures of welcome that take place in spaces of transit and gathering. To do this, I will engage in readings of welcome as they are performatively enacted upon the page and physically manifested in public space. While I will examine several instances of welcome, from welcome figures to choreographic gestures in Vancouver Opera's Indigenous adaptation of Mozart's opera the *The Magic Flute*, I will also treat this space—these pages—as a space of welcome and unwelcome. This is a space where we might come together, but also, as I will shortly describe, a space that will require remaining apart. It is a place of gathering that takes place not at once, but over time. My words here seek to gather. Together, they are an *act* of gathering, of gathering strength and acknowledging Indigenous voices and bodies, rather than a container for Indigenous content. They seek to modify the unmarked structures that define these pages as a space of being "on Canadian Theatre."

This essay is directed toward two specific readerships: xwèlmèxw/ Indigenous artists and scholars in the first instance, and non-Indigenous/ settler/xwelítem[1] scholars in the second. I name these readerships directly and distinctly (knowing well that identity is contingent and situational) in order to pose a series of questions: What is the place from which you read? What is the positionality of reading? How does this positionality situate your responsibilities as a reader and what you do with the knowledge you gain from this act of reading? I am not the first to ask such questions. Thomas King in particular charges his readers in *The Truth About Stories* with being responsible for each story they read. This charge takes as its premise the fact that relational operations of responsibility for knowledge are central to many Indigenous epistemologies. Indigenous writers including King, Lee Maracle, Leanne Simpson, and numerous others craft this responsibility through the orality of their writing and in doing so remind us that the page is not so far removed from other physical spaces—our big houses, longhouses, kitchen tables, and everyday spaces—where Indigenous histories are shared, documented, and affirmed.[2]

Lastly, this essay questions how reading and writing might be structured as acts of sovereignty. To situate sovereignty as constituted by action is to understand it through an Indigenous ontology wherein sovereignty is not held within documents/objects but instead within "doing." Though some might consider reading a somewhat passive and also post-contact form of such "doing," it is merely the modern iteration of interpreting signs (pictographs, pictograms, inuksuit) intended to convey information about places of

---

1   I am using xwelítem here in its dual sense of non-Indigenous person and "starving person." Historically, newcomers who arrived in S'olh temexw (our lands, Stó:lō territory) looking for resources such as gold were starving; we fed them.

2   I acknowledge that the contributions in this volume are by Indigenous performance makers, playwrights, and scholars who explicitly bring our stories and lived experiences to life in their work. My interest here is the ways in which such experiences, and the experience of sovereignty in particular, might be constituted performatively upon the page.

spiritual power, sustenance, and danger. Indigenous interpretation of signs—Indigenous hermeneutics—continues to provide us with this information. Reading, understood as an action, is thus not merely a conceit in order to allow me to talk about the performative relationship between writer and reader and the ways in which our voices are embodied in texts. Charting the history of sovereignty in Indigenous performative writing and textual orality are also not the end goals of this essay. Rather, this essay seeks to enact sovereignty with readers, through a particular action of refusal that begins with an injunction not to read:

> If you are a non-Indigenous, settler, arrivant, ally, or xwelítem reader please stop reading by the end of this paragraph. I hope you will rejoin us on page 16. The next eight pages are sovereign space, written for Indigenous readers.
>
> For those readers who are Indigenous, I welcome you to continue reading, to turn the page and enter into a different place of gathering.

SPACE #1: GATHERING TOGETHER

Ey swayel el sí:yá:m siyá:ye. Barbara Holman el ta:l. tl'elaxw li te Ts'elxweyeqw, yewa:lmels, tem mímele. Ruth Gardner el sí:le. teli te Skwah. Barbara Evelyn Garner sts'o:meqw qe Robert Craig Gardner sts'o:meqw. Qwotaseltil Charlie Gardner el th'ép'ayeqw—te má:ls te Robert Gardner. Elvira Jane Garner el th'ép'ayeqw—the tá:ls te Robert Gardner. tel'alétsechexw?

éy kws hákw'elestset te s'í:wes te siyolexwálh: it is good to remember the teachings of our ancestors. I open this place of gathering with a phrase used often to open meetings of upriver folk, and in order to acknowledge the previous work our Elders (artists and ancestors) have done in order that we can be in the place of creative and intellectual possibility we are in now. The fact that eighteen Indigenous scholars and theatre practitioners have contributed their work to this collection is a fact made possible because of those who have gone before us, our Elders, writing Indigenous spaces into being, chipping away at the colonial foundations of western institutional systems, building new structures that provide space for younger generations of Indigenous scholars and artists. This has been done with the help of many non-Indigenous allies, while made precarious by others. It feels both good to affirm the hard-won existence of this space at the same time as it feels as if we are celebrating the minimal, the basic, the single seat at the table. We celebrate as if the table regularly consisted of artists from across our nations, gathering together. This history of absence, combined with the more recent felt exceptionalism of inter-national gathering, is what makes our voices joined together here in this textual gathering place exceptional. Similarly, it is the relative absence of Indigenous representation on the stage that makes more recent Indigenous inclusions in performance stand out.

Such is the case in Vancouver Opera's 2007 adaptation of Mozart's opera *The Magic Flute*, a Northwest Coast First Nations adaptation that involved a large number of First Nations artistic collaborators as well as the First Peoples' Heritage, Language and Culture Council (now the First Peoples' Cultural Council). Living in London, England, at the time of its first performance, I did not attend the performance, but learned much about the

production through colleagues' stories of their involvement, and in particular from Marion Newman, a Kwagiulth mezzo-soprano who had been a part
of the production:

> There was a scene during one of the dress rehearsals of the opera,
> when I wasn't on stage, and I took that opportunity to take a look
> from the audience at how the set and costumes all looked on stage.
> This was the moment when the chorus came in wearing different
> regalia, ranging from the North to the West, as if they were arriving
> at a potlatch. They all came forward in a half circle as the curtains
> parted and I was completely taken aback at the emotion I felt come
> over me. I realized that this was the closest I'd ever come to seeing
> just how beautiful it must have been to see the different villages ar-
> riving at a special event, back in the day of my great-grandparents
> and before. An event that I have never had the chance to experience
> because for a long time the potlatch was outlawed, the masks and
> regalia confiscated and people were forced to give up their religious
> ceremonies, their form of government and their way of keeping a
> record of the important moments in life. (qtd. in McQueen 323)

Newman had twice described the second act's first scene, this gathering
of our nations, to me as profoundly moving. Without having attended the
performance, I was transported by her experience of witnessing our history—as in a potlatch itself—a history of abundance and fullness of nations
and communities gathering together. The longing and pride mixed within
her telling gave me with a glimpse of the powerful affective experience she
had. When Vancouver Opera announced that they would remount the production in 2013, I eagerly anticipated seeing it and, in particular, the scene
of gathering Newman described.

The work of so many of Indigenous collaborators on *The Magic Flute*—
the designs by Kwak'waka'wakw artist John Powell; choreography by Michelle
Olson of the Tr'ondëk Hwëch'in First Nation and Artistic Director of Raven
Spirit Dance; and leader of the Squamish dance group Sp'akwus Slulum,

S7aplek Bob Baker, amongst many others—was indeed beautiful. And yet, emerging from the audience at the end of the performance, I felt similar to an Indigenous audience member who noted to me in a post-show group interview: "I attended the Opera hoping to see an Indigenized *Magic Flute* that was infused with Coast Salish logic and referenced stories in the hənq̓əmin̓əm̓ language; instead I saw *The Magic Flute* all dressed up." Continuing on, the same audience member conveyed how she was

> . . . elated by the beauty of the Coast Salish design. It's grand and it's impressive and it's really striking and beautiful. For those who live here, and who are familiar with local ceremonies, there are points of recognition when you recognize the setting, when you recognize the ceremonial display. That being said, despite these moments of recognition, my overall reaction to the opera was that of alienation. It seemed to me to be *The Magic Flute* in Coast Salish drag. (*The Magic Flute*, audience member)[3]

This fact of "dressing up" the opera in "Coast Salish drag" conveys the sense of playing with identity, yet here not in the intentional way in which drag operates.

In the space of inter-national gathering represented in the longhouse scene, what most fascinated me was what could be called a kind of "gestural drag" or "wannabe affectation" where non-Indigenous opera singers embodied the gesture that I will spend the remainder of this essay focusing on: raising up one's arms in thanks or recognition. A gesture that has become synonymous with welcome. In gatherings held by Stó:lō, xʷməθkʷəy̓əm, Skwxwú7mesh, Səliĺwət, and other Pacific Northwest nations, the gesture affirms the message of a speaker whose words have been particularly powerful. The same gesture when it is embodied by carved welcome figures has come to signify welcome.

---

3   It is important for me to note that the group discussion held after *The Magic Flute* was also a space of sovereignty, and I would like to believe that our discussion there was qualitatively different than it might have been in the company of non-Indigenous participants. At the very least I can say it felt this way for me.

In an operatic adaptation of the gesture in *The Magic Flute*, Vancouver Opera's chorus members raised their arms up to each other as a kind of handshake. In "costume regalia," the singers walked up to each other and waved their arms up as if to say, "Hey, how are ya?" and repeated the gesture to each person they met. Made into an everyday greeting, the gesture speaks to its gradual proliferation by settler Canadian publics as a gesture of thanks decoupled from its power to demonstrate deep respect. And in such a way, perhaps it also speaks to those of us who were part of the opera's Indigenous audience able to recognize the infelicity of the gesture as the "trying on" of Indigenous drag. It signals an epistemological limit, and the important fact that this gesture cannot simply be "picked up" and deployed. Its failed deployment speaks of its importance as a lived gesture, as a felt gesture that speaks in sovereign recognition of those important words spoken by sí:yá:m when Stó:lō, xʷməθkʷəy̓əm, Skwxwú7mesh, and Səlílwət communities gather together.

This one-minute scene exists before the "action" of *The Magic Flute*'s second scene begins, but its importance as a failed marker of welcome—and evacuated of its significance as a gesture of respect—has stayed with me. In important ways the gesture resists the global migration of Indigenous welcome that has come to exist in post-contact carved figures now commonly known as "welcome figures" and "welcome poles." Such figures work to extend atmospheres of welcome to settler and tourist publics, and as I will later argue, are mostly unrecognizable to non-Indigenous members of the Canadian and tourist publics as figures that demarcate the sovereignty of the people whose territory they are guests in. While these figures might be understood as a kind of "immigration checkpoint" for Pacific Northwest First Peoples, the settler gaze consumes them as cultural display.[4] Like immigration officials, they ask us to remember our responsibilities as guests. And yet, because of the way that such figures are put to work in legitimizing the agendas of the nation and the neo-colonial force of the crown and its corporations, although

---

4   And yet, following Richard Rath (2014) who warns against analogizing wampum to a kind of written document or financial currency, it is important to refrain from representing our traditions "as like" other western forms, in order that we continue the ontological specificity of the thing/action itself.

I can understand the potential sovereignty of these welcome figures I often do not feel their sovereignty extend across the spaces they are located in. I do not feel their incursion upon the logics of the state. Despite the masterful work of the carvers and artists who bring these figures to life, the figures' placement often acts as an Indigenous stamp of approval. Such is the case for the 2010 Olympic and Paralympic Games, the entryway of the BC Hydro building in downtown Vancouver (taking part in a wilful amnesia of BC Hydro's Indigenous land expropriations), and as tourist spectacle in photo-op encounters with the welcome figures at the Vancouver airport. I am not in any way claiming that this is the intention of the carvers who deserve praise for their work. Rather, what I struggle with in each of these instances is the co-option and of the works as statements of sovereignty by their placement within structures that overwhelm their presence. The spaces in which they are placed neutralize their political intervention through architectural and institutional frames of political recognition. In airports, opening ceremonies, and crown-corporation building foyers, they are claimed rather than themselves making claims upon the sites they are situated in. Rather than acting as figures that question sovereignty—the equivalent of immigration officers who ask visitors about the nature of their "visit" to the unceded territories now called Vancouver—against their will the figures are made to perform a politics that supports the very structures of the state that they are created to challenge.

To resist the claiming of frames we must not be content to be included, and instead define new spaces of sovereignty. To do this here, in this gathering, I've asked non-Indigenous readers not to join us. Perhaps this makes you feel uncomfortable. It does for me. Aren't we supposed to be working hard at forming new relationships, seeking alliances, pursuing goals of radical inclusion, working toward including everyone in this time of reconciliation? We seem to be celebrating reconciliation these days with increased conviction, celebrating the change of federal government with hope, celebrating Indigenizations of the academy and other organizations. Yet in doing so we also celebrate forms of our mere recognition and inclusion. This is not to say we should negate the "reparative" (Sedgewick), "utopian" (Dolan, Muñoz), and "affirmative" (Braidotti) work that continues to give energy to the daily and extraordinary actions of sovereignty we practise.[5] Yet complete celebration is premature for reasons I do not need to name to those of us gathered here together. In this space with those of you whom I know, those whom I am related to, and those whom I hope to affirm kinship with, I continue to work through the potential of creating Indigenous sovereign space, what Métis artist and scholar David Garneau calls "irreconcilable spaces of Aboriginality," as spaces that provide "moments where Indigenous people take space and time to work things out among themselves," moments that exist outside of the colonial attitude " . . . characterized not only by scopophilia, a drive to look, but also by an urge to penetrate, to traverse, to know, to translate, to own and exploit" ("Imaginary," *Arts of Engagement* 13). Through inventing and constructing different forms of sovereign space we provide each other with a means to work things out with each other, finding ways to work outside of the gaze of knowledge production, and refusing forms of Indigenization that do not serve the needs of Indigenous artists, scholars, students, and communities. Our words, like welcome figures, are still too often used to legitimize other non-Indigenous actions and institutions. At the very least, I hope that this space of gathering will prompt discussion of how we might develop other models for creating Indigenous spaces that refuse to feed the hungry gaze of xwelítem. Many have already been developed, including Rebecca Belmore's touring of *Ayum-ee-aawach Oomama-mowan: Speaking to Their Mother* to Indigenous communities; David Garneau's provocative call for sovereign display territories ("Imaginary," *Arts of Engagement* 34–36); Ogimaa Mikana's large billboard of black text on white background that reads in untranslated Anishinaabemowin, "Gego ghazaagwenmichken pii wii Anishinaabemiyin" (Barrie, Ontario, 2014)[6]; and by the exhibition *cʼəsnaʔəm, the city before the city* at the Museum of Anthropology at UBC curated by Musqueam curator Jordan

---

5   For more on these positions of writing, see Robinson, "Enchantment's Irreconcilable Connection: Listening to Anger, Being Idle No More." Forthcoming, McGill-Queen's University Press, 2016.

6   Following Ogimaa Mikana's refusal of translation on the sign itself, I will not translate this message here.

Wilson and Museum of Anthropology curator Sue Rowley. Enacting sovereignty may feel like a precarious undertaking for the force by which non-Indigenous readers, spectators, and listeners experience their exclusion. However, as many of these projects demonstrate, not all irreconcilable spaces of Aboriginality require the exclusion of settler presence. Many of these spaces are defined by a refusal to take up the logic of settler systems, whether that be the refusal of translation (Ogimaa Mikana), or the refusal for Musqueam belongings to be displayed for the desire of museum spectators' gaze (cəsnaʔəm).[7] For those spaces that do require xwelítem, O'serón:ni, k̓amksiiwaa, Zhaagnaash, and other settler subject exclusion—exclusions of the settler gaze, listening, presence, and occupation of space—as in the gathering you have joined here, the point is not so much that exclusion is felt (though that can be a useful teaching), but that the space is structured and guests determined according to what we deem necessary for our work to commence.

Musicologist Suzanne Cusick opens her essay "On a Lesbian Relationship with Music: A Serious Effort Not to Think Straight" with language that remains untranslated. Cusick's essay seeks to inscribe space for speaking differently, "to try to speak both truly and helpfully," despite her great fear of what she might say—and perhaps what she can convey—in attempting to do so. I have always read Cusick's opening paragraph as her resistance to translating being, as a sovereign act, and in many ways as containing a knowledge that was intended to lie beyond many readers' (or at least my own) accessibility. A choice to intentionally speak to a specific community of something personal. Writing here, my choice to define a sovereign space of reading, I feel a similar pressure to try to speak both truly and helpfully, to convey something uniquely Indigenous, perhaps a teaching that has been shared with me, perhaps some kind of essential Stó:lō values or epistemology. I have previously been asked—and internalized the demand—to rationalize the creation of such space through a program of work intended to achieve specific goals

---

7 The word "belongings" is itself an important choice made by Wilson and the Musqueam community that both refuses the word "artifact" and its location of First Peoples' culture as part of history rather than the present. "Belongings" also names the fact that these belongings continue to belong to Musqueam ancestors despite their location in the museum.

or to continue the project of collecting content (knowledge). To capitulate to these demands is to undercut the usefulness and potential of such spaces for thinking and speaking without the end goal of knowledge production and dissemination. Such spaces do not need to be content-driven; they are not spaces to say essentially "Indian things" in essentially "Indian ways."[8] Nothing that I write here is a secret or confession. I offer nothing confidential or sacred.[9] By creating these spaces we offer the possibility to say things differently, for different ways of speaking to emerge in spaces that work hard to deter the feeling of being watched, listened to, or what we might think of as "settler atmospheres." This is the point. For even when settler readers have worked hard to decolonize the desire for knowledge and the extractavist drive to accumulate embedded within settler modes of listening, looking, and gathering, the *feeling* of the settler gaze remains. The degree to which we have internalized this gaze, and the degree to which it is present in the materiality of the non-Indigenous spaces we occupy and the normative western forms we use to share knowledge (the essay, the conference, the class)—these structures necessitate sharper anti-colonial interventions than welcome is able to provide us with.

th'ítolétsel el sí:yá:m sí:yáye. I thank you for joining me in this space, and I hope we will have other opportunities for conversation and work together in other spaces. On the next page we will rejoin non-Indigenous readers. In the remainder of the essay I will focus on scenes of welcome, focusing particularly on the ways in which welcome figures are made to participate in state welcome.

For any non-Indigenous readers who chose to read within this space of Indigenous sovereignty, who chose to cross the boundary of unwelcome, I ask:

What are the reasons you continued to read?

---

8   In fact there is also a great need to problematize the necessity for Indigenous writing always to demonstrate an essential orality. As an Indigenous scholar, artist, and language learner, I am already speaking in an "authentic voice." It is the voice I use every day in English with a smattering of Halq'emeylem, sometimes using what some consider academic jargon, and adopting a more polemic timbre.

9   I recognize this may be disappointing to any settler readers who decided to read this section.

SPACE #2: FIGURING THE CITY'S WELCOME

For settler and arrivant readers who have just turned eight pages, I thank you
for supporting and respecting the sovereign boundaries established within
this chapter. My request was a necessary act of exclusion not done merely to
exclude or to incite unwelcome feelings for that result in and of itself. This
essay's unwelcome action might seem to go against Indigenous protocols of
welcome that remind guests that they are guests. To welcome presumes the
authority and right to determine the proceedings that occur within the space.
We welcome people into our homes, onto Indigenous lands, into countries,
and to events we have organized. To welcome guests into each of these places
is, to varying degrees, to signal sovereign control over the rules of the space
and the authority under which such rules are enforced. And yet, welcome's
sovereignty is equally undermined by its misrecognition as a friendly gesture of greeting.

Indigenous gestures of welcome have found their way into increasingly
unexpected spaces over the past several decades, perhaps most strangely including eighteenth-century opera performance. The second act of Vancouver
Opera's 2007 adaptation of *The Magic Flute* opens with what its director, Robert
McQueen, describes as a " . . . council meeting where the fate of Tamino is to
be discussed. We decided that the feeling of place, or location, that best fit the
environment of the scene was a long house meeting" (316). Vancouver Opera's
program note synopsis for this scene reads, "Sarastro's council approves Tamino
for rights of purification" (Vancouver Opera 2007 and 2013 9), without the
mention of the longhouse context. The stage action of this scene begins with
members of this council (played by a number of non-Indigenous chorus members) arriving at the longhouse, each wearing a costume designed by John Powell
(Kwak'waka'wakw) to represent one of ten different First Nations in coastal
British Columbia. As they approach one another each performer raises both
arms upwards, palms facing the sky. These gestures toward each other are used
here as a form of individual welcome but are drawn from another gesture used
by many First Peoples in the Pacific Northwest to give thanks and acknowledge
important words shared by speakers.

The migration of this gesture provide the impetus for me to question how the performance and performative address of Indigenous welcome has been taken up in multiple contexts on the west coast of Canada for local and global audiences. In Vancouver in particular, welcome's performance circulates across a range of platforms. Here, in the world's first "city of reconciliation," the language of acknowledgement, of claiming the status of "guest" and thanking one's hosts—either xʷməθkʷəy̓əm, Skwxwú7mesh, and Səlíĺwət Nations, or naming all three with the misnomer "Coast Salish people"—has increased in academic, civic, and business contexts since the official declaration by the city of its location upon "unceded Coast Salish territories."[10]

Alongside my examination of welcome, the remainder of this essay will consider the political efficacy of enacting gestures of un-welcome in order to re-situate the assumption from being a welcome guest to the actuality of assuming welcome as an "uninvited guest." In particular, I draw upon Métis artist and art critic David Garneau's concept of "irreconcilable spaces of Aboriginality," based on the premise that " . . . while decolonization and Indigenization is collective work, it sometimes requires occasions of separation—moments where Indigenous people take space and time to work things out among themselves, and parallel moments when allies ought to do the same" ("Imaginary," *Arts of Engagement* 23). Garneau here proposes a break with both the current climate of reconciliation and a national ideology of multiculturalism that understands the primary work between Indigenous and non-Indigenous peoples within Canada as necessarily taking place through forms of intercultural dialogue and relationship building. While I acknowledge that such nation-to-nation relationships are essential on both the level of national politics and on an individual basis between members

---

10   On 8 July 2014, Vancouver city council designated Vancouver a "City of Reconciliation." In February 2016 Mayor Gregor Robertson noted, "Vancouver is proud to be a City of Reconciliation, and we are committed to strengthening our relationships between our indigenous and non-indigenous peoples. . . . We have come so far in recent years, but there is much more work to do. As Mayor, I am committed to ensuring Vancouver is a City of Reconciliation, one that values mutual understanding, respect, and empathy" (City of Vancouver, "Vancouver Takes Next Step").

of Indigenous communities and the non-Indigenous Canadian public, I am acutely aware that such a focus upon notions that "we are all one" ("Home") and friendship-building models have developed their own hegemony that can have the tendency to elide forms of sovereignty. Sovereignty in its micro- and macro-political instantiations is at odds with models that focus on coming together, on sharing, on not being separate. Spaces of sovereignty might similarly be understood as spaces of segregation that contrast national, mulitcultural ideologies of inclusion that structure Canadians' political, artistic, and interpersonal values. And yet, it is important not to assume that spaces of reconciliation and multicultural gatherings are, simply in their existence, devoid of power relationships. As Garneau notes, "When Indigenous folks (anyone, really) know they are being surveyed by non-members, the nature of their ways of being and becoming alters. Whether the onlookers are conscious agents of colonization or not, their shaping gaze can trigger a Reserve-response, an inhibition or a conformation to settler expectations" ("Imaginary," *Arts of Engagement* 27). While spaces of reconciliation and multicultural spaces do not explicitly foster structures of surveyance, there is nonetheless often a perpetuation of scopophilia:

> The colonial attitude is characterized not only by scopophilia, a drive to look, but also by an urge to penetrate, to traverse, to know, to translate, to own and exploit. The attitude assumes that everything should be accessible to those with the means and will to access them; everything is ultimately comprehensible, a potential commodity, resource, or salvage. The academic branch of the enterprise collects and analyzes the experiences and things of others; it transforms story into text and objects-in-relation into artifacts to be catalogued and stored or displayed. (Garneau, "Imaginary," *Arts of Engagement* 23)

There are many forms through which sovereignty might be spatialized, including the return of Indigenous lands. Sovereign spaces, or spaces "unwelcome" to non-Indigenous desire—ones that operate outside of the colonial desire to know—are essential not simply in order to share Indigenous knowledge not appropriate to share with the public. They are necessary in order to offer spaces without a predetermined program that allows for a different kind of "working out" of ideas/issues/futures for Indigenous folks, a working out that does not take place under the gaze of national and institutional scopophilia. Such spaces do not, as might be assumed, stand in contradistinction with the idea of "radical inclusion" as advocated by Cree/Métis artist Cheryl L'Hirondelle and others. The concept of radical inclusion, as I understand it, does not mean unlimited inclusion, but instead forms of inclusion that can extend toward our other-than-human publics, including ancestors and non-human forms of life around us. el sí:yám síyáye, Cheryl L'Hirondelle, explains how " . . . because of the animacy of nêhiyawin (Cree worldview) saying 'kiyânaw' (all of us together) includes not only everyone (hence not excluding any people or animals), but also includes all the animate 'things' present as well" (*Why* 50). In "Why the Caged Bird Sings" L'Hirondelle details her many years of work with incarcerated Indigenous women, men, and youth to compose freedom songs. L'Hirondelle's collaborative song-writing has also included prison guards when guards have shown interest to be included, recognizing that "the program staff and guards were to some degree, 'caged birds' themselves since they had been there day after day, year after year" (51). As L'Hirondelle notes, "as a generative approach to radical inclusivity, my project started out to be about women, then I realized the prison program staff were 'lifers' and needed to be included, and then youth, and then men" (Personal). Additionally, L'Hirondelle and the Indigenous women and men she works with write the majority of their songs in English, with other lyrics in Indigenous languages interspersed, since,

> To write a song in English is also ironically and contentiously to be radically inclusive—since it could be construed that to write lyrics only in one specific Indigenous language could be excluding others. To extend the thinking, the "inclusivity" of English in terms of sharing the song most widely applied not only within the core group of songwriters and collaborators but also by extension to other inmates at the correctional facility and/or others who might wish to sing the

song in the future. To leave that inclusive legacy, it was ironically important to use the widely understood medium of the English
language, despite the political connotations of using the "colonizer's
tongue." (*Why* 51–52)

An important distinction in these choices is that they are decided upon by
L'Hirondelle and the women and men with whom she works. Radical inclusion, then, is not a call for everyone to be included at all times and all places
(a call which would contravene many traditions across different nations), but
instead a call for openness toward including those who are not granted legit-
imacy or status within the systems of work we participate in. Here, the power
dynamics between extending welcome when interest is shown, and *requiring*
inclusion when that inclusion is not welcome by Indigenous people, must be
distinguished from each other.

To enact settler exclusion is a strategy of sovereignty that defines a space
outside of Indigenous knowledge extractivism, where our knowledge is not
simply a resource used to Indigenize. Exclusions are seldom enjoyable experiences. The call for non-Indigenous readers to absent themselves from
the space between page 8 and page 16, demarcates a boundary not merely to
enact a performative gesture of unwelcome, but in order to assert and affirm
the fact that, in this era where, as the popular slogan has it, "information
wants to be free," there is a need to define Indigenous space ungoverned by
the prerogatives of multicultural enrichment. Such spaces take shape through
sovereign re-marking of boundaries and borders that contrast the ways in
which Indigenous traditional and ancestral territories are traversed every day
without thought. Indigenous gestures of welcome have sought to materialize
sovereignty in public spaces. However, not every marking of welcome effects
the same degree of sensate sovereignty. Sovereignty can equally be elided
through what Sarah Ahmed would call the non-performativity of welcome, a
form of welcome that does not unsettle naturalized entitlements to play host.

CROSSING BOUNDARIES

Unlike the crossings of Indigenous territories, crossings between municipal, state, and international boundaries are prominently marked, and often accompanied by some form of welcome. As we move across state boundaries, drive across city and municipal boundaries, and arrive in countries we are greeted by signs that announce identities of place. These signs do not merely mark the history of what is already there—the history of the city, country, or state—but often perform a desire for what these places are not, actively constructing the identity of place.

Figure 1. "Welcome to Ontario. More to Discover."

As just one example of this, after answering a US immigration agent's skill-testing questions upon flying out from Toronto International Airport in October 2015, the traveller encounters the values of the border writ large. Here, in the liminal zone of declared US sovereignty in the Canadian state on the traditional land of the Mississauga originally occupied by the Neutral, Petun, and the Wendat (Dickason 65, 70, 130, 434), the traveller is confronted by a display that includes a human-size replica of the Statue of Liberty, the American flag and homeland security flag, and a large statement that reads: CORE VALUES. These

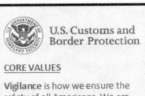

U.S. Customs and Border Protection

CORE VALUES

Vigilance is how we ensure the safety of all Americans. We are continuously watchful and alert to deter, detect and prevent threats to our nation. We demonstrate courage and valor in the protection of our nation.

Service to Country is embodied in the work we do. We are dedicated to defending and upholding the Constitution of the United States. The American people have entrusted us to protect the homeland and defend liberty.

Integrity is our cornerstone. We are guided by the highest ethical and moral principles. Our actions bring honor to ourselves and our agency.

Figure 2. US Customs and Border Protection: Core Values.

values are those of US border control, but they also speak strongly of the value distinctions between the identity of the place one has come from, and the place to which one is arriving. These particular signs also name the rules of welcome. The display says: you may enter if you do not pose a threat to the safety of those of the territory you are about to cross into. It says: this boundary is a space of continuous watchfulness, of vigilance, of protection and defence. This vigilance is legitimated by "the highest ethical and moral principles" of those who enforce it. This is not, obviously, the friendly welcome of civic signs where, for example, one is made to feel welcome to cross boundaries with ease, where that crossing represents the economic benefit of tourism dollars.

Figure 3. "Welcome to Vancouver."

Figure 4. "Welcome to New Mexico."

Border signs thus serve the function of boundary identification or enforcement but also of gratitude: city entrance signs announce the pleasure that awaits us now that we have arrived; we are thanked for visiting when we leave the city, and told to "come back soon." When we move from the city to the provincial or national park, we are greeted by rustic signs made of wood, sometimes with an animal or flower that is prominent in the park. Neighbourhoods in Vancouver are identified by community and neighbourhood flags that attempt to capture the feel of the area and encourage us to "explore" and "play." These are all signs that seek to foster "welcome feelings."

To walk down any city street or into parks and public plazas across Canada and the United States is to be reminded that civic amnesia operates through the visual normalization of colonial signs: street signs named after a city's "founders," statues of famous statesmen and explorers, and buildings named after companies who profit from resource extraction in Indigenous territories. The early colonial development of North American cities was in fact often accomplished by the resourcing of Indigenous civic infrastructure; ancient shell middens were used as the base material to construct roads (Kidder; Ceci; J.S. Matthews) while mounds were used as landfill (Young and Fowler). In refusing the city's desire to erase its violent colonial foundations, Indigenous artists such as Edgar Heap of Birds have intervened to weave our histories and futures back into the fabric of civic infrastructure.

Figure 5. Mount Pleasant flags, Vancouver, BC.
Photo by Dylan Robinson.

Marking these boundaries is of course not just a development of the modern nation state, or of contemporary Indigenous art that takes part in what Keren Zaiontz and I have called the "civic infrastructure of redress." Through inuksuit, pictographs, and pictograms, Indigenous peoples have always marked places of abundance or spiritual power, and issued warnings of unsafe spaces. We have also taken part in marking our welcome and unwelcome. On the Northwest Coast, one way in which this has taken place is through welcome figures.

Figures 6a and 6b. *Native Hosts* by Edgar Heap of Birds. UBC Campus, Vancouver. Photos by Dylan Robinson.

WELCOME FIGURES

Welcome figures have gained increasing prominence in spaces of public gathering, from Olympic opening ceremonies and foyers of hydroelectric companies to the Vancouver airport and opera stagings. With outstretched arms, at first glance these figures seem to extend a gesture of hospitality and generosity toward settler and tourist publics alike. At Vancouver International Airport in British Columbia, Canada, Musqueam artist Susan Point's welcome poles greet visitors to Vancouver immediately prior to the immigration checkpoint. Their position before Canadian immigration is significant as an acknowledgement

Figure 7. Welcome figure at sen̓aqʷ under Burrard Street Bridge in Vancouver, BC. By Squamish artist Darren Yelton, 2006. Photo by Dylan Robinson.[11]

O134|166|7280.

of whose land upon which the visitor first stands. Notably, these figures do not wait with open arms extended toward the millions who manoeuvre their carry-on suitcases around them. Standing directly in the arrivant's path, these figures require slight negotiations on the part of those who pass between them. They are an important acknowledgement of territory for those who recognize them as such. They also assert cultural vitality, an affirmation that is not insignificant for xʷməθkʷəy̓əm, Skwxwú7mesh, Səli̓lwət, and Stó:lō people who may identify Point's work as a marker of *our* "core values" (to return to

---

11   See " 'Welcome figure' goes up on seawall as sign of ownership" for further details. Siyám Bill Williams's statement was given following a court case ruling in favour of the Squamish Nation's land-rights claim to sen̓aqʷ, a village site that is now directly under the Burrard Street Bridge. Susan Roy writes how "in 1977 the Squamish Nation initiates legal action to reclaim parts of the reserve that have been sold. Following years in the courts, which also hear counterclaims by the Musqueam and Tsleil-Waututh First Nations to interests in the reserve, in 2002 the Squamish secure control over a misshapen fraction (the railway rights-of-way) of the earlier, larger reserve" (92). Given the counterclaims of the Musqueam and Tsleil-Waututh people to the site, the Squamish welcome figure acts as a particularly fraught political marker of unwelcome to these nations whose ancestors also lived at sen̓aqʷ.

the US immigration statement). And yet, without explicitly naming that sovereignty to the general public the figures are also arguably co-opted within the larger beautification project of the Vancouver Airport Authority. For the tired tourist eye the figures' visual incursion into the sovereign narrative of the Canadian nation-state is far less unsettling than it might otherwise be.[12] Moreover, Point's poles, situated after rooms full of more northern nations' carved works might similarly be reductively seen as "Indigenous culture"—a cultural enrichment of airport interior design consistent with the city's ongoing gentrification and branding through formline design.

When welcome is reduced to friendly greeting, its political assertion of sovereignty elides the question of who holds the "right to the city." The Vancouver newcomer's guide given to those who have recently immigrated to Canada notes, "You may have seen the Welcome Figures at the Vancouver International Airport. Musqueam artist, Susan Point, designed these traditional Coast Salish figures to welcome travelers to Coast Salish Territory" (City of Vancouver, *First Peoples* 14). The language here again emphasizes that these figures have been designed to welcome, rather than designed to assert xʷməθkʷəy̓əm sovereignty.

Figure 8. *Female and Male Welcome Figures* (1996) by Susan Point. Vancouver International Airport. Photo by Dylan Robinson.

---

12   As Musqueam curator Jordan Wilson noted to me, given that these figures have more in common with house posts, the phrase "welcome poles" may speak more to a contextualization of the poles by the YVR airport authority than to Susan Point's own contextualization of the poles.

Figure 9. *Welcome Figures* by Joe David. Vancouver International Airport, International Arrivals. Photo by Dylan Robinson.

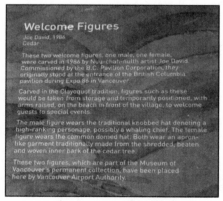

Figure 10. Welcome Figures, Interpretive Material. Vancouver International Airport, International Arrivals. Photo by Dylan Robinson.

The second set of welcome figures to greet international guests at Vancouver International Airport are those of Nuu-chah-nulth artist Joe David. The interpretive plaque placed in front of the figures reads, "Figures such as these would be taken from storage and temporarily positioned with arms raised, on the beach in front of the village, to welcome guests to special events." Notable here is the use of "guests" rather than "nations"—a focus on individuals that avoids the way in which these figures mark the relationship of sovereignty between nations who are hosts and those who are guests. Additionally, in using the open language of welcoming guests to special events, the figures are made relatable to any situation where a guest (visitor or tourist) might come to any of the city's "special events." It is significant in this and other contemporary welcome figures to note that the arms are permanently fixed (or locked) in a raised position, demonstrating permanent welcome. This permanence of welcome is most striking in George Hemeon's figures in the front of the BC Hydro building in Vancouver (pictured in Figure 11), where it is essential—especially given First Nations opposition to the Site C Dam at the time of writing this essay—to question what exactly is being welcomed, given the history of land expropriation and development across First Nations territories in BC by BC Hydro.[13]

Returning to the scene of Vancouver airport, the phrase "special events" located below Joe David's figures might also be understood as a stand-in for "mega-events," given that David's figures were originally commissioned for Expo 86 before they were moved to the airport. With the rise of the twenty-first century mega-event, welcome figures literally rise to give mega-welcomes

---

13   "In February 2010, BC Hydro underlined its commitment to building sustainable relationships with First Nations by constructing two 16-foot tall Coast Salish Welcome Figures in our Vancouver office lobby. The Welcome Figures, which will remain in perpetuity, were designed by George Hemeon, a BC Hydro senior Aboriginal procurement advisor and member of the Squamish First Nation" (BC Hydro, "First Nations"). While the large figures we know today are a product of modern carving practices, BC Hydro notes how "Welcome Figures were traditionally erected outside the entrance of a Coast Salish community, signaling to visiting people, with their outstretched arms free of weapons, that they were welcome to enter as guests." The inclusion "free of weapons" is conspicuous here, contrasting historical scenes of protest for land development like Oka, as well as confrontations surrounding resources that continue today (BC Hydro, "Traditional").

Figure 11. Welcome figures at BC Hydro by George Hemeon. Photo by Dylan Robinson.

to global audiences. Thus in the fourteen years between Expo 86 and the Vancouver 2010 Winter Olympics we see a jump in scale and number, as four giant welcome figures were cast in the Olympic opening ceremonies. Although not permanent, these figures temporarily presided over the Olympic's welcome that required Aboriginal people from across Canada to participate in a feat of endurance, dancing under their raised arms. These four welcome figures represented the four host First Nations: the xʷməθkʷəy̓əm, Skwxwú7mesh, Səliĺwət, and Lil'wat7úl. As a representative of each nation spoke a welcome, the arms on the pole behind the representative were raised.

I would like to make clear here that my critique of the compromised situation of these works within spaces that deny Indigenous sovereignty does not negate the skilful work of Susan Point, Joe David, and the carvers who designed the Olympic poles. Nor does it negate the individual pieces as sovereign expression, despite their circumstances of display. What I question in the situation of all of these figures is what is to me the expedient use of welcome to make comfortable the arrival of guests to what the city of Vancouver has now officially called "unceded Coast Salish territories." It bears noting that while these works by Point, Hemeon, and those who carved poles for the 2010 Olympic opening ceremonies have the potential to materially reflect the values of xʷməθkʷəy̓əm, Skwxwú7mesh, Səliĺwət, and Lil'wat7úl peoples back to the people, David's figures in speaking to/for Nuu-chah-nulth values have as much potential to reflect back the ongoing conflation of the specific values of these peoples with the generalization of "Indigenous people." That is, the continued prevalence in Vancouver for the public installation of Indigenous work by non-xʷməθkʷəy̓əm, Skwxwú7mesh, Səlil̓wət, and Stó:lō people demonstrates to those of us from these nations how the carving, art, and form of other nations is often used simply for its design, rather than thinking of such design as a sovereign claim.

In turn, for non-Indigenous visitors and settler publics the situation of these figures extends an atmosphere of recognition, and in doing so elides any uncertainty about what responsibilities are expected of them as guests. Rather than acting as the equivalent to unwelcoming immigration officials, these welcome figures do not through their materiality explicitly ask what responsibility settlers and visitors have while visiting or residing on xʷməθkʷəy̓əm, Skwxwú7mesh, and Səlil̓wət lands. By avoiding such challenging questions, the inclusion of these figures forecloses upon productive feelings of uncertainty about what it means to be a guest. Now that I have named this lack, I'd like to ask how those who are settler readers to consider more deeply the Indigenous history you walk over daily. How are you accountable to the welcome you have overstayed? In relation to the Indigenous communities whose history underlies the physical spaces you occupy how might you not merely consider what it means to be a guest in the territory you live in, but consider how you might address in some way, either small or significant, the daily invisible fact of Indigenous history and territory? How might you address this beyond acknowledgement?

CONCLUSION

The feeling of welcome, or of what we might otherwise call an entitled "right to the city," on Indigenous territories, is not only perpetuated by the monumental gesture of welcome figures. It is woven into the fabric of the city through the more everyday gestures of civic beautification. Such civic beautification takes place through gentrification processes across cities, but in Vancouver this has specifically meant including a variety of non-xʷməθkʷəy̓əm, -Skwxwú7mesh, and -Səlil̓wət works and design across the city. The City of Vancouver and the Downtown Vancouver Business Improvement Association oversee the creation

Figure 12. Granville Street Flags by Don Yeomans.
Photo by Dylan Robinson.

and installation of street banners across the city that seek to effect the city's beautification. Curious as to the ways in which friends and colleagues see the inclusion of one particular banner by Haida artist Don Yeomans, in October of 2015 I posted a photo of the banners on Facebook asking the open-ended question: What does this mean? The answers were varied, at turns humorous and angry. One person said it was an Indigenous version of the Canadian TV show *Kid's in the Hall*'s comedy sketch "I squish yo head." Another person's anger launched a more serious conversation about the representation of xʷməθkʷəy̓əm, Skwxwú7mesh, and Səlilwət people in the city. That person, an artist and member of one of the Coast Salish communities Vancouver now occupies, noted that the inclusion of these flags by a Haida artist was unacceptable and disrespectful. Moreover, they asserted that if the reverse were to happen—if they were to fly a xʷməθkʷəy̓əm, Skwxwú7mesh, or Səlilwət flag on Haida territory—they would be asked to leave. The artist noted that there was neither conversation with nor consent given by anyone from one of the Nations whose territory in which the flags were raised.

The hyper-visibility of Northern Indigenous artists' work in Vancouver has long been part of the tourism agenda of situating artwork by northern Indigenous artists upon xʷməθkʷəy̓əm, Skwxwú7mesh, and Səlilwət land. Historically, northern artwork was deemed more aesthetically developed than

the work of xʷməθkʷəy̓əm, Skwxwú7mesh, and Səlílwət people. Many poles
by artists from Pacific Northwest nations have been raised across Vancouver
over the years for this very reason. The result is that despite the prevalence
of Northwest Coast iconography in the city, xʷməθkʷəy̓əm, Skwxwú7mesh,
and Səlílwət people are not visible in their own land, while their territories
are entered and crossed daily, often without thought, without the knowledge
that any boundaries exist. Many of the theatre artists discussed in these essays challenge the invisibility of our people and histories through their work.
But I would argue that we need also to think beyond the sanctioned spaces
for Indigenous artistic inclusion and address the very composition of the
city itself. To do so would mean going beyond the city's acknowledgement of
Vancouver as "unceded territory" to instead acknowledging its responsibilities as a guest that may be unwelcome (or the fact that the role of guest has
been assumed). It also means finding new ways to engender public, felt forms
of "un-rightfulness" to the city. Lastly, it may mean exploring the creation of
"unwelcome figures" and figures that, like border agents, would require the
public to answer questions about why and how they have assumed the right
to the city. It would require members of the settler public to further consider
how spaces of sovereignty might not include their presence, and, paradoxically, advocate for and initiate their own removal.

SOVEREIGN PROCLAMATIONS OF THE TWENTY-FIRST CENTURY: SCRIPTING SURVIVANCE THROUGH THE LANGUAGE OF SOFT POWER

JILL CARTER

For thousands of years in this country, we've learned to live here. Because our need for this water is so great to our families and to our people, to our nations, most of our songs are about our greatest need. . . . I listen to a lot of American music. Seems like most American music is about love. . . . Is that why? Is that because you don't have very much?

—Fred Coyote, *Native American Testimony* 393

The understanding of Story as a vessel that contains the life and essence of a people is the cornerstone upon which Indigenous Knowledge (IK) is built. In the project to decolonize—which, perforce, entails the creation of a "new language . . . a new humanity [. . . and] the veritable creation of new men" (Fanon 36)—Indigenous playwrights in Canada and abroad have crafted a robust collection of performative interventions on the colonial project through potent articulations of reclamation. As they re-member their connections to community via their recovery of ancestral histories, languages, and aesthetic principles, these artists perform a "Sovereign Proclamation" in this historical moment—a collectively crafted oration for the coming generation of new, sovereign human beings. They, like us, will be "what we imagine" (Momaday 103).

The original peoples of these lands held fast to their creation stories. The narratives they shared could be viewed as a means to active resistance against the onslaughts of famine, natural disaster, and intertribal warfare that decimated populations and sometimes threatened to eradicate tribal nations, or as expressions of passive resistance against the agents of colonization and assimilation who came after them. These stories contain the spiritual mandates, histories, cultural practices, mores, ethical principles, and knowledge systems of the people. As they have been passed down in oral performance from generation to generation, they have evolved as the land has evolved and have grown with each new happening that affects the people. Tools to teach children how to behave, how to speak their language, and how to survive, these are the legacies that testify to the endurance of the community. They have afforded hope in the bleakest moments. They connect the people to the creation. And they have afforded meaning in times of unspeakable horror, crisis, bloodshed, and despair. When agents of the "New World" order set each of our Nations on its own "trail of tears," the ancestors told each other these stories over and over again; they imagined themselves in the stories, and they were able to keep walking. Indigenous peoples who live today are the seeds of those imaginings, and the creation stories are as vital for us and for the children for whom we dream as they were for those who dreamt our coming. Indeed, story ("thought and word") is our "last site of sovereignty" (Weaver, Public).

> "I would ask you to remember only this one thing," said Badger. "The stories people tell have a way of taking care of them. If stories come to you, care for them. And learn to give them away where they are needed. Sometimes a person needs a story more than food to stay alive. That is why we put these stories in each other's memory. That is how people care for themselves." (Barry Holstun Lopez, qtd. in Borrows 646)

The creation stories, as Anishinaabe educators Leanne Simpson and Edna Manitowabi remind us, are not simply speech acts upon which we are invited to theorize. Rather, they "set the 'theoretical framework,' or give us the ontological context from which we can interpret other stories, teachings, and experiences" (280). Appropriate engagement with our creation stories, as

Simpson and Manitowabi further assert, will offer us "a new way" of seeing the world, of theorizing our experiences, and of recreating ourselves (and the children we will raise) as new, sovereign human beings (281). Ultimately, they maintain, the live performance of these stories offers context for the "most powerful" expression of that speech act of (re)creation because "that context places dynamic relationships at the core" (281).

This paper explores the contemporary expression of re-creation in Indigenous performance produced in Canada through the existing theoretical and ontological frameworks offered by the creation stories specific to the nation(s) of their authors. As re-creation stories that speak to Indigenous sovereignty (of the artists, their nations, and the audiences with whom they enter into dynamic relationship), these speech acts are also heavily encoded with theory—theory which is too often left unexamined because of the artificial binaries that have been imposed to separate the subject under examination from the examiner's lens. As Barbara Christian has observed of Black literary criticism, "the academic emphasis on 'high' theory crowds out the voices of those who actually write literature" (cited in Simpson and Smith 36). And while Cherokee novelist and scholar Craig Womack does not summarily reject "high theory," he does caution us that the theories *produced by and encoded in the works of Indigenous artists and scholars* are the theories that must be privileged in our critical projects (*ibid.* 6).

Specifically under examination here are contemporary expressions of re-creation that illuminate the interface between love (expressed in the "language" of soft power) and sovereignty (which is so often regarded as a prize to be obtained only through the exercise of hard power). Political theorist Joseph S. Nye introduced the concept of soft power in the late twentieth century, arguing that many world leaders have remained blind to the force of persuasion, choosing instead to perpetuate a fruitless and destructive cycle through their unswerving faith in the force of arms (ix). In a discussion with Jeannette Armstrong about creative processes, Métis architect Douglas Cardinal builds on Nye's definition and credits his own creative genius with his investiture in "soft power":

The most powerful force is soft power, caring and commitment, together. You need that centre to make a contribution creatively. You
need to realize its power to make it realize your vision. You can have
visions and dreaming but how you realize them depends on caring
and commitment. Soft power is more powerful than adversarial or
hard power because it is resilient. By its nature, soft power is giving
and flexible but strong. It is woman power, female power. (Cardinal
and Armstrong 96)

The children of men live in "interesting times." Surrounded by pestilence,
war, and escalating communal rage, Indigenous peoples carry also the "interesting times" of our invaded ancestors. We bear great responsibility to those
ancestors, to our communities, and to our descendants. We are still under
siege. We are still governed by foreign invaders. We carry the (hi)stories of
our nations, and the struggle to retain faith in the midst of silent fears and
unaddressed resentments is considerable. Our nations' creation stories have
always provided the "script" of resistance—a script spoken in the language of
soft power—to fortify us against the "natural shocks" that accompany human
existence. In these fraught moments of settler occupation, the reclamation of
the Indigenous soul through the performance and reception of these "scripts"
(adapted for this historical moment) in accordance with traditional aesthetic
principles and original context provide a potent opportunity to softly trans-
gress within the belly of the colonial beast (see Simpson, *Dancing* 15–16).

Cherokee scholar Jace Weaver reminds us that our literatures address "the
part of us the colonial power and the dominant culture cannot reach, cannot
touch" (*That the People* 44–45). He imagines the sovereign exercise of creative
agency through which Native peoples re-member ourselves as Frantz Fanon's
"privileged actors" (36) who carry the power to create conditions rather than
to merely react against the conditions that have been created for us. With increasing urgency, our storytellers are beginning to *privilege* the imagination
of "human relationships: family, community, and that which transcends and
underlies human meaning systems" (Allen, *Off the Reservation* 81). As the
late Secwepemc-Ktunaxa playwright/educator Vera Manuel has reminded

us, supportive interrelationships, safe communities, and happy children are "every bit as important as Aboriginal title and rights; they go hand in hand" (41). Perhaps they are, in this generation, even more crucial to our continued survival and resistance than the gains to be made in the larger political arena; without the former, the latter seems, to me, an improbable and fruitless endeavour. Without the former—a conscious choice to embrace and act out of a personal *responsibility* to nurture and protect the children in our communities, to build healthy families, to support, defend, and befriend our neighbours' families, to lift each other up—we are stripped of all responsibility. Without this responsibility, which is our birthright—our *privilege*—we will relinquish the impulse and lose the capacity for independent action.

"Soul theft is a terrible crime" (Allen, *The Sacred Hoop* 204). And it is necessary for Indigenous peoples to invest as much vigour in the reclamation, protection, and assertion of those spirit-guided, internal mechanisms that direct our behaviour toward each other as we do in the reclamation of our sacred bundles, ancestral remains, repressed languages and cultural practices, and traditional lands. The Stories out of which we begin to imagine a "new human person" should strengthen and repair these internal mechanisms; they should speak to us, the people; and they should strengthen us in the knowledge that despite external impositions, inhumane treatment, injustice, and theft, we are creators not destroyers; we are generous, compassionate, and kind; we are beautifully human. We are loving, and we are loved. Leanne Simpson underscores this idea and reminds us, with reference to the Anishinaabe origin story that recalls the creation of the human and his/her first steps on earth, that these are the key lessons embedded in the (hi)stories that have been passed down to us through the generations. Love is the first gift and our greatest weapon in the struggle to endure:

Reclaiming the context of this means that rather than saying or thinking that Gzhwe Mnidoo lowered an abstract "first person" to the earth, if I am a woman, I say or think Gzhwe Mnidoo lowered "the first woman to the earth." . . . Again, our Elders teach us that this most beautiful, perfect lovely being was not just any "First Person,"

but that it was me, or you. We are taught to insert ourselves into
the story. . . . What does this tell us about Nishnaabeg thought? It
is personal. We were created out of love. . . . When interpreted this
way, our stories draw individuals into the resurgence narrative on
their own terms and in accordance to their own names, clan affiliations and gifts. For just a moment, they are complete in the absence
of want—decolonizing one moment at a time. Indigenous thought
can only be learned through the personal; this is because our greatest influence is on ourselves, and *because living in a good way is an
incredible disruption of the colonial meta-narrative in and of itself.*
(Simpson, *Dancing* 41; emphasis added)

THE "UNDERBELLY OF [MOTHER] LOVE"

But we are in the time of mist and fog. Those without grandmothers
swing on thin and twisted thread. Mothers without mothers spin in
squares hitting corners with every turn.
—Jani Lauzon, *A Side of Dreams*[1]

Toward the end of Turtle Gals Performance Ensemble's *The Scrubbing Project,*
Jani Lauzon's character Branda X declaims, "I will go to the underworld and
cross the raging river. I will reach out my arms and find my daughter" (Turtle
Gals 361). This is the "hope" that Lauzon promised, in 2002, for her broken,
semi-autobiographical mixed-blood character and that character's (unseen)
daughter who had been taken into care by the state. Lauzon's 2015 play *A
Side of Dreams* shows us just what such a heroic quest might look like and
just how necessary such quests may be.[1] Lauzon is a multidisciplinary Métis

---

1   In 2009, Lauzon held a playwright residency at Factory Theatre, and it was here she
began working with John Turner to develop *A Side of Dreams*. Developmental workshops
continued in 2011, in 2012, and then in 2013 when the National Art Centre's Sarah Garton
Stanley joined the project as director/dramaturge. In January 2015, Lauzon's epic confron-
tation of intergenerational trauma premiered at Native Earth Performing Arts, featuring

artist of partly Finnish ancestry who, in her more whimsical moments, refers to herself as "Finndian" (Turtle Gals 347). A fiercely dedicated single mother, she has raised a healthy, happy, and good-hearted young daughter who has grown into a fine young woman in the years between *The Scrubbing Project* and *A Side of Dreams*, and it seems that the life-role Lauzon has played is one that infuses itself into the projects she creates and co-creates—projects that speak to Indigenous healing within and despite the chaos and shame imposed upon Indigenous individuals, families, and communities by the colonial metanarrative.

In *A Side of Dreams*, Haisa, the daughter of a Métis waitress and a mixed-blood father, grew up in foster care. Mute since the violent murder of her husband, she has not spoken (in words) for much of her (now teenaged) daughter Aina's childhood. Living in the dark fog of her mother's silence, her murdered father's absence, and the terrible implications of the last words she ever heard her mother utter—"Not Again!" (Lauzon, *A Side* 10)—Aina has grown into an angry, confused, and resolutely "inquisitive" (13) young woman. Quiet, gentle, and humble, Haisa steps softly through life, speaking in offerings of apple pie and handcrafted dreamcatchers, but her silence, her humility, and the works of her hands with which she communicates exacerbate Aina's fury. Aina sees these gifts as physical evidence of weakness and surrender, not the exercise of hard-power resistance that she seeks. Shamed by such markers of ineffectiveness, she lashes out:

> After the circle is over I see an old woman walking slowly towards us and I think o.k. THIS is it! She's gonna have wise words of advice, I mean she's an Elder right? She's gonna make you all better. [. . .] What is that? She gives us Dreamcatcher supplies? That's as useless as apple pie. Pathetic. Flour and lard were hand-outs to the Indians—by

Lauzon, Jessica Barrera (as Aina), and puppeteer Trish Leeper. Most recently, it has toured to Big Medicine Studio in North Bay and to the University of Winnipeg, where it was presented by Sarasvàti Productions as part of FemFest (September 2015).

the government! And you can buy Dreamcatchers at the gas station around the corner. (2)

Aina, who (as she tells us) knows little about either her Finnish or her Métis heritage, has learned enough from the dominant culture to be ashamed of her métissage, and the symptoms of her dis-ease manifest themselves in her outburst. Dislocated from both community of origin and the lands that sustained her ancestors, her relationship with and perception of the world have become distorted. That she has brought her mother to an urban Friendship Centre demonstrates an instinctive desire to restore these connections, but these connections will not manifest themselves in the "pride" she seeks to inspire in herself for her Native identity, nor in the "quick fix" she seeks for her mother's muteness (2); she requires lessons in the language—as it is articulated and embodied—of soft power, or what Potawatomi plant scientist Robin Wall Kimmerer terms "the grammar of animacy" (48). To be restored to herself and to restore to herself the connections she seeks, Aina must be "re-storied."[2]

In *Braiding Sweetgrass: Indigenous Wisdom, Scientific Knowledge, and the Teachings of Plants*, Kimmerer reminds us that our Indigenous ancestors once viewed themselves as reciprocal partners within a thriving gift economy and cautions us that the generations who still occupy their traditional territories have been so severed from our biotas that some of us can "not even imagine what beneficial relations between [our] species and others might look like" (6). Severed by the forces of hard power from the languages through which those relations were articulated, we begin to forget the lessons of kinship; we begin to treat the natural world like an object, "absolv[ing] ourselves of moral responsibility and opening the door to exploitation" of our human and non-human relatives (Kimmerer 57). What is required here, on Lauzon's stage, is a *choice* on Aina's part to re-story herself—to cultivate the perception of self as a cherished relation within an immoderately abundant gift economy

---

2   Environmental scholar Gary Nabhan posits the idea of restoration (of right relationships between humans and their biotas) through "re-story-ation" (see Kimmerer 9).

and to eschew the desperate rage or the despairing paralysis that accompany the perception of self as an occupied and preoccupied casualty of conquest.

> What I mean of course is that our human relationship with [for example] strawberries is transformed by our choice of perspective. It is human perception that makes the world a gift. When we view the world this way, strawberries and humans alike are transformed. . . . A species and a culture that treat the natural world with respect and reciprocity will surely pass on genes to ensuing generations with higher frequency than the people who destroy it. The stories we choose to shape our behaviors have adaptive consequences. (Kimmerer 30)

Federal commodity handouts were a poor return for the theft of Indigenous lands, for the destruction of our biotas and lifeways, and for the state of abject dependency that was imposed on so many of our peoples. Delivered to our communities from across great distances, they constitute a material dissolution of ancient connections. And commodification of "exotic" Indigenous religious practices and ceremonial paraphernalia may inspire shame. But there are other ways to perceive these (hi)stories: flour, sugar, lard, and salt are all gifts from the earth, and Indigenous people have taught themselves to transform these strange gifts, proffered by a foreign hand, into gifts that sustain life and afford comfort. Frybread or apple pie may not be ideal forms of nourishment for an Indigenous body, but when they are crafted with care and offered with love, they keep hunger at bay and nourish the soul. Moreover, those (like Haisa) who have clung to the ancient ways, continuing their traditions and properly crafting ceremonial items, gently resist the colonial cultural violation that has worked to erode Indigenous relationships with the Creation. To allow shame and rage at such depredations to overwhelm our memories and to transform our understandings of the "gift economy" (in accordance with which our ancestors have always done life) is to utterly and irrevocably lose connection with all that we have been fighting to maintain.

Despite the wounds she has sustained through repeated encounters with hard power, Aina's mother has maintained her connections with the "gift economy." But although she struggles to pass on the lessons of connection to her daughter through her making and offering, her dis-ease (muteness) thwarts her efforts. She has suppressed the memories of her Métis mother ("Katherine with a K") and of her family history, blocking their passage through the generations in her silence. To remember and invoke her mother is to remember and invoke her murder and to remember and invoke its re-iteration in the murder of her own husband—Aina's father. By stopping her own mouth, does she seek to forestall any future reiterations of the violence that preponderates in her own "ancestral memory"? Perhaps. But her silence is, itself, a manifestation of hard power, exercised as she attempts to protect her daughter and cut off a violent inheritance. And this silence—albeit, less extremely manifested by Katherine with a K—is something that Haisa has inherited from her mother: "That one, that's your father; the one with the chiseled look like they have in the movies. I know. I should have said something. I was trying to protect you from being hurt" (16).

What should Katherine with a K have said? To whom? Should she have confronted Haisa's father about the "Indian gang" he was running with? Should she have told Haisa, long before her fateful seventh birthday, just who and what her father was? During this scene in which Haisa remembers her seventh birthday, the day on which she was orphaned, we learn that Katherine with a K was an innocent bystander shot by one of "our own"—caught by a stray bullet in a shootout between "Indian gangs" (17). Although Katherine with a K makes it clear that Haisa's "frozen," estranged father did not fire the fatal shot (17), as a gang member he is implicated in the murder of her mother. Moreover, this brutal event has been punctuated with a collective silence: "Everyone was long gone by the time the cops arrived, and of course, nobody said a word. That's what happens when we take our anger out on each other. Innocent people get hurt" (17).

That hurt reverberates through the generations. Rage and shame breed silence. And silence breeds more of the same in the generations that follow. Resistance to the hard power that undergirds colonial occupation finds its expression in a like hard power that inflicts even greater damage on those who struggle against the occupation. As Leanne Simpson so eloquently asserts,

Indigenous peoples living today carry a responsibility to break that silence, to articulate our (hi)stories, to seek redress, and to write a new world for the generations to come. And to effectively do this, we must push against and re-solve the conflict between the hard and soft powers—a conflict that has been imposed upon and internalized by Indigenous bodies since our first encoun-ters with the desperate bands of European adventurers who stumbled onto the shores of this continent:

> The cycles of shame we are cognitively locked into is in part per-petuated and maintained by western theoretical constructions of "resistance," "mobilization," and "social movements," by defining what is and what is not considered. Through the lens of colonial thought and cognitive imperialism, we are often unable to *see* our Ancestors. We are unable to *see* their philosophies and their strategies of mo-bilization and the complexities of their plan for resurgence. When resistance is defined solely as large-scale political mobilization, we miss much of what has kept our languages, cultures, and systems of governance alive. We have those things today because our Ancestors often acted within the family unit to physically survive, to pass on what they could to their children, to occupy and use our lands as we always had. This, in and of itself, tells me a lot about how to build Indigenous renaissance and resurgence. (Simpson, *Dancing* 15–16; emphasis in original)

Haisa's mother, while silent on many counts, sacrificed her dreams of escape and success to raise her own daughter alone. She tackled the menial labour of working in the local five-and-dime, enduring the racist comments of its customers with good grace because "[she] would have done anything for [her] little girl. [. . .] Sacrifice," as she tells us, "is the underbelly of love" (15). Haisa, who has silently endured the trauma of her mother's murder, a love-less childhood in an endless succession of foster homes, and the rage-fuelled disrespect of the teenaged daughter she has raised alone, is also no stranger to sacrifice. However, more is required of her if Aina is to be saved from the rage and confusion that threatens to engulf her. As Katherine with a K reminds her daughter, memory is a "duty" (17).

Like her mother before her, Aina has grown up without a grandmother (or the remembered invocation of that grandmother). Like her mother, she "swings on a thin and twisted thread"—a frayed lifeline, which threatens to twist itself into a noose, should her frenzied flailings intensify. To free her bound daughter, Haisa will have to "journey to the underworld" to meet her ghosts, "cross the raging river" of memory, and break the silence, which "swallows [them] whole" (8). The journey upon which Haisa embarks realizes itself on Lauzon's stage as a ceremony, invested with magic and whimsy and sweetened throughout by love.[3] Pulled through the vortex of a huge dreamcatcher that she has been making, Haisa returns to her seven-year-old self, played by a bunraku puppet, which is manipulated and protected by the elemental spirit of the dreamcatchers she has crafted, and by her own daughter Aina. Lauzon, who plays the adult Haisa, then takes on the roles of Haisa's ancestors and ancestral spirits—Pudlums the Fire Dragon,[4] Fog Man Giant, and Katherine with a K, Haisa's mother (see Figure 1).

---

3   Indeed, even within this most devastating memory, which exposes the genesis of Haisa's dis-ease, Lauzon does not allow Haisa to remain a prisoner. Katherine with a K comforts her daughter as her trapped spirit prepares to leave this place between worlds in which she has waited so long for Haisa to assume the duty that memory requires: "It's not how I dreamt our game would end, you being so very, very alone" (17). Now, "[she] can finish [her] journeys" (17). Haisa is tempted to follow. But Haisa, albeit imprisoned in her silence, is not alone. Her own daughter calls to her through the vortex of memory. Haisa is called to sacrifice the comfort of this "most delicious dream" by allowing her mother's spirit the freedom to move on from the realm of mortal concerns and to carry the lessons of her mother's love and irrepressible essence into a life fully lived with the daughter who needs her.

4   In Pudlums the Fire Dragon, Lauzon has imagined an elemental figure of mythical métissage through which she is able to "hold on" to the threads that connect her bloodlines (and those of her characters) and navigate a "bumpy" journey across the churning waters "where the blood mixes" (Lauzon, A Side 11). Pudlums is a "descendant of both [the Huron] Fire Dragon and Odin's banished dragon" (Lauzon, "Indigenous"). In her research for this project, Lauzon came across the text of a Huron creation story about a woman

Figure 1. "Blessed be your ancestors / We are calling you home": Jani Lauzon as Fog Man Giant, with (from left to right) Jessica Barrera, Haisa the puppet-child, and Trish Leeper in Jani Lauzon's *A Side of Dreams*. Photo by Samuel Choisy.

Temporal limens are dissolved on Lauzon's stage, as daughter-Aina encounters child-mother, grandmother, great-great grandfather, and the spirit beings that have directed the lives of her Finnish and Anishinaabe ancestors. With each encounter, Haisa learns "the taste of hope" that has been purchased for her by the soft power of love and sacrifice, and she learns of the killing power of silence, purchased by the "fear" and "drink" that arise from the despair of one who has "stopped believing in the ancient ways, the joy of life" (11). And Aina, who serves as helper to Haisa the puppet-child, connecting Haisa throughout to the present moment wherein she is a flesh-and-blood woman and calling her back to her "real" self when memory becomes too seductive or overwhelming, learns along with her.

---

who wished to marry a chief. She journeyed to the sky, married him, and bore a child. However, her husband suspected that this child was actually the progeny of a Fire Dragon, so the child was exiled to earth where he fathered the human race (Lauzon, "Indigenous").

We must take care not to confuse the imaginative representation of a tender remark, a gentle act, or the exercise of "soft power" with enervation or docility. We must take care not to confuse softness with weakness. Brittle strength without tenderness, gentleness, or compassion, is no strength at all. Wounded, broken, or dead children will not ensure the survival of our communities. Like their mothers before them, so many of our women continue to labour with herculean strength to maintain a home, put food on the table, and preserve the physical well-being of their children. But to nurture the emotional, spiritual, and intellectual well-being of those children, that strength has had to be tempered with "soft power"—a kind word, a gentle touch, a soothing, cool cloth on a fevered head, an indulgent laugh, a tight embrace, an embarrassing torrent of kisses in a public place, or a slice of homemade apple pie.

The Occidental patriarch had no use for soft power. He criticized Indigenous people for publicly displaying respect, leniency, and affection toward our children, just as he criticized us for the manner by which we accommodated ourselves to the lands we occupied, rather than assaulting the lands with hard power to "tailor" them in accordance with our whims (see Simpson, *Dancing* 138, note 208). We kissed our children too much: this he found repugnant. We listened respectfully to what they had to say: this he found incomprehensible. We corrected them gently and did not penalize them with harsh words or assaults on their person: this he adjudged to be foolish and weak. After all, children were to be seen and not heard; like "dumb beasts," they were to be "trained up" with blows: "Spare the rod, and spoil the child."

Is it any wonder that the children of Europe turned upon their own parents once they had reached adulthood? Note the preponderance of "evil witches" cannibalizing the young, and "wicked old misers" or elderly lechers blighting the hopes of their children and exploiting young virgins in centuries of European imaginings. The myriad collections of folk tales that come down to us today from England, Ireland, Italy, Spain, France, and Russia have been sanitized for popular consumption and labelled "fairy tales"; but these tales had teeth, and they fuelled and directed the deadly divisions that existed between young and old. This popular sixteenth-century Bolognese verse by

Giulio Cesare Croce trumpets this dark and hateful attitude toward the elderly that manifested itself across the "civilized," "well disciplined" continent:

A hundred old women found
Wrinkled, thin and poorly-fed,
Disgusting, bitter and ugly,
Who are no longer good for anything,
Come on, who wants to come?
And their names will have a place.
All into the vase!
And pull one out by chance.
Who will take the place?
Come on, who wants to come? (qtd. in Camporesi 44)

One hundred years later, savage praxis born of imagination and utterance continued unabated: The elderly, having outlived their utility, were targeted for destruction, and this publicly sanctioned "cleansing" was enacted on a regular basis throughout Europe until and throughout the eighteenth century (Camporesi 44). And it was *these* "human beings"—perhaps running from the memory of the atrocities they had recently committed upon their Elders or running from the atrocities that were in store for them—who mocked our soft power, who herded our peoples onto reserves, who "trained" our children with their "rod," and who broke so many of those children. The Europeans had imagined a world without soft power. And so it came to pass.[5] And with the passing of the feminine principles that had balanced out the hard powers, creative agency was dying. Drought, famine, and pestilence scourged

---

5   According to Amit Singhal, Senior Vice President and Fellow of Google, in 2012 the most frequently searched question on Google (over ten countries) was "What is Love?" In 2014, "What is Ebola?" "What is ALS?" and "What is Love?" were, respectively, the top three questions searched on Google (Al Arabiya News). It seems that disconnectedness and disease afflict the mind, body, and spirit of millennial humans, while the long-ignored solution now eludes us.

European soil. And the men who came to us and who professed to teach us how to be "human" were desperate in the knowledge of their own impotence.

> Among all the perils that conspired to bring about the decay and destruction of the human body, hunger was the cruelest; but like other calamities it escaped every mechanism of control. Man's sense of impotence in the governing of his own destiny became dismally more acute towards the end of the sixteenth century. (Camporesi 29)

For all their hard power, they could not govern their own destinies; so, they sought to shame us, rob us, and force us from the creative lifeways that had helped us to govern ours.[6]

Indigenous humans have always known that "we must care for the earth, not just for ourselves, but for all the generations to come. That nurturing and, in western eyes, feminine attitude is characteristic of both women and men" (Bruchac 34). This "feminine" attitude must be nurtured, cherished, feted, and shamelessly asserted with as much passion and conviction as we expend on land claims, assertions of sovereignty, and resistance movements against injustice. Overt displays of this soft power do not signal "weakness," "docility," or "ineffectiveness"—despite western assertions to the contrary. This generation of Indigenous people wrestles with the challenge of balancing

---

6   Statistics for the year 2000 in Canada indicate that one in twenty-five people over the age of sixty-five have reported abuse, while it is estimated that only one in fourteen abused elders actually report abuse (W. Scott, qtd. in Dumont-Smith 7). Health Canada statistics for 2000 indicate that the majority of incidents of elder abuse are perpetrated on older females, and 80% of these cases involve family members inflicting abuse on these women (Dumont-Smith 7). In reserve communities, these numbers increase dramatically. Claudette Dumont-Smith found in 1997 that over 50% of female elders living in reserve communities reported "that they had been or were victims of more than one type of abuse" (8). While much lip service is paid to the sanctity of the female and the importance of elders in Aboriginal societies, the truth remains that the processes of colonization (including residential schools, enforced structures of governance, relocations, and economic stressors) have contributed to the dissolution of right relationships and an increase in the misdirected exercise of hard power amongst all peoples that now share these lands.

the recovery of traditional values with the imperative of looking ahead, moving forward, and asserting Indigenous voice and agency within a dominant society governed by patriarchal powers. That many of us have internalized a deep-rooted shame for this traditional source of medicine and strength is highlighted most poignantly by Lauzon not only in the relationship between mute mother and raging daughter but also within the encounter between the child-puppet Haisa and a spirit-helper that Lauzon, like her protagonist, carries in her blood. Lauzon dubs this ancient Nordic-Huron fire-breather "Pudlums" (see Figure 2).

Confined for centuries in a remote cave and long forgotten by those who once carried her history, Pudlums is a tortured, raging (albeit cuddly) Prometheus of sorts, confined by vengeful gods and awaiting release and vindication. Haisa, who seeks release from her own "cave," in which she has silently raged against unaddressed injustice, is sent through the dreamcatcher vortex to confront this ancestral "cave dweller" and to learn about herself in the encounter.

Figure 2. "Let me be the Dragon in your ancient prophecies." Jani Lauzon as the Fire Dragon in Jani Lauzon's *A Side of Dreams*. Photo by Samuel Choisy.

Pudlums: Oh Gods and Spirits that guard the secrets of the universe
Let me be the Dragon in your ancient prophecies and
I will fight for peace.
I will conquer injustice.
I will . . . I will . . . (5)

But Pudlums has remained captive and alone for centuries, believing him/herself to be the last of his/her kind. As the expression of hard power with which s/he confronts Haisa ("Brandish your weapon, young warrior, and fight") is met with the mute vulnerability of a fearful, yet fascinated, child, Pudlums confesses his/her own vulnerabilities (s/he is not a warrior) and his/her own tragedy (s/he too is an orphan). In so doing, Pudlums enacts the most heroic deed of his/her existence, playing a key role in ensuring the survivance of the generations to come:

Pudlums: Ah, I see. Then what is it that brings you to the darkness of my cave? Oh! Silence. The deadliest weapon of all. I know that well. Dragons were silenced centuries ago; once strong and powerful warriors, once great and respected leaders, now just a distant flicker in the memory of mankind. Yet without us you would not exist.

What is it that keeps your thoughts locked up inside?

She wants to speak, even tries, but is unable to. She hangs her head, dejected.

Pudlums: But you were powerless to prevent it?

Haisa falls to her knees.

Pudlums: Perhaps the weapons of great warriors are not always swords but rather that which gives us the courage to speak our truth.
[. . .]

Pudlums: The Prophecies of a better world are still possible.

Haisa ventures closer to Pudlums, reaching up to touch his/her face. A gentle caress of the cheek.

Pudlums: You are my taste of hope. Perhaps you carry the generational memory of dragons in your blood. I take heart I may not be the last of my kind. (7–9)

Lauzon's lesson in Indigenous survivance is timely, crucial, and serious; nevertheless, its earnest urgency is rendered eminently palatable by its unique whimsy. She ushers us into a magical kingdom of apple pie, marionettes, aerial feats, stilt-walking giants, and cuddly dragons. We are at once profoundly moved and irresistibly charmed. She makes stringent demands upon us, reminding us of our responsibilities to our ancestors, to ourselves, and to our descendants, and she illuminates, for us, the treacherous path that we will have to follow:

There is violence in ancestral memory.
Your ancestors form a spine.
But sometimes they don't fit so perfectly
Some hurt, leave a mark, so turn that around! (12)

But the performative web she weaves is threaded through with the compassion born of soft power. There is much singing and dancing. And like the round dances that comprised the heart of Idle No More's Round Dance Revolution of 2012–13, the songs and dances that punctuate each of Haisa's encounters with ancestral helpers remind us that we humans have the power to sweeten life for each other and for the rest of the Creation with creative compassion and loving kindness. We can confront our dissatisfactions with killing words and instruments of death or we can embrace those with whom we contend, remind them of the connections we all share, and softly infuse such encounters with joyful reminders of just how sweet life is and how important it is to preserve that fragile sweetness for everyone and everything that lives (see Coates 61). "It's time to sing and dance [our]selves away from the darkness" (Lauzon, *A Side* 15). Dance, like love, is a transformative, (re) creative act. The conditions of oppression require us to love and to dance that we might continue to live; that is, to create and to actively participate in the processes of growth and transformation despite a concerted effort to paralyze our peoples and to cut us off from the process. Dance and love are acts of re-sistance—re-actions, creative responses. And so upon each encounter with the consequences of hard power—an imprisoned dragon, a drunken "asshole" of a grandfather (11), a murdered mother—Lauzon imposes a creative response. Each descent into memory is punctuated with a dance through which her characters affirm and celebrate life and the gift of fellowship—communion with each other.

At the conclusion of the play, Aina hears what she has long longed for: *her mother speaks her name* (19). Next, Haisa teaches Aina about her complex ancestry though a whimsical series of movements—"a combination of the gestures that she has acquired from all the ancestors she met, the reach to the sky in the rain, the swish of the dragon tail, the smudge with the fog from Finland, ending with the final gesture which is the mind to the sky" (19). As long as Haisa, Aina, and the generations that follow them remember and embody the "first few steps of the dance," they "carry the history of giants[, dragons, and ancestral lifeways] inside [their] feet" (12). Pudlums the forgotten dragon will not be the "last of [her] kind" (9). The generations of Haisa will carry a bone-deep knowledge of the northern seas and their treacherous fogs; the scent of the cedar smudge will always ground them; they will taste the underbelly of love in each sweet mouthful of kokum's apple pie; they will craft strong medicine to ward off bad dreams; and they will always be able to teach their children "how to fly" (19).

ARIA: A SONG OF THANKSGIVING FOR "A GIFT COME DOWN"

> We are looking for a tongue that speaks with reverence for life,
> searching for an ecology of mind. Without it, we have no home,
> have no place of our own within the Creation. It is not only the vo-
> cabulary of science that we desire. We also want a language of that
> different yield. A yield rich as the harvests of the earth, a yield that
> returns to us our own sacredness, to a self-love and respect that will
> carry out to others.
> —Linda Hogan, "A Different Yield" 122

Song and dance are part of the whimsical alchemy of love in Tomson Highway's performative decoctions. These are sweeteners that help the bitter medicine go down and numb the sting of Highway's incisive explorations into the causes of and cure for Indigenous disaffection. That he views his works as necessary, if bitter, medicine is evident in his epigraph to the published script of *Dry Lips Oughta Move to Kapuskasing* (1989), a play that magnifies the horrific dysfunctions and community breakdown on a fictional reserve. Violence, adultery, apathy, despair, alcoholism, and Fetal Alcohol Syndrome permeate the lives of his characters, and those who embrace traditional ways to active-ly push back against the destruction and disaffection that have overrun the community are utterly destroyed by the end of the play. It is a dark world into which he ushers us, and although he allows us to back away from this dark vision with the discovery that the horrific events that we have witnessed have all been part of a bad dream, Highway does not back away from his stated intention. He has exposed the root of the dis-ease that afflicts so many First Nations communities and their denizens, as he has promised to do, so that "the healing can take place" (Lyle Longclaws, qtd. in Highway, *Dry Lips* 6).

Highway's *The Rez Sisters* (1986) and *Dry Lips* offer a "window" onto life on a First Nations reserve. These plays are located on Wasaychigan (which means "window"), a fictional reserve that may be based, at least in part, on Highway's own community in the Pas and on other Anishinaabe communities in which he has worked. Highway's *Aria* (1987) takes place in no place or, perhaps, all places at once. Performed by one "diva" who embodies seventeen female characters,[7] the piece realizes itself as a unique ceremonial encounter that exposes the roots of the dysfunction we witness in *Dry Lips*, unpacks the fatal differences between "proximity" and "connection," and stories the people's re-creation through a re-invocation of feminine (soft) power. An aria is a solo musical composition to be performed by a female performer in either an opera or an oratorio. And Highway's *Aria* unfolds in the context of an oratorio—a sacred composition that consists of soloists, a choir, and an orchestra, delivering sacred texts as arias or recitatives straight out to the audience. On stage, we encounter a "diva" and her pianist. These are our conductors, taking us through the life stages of the flawed human and offended non-human females that sustain life on this earth. The "diva" never sings her aria, and the pianist sits inactive for most of the show; both "perform" with and for the audience. Perhaps, here, Highway has drawn on his early training as a concert pianist to design an encounter that is invested with sacrosanctity and ceremony without violation of the Indigenous communities for whom he writes.

 Aria begins in a moment of profound disconnection: a grandmother sits in a crumbling home, waiting to disengage from her corporeal self (81). Deaf, blind, and inert, she remembers a time of connection when the land and waters nurtured, sustained, and even conversed with her. When the "taste was sweeter than anything" she has ever known (81). But these memories bring her no comfort. Instead, they remind her of what she has lost, and she rages silently, hating the gaggle of alien grandchildren that "swarm" through the house and choking on the reek of unchanged diapers and stale liquor (81). Woman, it seems, has lost her place in this world. There is no mothering here. And no mother is in evidence. There is no grandmother(ing) either; there is only neglect and decay. A paralyzed female, isolated despite the bodies that surround her, mourns the loss of the world into which she was born and awaits her escape from this world in which she is dying.

---

7   When I saw this play at the Annex Theatre in March 1987, Makka Kleist played twenty-two female characters (including the Queen of England!).

Highway locates the cause of this dysfunction in the fall from Eden, which inhabits and directs the collective unconscious of the settlers who now govern this continent (*Comparing* 26). These strangers, he tells us, seek to control the "garden" of the fallen realm, rather than to partner with and "love" it. As a result, humans are destroying the planet and each other with displays of hard power. And the only way to halt this destruction, Highway posits, is "the death of the male god and the rebirth of the female" (*ibid.* 48).

Our communities are still reeling from the cataclysmic rape of the matriarchy by an invading patriarch. Our communities are still bleeding because the "sacred hoop," maintained by the Feminine, has been breached. As Paula Gunn Allen maintains, what has been lost here is a sense of rightful place within the circle. Feminine agency, which had instituted clan systems, appointed chiefs, birthed, raised, and educated the children, and envisioned the future of the community, lies soiled and battered on the ground (*The Sacred Hoop* 202). Our grandmothers have been vilified and accused of betraying their own people. Some, like Malinche, are branded as treacherous harlots.[8] Others, like Pocahontas, are characterized as romantically besotted nubiles, and while much work has been done to re-right these distorted images, this work has been undertaken by the granddaughters who live today (i.e., Beth Brant, Paula Gunn Allen, Monique Mojica, Yvette Nolan, and Cathy Elliot). In this regard, our men remain largely silent. Similarly, while much lip service is paid to the restoration of matriarchal values, violence against women continues to mount in our communities as the steadily rising numbers of missing and murdered Aboriginal women across Canada go largely unremarked by this nation's government and policing agencies. And while, statistically, more

---

8   Circa 1519, the Spanish defeated the Chontal Maya of the contemporary Mexican state of Tabasco; Malinche was taken into slavery by the Spanish, eventually becoming the enslaved mistress of and interpreter for Hernán Cortés. Remembered and mythologized as a woman of great beauty, she was also a valuable asset to Cortés for her ability to speak both Mayan and Nahuatl. She converted to Christianity and bore Cortés one son. In this, she may be said to be the mother of the Mestizos. For this, some might honour her; many others, however, have vilified her—characterizing her as a tool of conquest, as one who betrayed her nation for love of either Cortés or his power.

Native females can be seen in attendance at post-secondary institutions than Native males, the male voice is still privileged in publication—be it academic or creative (see Harjo and Bird 22).

To counter this imbalance, Highway ushers us through seventeen female life-and-lifeway stages, invoking the emergence of soft power and the re-establishment of the feminine principle. He takes us back to the beginning when life was "lovely," children were "a gift come down to [us]," and the love of the female earth for her human children was palpable. Here, a baby girl, reclining on her mother's loamy breast, articulates her first experiences of being in the world:

> Hello.
> Wonderful fun kind
> Of wonderful, wonderful sunbeam
> Fancy in the air there [...]
> I was playing lovely games with sun-
> Beam and the little stick . . .
> Lovely. (82–83)

Dissolution and disconnection begin as the "Lover of Men," who desperately wants to play the Virgin Mary in the (residential?) school pageant, enters puberty, awakens to desire, and learns to be ashamed of her natural curiosity and longing for intimate connection with the young men whom she encounters at school. That disconnection—from ancestral knowledge, traditional belief systems, from our fellows, and from our natural rhythms—is not an organic (albeit unfortunate) consequence of growing up. It is a crude and deliberate act of amputation.

Re-education within residential schools severed generations of Indigenous people from their languages. Many of us are in danger of forgetting, entirely, what Kimmerer terms the "grammar of animacy" (48), speaking now, as we have been taught to speak, in the scientific "language of distance, which reduces a being to its working parts . . . a language of objects" (49). When we forget the words that described for us the living character of the biota that sustains

us, we forget that what we take from the earth and what we make from the
earth are gifts freely given and gifts for which we "pay" through speech acts
that manifest human humility, gratitude, and conscientious conservation of
a precious relationship:

> THE WHITE WOMAN: The spirits.
> I see no spirits whatsoever
> On this cement, I don't know what this other woman is talking about.
> I walk on this cement, and the two
> The cement and I—
> Are distinctly separate and apart. (*Aria* 89)

The very loss of a three-syllable word like "Puhpowee," the Potawatomi word
for "the force which causes mushrooms to push up from the earth overnight,"
obfuscates our vision of a "world of being, full of unseen energies that animate
everything" (Kimmerer 49). The earth becomes Other—a foreign object—and,
no longer grateful, we begin to despise and disrespect her gifts (see Kimmerer
50–51). So spurned, she begins to withhold her gifts, and in the lacuna that
springs up between earth and human children, a destructive spirit of insa-
tiable craving begins to gradually move in.

As Highway's "diva" transitions from Lover of Men to Lover of Women
(the moon), and then to Bride, dissolution gains momentum. The young
woman who idolizes the Virgin cannot live up to her own ideal. She envies
other girls in her class; she looks longingly at boys (83–84). She gains a moment of connection as she enters her moon time, but it is fleeting and quickly
disappears as she becomes a bride:

> My white dress is like the dove
> That flutters, hovers and descends
> The last breath of airborne freedom, I feel.
> Pinned by male fuse to the soil
> Will I be forever bound
> to house

and bound
to giving my body night and day
and evening time . . . and teeming
life should sprout out from my flesh?
WHO IS THIS MAN?! (85)

Highway's lesson is clear. Just as humans insist on controlling the earth and all of her cycles through the exercise of hard power, so the human female presents a body to be "pinned" and "bound." Her body will "teem" with (other) life, not "gifts," and just as Highway's Kokum, at the end of life, views her grandchildren as unpleasant strangers, so the Bride is estranged from the bridegroom even before the vows have been exchanged.

The Wife settles into her new role as Hera Keechigeesik, wife of Zachary. Like Hera and Zeus of the Attic Pantheon, the "Big Skys"[9] are a power couple in their community of Wasaychigan. Hera feeds her children, takes care of her husband, pays the grocery bills, and takes care of the women who are her neighbours (86–87). She is proud of her role, of her feminine power, and she has gone to heroic lengths to resist the devastating consequences of the besotted and misguided exercises of hard power that threaten her community:

I, Zachary Keechigeesik's wife, walked 40 miles to the Anchor Inn in January through that blizzard to sober up Rosie Kakapetum the medicine woman to save this woman's own mother from the blood that accident, the gun in that drunken brawl this woman's own father was the one that pulled the trigger and just about shot her foot off. I walked that 40 miles. (87)

"This woman" is Gazelle Nataways, who has slept with Zachary Keechigeesik and now taunts the betrayed wife (her former saviour) with the knowledge,

---

9   Keechigeesik means "Big Sky" in Anishinaabemowin.

bringing his underwear back to Hera like a trophy.[10] Gazelle, throughout Highway's Wasaychigan series, is associated with dysfunction, community unrest, and marital breakdown. More troubling, however, is the power she exercises over this community's leading mother. Hera, enraged by Gazelle's gloating, attacks her pregnant nemesis, causing a miscarriage (87). This good mother has just murdered another woman's baby. When hard power takes over a community, the mothers disappear, and the children perish: "Ohhh, the breath of the Weetigo can freeze you [with despair] till you're stiff [paralyzed and silent] as a statue. Then the Weetigo enters you. Right into your soul. And you become. The Weetigo! And you eat people" (86). Like Gazelle Nataways and Zachary Keechigeesik, we forget—in our hunger, in our unaddressed rage, in our desire to exercise some control over our own lives—the sacrifices that others have made for us and the debts we owe. Like Hera Keechigeesik, we forget ourselves, sever our connections, and deny our spiritual essence to assuage the hunger of a foreign beast. When we can no longer imagine our connections to a loving biota that gives generously, then we can aspire, only, to "proximity" to the perceived power of the hard. As Highway demonstrates in the frenetic advancement of the upwardly mobile female and her evolution into the vengeful "Woman of the Rolling Head," proximity to hard power leads to its exercise and, ultimately, to the destruction of our communities (88–94).

Aria ends with an ambiguous, disjointed statement from Earth herself. Here, she draws upon key phrases, echoing back to us the stories she has witnessed of communal dissolution—stories of the grandmother, the mother, the child, the wife, the secretary, the executive, the vengeful spirit of an unfaithful spouse, and the battered prostitute. She sketches out the story of a gift that has become a curse within which we are doomed to perpetual seeking, reaching, and struggle. Earth remains. Earth remembers. But there can be no guarantee that we two-leggeds will maintain the loving connection and sustained conversation with her that we once experienced. If we forget to *live*

---

10 This would lead us to question, then, just which events of *Dry Lips Oughta Move to Kapuskasing* are dream and which are reality, as the adultery and the "boxer shorts" incident also figure prominently in *Dry Lips*.

the stories that she holds in trust for us, she may, in the end, tire of us and fall silent (see Simpson, *Dancing* 105):

> And the songbird paused.
> My spirit . . . like a mist.
> There was a gift came down to me.
> *(sings) Kees-pin ki-sa-gee-bin.*
> *(speaks)* Strange and mysterious goings-on.
> And pain becomes power.
> Here is the aisle.
> Me and him and him and me
> *U-wi-nuk-ee-pa-gi-ta-ta-moot.*
> Are separate and apart.
> Like ahmmm . . . so, anyway.
> I touch you and you speak.
> Closer proximity to.
> I can offer each member
> Ten thousand snakes.
> Oooh, how long?
> Starlight, moonlight and I'm alright! Hey! (Highway, *Aria* 96)

TRANSFORMATIVE ENCOUNTERS AT GRANDMOTHER'S HOUSE

In *Something Old, Something New, Something Borrowed, Something Blue*, a despairing silence that comes with disconnection is a deadly force that must be countered. Written and performed by Guna-Rappahannock playwright/performer Gloria Miguel—an octogenarian and respected Elder in the Indigenous theatre community—this is an intensely personal epic that recounts lived experience and gives voice to the experiences of other Elders who can no longer speak for themselves. It takes us through eight decades of urban Indigenous experience as it illuminates and resists a profoundly troubling gap between the generations that seems to be widening in this time and place.

> No more sounds
> No people coming to see her
> See another face
> Face like herself
> Older, wrinkled, no teeth. (Miguel)

The phone doesn't ring, relatives only visit when they require a babysitter, and the lessons this Elder (and those to whom she gives voice) has to teach about enduring the physical and psycho-spiritual shocks of hard power's exercise go largely disregarded by a preoccupied and "impatient" generation (Miguel).

But Miguel's intent is not to castigate those from whom she feels so intensely separated, and she does not simply seek a public platform from which to mourn her friends and her elder sister who have passed out of this life and so, it seems, out of reach and hearing (Miguel).[11] This is an important piece that communicates vital truths: *Old* truths that speak of how we came to be; *New* truths that whisper of the legacies carried by and promised to the generations who follow those aged storytellers; truths *Borrowed* from those who no longer have the voice to speak; and *Blue* truths that speak to our deepest fears around ageing, abandonment, and eventual death. In an undertaking of remarkable courage and generosity, Miguel performs a survivance-intervention, plunging into the darkest recesses of her life story and extending aged limbs across the thresholds of past, present, and future to connect the generations who follow her with hard-won lessons in endurance and with the creation stories that teach us that, despite the woundings we have inflicted or that have, in our mortal lives, been inflicted on us, we are all beings created in and out of love. The play opens with Miguel's embodiment of a Guna creation story that speaks of sacrifice and of vital teachings in survivance:

---

11   Elizabeth Miguel (a.k.a. Lisa Mayo) was with her sisters Gloria and Muriel one of the founders of Spiderwoman Theater—the long-running Indigenous troupe that is also the world's longest-running feminist troupe. Elizabeth Miguel passed away on 24 November 2013.

Ooh, ooh. I'm getting too old for this. It gets harder every time I come
down from the stars [. . .] I started later than the other girls, the Nis
Bundor, those first four sisters who came down from the stars. All the
Guna people come from the stars. My father told me so. *Degii.* The
youngest of the four sisters' name was Olonadili. She had a purpose
and a mission. She taught the people about plants and medicines, how
to feel emotion, to sing to the babies, to transform grief into verse.

As she enters her own story, Miguel warns us against absorbing the lessons of hard power and conforming to its ways. The violence of racism outside
her childhood home was carried into that home, and she carries its scars on
her person and in her memory. Called "the savage's savage" by her maternal
grandmother and "black bastard" by her maternal uncle, Miguel became, she
confesses, "dark inside," as "revenge [became her] weapon." Here, too, a gap
between the generations had insinuated itself, and, surveying it simultaneously through the eyes of Miguel-the-Child and through the eyes of experience,
Miguel speaks to its genesis and its repair. The child could not honour those
Elders who carried the violence they had encountered into their relations with
her: "Elders," this Elder cautions us, "must earn the right to be honoured."
And we do this, she shows us, by remembering the stories that teach us who
we were born to be: we learn to transform our "grief" into creative acts that
defy the destructive force of the hard powers that inflicted it.

In its execution, this performance teaches us what such acts might look
like and how we might remember the love that infused our creation in resonant action. When, at the age of eighty-two, Miguel began her work on
Something Old, Something New in 2008,[12] she was struggling with vision loss,
hearing loss, and compromised mobility. She had no work and felt isolated
and forgotten. Rejecting the role of the *vecchia inutile*—"useless old woman"

---

12   My own involvement with this production began in 2008 when I brought Miguel to
the University of Toronto's Robert Gill Theatre to perform a staged reading. In 2014 I directed its final developmental phase and Canadian premiere at Native Earth Performing
Arts's Weesageechak Begins to Dance Festival with Miguel's daughter Monique Mojica
as dramaturge.

(see Camporesi 44)—and refusing to settle into a rocking chair and wait for the darkness to overtake her, she wrote a one-woman show that she could "carry in two shopping bags" (as she said during rehearsals in 2014). She has been performing it across North America ever since. In the seven years that have passed since the play's first workshop, Miguel's health has declined, her mobility has lessened, and her fragility has increased. Still, she has something to say—a vital message for the generations that follow. And now, more than ever, she must sing and dance us out of the darkness and "transform [her/our] grief" into poetry, motion, and joyful noise. We *need* this "useless" old woman. We *need* her voice. And she needs us—her "community," her "family"—to help her to speak (Miguel). I could enumerate the behind-the-scenes supports provided to aid Miguel in her project—the longer rehearsal period; shorter rehearsal days; Miguel's dramaturge, the daughter who painstakingly nurtured this project; and so many other details. But these loving supports are invisible to those who witness the work. What audiences of *Something Old, Something New* were able to apprehend was the unabashed communication of these supports on stage—a performance of soft power: the loving hand of a strong helper, conveying the Elder through her story; the loving hands of the cellist (Cris Derksen) who responded to her every mood, doggedly following Miguel into the darkest recesses of memory, carrying her on music, and serenading her with sweet reminders of a life underscored by love; and the loving trust that infused the vulnerable storyteller's intimate connection with her audience. The teachings here are potent: we two-leggeds are infinitely precious creatures who are bound, carried, and ultimately worn away by time and all her capricious cruelties. We, who live in interesting times, facilitate our own survivance when we meet fragility with compassion—laying gentle hands on aged bones to dance them out of the darkness, on heavy hearts to coax another song, and on burdened minds to dream, with them, those moments of transcendence that carry us out of the exigencies of finite existence into those ceremonial spaces wherein all times are one.

AND THEY LIVED . . .

We encounter, here, three contemporary performances (of an ever-growing body of Indigenous works for the stage) that draw the Indigenous story-teller and her community of witnesses into intense relationship. In each of these re-creation tales, love (that is, the act of loving and the condition of being loved) informs and intersects in profound—albeit, sometimes, unex-pected—ways with the powerful assertion and manifestation of Indigenous sovereignty. Indeed, Lauzon, Highway, and Miguel (amongst many of the Indigenous storytellers who speak to us today) present, encoded in their re-creation stories, soft power (manifested as love) as the vital stuff of sov-ereign reclamation. All three have presented an answer to the call of Leanne Simpson and Edna Manitowabi to seek out and locate, in their nations' cre-ation stories, the mechanisms of this soft power—mechanisms that gently aid these artists and their Indigenous witnesses in the reappropriation of personal and political sovereignty. All three have answered Linda Hogan's call for a new, gentler mode of expression to heal broken relationships between

Figure 3. Aina (Jessica Barrera) smudges with her child-mother (Jani Lauzon) in Jani Lauzon's *A Side of Dreams*: "a true reconciliation circle." Photo by Samuel Choisy.

humans and the rest of creation. And all three have invested their *acts* with a feminine power (born of humility, gratitude, and stubborn endurance), breaching the silent void that separates the generations and forcing us into multiple encounters with soft power. Without such encounters, we are vulnerable to soul death and self-destructive acts. *Without them, our children will not survive to continue the struggle:*

> Love can be gentle as a lamb or
> ferocise [sic] as a lion.
> It is something to be welcomed yet it is
> something to be afraid of
> it is good and bad, yet people fight and die for this
> somehow people can cope with it I don'
> now [sic], I think
> I would not be happy with it yet I am depresed [sic] and sad without
> it. love is very strong. (Richard S. Cardinal, qtd. in Nabokov 417)[13]

---

13 This passage is the last diary entry of Chipewyan teenager Richard S. Cardinal, who hanged himself in 1984. His poem constitutes the final statement of a child broken by the abuses he suffered in twenty-eight foster homes and the despair that comes with isolation and neglect. His final thoughts challenge us to attend to our children, even if we have known only neglect; they challenge us to heal, despite the scars imprinted upon our own bodies; and they challenge us to love, even if we have been assaulted only with hate. Love is *the* vital act of resistance against the destroyer's onslaughts, and it manifests itself most potently in overt acts of intervention predicated upon soft power. Without it, Richard Cardinal warns us, further acts of resistance are unrealizable.

KIPPMOOJIKEWIN:[1]
THE THINGS WE CARRY WITH US
MARRIE MUMFORD

> In Nishnaabeg thought, resurgence is dancing on our turtle's back;
> it is visioning and dancing new realities and worlds into existence.
> —Leanne Simpson, *Dancing On Our Turtle's Back: Stories of*
> *Nishnaabeg Re-Creation, Resurgence and a New Emergence* 70

Sitting in Nozhem First Peoples Performance Space at Trent University during mid-winter ceremonies, I watch as the little boy water drum is being dressed by the shkaabewiskweg (women helpers to the Elder). A few of the children sit in silence in front of the drum, watching, sometimes helping, as they hear the stories of the little boy. The Elder explains why each part is needed in order to complete dressing the little boy, so that he is dressed in his best and ready for ceremony. It is Makwa Giizis, the Bear Moon, the time when the bear turns around in her den. She prepares her cubs to end their hibernation, as she begins to end her fast and search for food.

The drum sounds and the ceremony begins with the sacred teaching songs of the Anishinaabeg. The songs are sung in Anishinaabemowin (the Ojibwe language), and stories are told in the circle of Elders, with the shkaabewis-ag and families with their children, as well as with students from Trent. The feast is laid out on blankets in the centre of the circle in honour of Makwa, one of the clans of the Anishinaabeg. Makwa is the guardian and protector

---

1   I first learned this word from Leanne Simpson, who uses the title for the introduction to her book *The Gift is in the Making: Anishinaabeg Stories*. She credits learning the word kippmoojikewin in Anishinaabemowin from Maya Chacaby's thesis, *Kippmoojikewin: Articulating Anishinaabe Pedagogy Through Anishinaabemowin Revitalization*.

of the people, and now the guardian of Nozhem, our performance space that is named for the female bear.

The food has been brought by all the participants who have remembered to bring food that Makwa likes. Adults and children alike are admonished by the Elder who reminds us all that bears like more than sweets; they like fish too. Throughout the ceremony, bear stories are told, teachings are given, and, if we are lucky, we might see the bears dance. The ceremony is led by Edna Manitowabi, a revered Elder, a great-grandmother, a mother, an auntie, and a sister, who is also a fifth-degree Midewiwin teacher, as well as a residential-school survivor.

Edna is my mentor, a sister, a colleague, and a very dear friend. She is assisted in the ceremony by shkaabewisag, women and men whom she mentors and who will carry this practice forward into the next generation. Edna established the first Aboriginal Theatre course at Trent University, and it was her vision that brought Nozhem First Peoples Performance Space into being, which she was also invited with semaa (sacred tobacco used in ceremonies) to name.

As I sit in this circle, I hear a child behind me singing with the drum. She sings from her heart with confidence, with a clear, beautiful voice. She remembers all the words of these ancient Anishinaabemowin songs. As I look around the circle, I feel the energy in this space, where we not only feel safe to be who we are, but are empowered by each other to be the best we can be. I feel honoured to be here, to work in this community with the Elders and men and women who have mentored with the Elders, many of whom are artists from regional communities. As traditional performance specialists, they continue the work of the Elders, working with youth and their families, as well as with the students at Trent. Looking back I am reminded that it has not always been safe for our families and children, not for many generations. For many it is still not safe: for women in our communities, or for our youth on the street, or for those in prison, or for the many children still in care. But I know also there are many communities who have begun, as we who have gathered here in Nozhem, the process of respect, recovery, restoration, and resurgence. It is a growing movement that I hope will someday provide hope for all those who need to "come in . . . [to find] shelter from the storm" (Dylan).

Ceremonies—such as the Makwa Giizis ceremony—are the roots of Anishinaabeg performance cultures and, as with some roots, also the medicine. Indigenous performance cultures have evolved from such traditions through which Indigenous knowledges, languages, and cultural practices have been passed to future generations. In the words of Elder Doug Williams from Wshkiigimongaki (Curve Lake First Nation), "It is up to each new generation to reinterpret and to breathe new life into our teachings" (qtd. in Simpson, "Circles").

****

I did not attend an Indigenous ceremony, nor did I begin to work in Indigenous performance, until I was almost forty. I grew up in Redcliff, a small factory town of five thousand in southern Alberta where my father's family had lived beside the South Saskatchewan River since 1917. They were the children of the children who survived the Resistance—descendants of those who stood up and fought beside Louis Riel and Gabriel Dumont, for which they were discharged from Treaty 4 and forced off their land at Cowessess, Crooked Lake, Saskatchewan, in 1886 , one year after the Resistance. My grandmother's extended family moved between the Cypress Hills (when they had to avoid the North West Mounted Police) and Montana, living near large reserves to blend in as part of the four hundred Landless Chippewa-Cree[2] travelling throughout Montana with Chief Little Bear, son of Big Bear. They moved back and forth across what was then known as the Medicine Line in order to avoid persecution.

My paternal grandmother, born four years after the Resistance, remembers camping with her extended family in the Cypress Hills. Many of her young cousins died there. When you are that young, witnessing death has an impact that stays with you for most of your life. My grandmother's aunt,

---

2   Chippewa is how the Anishinaabeg people are known in the western United States.

Louise Boyer, whose family travelled with Chief Piapot's band, was the mother of my grandmother's cousins who died in the Cypress Hills. A newspaper in Red Deer reported that Louise Boyer lost an arm in a "skirmish" with the Mounties and was interned with her husband, Charles Boyer, and their surviving children in Regina for the duration of the Resistance.

In Redcliff, my extended family was identified as the only "Indian" family living in town. I suspect there were others, but perhaps not as noticeable as my father's family. His brothers were wild men, full of mischief. They called themselves the Dalton Brothers. My grandfather made sure they became boxers so they could defend themselves. My mother was an English war bride who was raised in an English orphanage from the age of three. Both of my paternal grandparents were motherless children and sometimes I also felt "like a motherless child, a long way from home" (Johnson and Johnson 30). I didn't feel truly safe until 1966 when I arrived at Brandeis University to study for a Master of Fine Arts degree in Theatre. Brandeis, a small liberal arts university of two thousand students located in Waltham, Massachusetts, was devoted to peace and social justice. I had arrived with my (now) ex-husband. We had received tuition scholarships and a living allowance for the time we were there. It was at Brandeis that the meaning, the possibilities, and the potential of theatre came alive for me. The program was led by Morris Carnovsky, one of the first-generation Stanislavsky teachers in the US. Being the eldest, at the age of twenty-nine, Carnovsky was considered to be the father of the Group Theater in the 1930s. The Group Theater was a political theatre based on humanitarianism and early concepts of cultural specificity as put forward by Stanislavsky (Ben-Ari), one of the founders of the Moscow Art Theatre. The experience of working with Carnovsky was transformative. It set me on the path that I continue on to this day.

Carnovsky was targeted and blacklisted for eight years at the height of his career for refusing to name colleagues during the anti-communist regime in the US and Canada in the 1950s. Wherever Carnovsky worked he created community. At Brandeis he brought with him a company of actors, directors, and teachers who had also survived the blacklist to work with twenty masters' students, creating an ensemble company that also included undergraduates.

The company of actors, directors, playwrights, designers, and teachers worked together in three theatres, with classes in the morning and rehearsals/classes in the afternoon followed by performances in the evenings once the plays opened. It was a two-year program and I loved every minute of being there. We were the first M.F.A. theatre students to graduate from Brandeis.

Carnovsky was an excellent teacher, as well as a very powerful actor, and I thrived under his guidance. The fire was lit. I felt safe in this environment, with the freedom to truly express from within myself without fear. Carnovsky loved us as if we were his grandchildren, but at crucial times he took on our resistances to take us beyond what we thought we could do. I was in a community of people who were also descendants of those who survived genocide. We were all survivors. I swore if I ever became a teacher I would teach as Carnovsky taught, creating a community with a positive, creative, encouraging working environment, learning how and when to challenge. I stayed in Waltham for two years after I graduated, working with fellow graduates in collectives creating and performing new work. Both of my daughters were born while I was there.

****

I returned to Canada to the city of Toronto in the fall of 1970 at the height of the implementation of the War Measures Act, with soldiers and tanks on the streets of Montreal, Quebec City, and Ottawa. My marriage had ended, and I was now a single mother of two. By the end of the decade I had studied with amazing teachers in the Stanislavsky tradition and, with that confidence, I worked in mainstream regional theatres across Canada, as well as in theatres, television, and small films in Toronto, including numerous television commercials to pay the rent. But there was a dark side to the industry, and it became easy to take wrong turns. The industry in Toronto in the seventies was not inclusive of ethnicity, let alone race. There seemed to be no end to "the illusion of supremacy" and stereotypes were everywhere, especially in film and television. Predators were also everywhere. Working in this environment anger and resentments grew. Whenever I could, I would go to New York City acting studios to study and be with friends from Brandeis to keep the fire burning. Eventually I walked away from the industry and established the Actor's Theatre Studio in Lois Smith's former ballet studio in Toronto, with two other acting teachers and a third to create a youth program.

It was during this time that I read *Halfbreed* by Maria Campbell. Her book has had a huge impact on my life. Her honesty helped me to see what was going on inside me, and the stories of her great-grandmother helped me to identify what was missing in my life. My family was concerned and wanted me to come home. I resisted, but my father convinced me when he said, "I hear your bitterness; just come home and be with your people. You don't have to stay; when you go back, you will see things differently." I stayed in Redcliff for two years working at Medicine Hat College, creating a two-year theatre transfer program to the University of Alberta.

****

When I returned to Toronto it was 1983; little did I know that in the next three years I would enter into three decades of working exclusively in Native Theatre, beginning with Tomson Highway. As far as I knew, the contemporary Indigenous theatre movement across North America began in the 1970s. I was not there at this beginning, but I have listened to stories from those who were. Among the stories I heard were of a group of Native men and women who advocated on behalf of Indigenous artists to establish a Native arts organization when the then Ontario Ministry of Culture launched funding support for twenty new Ontario arts service organizations in Toronto in 1972. This, I was told, is how the Association for Native Development in the Performing and Visual Arts (ANDPVA) came into being. It was designated as an Arts Service Organization (ASO) and was the only diverse ASO in the province of Ontario. ANDPVA was, I believe, the first Native arts organization in Canada that was directed and operated by Native people.

Cree Elder James Buller, who they say was an actor, an opera singer, and a champion boxer, was appointed Executive Director of ANDPVA. He then established the Native Theatre School (NTS) as a summer program in 1974, under ANDPVA's umbrella. In the early years, I was told, the summer program brought Indigenous cultural performance instructors together with western-trained theatre instructors working in performance practices derived from Augusto Boal's *Theatre of the Oppressed*, based in Paulo Freire's *Pedagogy of the Oppressed*. Students who became passionate about the practice of Native theatre returned for two or three summers and then, if interested, were offered an apprenticeship to work with a theatre company. Many of the graduates of NTS returned to their home communities to lead workshops for young people who were interested, and some eventually formed their own companies, such as the Awasikan Theatre, Four Winds Theatre, and Kehewin Native Performance.

NTS became the Centre for Indigenous Theatre (CIT), an independent organization, in 1994. Under the leadership of Carol Greyeyes, CIT went from a summer program to a year-round theatre-training program in 1998—four years after becoming an independent organization. In 1999 a second year was added, and in the year 2000 a third year of Indigenous theatre training was added with funding in place, all under Greyeyes's leadership. "1998 marked the launch of the Center for Indigenous Theatre's newest and most ambitious program. Based on the Native Theatre School model the Centre opened the new Indigenous Theatre School, the first full-time, 3-year training program in North America with a curriculum that integrates training in acting, voice, movement and traditional aboriginal cultural classes in dance, song and oral history" ("CIT at Artscape Youngplace").

To this day I continue to hear stories about James Buller from senior artists who say that they became artists because of him. They said he always had time to talk to them, encouraging each of them to follow a career in the arts. Through Buller's dedication and his years of service, he left a legacy for all of us. Within a ten-year period Buller had already reached beyond Canada to emerging theatres in Indigenous nations around the world. Through the beginnings of ANDPVA and NTS, Buller created a catalytic environment that fostered the development of innovative pedagogical methods to fulfill a vision to explore contemporary, culturally specific and trans-Indigenous performance that continues to this day. This work supported the creation of independent Indigenous theatres that spread across Canada within a twenty-year period, beginning with Native Earth Performing Arts (NEPA) in Toronto in 1983.

Key conferences kept the movement growing. From the formal Congress held at the first World Indigenous Theatre Celebration, created through Buller's work at ANDPVA, emerged the Indigenous People's Theatre Association (IPTA). The Celebration was held at York University in 1980 and included Native theatres across Canada, as well as international Indigenous theatres from around the world. In the summer of 1982, in an effort by Buller to continue work begun in 1980, Nogojiwanong (Peterborough) was the site of the groundbreaking second Indigenous People's Theatre Celebration: A Gathering of International Tribal People in Performance that brought together seventeen international Indigenous theatre companies from ten countries around the world. This second gathering, hosted by ANDPVA, lasted ten days and began with a Traditional Welcome, Pow Wow, and Native feast at Wshkiigimongaki, with performances throughout Nogojiwanong for the following nine days. The performances took place in the Peterborough Collegiate Vocational School auditorium and the Peterborough Square shopping mall, with outdoor performances in local parks. All performances were open to the public.

Ross Kidd, in the article "Reclaiming Culture: Indigenous Performers Take Back Their Show," suggests that in order to provide for the diversity of those companies participating in the conference to "shape their own cultural forms" (33), the focus was to be the celebration of culture in performance, rather than on western conventions of European genres or forms. This identified for me the beginnings of culturally specific work in contemporary Indigenous theatre. Colloquies were held in the mornings at Trent University and were led by professors in theatre from the University of Calgary and York University, who critiqued the performances of the previous evening. The fact that there were no Indigenous artists leading the colloquies was a huge problem. Perhaps it was these sorts of circumstances that prompted Lenore Keeshig-Tobias to suggest that non-Indigenous professionals such as university professors "have taken over the work of the missionaries and the Indian agents" (174).

James Buller passed away three weeks minus a day before the 1982 Indigenous People's Theatre Celebration began. He was honoured for "devoting his considerable energies and abilities to the development of the arts of the Native people in Canada," making a "unique contribution to the arts in Canada" (Matthews 150). The 1982 gathering sowed the seeds for the flourishing and highly regarded Indigenous performance landscape that we experience across Canada today. Seven First Nations in the Nogojiwanong region now participate in the Aboriginal Education Council at Trent University. They have a rich and vibrant history, beginning with the Teaching Rocks, oral traditions, and cultural practices of the Michi Saagiig Anishinaabeg, whose territory this is. Their support of Nozhem First Peoples Performance Space at Trent since its inception has played a vital role in supporting local, national, and international Indigenous theatre.

****

When I returned from Redcliff I wanted to avoid the mistakes I had made in previous years. I set up one class in the Firehall Theatre with former students and began to take classes myself, looking at different approaches to the creative process, studying with directors who worked directly with Bertolt Brecht, Peter Brook, Joseph Chaikin, Jerzy Grotowski, and Tadashi Suzuki. I had always thought of myself as a tragedian, so I took clown classes with Dean Gilmour and Mimi Smith. Clown classes were fun and gave me a whole new perspective on my life. Looking back, I realize now, at this stage of my life, I was intuitively looking for a creative family to work with. In the Anishinaabeg Seven Stages of Life Teachings, this stage of my life would be named the Stage of Wandering and Wondering. My oldest daughter, Darmody, explained to her friends that this was my experimental phase. When I was practising clowning at home, Cara, my youngest daughter, said to me, "Mother! It's very hard to have a serious conversation with you while you're wearing a clown nose."

In 1985 I accepted a job as a part-time instructor at the University of Toronto's University College Drama Program. I taught a second-year acting class and a third-year directing class and I moved my professional acting class to the Brooke Acting Studio. One of my daughters had already left home to attend university. When my second daughter left home I was in my forties and wondering what I was going to do in the next stage of my life. I was leaning toward moving to New York City to return to the studios and good friends from Brandeis who lived and worked there.

It was Tomson Highway who brought me into Indigenous theatre, and for that I will be forever grateful. Little did I know in the spring of 1986— when I was invited to perform Clytemnestra in a contemporary version of *Electra* directed by Alec Stockwell and produced by Act IV Theatre—that I was about to experience what Brecht would call a major turning point in my life. Working with Stockwell was a very creative experience; he was a good director and gave us lots of space to explore. It was a rewarding process, as was working with Jan Austin as Electra and Brian Smeagal as Orestes. It was my first time back on stage in a meaningful role in almost a decade. Both rehearsals and performances were fulfilling experiences. The play was presented at the Annex Theatre, which I believe had once been a Sunday school. The theatre had a walkway all around the second floor that overlooked the performance space. The dressing room was on the second floor (off the walkway), and in front of the theatre there were two large staircases coming down onto each side of the stage floor. This made for very dramatic entrances.

After one performance, the stage manager came to our dressing room and told me that Tomson Highway was in the audience and wanted to meet with me downstairs in the theatre. I was thrilled at the thought of meeting Tomson! I had heard, from the ladies of the theatre who met the previous summer in Vinetta Strombergs's garden for lunch, of the original work that both Tomson and his younger brother René were creating. Vinetta had worked in script development with De-ba-jeh-mu-jig Theatre on Manitoulin Island. During lunch she spoke enthusiastically about Tomson's work as the artistic director there. She said he was writing a new play and engaging very talented

Native artists from communities on the island. This was when I first began to hear of Tomson and René's work, as well as that of De-ba-jeh-mu-jig Theatre and Native Earth. Before I began to work on *Electra* I met with Vinetta; she had just returned from Manitoulin, where she had a cottage, and told me that Tomson had recently been appointed as the new artistic director of Native Earth Performing Arts (NEPA) in Toronto.

As I walked down the stairs to the theatre, I could see Tomson waiting below. I remember thinking that he reminded me of one of my father's younger brothers. I thought he was beautiful, and suddenly I felt shy. I can't remember what he said but he probably said he enjoyed the show, and maybe even my performance. But I do remember that he said he was working on a play that he was writing, *The Rez Sisters*, about seven women, and there was to be a reading on Sunday afternoon. He asked if I would be interested in coming and reading one of the parts. Quite calmly, I said, "Yes . . . I'd love to . . . " or something like that. But my heart was already bursting with enthusiasm.

And that was the beginning of what was to become a life-changing experience. I remember the first time I went to Native Earth's office. At that time their office was at the Native Canadian Centre on Spadina Road just north of Bloor, which I had never been to before. Sometimes when you're mixed-blood, you don't always know where you're welcome. I felt a sense of awe when I walked up the steps into the building. I asked the receptionist where I could find Native Earth's office. She pointed with her lips to the stairs and said, "At the top of the third floor." She didn't look at me as if I didn't belong.

I climbed the stairs on a hot spring day and when I reached the top of three flights stairs I followed the laughter to Native Earth's office. The office looked crowded, as if it was full of people. But when I stood outside the doorway of the office to talk to Tomson, I remember seeing only three people around the desk that seemed to fill the room: Tomson and Elaine Bomberry, the general manager; I think Tomson's nephew Billy Merasty was the third person. It was a very small office. I don't remember why I was there, perhaps it was to pick up a script. I don't remember details, or even what was said, but I do remember teasing and lots of laughter and feeling light and full as I left and walked back down the stairs.

As I was about to leave, the receptionist stopped me and asked if I would like to sign up as a volunteer, and as I said okay she handed me a form and escorted me to the volunteer office. "There are two volunteer coordinators," she explained to me as we were walking toward the office, "one who works with volunteers from Ojibwe communities and one who works with volunteers from Mohawk communities. You can choose to work with whoever you feel most comfortable with." At that point I was still unsure of my family's identity, other than we were identified as "Indian" in the town I grew up in, and as "Halfbreed" or "Breed" by our relatives who lived on Crow and Fort Belknap Reserves in Montana. Although we were living in Blackfoot territory, we knew we weren't Blackfoot; we thought we might be Cree. I was introduced to Sara Bagnato, who had previously worked as a nurse, who said she was Anishinaabe. Sara immediately reminded me of my favourite aunt, so I said I would like to work with her. As I began to fill out the form, Sara asked me about my interests. She then told me that she had been a board member of ANDPVA and she knew they were looking for board members. I said, "No, I don't think so, I have never served on a board before," and then I noticed on the form that you could volunteer to work in the kitchen for community feasts and gatherings, so I said I'd like to do that, as well as work with youth programs.

I was nervous as I approached the community centre where the reading of *The Rez Sisters* was to be held. When I arrived, Tomson was there and René and his partner Micah Barnes, as well as Larry Lewis, the director. There was lots of laughter and mischief in the room and I immediately felt safe and at home with everyone. It is hard to describe that first reading; so much was going on inside. (At this point I need to apologize, as I can only remember one of the actors reading: Nancy, and maybe that was because she was very kind and one of the first ones there. I think after that I was just overwhelmed to be there.) That evening, in that setting, surrounded by Native theatre artists, I felt as if I had found a home, an extended family, and a community in the theatre. It was a warm and welcoming space. The play touched me in a way that was very deep and emotional. It was the first time that I participated in reading a play that was written by a Native playwright, one where all the characters were Native, and were real, and none were victims. All were women except for Nanabush, the spirit who transformed him/herself into a seagull or blackbird or the Bingo Master, opening a door to a place that is often only felt by those in crisis. "Nanabush also made his stage debut in Highway's play apart from the major debut he had already made in the oral traditions many years earlier" (Manossa 65). That all of the women were related by blood, marriage, or adoption made them an extended family in situations that I could immediately identify with—both the humour in the familial relationships and the bickering, as well as the spirit and strength of the women. They reminded me that we are all survivors moving forward. Manossa writes that the women come from a community that has experienced loss. The eldest sister, Pelajia, says, "The old stories, the old language. Almost all gone . . . was a time Nanabush and Windigo and everyone here could rattle away in Indian" (Highway, *The Rez Sisters* 5). Within myself I understood that loss. "Highway's plays are realizations that Indian people, 'had a history, that we had a culture that was different' " (Manossa 83, quoting Highway in "Life and Times").

At the end of the reading, I was speechless. Reading the play made me think of Carnovsky, who said,

> Why is it that when we go out after some great experience in the theatre or the concert hall or whatever, we don't chatter to each other. We don't want to say, "Gee that was great," or anything of that sort. It's not necessary. It's because I think something has assisted us to reach a level of Self in our own experience which is unique. We're more than we were before. That is the purpose of art. To make the world of people more than it was before. That is the responsibility of the Self. (Carnovsky 33–34)

****

The Native Canadian Centre offered a respectful and welcoming environment under the leadership of Barbra Nahwegahbow. Working in the kitchen
with the women was fun—and these women could cook, often preparing
feasts for three hundred or more. It reminded me of working in the kitchen
with my aunts on special occasions. After the dishes were done, we would sit
around one of the tables with the Elders for coffee and cigarettes and listen
to their stories. There was always lots of laughter. I was also invited to sit in
on program meetings, including Elders' Council meetings, which were my
favourites. This was the beginning of my work with the Elders, who came
every month to the centre. I was drawn to the Anishinaabeg Elders, one of
whom, the late Gladys Kidd, became my traditional grandmother. I began to
attend her Full Moon Ceremony every month in Harwood, which is about
an hour outside of Peterborough.

It was then that I began to travel with Gladys and her younger sister,
also an Elder, the late Vera Martin. Vera had been part of the group who had
advocated the establishment of Native Friendship Centres across Canada.
Gladys and Vera were invited to First Nations territories throughout southern
Ontario to conduct Full Moon Ceremonies and hold Women's Circles to share
Indigenous Women's Knowledge. They often invited me to travel with them.
It was the dream of a lifetime. Besides being a lot of fun, as well as women
of knowledge actively working in communities when they were called, they
were positive about the journey of aging. I was learning so much from these
grandmothers. I began to have thoughts of leaving the theatre; somehow in
the future, I thought, maybe I could just work with the grandmothers. But
Vera began to talk with me about theatre. She had worked at Catalyst Theatre
in Edmonton as well as at the Nechi Institute in St. Albert, Alberta. She had
worked with Floyd Favel, Tantoo Cardinal, and Louise Halfe. She had also
acted in a film with Cardinal and Ken Welsh. Vera said that the Anishinaabeg
Elders at this time spoke of the Seven Fires Prophecy, and that the Elders
said it was up to the artists of this generation to carry the work of the Elders

forward—to share the oral histories, traditions, and cultural practices through their work—and she wanted to know what I was going to do about that.

On a deeper level, even though I wasn't aware at the time, I had begun hunting, searching for my ancestral roots. It was as if I turned a corner and, without knowing it consciously, I had begun the part of the journey that in the Anishinaabeg Seven Stages of Life Teachings would be called the Stage of Seeking. I was now about to gather knowledge that became very meaningful to my life; I named this part of my life Hunting & Gathering in the Twentieth Century.

As volunteers of the Native Canadian Centre, we were invited to form a crew to go to the Midewiwin ceremonies in Wisconsin on the southern shores of Lake Superior. Over four days I heard the water drums from the four directions, and the teachings, always first in the language, then translated into English to take pity on those of us who have lost our language. I listened to the oral histories of the Three Fires Confederacy: the Anishinaabeg, the Odawa, and the Potawatomi. I participated in ancient cultural practices, learning the stories, the songs, and the dances. We feasted. I became a shkaabewis. It was as if a door opened deep inside and I could feel the past in the present and could sense the future. I realized that this is where our theatre comes from; these ceremonies are the roots of our Tree of Knowledge; this is the medicine, the way in which Indigenous knowledges, languages, traditions, and cultural practices have been passed on to future generations. I was reminded of the teaching given by the mountain man, the spiritual leader of the Anishinaabeg, that we should search for this trail to find the gifts that the ancestors left for us to guide us on our journey. I was also reminded of my studies of Greek theatre during the master's program at Brandeis, the study of the Greek Elysian societies where the people gathered to learn about the Great Mysteries, out of which their theatre grew and became the festivals that celebrated their stories (and teachings) through the tragedies and comedies presented each year.

Two years later, as my volunteer work in the Native community increased, my traditional grandmother suggested that I put my tobacco in the fire at the next ceremony to find my ancestors. I did, but I did not have the faith that the grandmothers had. Our family had been in hiding for two generations because of the persecution of those in our family who participated in the Resistance. We did not know the names of our ancestors beyond my grandmother's father, and his last name was Thomas. When I went home that summer, I asked my father again if he could remember, and this time he told me he had papers from his cousin Mark McGillis, who had searched for his mother's family history. Mark was a tribal councillor with the Little Shell Tribe in Great Falls, Montana. They were recognized by the Montana tribes, but were not federally recognized. Mark's mother was my grandmother's sister. My grandmother's brothers and one sister stayed in Montana, and were registered on the Roe Cloud Registration as the Landless Chippewa-Cree. Mark said that his father told him that old people said to always remember the Chippewa.

Now that we had my grandmother's mother's name, my youngest daughter Cara began research in the Glenbow Museum archives in Calgary. Days later, she surfaced and found our family's journey back to Sault Ste. Marie in the 1840s. She found my grandmother's family's Indian name and also found that our family was part of the Anishinaabeg migration west. They were with Riel in Manitoba and fled with him to Turtle Mountain in 1869 when Prime Minister John A. Macdonald sent in the army instead of a delegation to honour the new province of Manitoba, named by Riel and legal within the British North America Act that established the Dominion of Canada. From Turtle Mountain my grandmother's family travelled to Montana with Chief Little Shell. They then travelled back across the Medicine Line to the North-West Territory (now the province of Saskatchewan). My grandmother's extended family were at the signing of Treaty 4, when they were assigned to Cowessess First Nation. I cannot find the words to say what it felt like after all those years to finally know my family's history, my ancestors, where we came from, where we have travelled to, and who we are related to through kinship. It affirmed so many things I felt deep within; it filled the emptiness that I felt in my heart.

****

In the fall of 1986, Native Earth moved into new offices on Jarvis Street. I had arranged to meet with Tomson to go for lunch to talk about workshops that he and Maaka Kleist were going to give at the University College Drama Program at the University of Toronto. I was given the tour of the new office, and then we walked to a restaurant. Tomson was in very good spirits and he announced to me that he loved working for Native Earth. I was surprised; I knew how hard he worked to keep the doors open and I said, "But, Tomson, you *are* Native Earth!" He looked at me with what I thought might be disappointment, saying (to the best of my memory), "Nooo, I'm not the only one doing this work; there are people all across this country doing what I'm doing. I'm not alone. If I thought I was alone in this, I would quit." As we continued walking, Tomson would share Cree words and concepts with me. I loved how he made me aware of the importance of Indigenous languages. For example, he would say, "Look at these trees; you never say, 'what are these trees'; you say, 'who are these trees.' Each tree is different; each has its own soul." We were stopped on the street by a Native man who asked for a cigarette and money. I remember Tomson taking him aside and talking to him and giving him both.

As we walked, Tomson told me that Native Earth and Act IV Theatre, the company that Larry Lewis worked with, were going to produce *The Rez Sisters*, with rehearsals in November and performances in December. I was excited for Tomson and Native Earth, but also devastated for myself because I would not be able to join the company, as several months earlier I had accepted a role in a play with a company that was going to perform at Factory Theatre at the same time as *The Rez Sisters*. I had this ethic of loyalty once I had made a commitment. But my loyalty was not rewarded. The production for which I gave up *The Rez Sisters* became extremely challenging, reminding me why I no longer wanted to work in mainstream theatre. And as for *The Rez Sisters*, well, that was an historical event, not only making Indigenous communities across Canada proud; it made the mainstream theatre, not only in Canada, but around the world, aware of the power of Indigenous theatre.

Personally, I was so glad *The Rez Sisters* was a hit; it meant I got to see the production once the play I was in had closed. Sitting in the audience at the Friendship Centre, I laughed and I cried. I was proud of everyone's work; ever since the first reading, I felt a connection to *The Rez Sisters* like it was part of my family. Or maybe it was that I felt part of this community. At the end of the performance, I was speechless—my faith in the importance of theatre was renewed and I think that night was the beginning of my commitment to work on behalf of Indigenous theatre. I was inspired.

Later that year I found out that the provincial government made significant cuts to the Native Community Branch, in the Ministry of Citizenship, which had secured the first core funding for Native Earth the previous year, making a minimum commitment of five years. Just after the major success of *The Rez Sisters* in their first season in 1986–87, the remaining four years of their core funding was cut. "Despite this great loss, Bomberry [the general manager of NEPA] stayed with Native Earth for seven months before she was put back on salary, while Highway was without salary for a year and a half" (Preston 12).

In the year that followed, I began to work on contracts with Native Earth, first as an actor, then as a dramaturge, eventually as a director, and an associate director with Tomson Highway. I loved every minute of working at Native Earth. Tomson was a wonderful artistic director and a great teacher. I learned through the stories he shared and his example. In many ways he saved my passion for the theatre. My work with Tomson gave me back the life in theatre that I felt I had lost.

Tomson is humble about his contributions. Although most people know about Tomson growing up in the North before he was taken to residential school, and most of the biographies of him focus on his work at Native Earth and the plays he wrote and continues to write, as well as his time at university and as a concert pianist, I think few know of his community activism. The biography in the Fifth House publication of *The Rez Sisters* in 1988 states,

> Once out of university, Tomson went to work for seven years with Native organizations and Native people . . . in London, Ontario, and The Ontario Federation of Indian Friendship Centres in Toronto.

During these years he worked with cultural programs, Native in-
mates in correctional centres and prisons, children's recreational
programs, and other Native enterprises. His work enabled him to
travel extensively around Canada—while meeting and working with
(and just plain falling in love with over and over again) Native people
on reserves, in friendship centres, in prisons, on the streets, and in
the bars . . . just generally familiarizing himself intimately with the
organizational network of Native lives and politics in this country.
(Highway, *The Rez Sisters* viii)

. I believe this is where his vision began, a dream for the people to hear the
stories of the ancestors and of the land and all the beings who inhabit the land
so we can laugh and cry with Weesageechak and all the brothers and sisters.
I thought of this when I was conducting research for a new course at Trent,
The Living History of Indigenous Dance and Theatre. I came across a report
that Native Earth had submitted to the Royal Commission on Aboriginal
Peoples (RCAP) in 1993. It was then I realized how much Tomson knew of
and worked with a network of Indigenous theatres in communities across
Canada, as well as international Indigenous communities.

The report is a valuable document that touches on the very early contemporary history of Indigenous theatre in Canada since 1951, when the "new"
government of the Dominion of Canada revised the Indian Act so that it
was now legal for Indigenous people in Canada to conduct or attend ceremonies, traditional or social dances, as well as other cultural practices.[3] Prior
to 1951, many Elders went to prison for dancing in protest, "and hundreds
of potlatch items were confiscated, a devastating loss to the community. . . .

---

3   "In 1884, the federal government banned potlatches under the Indian Act, with other
ceremonies such as the sun dance to follow in the coming years. The outlawing of the potlatch severely disrupted these cultural traditions, although many continued to potlatch"
(Hanson, "The Indian Act"). In January 1897, P.J. Williams, the Indian agent at Battleford,
reported that, "he had arrested 5 Indians of Thunderchild's reserve for holding a 'give away'
dance. Two had been given suspended sentences while three had been given a 2-month
prison term" (Titley 167).

Countless communities were similarly impacted by the restriction on ceremonies, facing legacies that continue to this day, in the form of the loss of
cultural practices, traditions and oral history" (Hanson, "The Indian Act").
According to Tomson, this revision of the Indian Act "marked the beginning
of a renaissance" of Native theatre in Canada (Highway, "Author's"). "Unlike
our ancestors, contemporary Native people are free to explore Native story,
song, and dance without persecution. We are free to learn to dance again"
(Manossa 76). And we are now free to participate in ceremonies.

It was around the time that I began to work with Native Earth that I first
heard of the Riel prophecy, "My people will sleep for one hundred years, but
when they awake, it will be the artists who give them back their spirit," at-
tributed to Louis Riel on July 4, 1885 (qtd. in Crean). And one hundred years
and seven months later, in February 1986, the play *Jessica: A Transformation*
by Maria Campbell and Linda Griffiths, based on Maria's book *Halfbreed*,
opened in Toronto at Theatre Passe Muraille, and won a Dora Mavor Moore
Award for Outstanding New Play that year. Maria was so "impressed by the
power of theatre and its potential to convey a spiritual world" she felt the
need to "create a thing of beauty from her painful past" (Pastor 36). On 26
November 1986, *The Rez Sisters* by Tomson Highway opened at the Native
Canadian Centre; it received rave reviews, and also won a Dora Mavor Moore
Award for Outstanding New Play in the 1986–87 season. Both were awarded
Floyd S. Chalmers Canadian Play Awards in the same year.

Drew Hayden Taylor, in the summer of 1995, wrote, "What was once barren was now bountiful. If in 1986 there was one working Native playwright
in all of Canada [I would add there were two, to include Maria], today [nine
years later] at least 3 dozen playwrights of Aboriginal descent are being produced and published" (256). I can't help but think, even though our theatres
continue to struggle and Native peoples still do not have their proportional
share of support, that the burgeoning of Indigenous theatre had something
to do with Riel's prophecy and the Seven Fires Prophecy . . . and it makes me
believe that we are now living within these prophecies.

In 1997, about a year after we had established the first Aboriginal Dance
Program at the Banff Centre, I was sitting in an advisory circle with Elders,

traditional performance specialists, and dance artists, when we were asked, "What is the biggest impact that colonization has had on us, our families, our communities, and our nations; what is the one thing that keeps us from moving forward?" After much discussion, we all agreed that the biggest impact was how divided we have become amongst ourselves, in our families, our communities, and our nations; that is what keeps us from moving forward. For me, the Anishinaabeg process of Naadmaagewin . . . the Art of Working Together in Our Communities has become a response to that question asked so long ago.

In " 'Bubbling Like a Beating Heart': Reflections on Nishnaabeg Poetic and Narrative Consciousness," Leanne Simpson writes, "We as artists and writers have the power to create decolonized spaces of resurgence within our communities. We have the power to vision alternative realities . . . [and] the responsibility to collectivize these visions in order to bring those dreams of our ancestors into realities" (116).

THE SEARCH FOR SPIRITUAL TRANSFORMATION IN CONTEMPORARY THEATRE PRACTICE

JANI LAUZON

It all started when I was in grade two.

I was a rambunctious child with a vivid imagination and clearly driven by spirit and impulse, so my mother determined I needed an outlet and registered me in a creative movement class on Saturday mornings. While other kids were watching cartoons I walked over to the local elementary school in Kimberley, BC (Lindsay Park), to join in the fun. To be clear, at that time in my life, the closest I came to cultural teachings was what the Lord Jesus had to offer. My father (Métis) had been highly influenced by his parents' devout Catholic faith, and by the priests at the residential school in southern Alberta he attended for over six years. That is until he ran from that world to attend the Vancouver School of Art (now the Emily Carr University of Art and Design), which led to a life of continual guilt and struggle trying to find a balance between artistic expression and the role of the church in his life. But I digress. One Saturday morning we were asked to improvise (through movement) the journey of a baby chick hatching out of an egg. We talked in a circle beforehand about how hard things get sometimes, how badly you just want to give up, but how you must find a way to keep going, just like the little chick trying to break open the hard shell with its beak. That made sense to me. The very nature of being a brown girl in a white world required that kind of tenacity, not to mention the grit required for navigating family dysfunction and generational trauma. I still remember the epiphany I had during those final moments when my chick cracked the imaginary eggshell: the adrenaline of persistence, yielding finally to a deep breath and a life of freedom. A birth.

I had no idea that a simple gesture, a sound, such deep, rich emotion could emanate from my body and be released into the universe for others to witness and share! The nod of approval from my instructor and fellow classmates sealed the deal. I was hooked on becoming a theatre-maker, for this was as a world of freedom unlike the world of confinement I had known.

Finding my artistic identity, my voice, required obstinacy. Disconnect with voice is epidemic among Indigenous youth. Generational trauma has crippled our feelings of self-worth. Coupled with the loss of my mother when I was twelve (my parents were separated) and the fact that my father had relinquished his responsibilities as a parent, making me a permanent ward of the government, I dropped deep into an internal world of silence and solitude. While this was not ideal, the positive outcome was that I learned to listen and observe. I developed a keen intentness for the study of sound, gesture, and image. I thought of myself as a photographer without a camera. I became fascinated with the beauty of nature. I spent countless hours observing my friends, family, fellow students and devoured books on the human condition. And although I felt alone I knew I wasn't for the loving arms of the natural world that surrounded me.

Figure 1. Jani Lauzon in her show *Prophecy Fog*. Photo by Samuel Choisy.

I also had a positive foster-care experience. My foster father was the high-school drama teacher and community-theatre director in Cranbrook, BC. I lived and breathed theatre, from helping backstage to analyzing plays (our casual dinner conversation) to spending nights listening to LPs of Broadway musicals in front of a roaring fire. Western theatre, European theatre, American theatre, I thought that's what theatre was. That is until I started devouring the books I discovered among my mother's belongings after she died. This created a shift in cultural teachings from Jesus to astrology, Edgar Cayce and Finnish Shamanism (my mother was Scandinavian), and although it made navigating identity and joining opposing worlds more confusing, I began contemplating ritual and how it may be applied to theatre. During her lifetime my mother kept secret these interests she had in what was then known as the occult. But her books opened my mind to a form of spirituality that I had always been drawn to. These theories would not only form the basis of further investigation into theatrical practice, but are similar to concepts I now understand as the foundation of an Indigenous world view and of my own Métis culture.

Because I lacked confidence I was not successful in securing a place at any of the national training institutions. In hindsight, the spirits were guiding me toward a more individual road. I studied with masters and settled in Toronto, as many of them were either based there or coming there to teach. I sought out instructors from all over the world whose methodology incorporated a spiritual practice, a ritualistic discipline, and the integration of body, mind, and spirit as a basis for the training. I will be forever grateful to Frau Til Thiele, with whom I studied modern dance at an early age. Thiele studied and worked with Mary Wigman in Germany before coming to Canada. "*To dance you must prepare your body so you can dance as you like, but first you must find your body,*" she would say (qtd. in Fraleigh).

Others who inspired me along the way include Patsy Rodenburg and David Smukler (both excellent voice/Shakespeare teachers), Kennedy Cathy MacKinnon (who helped reaffirm that Shakespeare was my thing), and Richard Pochinko, who opened my closed and broken soul to creative impulse through clowning. I began to contemplate pedagogy when I worked with Floyd Favel as Associate Artistic Director (with Monique Mojica) at the Native Theatre School. Favel was investigating the intersection of his training with Jerzy Grotowski and Indigenous performance culture. It was my first introduction to the concept of weaving theatre ideologies and Indigenous culture with the goal of creating something new and unique. Favel's work, along with that of Spiderwoman Theater, highly influenced Turtle Gals Performance Ensemble, a Native women's theatre collective I co-founded with Monique Mojica and Michelle St. John. Not only did we train extensively in ensemble creation with Muriel Miguel (of Spiderwoman Theater fame), but Muriel also directed our first play, *The Scrubbing Project*. Similar to Favel's, Miguel's work layered Indigenous world view over western construct, in this case transforming the work of Joseph Chaikin to an Indigenous training and performance process she calls Storyweaving.

But it would be Japanese actor/director Yoshi Oïda and Odawa Elder Sam Osawamick who would be two of my greatest influences in helping me find a deeper connection between my own artistic and cultural practice. Yoshi Oïda seeks to find the truth in his art. Immersed in Noh theatre at a young age and having trained for a short time as a priest in a Shinto monastery, he spoke (as did Til Thiele and Grotowski) of how we can learn something about our universe by exploring our body's movements. What made his pedagogy unique was that we started with tradition and ritual, and organically wove that into theatre practice and artistic expression through the repetition of rigorous physical sequences. Oïda often said that the magic was in the repetition. I remember one morning he taught us a short movement sequence along with a traditional Japanese song. We repeated this sequence for the next three hours. I went from enthusiasm to frustration to rage to bliss. This final stage was achieved only through abandoning my ego and allowing myself to experience nothing more than the immediate moment. I had never felt more alive in my life. This was what Oïda described as spiritual transformation. I think it's important to clarify here that we are talking about spiritual transformation and not enlightenment, which is different. Oïda's goal was to weave Eastern and Western techniques in order to engage the spectator. The training demanded that performers reach openness, a connection to mind/body/

spirit in order to be ready to play as a performer, not through bodybuilding or cardio training but movement motivated by breath and simplicity.

That certainly wasn't mentioned in any of the books I had read on actors' process, although some masters do talk about obtaining neutrality, which may be the same goal using different language. The word neutrality never worked for me. The concept of spiritual transformation did. I now had a goal as a performer, a process to explore.

This began a period of questioning for me as an artist/writer/theatre creator. I tried to apply the theory of spiritual transformation as a performer while playing Raven (a full masked character) in the Young People's Theatre production of *Whale*. During the rehearsal process I focused my energy on physical training (similar to what we did in Oïda's class) for two reasons: in order to achieve a spiritual connection and because the role itself required incredible physical aptitude. For a first concerted effort the outcome was more than satisfactory. I not only received a Dora Mavor Moore nomination for Best Actress, but audience members as young as eight years old were deeply affected by my character Raven. But it was exhausting and I knew I was over-analyzing the process. I also began to question whether mask work and performing for young audiences was already conducive to a positive outcome. By its very nature, mask work requires a heightened level of performance that one might argue already reaches toward spiritual transformation. All over the world Indigenous cultures have used mask as part of ceremonial practice. And while there are masks used specifically for ceremony I always approach the use of any mask with great care when performing or teaching, as I have experienced some incredible and powerful occurrences while using them. As for young audiences, they are smart and simply tune out if the performance does not engage them.

In my early career I spent time working for the De-ba-jeh-mu-jig Theatre Company based in Wikwemikong First Nation (now Debajehmujig Storytellers). During my time in Wiky, I spent many hours with Elders Justine Enosse and Edna Manitowabi, whom I turned to as ceremonial leaders and who also had a keen interest in the power of theatre. We talked about how before contact and colonization the function of both singing and dancing was spiritual in nature. There was no separation among creative expression, spiritual connection, and everyday life. We sang and danced to live, survive, pray, and entertain. This was our Indigenous theatrical practice.

As a measure of control and power, Church and State unravelled that connection. Rather than see creative expression as a form of spiritual practice—as the reason we exist—these institutions created sanctions around who had permission to do what, when, where, and how. We still deal with this form of censorship and disconnect today. We have created a divide in our human condition. There are those who call themselves artists and those who believe they are not. I would argue that we are all artists. We creatively express ourselves daily whether writing a play, giving birth to a child, or negotiating a contract.

In many ways, my resolve was to weave together what has been lost while being an artist in a society struggling to reconnect with its purpose. But I was bogged down in theory and analysis. I was beginning to understand how to achieve spiritual transformation, but how did achieving that state infuse a performance and ultimately engage audience? And what did all that have to do with the intersection of methodology and culture?

The answer came as most do: unexpectedly. I was visiting with Sam Osawamick, an Odawa Elder from Wikwemikong that I had met, not through theatre, but through the need for help healing my body. Sam's medicine and prayers helped where western medicine could not. He became not only the second of my greatest influences in developing the theories I continue to explore, but someone I grew to love as a grandfather.

One day, while helping him pound medicines, I asked him how he knew what medicines my body needed and how he could see aspects of my future (he had that gift of sight). He sat quietly for a moment, as he often did, and then responded, "Your body is like a book. I read and it tells me what I need to know."

It was Sam who helped me coin the phrase "Our bodies are our books." In some ways it's not a unique concept. Many of the masters I have worked with explored the value of accessing impulses through body work. But envisioning my body as a book was the missing link for me. My book contained muscle and generational memory, all that I had gathered through oral culture as well as the art of observation. I suppose a more contemporary phrase would be "Our bodies are our computers," our own personal electronic devices, but I like the tactile connection to books. The main point is that it's where all of our life experience, and more, is stored. And a more cohesive process evolved.

Step one: achieve spiritual transformation or neutrality.

Step two: from that state, access information in the body, including cultural and personal.

Step three: Use that information to inform character, relationship, and intention.

Step four: Share and engage with the audience.

I applied this while playing the role of Shylock in Shakespeare in the Rough's *The Merchant of Venice*. We rehearsed outside every day, and although not quite the same as BC wilderness I was surrounded by big, beautiful trees, the comfort of nature. I rode my bike to work and arrived early, taking myself through a physical warm-up so that I was open and ready to work daily. And I borrowed from my personal experience and generational memory to help inform the work. When my Shylock spoke the words "scorned my nation" I had a body reference to draw from. Was I a Jew in that moment? No. But my body knew the core issues: oppression, colonialism, assumption of religious superiority, and I could easily inform the moment with my life experience. Audience members saw what they wished. Some saw a side of Shylock they had never considered, others thought the performance was deeply connected to something much larger than they had seen in productions of *Merchant*, while others told me I was the best villain they had seen. What mattered most to me was that they were engaged. Another Dora nomination for my performance told me I was on the right track.

I continued these explorations, playing Mark Antony in Yvette Nolan's *Death of a Chief* (based on Shakespeare's *Julius Caesar*) and Yvette Pottier

in the National Arts Centre (NAC) production of *Mother Courage*, directed
by Peter Hinton: two performances I am very proud of. And I was familiar
enough with the process to use it more organically and effortlessly while playing both Cordelia and the Fool in the NAC production of *King Lear* alongside
August Schellenberg as Lear, also directed by Peter Hinton.

I am now at the point where the process has become an act of prayer and
the theatre a sacred space. The magic is indeed in the repetition.

None of this has been easy. My approach to the work was often misin-
terpreted. Some fellow artists were impatient with my inability to "get it"
quickly, and the demands of the shortened rehearsal period in English theatre
in Canada do not lend themselves to this kind of process. The key became
working on specific projects with specific people. I was drawn to characters
that had either a strong physical capacity or were exploring deep moral issues.
I gravitated toward projects that had multidisciplinary aspects, or comedy
within tragedy, and toward directors whom I felt I could dialogue with: Ruth
Madoc-Jones, Soheil Parsa, Marjorie Chan, Julia Aplin, Peter Hinton, to name
only a few who I have had the recent pleasure of engaging with.

With the closing of Turtle Gals Performance Ensemble I made the decision to invest in the creation of my own work outside of the collective format.
I dove in with a renewed sense of purposefulness, yet almost immediately the
doubt set in: writing from the body is a vulnerable process. When the material
is connected to your core, your soul, it's important to remember that criticism
may come, and your task is to separate that which is constructive from that
which contradicts your instinct. I learned to trust my body to guide me, and
find those that I trusted whose expertise could assist me in cultivating the
story I wanted to tell. I tried not to listen to others who judged me; we have
had too much of that already. I also tried to remember that our ancestors
persevered through great adversity, even facing imprisonment and death,
to tell the stories they believed needed to be told. I figured, in comparison, I
could learn to move past old trauma and loss to handle a little rejection and
criticism now and then.

My best writing periods are, in fact, nowhere near my computer. While
my work is not always linear, I am a big fan of structure and story. In order

to navigate that river and not get lost in too many tributaries, I find I must be out in nature—or, when I'm in the city, my bike suffices as my urban canoe. In no way does this replace the daily discipline of writing, but being in close proximity to water, wind, trees, and silence allows me the opportunity to best listen to my body. The answers to my questions come in pictures, emotions, and large concepts. The next phase requires time in the studio, where I use movement improvisation, borrowed from all the masters I have worked with, to help generate material. It is then my mind's responsibility to weave the threads of research, logic, and reason to create the structure of storyline and dramatic framework.

To date, my short film *eu·tha·na·sia* continues to tour festivals and I have four theatre projects in varying degrees of completion. *A Side of Dreams* incorporates an aerial hoop, a bunraku puppet, mask work, an incredible musical score, and text (see figures in Jill Carter's essay, page 33). *Prophecy Fog* is a storytelling/performance-art exploration of Star Beings and Sacred Spaces (see Figure 2). *I Call myself Princess*, the most conventional of all my work, is a two-act play with opera (see Figure 3). And finally *Only Virgin's Need Apply* (the working title) dissects the written work of Chester Beavon

Figure 2. Jani Lauzon in *Prophecy Fog*. Photo by Samuel Choisy.

Figure 3. Jani Lauzon in the workshop presentation of her "two-act play with opera," *I Call myself Princess*, at Native Earth Performing Arts's Weesageechak Begins to Dance Festival. Photo by Samuel Choisy.

and the paintings of his wife Daphne Odjig. I have a plethora of ideas. They are all stored within my body for safekeeping for when the circumstances are favourable to bring them to life.

Central to my writing are the themes of spiritual transformation, navigating identity, and the mother/daughter relationship. I would say that my biggest challenge as an artist has been the parallel commitment to being a single parent while staying true to my own needs. My daughter has grown up watching me struggle as an artist trying to carve out and delineate a space for myself in a very competitive and challenging environment. She has travelled with me everywhere, been backstage in most theatres in Canada, and has gone without on numerous occasions as a result of my lack of financial stability. There were many times when it felt too hard and I questioned whether it was worth it. But the more I put into it, the more I pecked at the hard shell, the more I was able to show my daughter that living your life creatively means engaging in life to its fullest. My daughter has grown up witnessing my determination to survive, succeed, and continue to grow, and as a poet/artist/

writer she is now inspired to do the same. What more could I ask for? The connective tissue to all my work is my desire to grow in spiritual transformation and, dare I say, hope my audience and those around me are inspired through my performance to reach for something bigger, something larger that dwells inside each and every one of us.

ON THE TRAIL OF NATIVE THEATRE

CAROL GREYEYES

I put you on this trail that you must now follow no matter where it leads.
—Chief Crowfoot to Poundmaker (qtd. in Sluman 294)

As a theatre artist and teacher for over three decades, I have had the privilege of being both a participant and a witness to the development of Native theatre in Canada. Native theatre has become my mêskanaw, my artistic trail, and my life path. At times it appeared to be wandering and random, but in retrospect it has been a clear and definite path, always leading me in a specific direction, even when I was unaware or unwilling to take it.

During my professional and sometimes vocational career as an artist, I've had the honour to act in numerous plays, many of them world premieres by award-winning Canadian Indigenous playwrights. I have collaborated on, directed, and produced Native theatre, and participated in the creation of a new theatre canon. I have been privileged to teach several generations of emerging First Nations theatre artists, and witnessed with great pride the contributions they have made to the genre. Whether on stage or off, creating or interpreting, or teaching and supporting others, I seem to have been constantly led in this direction. Looking back I can see just where the path took me, the detours, points where I stepped off, lost my way, and returned. This essay is a reflection on that very particular and at times idiosyncratic journey—my mêskanaw—on the trail of Native theatre.

Perhaps it is an anachronism, but I still refer to it as "Native" theatre because in its formative years that is what our generation called it. Besides, that is how my grandfather and mentor always referred to us; we were

Nehiyaw—Cree—or simply "natives." It was hardly ever "Indian," certainly not "Aboriginal," and not "Indigenous"; those terms came into vogue long after he was gone. And in the early days, no one even knew what Native theatre was, much less what to call it. There was simply no real definition, no category as yet for Native theatre, at least not in the mainstream theatre community or academic institutions. At the time Canadian Native theatre was beginning to emerge, and the standard definition of theatre had become so codified that any type of cultural expression or performance that didn't fit within those narrow parameters was not considered real theatre in the Eurocentric western tradition of theatre. Yet we had rocked the storytelling genre for thousands of years and I haven't come across a tribe yet who didn't tell their stories through dance and song, or who didn't put on some special outfit or mask to transform in order to perform a ceremony or tell a story. So what if we didn't have written dialogue? If the definition were expanded just a little, we felt that we most definitely had a rich theatrical tradition.

In the early days when the genre was developing, I don't think anyone had an actual definition for what we were trying to do. We were so busy trying to synthesize, to invent and transform theatre to make it our own, that we didn't spend too much time trying to define it. Eventually, in order to validate what we were doing, we found we needed a definition, or at least a way to talk about it so we could explain it to ourselves and to outsiders. Then the time came, at some theatre conference or similar event that I had been asked to attend, when the question was invariably asked: "So what exactly *is* Native theatre?" I remember a long silence as we, the designated practitioners and representatives for Native theatre (a label put *on* us, not *by* us), tried to figure out what to answer. Finally someone in our group blurted out that Native theatre was "Indians on stage." We all laughed. But after the laughter, heads nodded. That would work, for the time being. There seemed to be an unspoken agreement amongst us that this was as close as we wanted to get to a definition—we were inventing it as we went along, and still are. And after being silenced for so long there was this overwhelming need to express ourselves with as few limitations as possible. The attitude was, "Don't tell us what we can and can't do, just let us tell our stories in our own way. Let us see our culture reflected

back to us in whatever fashion, and in whatever media we want." As artists
we resisted set boundaries, rigid rules, and stifling definitions. Like the nature of art itself and the dynamic cultures it expressed, Native theatre was and
continues to be a work in progress.

****

> You are the same people who fought so well and so bravely on
> Cutknife Hill. But you are going to have to fight another kind of fight.
> —Poundmaker (qtd. in Sluman 284)

The emergence and development of Native theatre, the need to have "Indians
on stage," in many ways reflected the larger socio-political changes that were
happening in the country and all across North America. Native Canadians
were gaining more rights and freedoms and were no longer invisible, ignored, or shut away on reservations and in isolated communities. Here in
Saskatchewan, there seemed to be a defining moment when things shifted on
a socio-cultural level and we ceased to be invisible. In the summer of 1982 the
World Assembly of First Nations (WAFN) was held in Fort Qu'Appelle. This
gathering of Indigenous people from across the planet, the largest event of
its kind ever seen in the province, demonstrated this new visibility. Not only
did it change perceptions of the general population, it had a powerful impact
on the psyche of those, like me, who had never attended such an event. We
watched in awe as visitors from all four corners of the planet danced their
spectacular traditional dances, sang their songs, shared their stories, ceremonies, and cultural practices. Away from the WAFN site in the valley we
marvelled at exhibitions of traditional and contemporary visual art on display in galleries all over the city of Regina. For many, WAFN was a profound
psychic and spiritual affirmation of our Indigenous identity and it demonstrated we were no longer mere relics of the past: our cultures were alive and
flourishing. For me it was one of those spiritual awakenings that helped set

me on the path I still pursue: the exploration and expression of who we are as First Nations people.

In as much as the World Assembly of First Nations celebrated and affirmed our cultural identities, it also made some of us realize that we really didn't know what those identities were. Michael Lawrenchuk, a Cree actor, playwright, teacher, director, and former chief of Fox Lake Cree Nation in Manitoba asks:

> What are the factors involved in one trying to answer the question "who am I?" Where does one look when exploring the question "who am I?" The question may seem simple enough for most people, but for a people who suffer impacts from colonial infrastructures and policies, the journey to the answer is fraught with danger.

The need for voice and self-discovery in the post-colonial era had suddenly become critical. It fuelled our First Nations political and artistic agendas across the country, and it was out of this need for affirmation in an atmosphere of cultural reawakening that Native theatre emerged.

This cultural renaissance and the development of a Native theatre in Canada paralleled another shift happening in the Canadian theatre world: a distinctly nationalist movement was shaking up theatres across the county. Even big regional theatres and theatrical institutions such as the Stratford Festival were moving toward a more Canadian approach in their direction and programming.[1] In Saskatchewan, the clearest indicator of that shift was probably an unusual new play produced in 1977 by 25th Street Theatre called *Paper Wheat*. Similar to its stylistic predecessor, Theatre Passe Muraille's *The Farm Show*, *Paper Wheat* was not an American or British play from the European canon, but rather an original collective creation. A company of actors and the director went out and talked to local Saskatchewan farmers, politicians, and community members in order to develop the script. All of a sudden people

---

1 Especially under the artistic direction of Robin Phillips from 1975–1980, who, although an Englishman, was ironically credited with the Canadianization of the Stratford Festival.

were seeing their own stories reflected back to them on stage and the effect
was electrifying. For the first time an authentic Canadian voice was being
heard on stages that hitherto had been producing plays and telling stories
from cultures and countries other than our own. And in Indian country, our
future Native theatre artists were doing the same. In 1970 the Mohawk writer
Nona Benedict had her play *The Dress* published. In northern Saskatchewan,
a group of Métis high-school students formed Upsasik Theatre in 1976 and
told their own stories in their own language, and in New York in 1976, Muriel
Miguel founded Spiderwoman Theater. Although we would have to wait another decade until 1986 for the landmark production of Tomson Highway's
The Rez Sisters, the winds of change were stirring our collective consciousness,
and it was just a matter of time before the nascent Native theatre movement
would fully emerge and spread across the country.

In some ways my mêskanaw, my path to Native theatre, is a microcosm of
that larger story. I was born in Saskatchewan to a Cree mother in the 1950s,
right smack dab in the middle of all that societal change and those radical
movements. Initially I didn't pursue theatre. When considering what to do
with my life, I thought about being a nurse because my mother had been
one of the first Native women in the province to get a nursing diploma, and
I thought I might follow in her footsteps. Then I toyed with the idea of doing a geography degree at university so that I could help with land claims.
During that period, land claims were hitting the courts across the country
as First Nation bands (like my own) realized that they had been defrauded
not only of the land that the treaties had promised, but of many of the rights
and obligations supposedly guaranteed by the Crown in those (theoretically)
binding legal agreements. But I eventually picked up the theatre trail again
when my former dancing partner sat me down and demanded to know when
I was going drop distractions like geography and nursing and accept the fact
that I "belonged on the stage."

Dance had given me my first taste of performing on stage. When I was
only fifteen (I'm pretty sure I lied about my age at the auditions) I was cast as
a dancer in one of the very first plays produced by the newly founded 25th
Street House Theatre (as it was called then). *Covent Garden* was conceived,

written, directed by, and starred Andras Tahn, the company's founding artistic director. It was a huge, ambitious, eclectic production with actors, musicians, and an entire dance corps. It had scenes and soliloquies, dance numbers and songs, and in the transitions a lone sax in a single spotlight played a haunting melody. In another interesting twist of fate, my fellow dancer in the corps was a young man by the name of Layne Coleman. Layne's girlfriend at the time was another young actor, Linda Griffiths. Our paths would cross again many years later when the two of them, separately and together, would become major figures in the development of new Canadian theatre. Perhaps it was that early exposure to such exuberant creativity and unfettered experimentation that steered me onto my theatre path. Or maybe it was the tinfoil star that someone had lovingly stuck onto the door of our dressing room. But whatever the original impetus, my theatrical destiny was set. So in 1977, when *Paper Wheat* was causing such a stir on the Canadian theatre scene, I wasn't studying nursing or geography, but happily taking drama at the University of Saskatchewan.

****

> You must fight yourselves and this new way of thinking that we are
> less than we are because it is not true.
> —Poundmaker (qtd. in Sluman 284)

As exciting as it was to be back on the stage, I was beginning to become aware of a real split between my identity as a Native woman and what was being taught at the university. I felt like I was living in two very distinct worlds and I couldn't see how they could possibly be reconciled. Perhaps it was because I had no role models or couldn't see myself reflected in the type of theatre I was being taught, or that I simply lacked the imagination or courage to blaze a path of my own. But even then it seemed like whenever I would stray from my mêskanaw, I would be given something to nudge me back on the path. One such "nudge" came from of my first university acting teacher. On the very first day of classes, I was shocked when he proclaimed that in order to be an actor it was essential "to know who you are. Before you act, you have to know yourself first." My heart sank. I had wanted to become an actor so I could be anybody else but me. I was filled with self-hate and had such a negative self-image. I wanted to be an actor so I could simply become whatever character the script called for. I didn't have a clue who or what I was, and hoped that I could just skip over that step. I had long determined that the best way to succeed was to always blend in and hide my real self away. I had light-coloured eyes and a fair complexion, so I could easily pass as a moonias iskwew, a white woman. And I did. I had become a ghost, the invisible Native. Ironically, however, my invisibility allowed me to get some great roles in the days when there was no such thing as "colour-blind" casting, nor were there any plays with great roles for Native women (yet), and the very few plays that had parts for Native women were being played by non-Native actresses.[2] So after I graduated and started working in professional theatre, I reconciled myself to playing anybody but myself.

As exciting as my career as a newly minted professional actor was, I nevertheless felt like something crucial was missing. So in 1982, even though it wasn't an acting gig, when I was asked to be an instructor in a pilot drama program at the Native Survival School in Saskatoon, I jumped at the chance. Ruth Smillie, former artistic director of Persephone's Youtheatre, and Kelly Murphy, the school's English teacher, had created a special program for students that would enable them to tell their stories using popular theatre techniques. Also on the team were Maria Campbell as the storyteller and Tantoo Cardinal as the actor/mentor.

In an interesting twist of fate, I had finally come face to face with Maria Campbell. A number of years earlier, I had read an article published in *The Weekend Magazine* profiling her book, *Halfbreed*. It struck a deep chord: finally something that spoke to my identity. So deep in fact that when they mentioned

2   The character of Rita Joe in the premiere of *The Ecstasy of Rita Joe* at the Vancouver Playhouse in 1967, often considered the beginning of "Native theatre" in Canada in spite of its having been written by George Ryga, a Ukrainian Canadian, was played by Frances Hyland, a non-Native actress.

that a movie was in the works based on *Halfbreed*, I wrote an ardent letter to Maria Campbell, sent via the publisher, asking to play the lead. I felt so passionately, as one does at age thirteen, that I simply had to play that character. It was the first role that I could truly identify with and felt I knew from the inside out. When I heard nothing back, however, the idea faded into the background and I eventually forgot about it. But then, here we were, over a decade later sitting across the table from each other in a classroom at the Native Survival School. More of a coincidence, Maria told me that only the day before, while cleaning out her desk, she came across my letter and reread it. I was astonished because I had assumed it was never delivered. I took this synchronistic encounter as another sign that I was indeed headed in the right direction.

Looking back, I think my involvement with this project set me more firmly on my future path as an educator and animator for Native theatre. I learned first-hand just how powerful community theatre could be in changing people's minds and lives. The final show, created and performed by the students, had a real impact on Saskatoon audiences when it was performed publically. It opened people's minds to a new reality and whole new community that heretofore had been unacknowledged. The project also changed the school and the students' lives. Educators could see the value of the program when things like student attendance improved and English test scores increased substantially. "Story Circles," as the program was called, even created a few theatre stars. Floyd Favel, a former student at the Native Survival School, is the most famous. He went on to become a well-known actor, director, and playwright. Many years later, in another synchronistic interweaving of paths, Favel directed me in the premiere production of his play *Lady of Silences* at Native Earth Performing Arts.

A few years prior to the Native Survival School project there was another English teacher in northwest Saskatchewan, Lon Borgeson, who was also encouraging his students at Rossignol High School in the Métis village of Île-à-La-Crosse to tell their stories. In 1976, this group of energetic students, directed by one committed teacher, officially formed a company called Upsasik Theatre. Borgeson's students were creating plays that reflected their own experiences and for the first time were being performed in their own language,

Cree. The Upsasik productions received such positive responses locally that they eventually toured across the north to enthusiastic First Nations audiences. When I heard about their work, I had to go to see a show in Île-à-La-Crosse myself. I knew intuitively that this was a pivotal moment in Saskatchewan Native theatre history. Although I wasn't a fluent speaker, it didn't matter. Even if you couldn't understand what was being said or didn't know the local people they were lampooning, the shows were nevertheless entertaining and powerful. The characters were identifiable, the plot and themes universal. And despite not achieving professional status as a theatre company, they still were the first Native theatre company to produce collective plays in an Aboriginal language, therefore they made significant contributions to the advancement of Native theatre not only in Saskatchewan but in Canada as well.

****

It would be far easier just to fold our hands and not make this fight.
—Poundmaker (qtd. in Sluman 295)

To the west, in Alberta, there was another theatre company doing popular/ community theatre. Based in Edmonton, Catalyst Theatre's mandate was "to practice and promote theatre for public education and as a catalyst for social change." So when an isolated Cree community in northern Alberta reached out for help with their troubled youth, Catalyst Theatre responded by putting together a team of theatre professionals, both Aboriginal and non-Aboriginal, who would move to Wabasca-Desmarais to do a community-theatre project there. After my experience in the Native Survival School project, this seemed like a natural progression and so I signed on. Besides, I wanted to learn Cree, and this isolated Cree-speaking community seemed perfect. After doing some basic theatre training in Edmonton, we all went up north for what we thought would be a fairly short project. The plan was to offer drama classes in the high school, get the youth involved, find out their concerns, create a play, rehearse the play, then perform the play for the community, and voila, issues would be brought out into the open and the community healed. Of course it didn't work out that way. We couldn't get the teens to participate, the alcohol abuse and suicide rates continued to climb, and no one in the community seemed to care about us or the project. Not only that, the project funding was coming to an end. For me, it was a very steep learning curve: Popular Theatre Boot Camp.

However, despite a very unremarkable ten months, we were able to convince the theatre company and project funders that the project needed more time and money. We needed time to build relationships and trust in a community that was sadly all too used to broken promises and government Band-Aid programs. They distrusted us outsiders, moving into their community and preaching our gospel of theatre. But like faith, theatre also has the power to transform and heal, and after three long years of holding the vision, project leader Jane Heather achieved our initial goals. Out of the original team, only Jane was able to see the project through. But as a reward for her steadfast commitment and hard work, Jane witnessed the eventual engagement of the youth, the creation of a collective play, even a tour. The project not only empowered the young participants of Wabasca-Desmarais and changed their lives forever, but it had an equally profound impact on those of us who worked on the project. The lessons I learned in Wabasca about the power of art to connect and transform would continue to inform my thinking and my career as I progressed even further along on the trail of Native theatre.

****

Our old way of life is gone, but that does not mean we should just sit back and become imitation white men.
—Poundmaker (qtd. in Sluman 284)

A decade previous to the work being done in Alberta and Saskatchewan, in Ontario there was a new training program that would eventually become another major step in the development of Native theatre and also of my career path. In 1974, the first Native Theatre School (NTS) was established by

James H. Buller. A Cree also from Saskatchewan, Buller believed that if First Nations students could have access to professional training in theatre arts—acting, playwriting, directing, and design—Native theatre would develop and flourish across the country. And this concept worked; some of our most renowned Native theatre artists got their start in the barn at Kimbercote Farm. Many creative fires were lit during those transformative weeks in rural Ontario. As a result of this unique program, when NTS students returned to their home communities, the work continued to grow and spread across the country. Even if many of the NTS graduates didn't continue in theatre per se, they became performers in other genres like dance or music, or became filmmakers, performance artists, writers, or radio and television producers. Native Theatre School became the springboard for First Nations artists to share their cultural identities, realities, and vision with the rest of the country and the world. Many of the early NTS graduates like Gary Farmer and Graham Greene began the work of creating a Native theatre presence in the east and in their own communities. It wasn't surprising therefore that after the establishment of NTS and after several cohorts of students had received training, Native Earth Performing Arts, the first professional Native theatre company in Canada, was created in Toronto in 1982.

My involvement with the illustrious Native Theatre School didn't happen until 1995, by which time it had been renamed the Centre for Indigenous Theatre (CIT). I had moved to Ontario in 1990 to pursue an M.F.A. at York University and was working as an actor and story editor in Toronto. My cousin, Warren Arcan, who was Artistic Director at the time, invited me up to Kimbercote to teach his "kids" at the summer school program. I taught at the farm for two weeks and completely fell in love with the students, the atmosphere, and the thrill of doing culturally affirmative, cutting-edge theatrical work. So when Arcan left CIT and suggested that I apply for the position of artistic director I jumped at the opportunity. In those days, however, the job consisted of only eight weeks of work: six weeks at the farm teaching and running NTS, and two weeks in December to write and apply for grants. But since I was happily pursuing a professional acting career during the rest of the year, coordinating CIT and the summer school was the best of both worlds.

After my first year of teaching and directing at the summer school, however, it became obvious that a six-week program was simply not enough. A
first-time student could not realistically master the art form in such a short
time period. Students would just be beginning to develop some performance
skills and getting excited about the work when the session would be over.
They really wanted to continue, to go deeper in their study and training, but
couldn't because it was merely a summer program. And at that time, there was
nowhere else for First Nations students to go if they wanted culturally based
theatre training. So in response to that need, CIT created Indigenous Theatre
School (ITS) in 1998. Built on the NTS model of blending Native culture with
training in acting, voice, and movement, ITS became the first post-secondary
Indigenous theatre-training program in North America. The basic goal was
to provide Indigenous students with a culturally affirming and a pedagog-
ically sound curriculum. By that time in my career, I had seen how theatre
could build ideological bridges and heal communities, and most importantly
I saw its power to shift and affirm a sense of self-identity. I never forgot how
bereft I had felt during most of my theatre training, and I was determined
that our ITS students wouldn't have to feel that way. We also wanted to provide professional training in order to supply actors for the growing number
of Native plays and for the media industry; we aimed to grow and develop
the Native theatre canon by creating new work, and equally importantly we
sought to expand the larger society's understanding and perception of First
Nations people.

As idealistic and successful as ITS was there were still major challenges. CIT and ITS were based in Toronto, and therefore students had to move
to the large urban centre in order to take the three-year program. Even for
me, after living previously in cities like Saskatoon and Edmonton, living in
Toronto was a huge adjustment. For many ITS students, leaving family support systems in tight-knit rural communities and coming to such a huge
city caused a multitude of problems. The most critical challenge we faced
was encouraging students to open up physically, emotionally, spiritually, and
mentally when they were being assaulted, sometimes literally (one of our
northern students was robbed at knife-point coming home from the studio

in broad daylight), by a huge metropolis. It was too jarring, too difficult to navigate for many of our students. Yet from those first cohorts, even though they struggled to adjust, there also came excellent work. *Dark Loves To Play* was the collective creation of our second group of ITS students. Based on a collectively created poem, it incorporated dance, clown, and original music. Other ITS student productions such as *Songs*, a series of new dance pieces created by Michael Greyeyes, and *The Witch of Niagara*, a play by Daniel David Moses, were innovative and artistically strong. And like graduates of the NTS summer program, Upsasik Theatre, the Wabasca-Desmarais theatre project, or even the Native Survival School theatre program back in the eighties, ITS students used their theatre training not only to advance and develop Native theatre, but to become community and artistic leaders. ITS alumni have formed their own theatre companies, performed on national and international stages, made films, opened daycare centres, choreographed new dance pieces, started community youth theatre groups, made records, written plays, starred in their own TV shows, toured the country doing stand-up comedy, received university degrees, and won national awards for their art. One has even become Grand Chief.

****

> We all know the story of the man who sat beside the trail too long and then it grew over and he could never find his way again. We can never forget what has happened, but we cannot go back. Nor can we just sit beside the trail.
> —Poundmaker (qtd. in Sluman 296)

When I left Toronto and moved back to Saskatoon for family reasons in 2001, I was happy to be back in my home territory. I was also eager to apply what I had learned at NTS/ITS and to fulfill an obligation I had made before I left to do my master's degree at York University. This obligation—or responsibility, as I had come to think of it—stemmed from a conversation with Harry

J. Lafond. Lafond was the chief of our reserve, Muskeg Lake Cree Nation, and was very supportive of education; he himself had a Master of Education. Although I didn't understand it at the time, his comments had an enormous impact on my perception of Native theatre and training. Over lunch, I asked him what he thought about my leaving teaching and doing graduate work in Ontario. His response (as I remember it) was: "Yes. Go get your Master of Fine Arts. Because then you can come back and open a school of fine arts for Native students." He went on to say that "the education system has failed our people. So many of them drop out and leave—they fail at reading, writing, and arithmetic"—a damning statement coming from an educator. Then he mitigated that statement by saying, "But they have so much talent as artists, musicians, in painting, drawing, as dancers. Our young people need to feel they have something of value to offer. Art will give them that opportunity."

His comments stopped me in my tracks. I hadn't expected such a response; I think I just wanted him to rubber-stamp my plans to leave and get more education. I wasn't looking to be handed a life mission or the responsibility of transforming the education system. I simply wanted to move to Toronto, get my M.F.A., get a talent agent, and work in the film and television industry (read: become a movie star). Further, I reasoned that if I couldn't make it as an actor and had to go back to teaching, at least I could make more money with a master's degree. But once again, whenever I wandered off my mêskanaw, if I sat beside it too long, or got distracted, something always intervened and guided me back. In this case it was Harry Lafond and his radical ideas about what I should do with my life. Maybe he knew something I didn't about my future or maybe he simply sensed that I would do what he suggested. Because even though I went ahead with my plan and temporarily ignored his ideas, the words had been spoken. And even though I tried to forget them, they had a life of their own and were rapidly gathering energy in my subconscious. So inevitably the time came when I returned to the trail and to Lafond's counsel. One could justifiably argue (and I often did) that I had, in fact, accomplished his directive. I got my M.F.A. and established an art-training program for "our young people," one that allowed them to express themselves creatively and experience success. We even brought Native Theatre School to Saskatchewan for two summers in order to train Saskatchewan youth. But despite all of this, there was a nagging sense that I hadn't really done what he had originally asked me to do. Therefore fulfillment of that commitment became one of my main purposes when I resettled back in the Northern Plains.

****

> Our beliefs are good, our gods have served us well. No white man has showed me anything that is better . . . I am more prouder than I ever was before that I am a Cree.
> —Poundmaker (qtd. in Sluman 284)

It wasn't immediately clear how I could create another ITS in Saskatchewan and I ended up pursuing many false trails that quickly petered out or led nowhere. Still the idea seemed to have a life of its own, and had already been developing in the minds of a number of other people. One of those people was Dwayne Brenna, who was the head of the Drama Department at the University of Saskatchewan. Brenna approached me in 2001 about incorporating an Aboriginal drama program into the existing Drama Department. I was quite excited about this idea since one of the major obstacles that NTS and ITS encountered was the lack of accreditation and the inability to access funding that goes along with being a degree- or certificate-granting institution. Unfortunately, we hit some roadblocks and the idea was moved to a back burner at the university. It seemed as if we were back at square one, and as a result I began to develop a somewhat fatalistic attitude; if it was indeed meant to be, it would happen, and in its own time. My job was to hold the vision, do whatever I was asked to do, and then get out of the way. After a number of years of gestation, however, the idea was picked up again at the university by two subsequent department heads: Jim Guedo, followed by Dr. Greg Marion. Under Marion's leadership, the idea really gained momentum and over several years we developed the concept and expanded the conversation, gradually winning over more and more people at the university to our proposal. In another elegant bit of synchronicity, the original founder of Upsasik Theatre, Lon Borgeson, joined one of the community advisory circles that we created to guide the program development. Finally, through many ups and downs, Harry J. Lafond's visionary idea, set in motion over twenty-six years ago, was finally achieved. In the fall of 2015, the University of Saskatchewan officially launched *wîchêhtowin*: Aboriginal Theatre Program in the Department of Drama. Although it is not a school for all of the fine arts, it is an opportunity for Indigenous students in Saskatchewan to take a certificate program in theatre arts at a university level. And who knows? This two-year certificate in Drama may be the beginning of other Aboriginal certificate programs at the university, perhaps in Art and Art History, Music, or Creative Writing. With *wîchêhtowin*, a Cree word, a noun that names a process—we live together in harmony; we help each other; we are inclusive—I feel I have done my part. And in an appropriate act of closure, I have been hired as an assistant professor and the coordinator of the program.

Returning to Saskatchewan and to the Drama Department is in many ways like coming full circle. I am back where everything started, at the head of the trail. But I prefer a more three-dimensional analogy: the spiral. I am back at the starting place, but it's different because my perception has shifted. It might look like the same starting place, but a spiral takes you deeper and deeper into the centre, to the heart of things. Like brilliantly outfitted pow wow dancers spiralling into the centre of the Grand Entry, we are advancing Native theatre step by step, building capacity, complexity, and diversity while accommodating all styles of expression in a unified whole. And I for one can't wait to see what lies ahead of the next bend in my mêskanaw, spiralling along the trail of Native theatre.

SAINTS AND STRANGERS: A RAPPROCHEMENT FOR INDIGENOUS PERFORMANCE

MICHAEL GREYEYES

The search for *precision* in performance is vital and ongoing. If an acting performance would be recognized for its technical merits the way a violinist's playing is measured or the way we marvel at a dancer who can complete multiple turns, finishing on one leg, fully on balance, then it is safe to say that within the North American context, at least, the entire training paradigm would have to change. Across the globe there is a staggering array of performance traditions and each tradition is produced through a training system that is intrinsically aligned to the social, political, and artistic concerns of the culture from which it emerged. The training apparatus, through its methods and personnel—often retired performers or directors—feeds back into the system further shaping and reinforcing the curriculum, which was already shaped and reinforced by the professional theatre and the canon that it serves. It is rare for any theatre school or training institution or theatre company, for that matter, to hire people who are seeking to dismantle the entire apparatus. But if Indigenous performance communities are demanding revitalization, then perhaps the role of senior artists and educators is to unleash our wrecking balls upon systems built by others and rifle through the debris for clues about the path forward and to examine the uncovered spaces for a place to build something new.

Anyone's journey through a system of training is fraught with numerous impediments (personal and institutional), but I assert that Indigenous students face a double bind in North America in that our culture and protocols have safely been ignored for a very long time, and that any system of performance training available to them will come to them from outside their personal experience and be delivered by people who, for the most part, don't reflect them ethnically or culturally.

A few months ago, I was privileged to attend *The Study/Repast*, sponsored and organized by the National Arts Centre at the Debajehmujig Creation Centre on Manitoulin Island and curated by Yvette Nolan and Sarah Garton Stanley. I was invited to speak about precision in performance training, which in turn has inspired many months of further rumination. I stood with my peers, leading them through various exercises and wide-ranging discussions about training in general and our personal journeys, as Indigenous people, through the academy. I was struck, of course, by the similarities between their paths and my own as a student at Canada's National Ballet School in the late seventies and early eighties. I was struck, too, by the fact that the instructor before them was Aboriginal. We had all been strangers in a strange land. Yet now we were gathered from distant lands in the territory of the Three Fires Confederacy training together, and my thesis to them was provocative: *excellence* is *not* a western concept; it is already embedded in our cultures' art practices, but we have eschewed the rigour of those traditions in favour of a misaligned cherry-picking of western methods. Perhaps this turning away from the costs of rigour (and there are many for both teacher and student) seems expedient to our students, who come to us already bruised by numerous legacies of the colonial project, or perhaps it is all we can muster within our woefully underfunded, ill-resourced training centres. But in a final tally, I am an educator realizing with quiet dismay that whichever methods we've chosen have not challenged our students to be better than us. The instructor generation is still way out ahead of the ones that follow in terms of ability and rigour. Where is the next August Schellenberg, Margo Kane, Jock Soto, or Santee Smith? Or even me?

There on Manitoulin, I stated that as a professional director I needed actors who were precise in all aspects of their work, who could repeat actions easily, again and again, rehearsal after rehearsal, night after night, performance after performance. And I said that the systems of training that brought me to this appreciation of precision may have come from outside the Cree culture of my background, but I have benefitted from those systems in a professional career that has lasted for over thirty years. I have, however, had to do a translation of my training—*a translation that has been in process for thirty-five years* and will continue unabated until I am a very old man, still unpacking memories of canvas ballet shoes carving geometries on a wooden floor and beautiful black hair plastered with sweat against dark brown skin in a room full of other skin and hair unlike mine.

It is here that I state my next thesis: as an Indigenous performance community, we must produce an entirely new model of actor/performer. I'm not asking for another training academy like the National Theatre School, or York University, or Ryerson, but now run by Indigenous artists and teachers. I am asking for one entirely suited to the demands of the Aboriginal theatre companies that have emerged in the last decade: Kaha:wi Dance Theatre, ARTICLE 11, Raven Spirit Dance, Compaigni V'ni Dansi, Red Sky Performance, and my own Signal Theatre. In my opinion, these companies are leading the community in terms of energy and public reach. All these companies demand physically adept performers, but all have cast outside the ethnic boundaries of Canada's Indigenous population because the requisite performers—physically virtuosic actor/dancers—do not exist in abundance. We haven't trained them yet. And there is our task.

My thesis expands outward from this into a nascent pedagogy, a pedagogy required for a professional environment that *already* exists here and across the planet. A recent performance from Australia's Marrugeku Theatre and performer Dalisa Pigram called *Gudirr Gudirr* should have been a wake-up call to every Indigenous actor in Canada. Her work was incredibly physical, emotional, and seething with intense energy. *This* is the new playing field. I propose two primary avenues of concentration: through the body and through language. This, of course, resembles nearly all performance programs in the world, which often divide their course work in the Holy Triumvirate of "Acting," "Voice," and "Movement." I need us to leave "Acting" out of the pedagogy because the requirements of the new stage need a much greater level of physical and vocal proficiency and that takes a lot of time and effort (see my earlier mention of the "costs of rigour," or ask any high-level dancer or musician how long it took them to find that proficiency).

PHYSICAL TRAINING

We are desperately out of shape.

I can say this because *I'm* out of shape. Sadly. If I was asked to step in to replace Pigram in *Gudirr Gudirr* I'd last about ten minutes before they called in a team of health-care workers to revive me. But that is, thankfully, changing for me, having spent the last twelve weeks in an intensive conditioning program for the television project I am working on in Cape Town, South Africa. The project in question, a four-hour movie event for the National Geographic Channel, is called *Saints and Strangers*, written by Eric Overmyer and Seth Fisher. *Saints and Strangers* is a provocative retelling of the mythology of the voyage of the *Mayflower* and how the Atlantic coastal nations reacted and responded to the settlement of Plymouth. *Saints and Strangers* looks at the passenger manifest of the infamous *Mayflower* vessel through a new lens. It asserts that half of the passengers were religious zealots, fleeing persecution in England, while the other half were con men, fleeing justice. The miniseries proposes that the *Mayflower* and the settlement of Plymouth provided the American nation with a DNA blueprint that is still resonating across the headlines to this day.

The physical discipline required by this project has changed my body and it has changed my capacity to perform. My acting has been elevated by my new-found physical condition. If you take any Indigenous actor working in Canada at the moment, male or female, and cast them in a film or theatre project in which they wore next to nothing—a bathing suit, for example—would they balk and say, "Really? That's the costume?" I can almost hear the litany of excuses across Turtle Island: "Well, I'm not in great shape right now." "My back is messed up." "I was running, but then I hurt my knee, and now I've put on a few extra pounds!" Of course, a lot of the plays that exist in our canon don't require athletes to perform them, but the terrain of work that excites me—primarily physical, uniquely Indigenous—requires a different kind of actor. And yes, many of the companies I've mentioned require highly trained *dancers*. Dancers who take class nearly every day, exactly like musicians who practise their instruments every day, but if our actors were required to hold physical practice in this way, imagine the potential for staging, for dynamic physical action, that would be available! I am, in fact, suggesting that the distinction between actors and dancers, in the Indigenous context, be obliterated. Such delineations, entrenched in western systems of training, are already becoming less and less useful to professional practices, so let us lead toward a more holistic conception.

When I was asked to direct the seminal *Almighty Voice and His Wife* by Daniel David Moses for Native Earth Performing Arts (NEPA), I brought kettle-bells to the first rehearsal and made the two actors lift them at the start of each day to warm up and would often have them blast through a few sets of swings and squats before rehearsing a scene. Our venue was Theatre Passe Muraille, with its multi-level mainstage and its four-foot drop at the front edge of the stage. I envisioned the actors racing up and down its steps, never pausing for a breath, and leaping off the edge of the stage with careless abandon. Moses's play has numerous songs and dances in addition to his high-octane physical action. It demands dynamic actors—in fact, *athletes*. They *were* athletes in this production, and the physical and vocal conception I had for it toured across Canada, albeit with a new actor playing White Girl. Donna-Michelle St. Bernard, then General Manager of NEPA, called it "The little show that could!" Apart from the fact this play stands atop the canon and can be considered to be our *Fences* or *Buried Child*, the version we created had an energy that was borne of its physical daring. And audiences always respond to such focused energy.

So basic fitness is one aspect of the new path. And there are many ways to get there, but within formal training we need more than this, acknowledging that we cannot borrow existing systems of movement training, particularly western-based systems, since we know they are aligned to the purposes of the western stage. For example, classical ballet—a staple in many programs still—is an ideal training platform to address postural alignment for this slumpen generation, as well as to gain flexibility and strength. But I no longer teach it as part of my curriculum because its strength comes with a cost for Indigenous performers. The term used is neuromuscular patterning. It's how we learn to do any physical action. Author Mary Ann Foster, in "Changing Neuromuscular Patterns," describes it:

A neuromuscular pattern is a sequence of muscular contractions that results in a specific movement. These patterns are stored in the brain's motor cortex. The more a pattern is used, the stronger it becomes, due to the myelination of the motor nerves used in that pattern. This is why habitual patterns of posture and movement are often difficult to change.

In other words, any system of movement is creating rivers within our interior landscapes, along our nerve pathways, in our joint capsules, in the sinew of our muscles—robust highways of activity and conduction. The more these are used, the more robust they become. And like rivers in any landscape, there is rich growth near them, fertile valleys along the path of the colonial invasion. As I said previously, I've been unwrapping this myelination, this codification of my body for thirty years now, forever questioning where a physical impulse is coming from. And with media pumping us full of image after image, we must curate with even greater scrutiny if we are to have a choice in mapping our own performance paths. Fortunately, the options for a new physical curriculum are endless, many of them emerging from our own history: combat, dance, and games, with others from around the world to augment and intermingle. We simply must accept their inherent rigour and commit to the increased span of time that such training would require.

LANGUAGE

If you could only speak one language, I'd like to propose that English is probably your best bet. In addition to its widespread use, English is particularly notorious for its ability to "amalgamate" and "borrow" from other languages. It is the Borg of the planet's languages. In English usage, the word "noggin" means head. It's also the Maliseet word for head. "Mosey along people!" Another Algonquin word (Abenaki), "mosey" means to "wander" or "travel." But English goes beyond simply taking other people's words as its own. It also anglicizes pronunciation. Do the cities "München" or "Москва" mean anything to you? They should. München is a city in "Germany" (Deutschland, actually) that the English decided to call "Munich." "Hmm, yeah, that sounds better!" Same with Москва (a.k.a. Moscow, but pronounced "Moskva")! It takes some brass to change the name of a city and country to your preference. "Hello, my name is Hussein." "A pleasure, I think I'll call you 'Harold.' It's easier on my English tongue."

Putting the stunning arrogance of that aside, it's also lazy. As a choreographer, if I show a performer a fall to the floor, where they lay their ankle, knee, hip down in succession *before* their hands, I really don't expect the performer to say, "I'm gonna go ahead and put my hands down first as that is much more stable," or worse, refuse to try it. And conversely I refuse to allow them to give up on it if they cannot master it on day one. There would be no kids on bikes on any street in Canada if that was our usual approach to difficult tasks. This has led me to think there is an inherent weakness in training our actors in the common tongue. And that is my next thesis: we must train our actors in Indigenous languages, first and foremost (and leave "English," like "Acting," on the sidelines, as we've got waaay too much work to get on with!).

As I finish work on *Saints and Strangers*, I can acknowledge that it has been a game-changer in terms of my thinking about the use of original languages in filmed media and realizing its potential as a training platform. The cast was taught by a brilliant language specialist, Jesse Bowman Bruchac, who is one of twelve Western Abenaki speakers left in the world. We spoke this dialect as the language common to our various tribal nations (Narragansett, Pokanoket, among others) circa the seventeenth century, as depicted in the show. It was difficult. It is an Algonquin language, but with unique word sounds, and grammar that I have not yet encountered in over twenty years working in the film industry. To say the cast was challenged by the language is an understatement. We were terrified. Because we understood the political and artistic importance of doing it right. We are not speakers, so we are relying upon the precision of the teaching and our ability to precisely mimic the sound combinations we are hearing. Here are two examples from the script:

N'nodabnob Iglismonak wijokahalid jiligiliji Namasket. Ni, Nalag-
onsek kadawi sôgenaozin ta gwezioholit.

Kizilla, ônda n'wawaldamowen, kanwa n'wawinawô Kinjames.
W'wizwôgan. Ônda nidôbanna, ônda kindôba Teskwatem. (Overmyer and Fisher)

The "i" is pronounced "ee," as in "beet." The circumflex above the "o" turns
that letter into a double sound "o(n)," as in "bone" with an unvoiced "n," as
in the French nasal "n" in "un." The accent is on the final syllable, unless it
is a greater-than-three syllable word (which are common), when it is on the
third syllable. A "w" followed by a consonant is pronounced "oo," as in "cool,"
but if it is followed by a vowel then it makes a regular "w" sound. (These are
just a few of the language rules!) The language coaching was laser-like in
its precision and our approach as actors was religiously accurate. We were
competing with each other to sound more fluent than the rest. We were driving each other to excellence. And it took hour after hour, coaching session
after coaching session, day upon day, individual practice, walking on Cape
Town's streets with Bruchac feeding us lines, while we dodged pedestrians
and traffic and hazards, so that when we arrived on set, we were assassins.
Two takes usually, but never more than three or four for language accuracy.
If we needed more takes it was camera or sound based—never for the language. The pilgrims were played by English and Irish actors, who are famous
for their professionalism and crisp technique. They stood at attention when
we spoke—our words flowing out with energy, conviction, and power. Deadly
accurate in our mastery of language. And this is language we don't understand! We did double translations, parallel understanding of the text—what
we were saying vocally and how it translated in our minds in relation to the
English text, which itself was not a one-to-one translation, since the Abenaki
required us to learn another intrinsic Indigenous thought process, embedded
in the structure and words themselves. I am very professional; I always know
my lines when I go in front of the camera or step onto the stage. But this was
work at another level, a more rigorous and exacting level than I think any

one of us, veterans of numerous high-level projects, had known. We were on the ground floor of a new paradigm.

Saints and Strangers poses complex questions for me as an Indigenous artist and scholar. On the one hand, such work represents more than half of my professional output as an actor, while at the same time I resent our depiction in period films as it entrenches, for a worldwide audience, the belief that our cultures and communities exist primarily in the past—vestigial. Indigenous characters are usually written by non-Indigenous writers with little practical or artistic connection to our cultures. There are exceptions to the rule, John Fusco obviously coming to mind, but without that type of cultural knowledge or experience, writers usually have only one choice (since they can no longer safely depict us as savages): writing us as some version of "noble." The problem is that we are all so depicted; our community depiction is monolithic. We're all wonderful. But there is no community, or family, like this in existence. Where is the crazy uncle? The slightly demented grandmother? Or the maniac cousin? Yes, those are all clichés too, but writers from outside the community steer entirely away from them in fear of offending or painting us negatively. *Saints and Strangers* took another path. In it, the Indigenous characters vary widely and the characterizations are complex and sophisticated. It featured easily some of the best writing for Indigenous characters I've seen coming out of Hollywood in eons. This was especially true of my character, Canonicus. He is quite paradoxical. On the one hand he is insufferably arrogant and ambitious. He is power-mad, and with a nation that at that point was untouched by disease, he was literally the most powerful sachem in the region. By taking a risk to create a foil in Canonicus, Overmyer and Fisher gave the Indigenous actors in the miniseries three dimensions to work in. And in the end we see that Massasoit was neither a villain, nor a fool, but his decision to help the settlers was based on immediate needs and borne out of urgent political necessity. This is not usually the kind of room we are given to play in period films.

Even Canonicus, a seeming blowhard, was allowed room to grow and change and contradict. In a crucial two-page scene near the end of hour three, he confides to Massasoit that he is actually afraid of the English. He sees in them the "end of us all, our ways, and our future" (Overmyer and Fisher). For me, the level of discourse and the range of intention and backstory for Indigenous characters in this project was finally equal in complexity to the range of characterization and intention in the non-Indigenous cast. *Saints and Strangers* represents a détente of sorts within the hotly contested terrain of media representation—at least it does so for me, an insider to its processes and personnel. Perhaps we are in the midst of a sea change or can actually see one in the distance. And however you see this—a one-off, a blessed relief soon to be replaced by a return to the status quo, or a paradigm shift, it has allowed me to articulate a way forward for us in terms of performance training.

In the spaces provided by a rapprochement between our community and the image brokers, I can see a foothold for a pedagogy embedded in professional contexts. It's like training an actor how to ride a horse, drive a car, or handle a firearm safely and fluently. Those three skills alone are used again and again in movies that feature our communities. And if we teach our emerging actors through the use of Indigenous languages, we teach them a methodology for working in *any* language with precision and craftsmanship. If we train our actors through an intensely rigorous physical lens, we train them to connect to cultural practices that emerged, too, from vibrant physical terrains. And if we do both, we will teach them something else—that *excellence* is embedded in ourselves, our cultural practices, and our ways of doing things. We just somehow forgot.

ARTHOME
TARA BEAGAN

Throughout my time in this life, I've had difficulties finding a perfect home. Not to say I didn't grow up in love and goodness. I did. I am that rare person whose parents are still together, and I am friends with both of them. I have a brother and a sister who I dig, and they enjoy my company. My older sister did us all the favour of having two offspring, anchoring us all in the present and lending us hope for the future. Not a day goes by that I don't share a laugh with family. This solid base has allowed me to connect to what I know, and pursue that which I do not.

I inherited a lot of qualities from my gene pool that I truly appreciate. A soundly balanced set of assets has been counterweighted by being an artistic soul housed in the body of a halfbreed. As a halfbreed, I often saw myself somewhat in stories and yet felt on the outside of them at the same time. I, like Anne of Green Gables, love words and have roots in PEI, yet why did she never speak of the Mi'kmaq of that red soil? I was there, but I wasn't.

I've identified as a halfbreed for quite some time, aware of the internal conflict inherent to my reality. It is likely because of living this rich tension that I have never found fulfillment working within the prescribed norm. I keep relearning this. The more I learn I must build my own arenas, and succeed within them on my own terms, the more I learn of others who have done so. Maria Campbell's remarkable *Halfbreed* was introduced to me by Yvette Nolan because of my choice to own this term. Since the day Nolan gave me a spare copy, which she keeps on hand for this purpose, I too have collected them for passing along to others.

Nolan was in the early days of her long term as Artistic Director at Native Earth Performing Arts (NEPA) when we met. She had heard of me as a playwright/performer from Michelle St. John, who had seen my professional theatrical debut in Toronto. When Nolan and I clapped eyes on one another she connected my face with the cracked-out troublemaker I had played on a CBC TV show earlier that year. She remarked she was impressed that the casting folks had had the vision to choose an actor who "could pass." With that, she introduced me to the term I had lived for many years, but had never named. I could pass for white, but, like Nolan, I never had the desire to. As Nolan jokes, this likely means we fail at passing.

I didn't know Native Earth at that time. In my late twenties, the only Indigenous theatre artist my education had introduced me to was Tomson Highway. The company he was instrumental in founding simply did not come up in the classes that included his work. The company hadn't become legendary in my mind, the way Theatre Passe Muraille or Factory Theatre had. I didn't know the storied history of NEPA, and having lived in Alberta until that point, only had an onscreen familiarity with some of the actors who had trodden its boards. My writing brought me to NEPA, and very quickly I learned of a new way of working, and of scripts that reflected versions of my own experience. In Nolan I found an ally with whom I had much in common.

In 2011, Nolan resigned from NEPA, having tripled the company's operating budget and increased its staff to support said growth. NEPA was poised to helm a rental venue the following year. In short, Nolan's leadership blew NEPA up in profile, productivity, and creative scope. The search for a successor was a little fraught, no doubt in part because of Nolan's intimidating track record. How could anybody match what she had done? How, even, could anybody other than Nolan maintain what she had accomplished for the company? Big questions for a community of artists rich with art yet suffering a scarcity of skilled and available administrators.

The initial call for applicants yielded no results. Not one person applied. NEPA, with Nolan, had invested in training of every kind in anticipation of this moment—the time for somebody to step up and serve. Naturally, the lack of applicants was partly a wonderful result of great artists founding their own companies or plying their skills to new avenues. Still, a company of nearly thirty years of age needed an artistic director (A.D.).

We rallied some likely suspects and held a round-table discussion. Fears and hopes were voiced. Indeed, every person in the room felt hobbled by the knowledge that s/he could never be Nolan. Nolan and her trusted friend and colleague Franco Boni, A.D. of Toronto's Theatre Centre, assured us that no A.D. would want a clone to succeed her. We ten or twelve artists (all under forty) emerged from the session agreeing to apply for the position. Further, we agreed we would be the support network of the successful candidate regardless of whether that person came from our little meeting or not.

When applying for the position at NEPA I submitted a visioning statement. Imagining seasons was a joy. I also dreamt of a pay scale, wherein veterans would be honoured for their trench warfare and their leadership, whether or not they took on formal mentorship in the rehearsal room. In my perfect future, emerging artists would be paid an industry standard, and pay would increase with experience. To me, this reflects an acknowledgement of generations and our responsibility to one another. I wanted traditional values written into all contracts, as NEPA had sometimes done, to employ as helpful talking points should conflict arise. I served as Artistic Director of NEPA from February 2011 to December 2013. Just shy of three years. I was in awe (I still am) of Nolan's nine. In some ways I'm still recovering. The 2015/16 NEPA season marks the first year none of my programming as A.D. is on the slate. I am finally breathing at full capacity again. Better yet, I am able to see what my time as A.D. taught me about the kind of company I am best suited to lead.

My artist self has been resuscitated by refocusing my energies on a company that enriches me and exists within my value system. This company, ARTICLE 11, I co-founded with the greatest artist known to me, multi-faceted designer Andy Moro (Cree.) As a halfbreed in this colonized nation, I live day to day within an imposed structure. The history of this country has been recognized by the United Nations as being rife with genocidal practices. Canada does not acknowledge this. It is no wonder that this country was one of the last holdouts on agreeing to work to abide by the *United Nations*

Declaration on the Rights of Indigenous Peoples. In this hostile land we create our own space for our storymaking as much as we can. So grows this
self-created home.

> Indigenous peoples have the right to practice and revitalize their
> cultural traditions and customs. This includes the right to maintain,
> protect and develop the past, present and future manifestations of
> their cultures, such as archaeological and historical sites, artifacts,
> designs, ceremonies, technologies and visual and performing arts
> and literature. (United Nations)

ARTICLE 11 has a mandate and mission that we revisit, with this article—
Article 11 of the *United Nations Declaration on the Rights of Indigenous
Peoples*—as a touchstone. It is a living and evolving mandate and mission,
and so we treat it as a living, working thing. Core to our creation processes are several non-negotiable things. These items are what we see when the
eleventh article of the UN's declaration is unpacked:

1. REPRESENTATION

At every step we work to hire Indigenous collaborators. Crew, designers, performers, all. Our voices are under-represented, and so we give them a platform
with our work. In our two years of existence, we have filled sixty-one positions
with Indigenous collaborators. We are especially proud of the inclusion of
all generations. A great moment of advocacy for us was while working at the
Royal Ontario Museum (ROM) in Toronto, with our large-scale performance
installation piece, *DECLARATION.* The ROM provides text for its patrons in
both government-sanctioned languages. We insisted on adding an Indigenous
language, representative of the lands we were on. Elder Ernie Sandy (Ojibwe)
was brought in to translate the text I had written for the didactic panels, and
throughout the show we felt very proud to have Anishinaabemowin included
in the declarations on the walls.

Anishnaabek Diyaanaawaa chi zhitkewaat miinwaa chi maajiiskaa-
toowaat gaazhi nebmoowaat miinwaa gaabi naadziwaat. Ed goosin
chig noowenjgaadek, chi koowaamjigaadek miinwaa chi maaji-
iskaatoowaat gaazhi webak giinaagoh, noomgoh ejiwebak, miinwaa
giiyaabi waabiiyaamgak, gaabizhi maadzhiwaat meyeozha gaateg gin,
zhit kanan, gaazhi dewewaat miiwaa ewaabji gaadek miinwaa eginj
gaadek"aad–aadekkaadekkkkgaadekzhi aazhi Article 11.

On the other end of the age scale, we have Production Manager Brittany
Ryan (Métis). A recent grad of Ryerson University, Ryan has been working
for ARTICLE 11, Signal Theatre, and other First Nations–helmed companies
since her second year in school. ARTICLE 11 made a point of paying Ryan as
an emerging professional, because her output was very nearly at a professional
level. Still learning, Brittany also goes above and beyond to earn her place in
the process, and often proves an insightful voice during the development process. Our youth and our Elders work with us, and work hard. We value this.

A person's role is creatively considered when listing credits. Sandy, for
example, was named as Translation Collaborator, for that is what he was at the
ROM. When having a workshop production of our project *RECONCILIATION*,
we had the privilege of working with Paul Chaput (Métis.) An academic, actor,
musician, filmmaker, healer, and young Elder, Chaput had a grounding influence and helped us feel safe in the subject matter. His title was Elder Research
Collaborator, whereas, in the past, some productions featuring Indigenous
voices might have named him a consultant. As Diane Roberts beautifully
stated on a panel at Full Circle's Talking Stick Festival, "We're way beyond
consultation. We collaborate. Consultation is bullshit."

2. PAYMENT

Administration of the arts is invaluable. Without the art, however, there would be no administrative work. We reflect this reality in our pay structure. To date, we have written of our commitment to pay above industry scale in our grant applications, and have received much support from granting bodies. Indigenous artists are specialized by our very existence. Retaining an Indigenous artist on any given project can be challenging due to demand, and so we aim to be competitive by offering a rate comparable to that of an indie film project. This eliminates one variable from the artist's tough decision should overlapping offers arise. We have yet to pay ourselves (Beagan and Moro) equitably for administration and royalties, but that will come with time. As artists who work several positions, we do make a living wage when we work on our own projects, and that is the goal. ARTICLE 11 works with a pay scale that reflects the experience—not the profile—of the artist.

A simple example of reflecting this pay scale is that for performer Sera-Lys McArthur (Nakota.) McArthur has performed ARTICLE 11's *In Spirit* on half a dozen different engagements. Her value to the production increases as her experience with the show—a work for a solo performer—gains ground. We increase her pay every time we engage her as the performer for the show. Her presence contributes to the merit of the work, and so her remuneration reflects this.

At times ARTICLE 11 gifts collaborating artists, in addition to paying them an equitable rate. This gifting is a practice Indigenous peoples have honoured for thousands of years. For us today, it's a way of thanking artists for their unique talents, without requiring a percentage of cash to go to a union or agent. It is a way of inspiring feelings of appreciation among us, and it's something we enjoy.

3. PRINCIPLES

Every person involved in our projects has a voice. Decisions have to be made eventually, so conversations can't go on indefinitely, but conversations are had, and anyone who wants to participate in them does. We've had visiting students from the University of Toronto, Rosedale Heights School of the Arts, and Ryerson University. As I learned at Nolan's NEPA, the room can be an open place and a fruitful learning environment. When an auditing student was so moved by our work that she jumped up to help with room set-up and strike, we offered her an honorarium. This mutual generosity goes a long way.

An unofficial rule of ARTICLE 11 is "no assholes." This means we have to keep our own stress in check, so that we don't snark at anybody during the work, but it also means we don't hire people unless they are kind. The theatre community is a small world, and the Indigenous theatre community even smaller. All people make mistakes, yet not all people bother to correct harmful behaviours if they seem to get away with them. We choose not to invite those people into our projects. At every step we want collaborators who treat the venue staff and one another with kindness. When venue staff don't have the capacity to do the same, having a reliably generous person on your side is a wonderful way to diffuse a problem before it becomes a crisis.

Our projects are taking shape around this way of working. In its turn, the work reflects the goodness in these ways. Our project *DECLARATION*, when at the NAC, boasted a number of remarkable collaborators, including founding ensemble member of NEPA Monique Mojica (Guna and Rappahannock). In a moment of calm during a hectic week of exploration, Mojica was surprised by tears of joy. She looked about the room—a room full of brilliant colleagues, a room transformed by Moro's design work—and said, "This is how we used to work. This is how we should always work."

The work brings hope. Creating hope through the work lands an artist a home.

THANKSGIVING
FALEN JOHNSON

In 1994 I made my first cornhusk doll. Cornhusk dolls are a traditional art form in my community of Six Nations in southern Ontario. The faceless doll teaches us to remain humble as we walk through the world and to honour our commitments. Making this doll was just about the most cultural thing I had ever done in my twelve years. I made the doll at a summer camp on Six Nations called the Red Barn that taught traditional arts to kids. The creation of the doll also coincided with my first ever fainting spell. As I folded the cornhusks over each other to create my doll I felt an odd sensation come over me. Everything slowed down and sped up at the same time and before I could think what to do I collapsed. Word spread throughout camp that I had fainted, but not really. The official word was that I had faked it and for the rest of my time at the Red Barn I was referred to as "Faker." It wasn't until later in my adolescence that I discovered why I fainted that day. Unbeknownst to me or to anyone else at the time, I had severe anemia. It would take me four more years before I was diagnosed. Fainting aside, the doll turned out well. She had a bright yellow beaded crescent moon across her dress and long black yarn braids that lay over her shoulders.

Six Nations, like many Indigenous communities in Canada, is a polarizing place in terms of culture. In crass terms one might say you either have it or you don't. My family does not. At least in any formalized sense. For many people on any reserve across Canada this is the case. You pick up bits and pieces of culture as you walk down the dirt roads of the Rez. You learn to recognize edible plants that grow in the ditch; you hear the old stories from your grandparents as you head into town for groceries; you watch the funeral in the longhouse and try to make sense of what is being said in a language you have been long disconnected from.

When I moved to Toronto to work in theatre my connections to culture began to shift. Suddenly I found myself around people who practised tradition. Some of it was from their specific nations, some of it was adopted, but nonetheless people had rules and protocols they followed. Skirts during ceremonies, sage burning, and walking around the circle clockwise or counter-clockwise were all things that I began to consider. I had questions but no one to ask. Again my family didn't practise any sort of traditionalism. This was shame-making for me. People would turn to me in the rehearsal hall for some kind of cultural knowledge and I had none to give. It seemed hard for some people to understand that someone who had grown up in their community didn't know the story of Tadodaho front to back or know how to smoke dance. I googled and lied a lot of my way through those times.

Over time I attempted to piece together what knowledge I had or had heard about to make some kind of patchwork cultural knowledge I could use in the rehearsal hall. It worked some days, but there were many days I left frustrated by what I didn't know. Sometimes I didn't want to smudge or be told not to smudge if I were on my menstrual cycle. A no-no in some Indigenous cultures. Most of the time I just wanted to walk through the world trying to be a good person and still be considered a part of the community. I wanted to be supported by my community as a colonized person who was trying to find her way back to something that she didn't fully understand.

In 2014, twenty years after I made my first cornhusk doll, I made my second. The Setsuné Indigenous Fashion Incubator announced a series of courses to be taught in Toronto and one of these courses would be on the creation of cornhusk dolls. I signed up. The course was being taught by Elizabeth "Betts" Doxtator, who is a master of cornhusk. Her work is renowned and incredibly intricate. Tiny baskets, real pottery, and authentic brain-tanned hide are all used in her creations.

The first time I met Betts and saw her work I felt an immediate connection to her and her dolls. I introduced myself and told her I was from Six Nations. She began cracking jokes and taking jabs immediately. I felt like

I was at home speaking with her; she felt like family. Betts showed me her dolls and explained the traditional stories they tell. I felt like for the first time ever someone was teaching me, and, as Betts would explain, with traditional tools. The cornhusk is a traditional medium. It is something our people have worked with for as long as memory stretches. I felt like I had the room to not know with Betts and to be able to ask questions.

On the day of the cornhusk doll workshop I said hello to Betts and chatted with her. She asked me if I knew the thanksgiving address, a traditional Haudenosaunee address that opens many traditional gatherings. I told her the truth: that I did not and I had never spoken it. She said, "Really?" and reached into a bag and handed me her traditional Haudenosaunee outfit and told me to go put it on. I thought about protesting, but quickly thought better of it. I felt shy and thought that the outfit wouldn't suit me and I would look out of place, but I decided to accept this potential teaching. I put on the cotton leggings, tunic, moccasins, and even a beaded floral barrette. I stood in the bathroom looking at myself in the mirror, and as I took in my reflection my old nickname "Faker" ran through my mind. I walked back into the room and Betts handed me a printed copy of the thanksgiving address and told me to stand at the front of the room and read it. The address gives thanks to the water, the animals, the trees, and everything in the world; it asks that the group of people listening to the address come together and be of one mind to do the work that they need to in a good way and that those in attendance must be joined in their purpose. The address is not a short one—it was many pages—and as I stood at the front of that room reading I felt an odd sensation, like sinking. I worried I might faint again like when I was twelve at the Red Barn. But I didn't. I took the words in and let myself feel the legacy of the address. When I finished reading I looked to Betts as to what I should do next. Betts announced to the group that there would be a closing portion of the address at the end of the day after we completed our dolls.

As I made my doll, questions knocked around in my brain and I spoke to Betts about them. I told her about ceremony in the city and how I came to my teachings through the arts and performance community because I didn't really know anything from back home. I spoke with her of how the address had stirred something inside me.

I told her about my work with Native Earth Performing Arts over the years and a type of ceremony that was created between the artists in the room. I recalled working on a piece titled *A Very Polite Genocide* by Melanie J. Murray. The play is about the residential-school system and the subsequent generational fallout. The work was, not surprisingly, emotionally taxing. The rehearsal day began with a smudge and the abalone shell we used for smudging would remain in the room for the duration of the day in case anyone felt the need. We did a check in at the beginning and at the end of each day. Traditional medicines were always present in the room. After our check in at the end of the day upbeat music would be put on and the cast and crew would dance together with the intention of letting go of the work we had done. Working in performance is ceremony much of the time. One opens oneself up to experience and feels things intensely. It can be emotionally dangerous to attempt to walk into the world so open and so vulnerable; we took this moment to, in a way, close ourselves back up. It can be difficult to grieve five hundred years of genocide and then get on the busy streetcar where you are being yelled at because your backpack touched someone's arm. Like teachers do, Betts nodded as I spoke, and watched me put the pieces of what I was learning together myself.

At the end of the day Betts asked her son to speak the closing of the thanksgiving address. Her son, who had been in the room all day as her teaching aid, stood and spoke the closing in Mohawk. His words were humble and quiet, the way traditional languages are frequently spoken. He then explained to the room what he had just said, that we had all come together in a good way to work on a common goal, to learn something, and now we must break our minds so that we can go into the world and be of our own minds. The parallels between the performative ceremony and traditional Haudenosaunee thanksgiving address were all of a sudden so apparent to me.

On my walk home I thought about my relationship to ceremony and how it has been tied to theatre and performance for so long. These days I find myself out of the rehearsal room and more and more in my office or in a coffee shop writing. I frequently wonder about my relationship to ceremony. I have moved away from many of the practices that used to feel so very urgent. That community doesn't exist for me in the way it used to. I rarely feast; I never smudge unless I'm in a group of people at a gathering and it is already present; and I have never been one to pray. If my relationship to ceremony has been tied to performance and now the performance is out of my life, then what now? I still have a box of traditional medicine in my house and I do believe there is merit to it, and I think there are teachings to be gained from sweats and fasts and feasts. But it's all a little unclear to me right now. I remember in theatre school my instructors would say, "We are just providing you with a tool box; take what works for you, leave what doesn't." Could it be that easy?

BRINGING FORTH THE SACRED, SPEAKING FOR THE SPIRITS: A BRIEF BRAID

ANDRÉA LEDDING

I was honoured to be asked for some thoughts on theatre and performance: I had many thoughts on the matter, but did not know what I had to offer besides myself, and so that is what I have brought to the page. Traditionally who you are is what you bring, so I will try to come from that place that is authentically me, connected to others.

ACT 1, SCENE 1: THE BEGINNING

I was conceived in St. Boniface, Manitoba, born on 20th Street in St. Paul's Hospital, Saskatoon, Saskatchewan, and grew up in small towns, bouncing between city, rural, and provincial boundaries.

In one province Louis Riel was a hero, founding father, and martyr; in another he was a traitor who'd been hanged and declared mad.

Having an accent on my first name and brown relations as well as white ones, French and English and other languages which were somewhere in-between, mixed marriages in many ways and directions, and formative years in a KKK prairie town where I was one of the targets, the warp and weft of my identity was on the sash long before I entered this world, and continues to be swiftly woven in many colours and threads. Red, white, brown, orange, black, green . . . at the bottom the threads hang loose, dangle with possibility. I write my bio for an award nomination, stating that I am proud of all my relations and ancestors which include Irish, Scandinavian, Michif (Métis), French, Haudenosaunee (Mohawk), Nehiyaw (Cree). I am called Métis in all copy and at the awards ceremony, because in this world you can only be one thing, and they want to show how they are celebrating (ironically) "diversity." Nobody else is me, can I just be Andréa? That's hard enough, believe me. This is not shame or pride, but if my parents consider themselves "mostly Irish" and "lucky to be Canadian," who am I? Where do I come from? Who are my people? When I was a little girl I thought the Golden Boy on top of the Manitoba Legislature was Louis Riel. I used to pray to him as I prayed to other saints and dead relatives; my great uncle Pat in heaven, my cousin Pat who died when I was three, my grandmother I never met, for whom I was named.

"You are sentenced to be hanged by the neck until dead, for treason to the crown." "Treason to the crown? That crown belongs to King Richard." (As a child I would get Disney's *Robin Hood* conflated with the trial of Louis Riel. I saw the emotional logic.) Louis Riel has inspired over a century of art, from his trial held annually in Regina as a re-enactment to and including Harry Somers's opera *Louis Riel*, Carol Bolt's play *Gabe*, the current National Arts Centre French Theatre extravaganza in development *Gabriel Dumont's Wild West Show*, and many other scripts and performances at local, provincial, national, and international venues. Martyred visionaries are impossible to kill.

ACT 1, SCENE 2: THE MIDDLE, THE MUDDLE

There is conflict in the room/house/community/city/country. Man against woman, woman against child, in-law against out-law, green against orange, atheism against religion, white against brown, teacher against student, student against student against student, men in white sheets against people who aren't white enough or the right kind of white, French against English against Indian, but only one group is sauvage; this word means wild, this word means free. Feel it, absorb it, try to understand it; learn to pretend it's not there. Work at clarity, intention, motivation in all people. Translate as necessary. Know the stakes at any given moment. Assess danger at all times. Watch it all unfold around you every day. You are living in a war zone and words are bullets. Bullets are ammunition. Ammunition either misses, wounds, or kills, until it runs out. Ponder it in your heart. Act like it never happened. Don't act at all: BE.

A South African teacher organizes a reading of "The Three Little Bears" in various languages to try to emphasize the strength in diversity, pushing against the WASP racism he sees in the community. Tante Marie-Paule on the phone, checking translation of her first languages with sisters because the wrong kind of French got them strapped. You read it on risers, wearing your best dress, homemade by your mom, and your knees aren't together enough because the boy in grade six that you love is pointing up your skirt to his friend, and whispering about the colour of your panties. Your face flushes less as you read the language you weren't supposed to speak in this town, silent accent aigu on your first name. Trembling hands, shaking knees, steady voice. Stage directions.

Memorize poems for music festivals. Say them out loud. Feel the power in words, voice, memory, and a room of people who want to hear what you have to say. You have always memorized by sight and sound the things you wanted to keep, and the things you couldn't lose no matter how hard you tried. Join high-school drama (the on-stage kind); your first kiss is a stage kiss; you finally quit in grade twelve because the scripts have gotten worse and worse. On stage and off. You have an ear for music, and an ear for dialogue. Hate to be patronized. You do know what that means, don't you?

ACT 1, SCENE 3: A MINOR CONCLUSION

There is identity. There is community. There is story. There is voice. And there is theatre, which is all four and yet something else of itself. Of all the experiences in your life, writing and performing are perhaps the most like having that boy you loved looking up your dress at your underwear.

ACT 2, SCENE 1: OTHER BEGINNINGS

I was invited by a warmly enthusiastic and supportive English professor to compare my process of developing a play with Shakespeare's process, particularly since my play *Dominion* had been workshopped at the University of Regina in its early days. I felt incredibly intimidated to compare myself with Shakespeare, especially since I would have to present my essay to the entire Honours class, and I wasn't sure what she thought I would discover.

Dominion has since gone on to be workshopped and dramaturged as part of the Weesageechak Begins to Dance Festival at Native Earth Performing Arts in Toronto and the Saskatchewan Playwrights Centre's Spring Festival of New Plays. A condensed version of it ran across the country with eight other short plays in Canada 300, an ambitious attempt by PEI's Watermark Theatre to capture an essence of Canada along with hopes dreams and visions of a shared future, and to engage audiences in conversations about what sort of country they want to build. But *Dominion* was my first play, and as a first-born it continues to demand my attention in various ways, even as I continue to work on other projects.

How I came to write the play was interesting. Leeann Minogue (author of *Dry Streak* and other plays) had heard me read fiction and poetry and said more than once that my dialogue and staging in these pieces would work well as plays. While attending the Indian residential school apology broadcast at White Buffalo Youth Lodge in 2008, I was witness to one response that spoke in part about the history of this country and how the original inhabitants had been locked in the bathrooms of their own homes without access to even the basic necessities of life: in discomfort, inconvenience, and shame. That haunted me, and I knew it was a play but had no idea how to write it. Many times I'd thought that the Canadian government's treatment of Métis and First Nations peoples was similar to an abusive domestic arrangement, and that was why it would not stop haunting me. Canada as an abusive Anglo spouse/patriarch cutting deals with an unhappy Francophone wife was easy to imagine, but writing characters locked in a bathroom was harder. Also I had no idea how to write a play and wanted to avoid mistakes and time wastes.

So I audited an online class through the University of Regina and met with a lot of excitement over the play, including from the Indigenous readers who helped workshop it. I also met some resistance over the play, from people such as the non-Aboriginal woman who said as a white person she found it offensive. I found historical and contemporary realities offensive, so I tried to ignore that comment, but being a good little societally conditioned female Canadian I hated the thought I was giving offence, and after the workshop I buried the play completely until Yvette Nolan became writer-in-residence at the City of Saskatoon Public Library shortly after. When I showed it to her she congratulated me: "You're a playwright." I was a little alarmed, but most-ly relieved. As in all things, I owe the people around me and the Creator or creator or creative impulse or however you prefer to describe the beauty of the life force behind, within, and around each of us. It went forward from there again, and where it will land finally, nobody knows. It's not mine; I just started to write it down. It's everyone's. And that's the ugly truth/profound beauty of a shared story.

Well, in the very intimidating-to-me process of comparing myself to the western world's playwright-of-playwrights for a class presentation/seminar, while processing my own feelings about my play, I was surprised to learn that Shakespeare was not in the least welcome at Oxford. But then neither were the general unwashed masses welcome. (I wondered if the professor knew that all along and wanted me to know it too.) Shakespeare's theatre served a pur-pose, but it was never academic, nor was it considered by the academy (at the time) to be something worth studying or collaborating with, let alone hosting or supporting. Shakespeare wrote for the people: all the people. Shakespeare wrote to work things out, to reflect the histories of the land, to capture the relationships and complexity of humanity, to entertain, to provoke, to tell stories, and to make language sing. Shakespeare contributed to the creative development of the language itself, either capturing or creating words and bringing them into usage that is still reflected today. Despite being shut out of academia and looked down upon, Shakespeare's contributions arguably exceeded and outlived those of many academics. And now Shakespeare is part of the modern academy and almost every curriculum.

ACT 2, SCENE 2: THEATRE IN SASKATCHEWAN

In Western Canada, we have local theatres that strive for avid subscribers, patrons, reviewers, mass appeal, artistic integrity, economic success, and vibrant, diverse productions. A lot to balance. Globe Theatre, Dancing Sky Theatre, 25th Street Theatre, Persephone Theatre, and so many more. Small towns have theatres and summer players, and there is an adjudicated theatre festival for elementary and secondary school students. Both the University of Saskatchewan and University of Regina have lively drama departments.

And in Saskatoon where I currently live, the late, great Gordon Tootoosis helped found the highly successful Saskatchewan Native Theatre Company (SNTC), recently renamed after him as the Gordon Tootoosis Nīkānīwin Theatre (GTNT). Their Circle of Voices program for youth is but one of their many success stories. They provide training grounds for Aboriginal actors, and opportunities for Indigenous writers and stories to be showcased, from Tomson Highway and Drew Hayden Taylor to Curtis Peeteetuce and Kenneth T. Williams. Just as the displaced flora and fauna of the prairies still gently but persistently push up and through the colonial impositions of grids and fields and cement, so do the stories of the original peoples echo forward and insistently push into the mainstream theatre spaces. 25th Street Theatre produced *Jessica* by Maria Campbell and Linda Griffiths; La Troupe du Jour and GTNT share office and theatre space; and Persephone will often run the box office for GTNT productions even if they aren't being held in the actual Persephone building. Cree actress Carol Greyeyes has been an actor at Persephone on both stages in roles that aren't necessarily Aboriginal. Kenneth Williams has been produced twice at Persephone Theatre, not just SNTC/GTNT, with his plays *Gordon Winter* and *Thunderstick*.

I once did lunch and an interview with Lorne Cardinal when he was in town performing Kenneth Williams's *Thunderstick*, and I remember him saying something along the lines of, "We could do an all-native Shakespeare. We have the talent and capacity for that too, but so often the parts for anything go to the non-Indigenous, whether the parts themselves are Indigenous or not." While I had significant street cred with my kids for having lunch with

Davis from *Corner Gas*, Cardinal was articulate and passionate about a field he stumbled into from being the quiet techie climbing on ladders to adjust lights in Edmonton. His character on Brent Butt's *Corner Gas* was memorable because it was no big deal that he was Aboriginal—that wasn't why he was playing the part. He just: happened to be, while being a great character actor. For so long on- and off-screen, Aboriginals have been largely invisible unless they were the hostile Indians or the amiable sidekicks (Tonto means "stupid" in Spanish, if you can recall the Lone Ranger's silent pal. Interesting fact.) A Saskatchewan production played no small part in making Aboriginals everyday accessible stock actors—thanks, Brett Butt and Lorne Cardinal. Here's to the future continuing on stage and screen in this vein.

ACT 2, SCENE 3: WHAT I WANT FROM THEATRE IN SASKATCHEWAN

At this writing and in my entire life's memory, every production and performance in this city anywhere generally ends with one response: the standing O. Rarely is it not given, no matter what, so I once decided as a cynical youth this was because we were incredibly grateful to any people who bothered to create artistic performances of any kind in such a place. Whether you are reflecting on the past and current history, or the climate: generally warm people, generally hostile environment.

By this rationale, or so I figured, almost every attempt deserves a standing O, just like all the kids in soccer games get medals for showing up and trying. I can be persuaded this is good practice. But I do confess to one day refusing to stand. It was a theatre piece, and the writing and the performance was so disappointing to me personally after the hype I'd been fed that I feigned an injury and clapped from my chair. Or maybe I was seated on a riser and didn't want anyone looking up my skirt. But that day on either side of me two other people also did not stand, as a result of my example. I counted it my one act of theatrical treason for which I could quite likely swing on a bad-judge day, like Louis Riel, the man who inhabits a lot of space for being dead over a century.

But part of me always deeply hopes to be carried away by the performance before me. I don't just want to stand up and clap at the end. I want there to be a profound silence. Followed by people standing on their chairs, whistling and cheering and ululating. (I'm an all-or-nothing kind of gal when I'm allowed to get a little bit idealistic.)

However, that is theatre as performance, as spectacle, as entertainment. Theatre as practice is something else entirely. By rigorous play—elements of both artistic discipline and study combined with a spirit of joyful, childlike dedication—it elevates the everyday into a public act of consecration whereby people and words and objects are transformed into Something More Than They Were. The audience becomes part of this transformation, and the energy creates, changes, shifts paradigms. The sum is, or at least should be, greater than its parts, if most or all parts are in good working order.

A living, breathing audience changes every day, just as the work in progress goes deeper and the actors learn more about who they are becoming. Theatre, like life, never arrives. But it should keep getting better, or at least this is the hope that keeps most of us going in both life and theatre. As in life, a theatrical disaster is actually a giant learning opportunity, critics be damned. The most interesting theatre I ever saw at a Fringe festival involved the writer/director standing up mid-performance and critiquing the actor. What followed was some of the best live theatre/drama I've ever seen in my life, and although I have tried to write that scene as a performance of its own, I doubt it will ever live up to the original. So much was at stake for everyone. We were all on the edges of our seats. Was this part of the performance, or was it real? And that is what theatre must be: a balance of the real, and the suspended (dis)belief.

ACT 3, SCENE 1: TO TIE A BRAID

To tie this into Indigenous practice is to also enter the realm of what is, to me, the spiritual, the ceremonial. I am not going to tout myself as some kind of expert on that, nor am I going to write about it directly because I believe experience itself should be the teacher, not words in a textbook or collection. But some practical elements could and should be included: a sacred space for Indigenous actors and perhaps even audience members to enter. It could be as simple as bypassing a theatre space's no-smoking rules to allow a ceremonial smudge beforehand, to acknowledge that they are cleansing themselves of the stench of self, ceremonially, to bring to one another and to all others the gift of self, offered in a good way with purpose and good intent. It is not for me to say that all playwrights and directors should do the same, but I do suggest that it wouldn't hurt. Especially before those really painful bleed-out editing and directing sessions where every second word is "cut!" It is already standard practice for some directors and theatre artists and could be more widely embraced.

Theatre space largely is the realm of the spiritual and the ceremonial. No matter their particular spiritual beliefs or lack thereof, each person walks into a dedicated space where they are asked to be a part of something greater than themselves: where they suspend, at least temporarily, some of their beliefs to enter into a created world to learn something about themselves and/or others, and the world around us all. To smudge out that space beforehand and to cleanse it in preparation for others is to honour the very real work being done in hopes it will be a positive experience. Many Indigenous practitioners smudge the space before they work. These ceremonies can be shared by all, Indigenous and non-Indigenous alike. They help make tangible some of the very real magic that the theatre brings to life, and honour that tradition.

ACT 3, SCENE 2: THE UN-SILENCING OF THEATRE

It is no easier to unravel the mystery of theatre, let alone Indigenous theatre, than it is to define oneself. We choose words, stories, and actions to highlight or illustrate aspects of the task at hand, and we let the rest remain, like the icebergs, submerged below, in darkness and the Great Mystery. But what we show should be illuminating enough to reference the vastness of the unseen.

To tie in the third strand of Indigenous theatre and self in order to make the final strand of a quick essay braid: Helen Betty Osborne was the first Aboriginal women I knew to be disappeared, a hole dug which I was born into, but there have been many others before and since, and it is a deliberate and ominous silencing. Missing and murdered women, and men, number like the stars, adding the weight of their voicelessness to those of us who still have tongue. She was brutally killed after being approached and violenced, a fate many of us have suffered but survived. She did not live to tell. Her murderers largely got off without consequence. The message being sent: her life doesn't matter, nor does yours. You are disposable. We can, and will, silence you. Theatre is a space where un-silencing can happen, and voices can be regained.

In Indigenous theatre, as in all spaces Indigenous and non-Indigenous, women need to be calling the shots and being given the voices, not just in the communities—and yes, many Indigenous communities were strongly matriarchal and Euro-feminism itself borrowed heavily from that and then forgot—but as playwrights, as directors, as actors, as producers, as professors, as Elders, and as the community leaders they always have been and always will be. Men need to learn how to listen, if they don't already know. Indigenous and non-Indigenous. Not to be the audience trying to look up skirts, but respectful listeners to a variety of voices.

ACT 3, SCENE 3: TYING THE BRAID

So, quietly, I welcome you in and I offer you this small and very humble reflection on prairie performance and Indigenous theatre: excellence and respect in all things, because you are bringing forth the sacred and you are speaking for spirits—your own, or others—when you step onto the stage or page in any way.

The audience is equal partner in every performance and has to realize their individual and personal lenses will affect how they perceive what they are shown in that half-space that is the real world, and not. Just one response impacts all those around it, and everyone in the room has some kind of stakes and some kind of responsibility to their spirit and to other spirits.

The classrooms and courtrooms and office spaces of the world are performative spaces that are occupied every day in an infinity of configurations; drama is everywhere, but theatre is one sacred space where we deliberately gather to seek it and to make new sense of the world. Hiy hiy.

SPINE OF THE MOTHER: MOVING MOUNTAINS ... CREATING DANCE

STARR MURANKO

Spine of the Mother premiered in Vancouver, BC, in November of 2015 and was the culmination of a multi-year collaborative exchange project between dance artists, collaborators, mentors, and cultural advisors in both Canada and Peru. The project resulted in a multimedia dance piece that, while contemporary in form, is firmly grounded in traditional teachings connected to Andean cosmology and an Indigenous world view. The piece explores our connection and relationship to Mother Earth and the Cosmos, to ourselves and to each other. Inner to outer. Micro to macro. And everything in between.

BACKGROUND

I first began travelling to Peru in 2002, inspired by an invitation from a dear friend to come and visit his land, his home, the Andes. From the first moment I landed in Cusco, twelve thousand feet above sea level, I felt as though I could exhale in a deeper way. The land herself was holding me so close that I could only sink into her body. I could exhale. I could see my relationship to the Apus, the mountain spirits as the Quechua people refer to them. Over the weeks, months, and later years that I would travel back and forth between our two continents I would discover that those same mountains would allow me to dive deeper into my own personal process because I knew that she, Mother Earth, and therefore the Andes mountains themselves, would catch me; she would hold me; she would let me shatter into a thousand pieces to only be built stronger again. She became my touchstone, the place I would go to, even sometimes in spite of myself. She would call to me like a mother to a child and I would go, unwillingly at times and at other times running at the speed of light to be held in her soft yet powerful embrace.

It was early on in those years that I learnt of the traditional teachings and understandings that the Wisdom Keepers of South America hold and that would later be reaffirmed by my Elders here in the North. Those teachings are that the Andes mountain range runs from the base in Argentina, up through the Americas, ending at the tip of Alaska. It is understood that this is the "Spine of Mother Earth," and that there is an unbroken line of energy that travels up and down the spine that has connected us as Indigenous people for tens of thousands of years. That spine mirrors our own spines and the Kundalini or serpent energy that travels up and down our central nervous system. It has been activated, utilized, and travelled along through trade routes and ceremonies and the transferring of oral histories and knowledge. It holds the teachings and Prophecy of the Eagle (the people of the North) and the Condor (the people of the South) coming together. It speaks to the times that we are living in now as being a time for remembering each other and remembering that we have flown together before. It is a coming together of our minds and our hearts and working together as one human family for the betterment of all. As Indigenous people we have always known of each other; we have always been connected, and it was only in the past five hundred years or so of colonization that it was agreed upon that we would "disconnect" or hide the fact that we knew of each other, as a way to protect the traditional teachings. Jhaimy Alvarez-Acosta, a traditional curandero (healer) from Cusco, Peru, (who would later become our cultural advisor for the project) would often share with me in those early visits to Peru that the Andean people believed that it was during that time of colonization that sacred temples were covered, traditional knowledge was buried as a means to protect it, and medicines were concealed or "swapped" between the North and the South to avoid being discovered. Now this energy is being unlocked and is travelling along the spine of the mountains and along our own spinal columns. It is an energy of re-connection, of re-membering who we are and where we came from, and it is grounded in a strong reverence for Mother Earth. It is a remembering of cosmic maps of time and space that were intricately woven into both our sacred sites and ourselves, and it has never left our DNA.

It was a compelling image that not only captured my imagination but that also, on a visceral level, I knew to be true. This image and the traditional teachings shared during my times in Peru tugged at me for years, nudging me at times and at others picking me up and putting me where I needed to go . . . to complete the next step, the next stone, the next piece. At the time I didn't know the process of creating this dance piece was already beginning, but like all epic journeys it begins with one step.

From the very beginning, working with Alvarez-Acosta was key in grounding the piece in the traditional teachings of the Andes that include both South and North. Although we would begin to approach the work through the lens of the teachings of South America it became very clear, and very quickly, that, as Alvarez-Acosta said, "Nothing goes one way." There is a Quechua term that describes this connection: Yanantin-Masintin, which could be roughly translated as yin-yang, two sides of the same coin, or one cannot exist without the other. This has become the essence of the work that we have done together as a creative team; it has become the embodiment of that teaching within the work itself.

Spine of the Mother is a duet for two dancers, two woman embodying their individual yet interconnected lives, stories, and memories on opposite sides of the world (see Figure 1). Two continents, connected by a range of mountains and a thread of energy that is timeless, patient, and ruthless all at once. It is a dance piece that requires the dancers to dig

Figure 1. Tasha Faye Evans and Andrea Patriau in *Spine of the Mother*, video/media design by Sammy Chien. Photo by Chris Randle.

deep in order to find their own connection to self and to each other. It requires a deep presence and listening while exploring the inner landscapes of our own bodies as women and connecting to an outer landscape that is as immense as the Cosmos herself.

Early on in the research and creation period of the piece, a short poem came to me that encapsulated the process that we would be exploring and that would ultimately become our touchstone to the piece:

Women, Mountains, Moon
Tumbling Rocks, Bones and Stories
Breathe and I am here

It was always my desire to work with artists, with women, who could go on this journey with me not only artistically but spiritually as well. Who would not be afraid to look into themselves and find those tumbling rocks, bones, and stories that wanted to be unlocked and embodied through movement. I knew intuitively it was going to be a long journey and that we would need to not only be committed to the process but that we would need to create a safe space and container for each other to go to some of those places. In hindsight now I believe that we were all brought together at this specific time in our lives to create this dance piece together. The women who completed this journey with me were Tasha Faye Evans (Canada) and Andrea Patriau (Peru). Two women on opposite ends of the mountain range, travelling along the Spine and working with me to discover how we could re-connect to ourselves, to Mother Earth, and to each other.

THE IMPORTANCE OF CEREMONY AND RITUAL

In the beginning we sent each other bundles from our respective countries, carefully wrapped and hand-chosen by each of the dancers to send to the other. Rocks, memories, photos, poetry, chocolate, tea, pieces of our lives and of our land that met each other before we physically did. While I was the one that would travel back and forth between Peru and Canada in the beginning it also was those small bundles that made the long journey, often without us, as they would be carried by friends and family that we knew would be travelling and that offered to carry them for us.

As we patiently waited for grant requests to be approved, for schedules to line up, and stars to align, we danced with those stones and with each other through virtual studio time with Skype cameras and projectors set up in studios in Vancouver and Lima. We went through the changing of the seasons together, sipped on hot tea in the wet, dark winter months in Vancouver while peering through a video screen to our sister in the hot summer months of Lima with lemonade in hand. And of course six months later we had flipped seasons again between the North and the South and giggled together as we huddled around the computer screen, Faye Evans and I now in tank tops and sunshine in the North with Patriau wrapped up in woolly leg warmers and gloves. Interruptions by frozen Skype connections, dropped calls, and slow Internet speeds in the South reminded us that all things are not equal, and that if we wanted to work in this way—to connect from so far away—we would need to work through those things. It would have been easy enough in those early months to give up, to decide that it was too hard, that we should just try to work with artists in Canada, closer to home. And yet I knew in my bones that was not what this piece was meant to be. The whole purpose and reason for embarking on this research and exploration was to live the experience of trying to connect the North and the South. And that meant it would often not be easy.

We were reminded that this "new technology" that we were using to communicate was actually only an infant in comparison to the larger "net" of communication that was actually happening between us. Alvarez-Acosta would remind us often of this net, this energy through the teachings and traditional knowledge, this line of energy and connection that was indeed tens of thousands, and likely millions, of years old. The land was bridging that communication, those stones were carrying us and their stories, our shared stories, in ways we could only begin to imagine.

When we first met in person in Vancouver as a group it was like a reunion of long-lost relatives, of sisters, of friends who had been thinking of each other for a very long time. Both Faye Evans and Patriau commented often that they couldn't believe that they hadn't actually been physically together before. They had danced together virtually for months, women on opposite ends of the earth, and had felt each other. They had held each other's stones, each other's stories, with so much care and ritual that the actual physical meeting of each other really became a formality. The connection was already there. It had been weaving itself together over all of those months and years.

And so it was that thread of connection that we held on to. We waited, we danced, we prayed, we lit sage, we placed tobacco, we shared the teachings of our Elders from both the North and the South, and we put those teachings

Figure 2. Olivia Shaffer and Tasha Faye Evans in *Spine of the Mother*, video/media design by Sammy Chien. Photo by Chris Randle.

into practice. We were kind with each other, we were generous, and we were strong, even when we wanted to give up . . . those stones that we would carry continued to multiply, they continued to nudge me in the direction of this piece and this unfolding.

What began as a handful of small stones in Vancouver now create a long and strong line diagonally across the stage with stones that have been gathered from North and South America over our years of working together (see Figure 2). It is one of the most poignant moments for me in the dance piece when Faye Evans carefully and methodically places each stone, each story, each point in the Cosmos in a precise mapping of the stars mirroring the Spine of Mother Earth and our bridge of re-connection. It reminds us of how we have carried each of those stories with us both literally and figuratively in our lives as women. Sometimes we carry them for ourselves and at other times for those who cannot. We carry the stones for those who have come before us and who will come after us. And as the teachings in the Andes share, each kuya, or stone, represents the essence or spirit of that Apu, or Spirit of the Mountain/Land from which it came. It is not something to take lightly, and we have learnt that time and time again over the years of creating this dance piece together.

THE ANDES

Edgardo Moreno, composer for *Spine of the Mother*, writes:

> I was born in the foothills of the Andes and have grown up with it as a constant, if not always real, presence. When I travel to Chile I'm in awe of the beauty of these mountains. In winter they are snow covered and in summer a desert. They change colour as the light of the sun grows stronger in the mornings and diminishes in the evening. From a bright yellow to a deep blue at dusk. Most people in Santiago's central valley gaze at them when in contemplation. It is our psychic backdrop, our compass.

The mountains were a constant reminder of the macro and the micro that we live in our lives. How we are so small and so huge all at once, how we are like the small star in the Cosmos and the whole Universe herself. It was overwhelming at times to connect with the immensity of this concept and to try to conceptualize it and distill it down into a single dance piece (see Figure 3). And yet it was this challenge that kept us engaged, connected, and striving to understand it in some small way. And so each time we would get back into the studio, or have the opportunity to travel to the Andes either physically or through the traditional teachings, we would have the invitation to go deeper into ourselves, into our own bodies, our own Spine to find that connection to ourselves, to each other and to Mother Earth.

And as art imitates life or the other way around we would quickly realize that the stories that we were carrying at that time in our life, our triumphs, our losses, our rising again, our crumbling, our moments of being overwhelmed, have all been woven into this piece. How could they not? The challenge has been to realize that it is all of this and none of this. It is staying true to the moment, and connecting deeply with our bodies and with the pulse of Mother Earth. To carry those stones with as much reverence and responsibility as they deserve and yet to not be precious about it. To realize that, as in life sometimes, it becomes too unbearable to carry and that things must shatter to be broken apart, to be built again. And how do we allow for each other to do that in a safe place? There is a fine line between art, ceremony, therapy, and indulgence. A fine line to dance indeed.

Figure 3. Tasha Faye Evans in *Spine of the Mother*, video/media design by Sammy Chien. Photo by Chris Randle.

BRINGING IT ALL TOGETHER

As we moved out of our research and creation phase and began looking forward to our premiere I began to gather the team that would further bring our vision and explorations to life on the stage. With nurturing guidance and direction from Dramaturge/Mentor Alvin Tolentino, I began to seek out who I would be working with in the areas of sound design, lighting, and costumes. I also had an intuitive sense that there would always be some type of video or projection in the piece, but I didn't quite know what that would look like at first. I was encouraged by other senior artists and mentors to look at exploring the actual research items and images that had inspired the choreography and shaping of the dance as part of the final piece, either through projections, or set, or other elements. I surrounded myself with a strong community of talented and sensitive artists who took the time to understand and connect with my vision and with the traditional teachings that inspired this piece. We took the time together as a community to explore ideas, to deeply listen to one another, and to be in ceremony together. For this I am grateful.

The result was beyond my expectations, with an original sound score created by Chilean-born/Hamilton-based composer Edgardo Moreno, who recorded the sounds of the stones, our voices singing as women, and the sounds of the environment while at his parents' home in Chile at the foothills of the Andes. That score held and framed the dance and further inspired the choreography and spatial tension that was building in the piece. Lighting design was by senior artist John Carter, who created worlds and states for us to dance in that I had only imagined. Designer Ines Ortner created beautiful costuming for the dancers that incorporated natural fibres, dyes, and hand-painted elements. And my desire to create environments and landscapes through video projections was fully realized through my collaboration with video/media artist Sammy Chien, who had an incredibly innate sense and ability to listen deeply and to incorporate the traditional teachings into a video score. Sammy's work became integral to the final production of the piece and created dynamic and epic landscapes for the dancers to dance within while harmonizing the delicate balance between the live performer and the visual that was being projected behind them (see Figure 4). Further insights and encouragement were offered throughout our process during several work-in-progress development showings and in particular from artists that I deeply respect, including Michelle Olson and Alejandro Ronceria. The creation of this dance piece was never meant to be a solo journey; this I know to be true, and it was demonstrated to me time and time again.[1]

Figure 4. Tasha Faye Evans and Andrea Patriau in *Spine of the Mother*, video/media design by Sammy Chien. Photo by Chris Randle.

---

1   We also had the great fortune to integrate Vancouver-based dancer Olivia Shaffer into the project as a performer who would dance the role of Andrea when it was not feasible for her to fly up from Peru for certain performances. Olivia contributed greatly to the final development of the piece and confirmed that the journey of these two women was something that was universal and that could be connected to in a deep way through the movement and the piece itself.

HOW DOES A SPINE GET BUILT?
FINDING MY VOICE

Building a spine, whether in a dance piece or in your life is not an easy task. It means standing strong and true to your convictions. It means finding the dynamic of both flexibility and strength at the same time. It means knowing that each piece is connected to the other. It means listening to your Elders and listening to yourself. It was something that I wasn't prepared for when I started the journey of this piece and yet it was something that was inevitable. Was it worth it? Absolutely. Finding a way to process my own experience of travelling between these two continents, of having my heart feeling as though it needed to span two sides of the world at the same time was perhaps the reason that I began this journey. Thinking that it would be an epic story told on stage when in the end it became an intimate and, my hope is, honest, sliver of time and space. A sliver of our experience as women searching for a deeper connection to self and other, of finding strength through teachings that are older than time and remembering that there is a thread that connects us to that trajectory. Each stone representing a part of my story, our story, and being carried only for a moment in time while being danced in an eternal ceremony.

We often don't understand what pulls us toward certain ideas, people, images, teachings, and yet we go there. If we give ourselves the time and space to explore those stirrings, and if we "walk, don't run," as Alvarez-Acosta would say, then we find the space and the breath in between where it all seems to make sense, even if just for a moment. It makes sense in the body, in the breath, and that is all that we really have in the end. Body. Mind. Spirit. The Spine of our Mother.

A COMEDIC HISTORY OF ABORIGINAL PROPORTIONS
DREW HAYDEN TAYLOR

If memory serves me correctly, I was in our nation's capital, just outside the University of Ottawa. A performance of my play, *The Bootlegger Blues*, had just finished and I was watching the audience members exit and trying to gage the after-effects of my comedy. There had been plenty of laughter, but I wanted to see if the patrons were laughing with the play, not at it—an important distinction. That's when I noticed this old man with a cane hobbling out. I could see him say something to a small gathering of people hovering near the door. Almost immediately, they all pointed at me. The man then approached me, walking as fast as a man in his condition would allow.

"Did you write this play, young man?" he asked. I answered yes, wondering what was up. Horrible things have happened shortly after a question like that. The man then stuck his hand out, wanting to shake mine.

"Your play made me homesick," he said, no doubt referring to the kitchen-sink nature of the play and the homey atmosphere the humour generated. I have no idea who he was or where he came from, but to date I consider that the best review I have ever received as a playwright. That was the late summer of 1990. Oka/Kahnehsatake was still raging, and I had just written what had been described as essentially an Aboriginal version of a British farce. It was either the best of or the worst of times for a theatrical contradiction in terms called a Native comedy. That single play started me off on a unique trajectory.

Up until then, I had written only three plays—all one-act plays for young audiences. This was my first two-act adult comedy. As a playwright I was still green. In fact, I was practically dripping with chlorophyll. I had been a playwright for almost exactly one year. I knew little of what I was doing as a teller of theatrical tales. As a result of that inexperience, that first play is perhaps my rawest. I threw every possible kind of joke or amusing situation or vague attempt at humour into it. Some of it was forced, probably borderline sexist too. The play was probably the equivalent of a first-year drama student's effort, but, at the time, Native theatre was so hot the market exceeded the supply.

It all started for me with a man named Tomson Highway, with a grant from the Ontario Arts Council's Playwright-In-Residence program. He approached me about working with a theatre company called Native Earth Performing Arts. At that time, my writing resumé consisted of exactly one episode of a television series called *The Beachcombers*. Theatre . . . what was that? The education I had on the reserve and later in a nearby high school we were bussed to had taught me that theatre was essentially dead white men. I did not know any dead white men, and did not speak iambic pentameter, so I was not interested.

To make a long story short, I opted not to disagree with Highway's reasons for asking me and accepted the position. An angry and hungry landlord can also be very instrumental in convincing you to accept dubious contracts. Thus my life changed. It's quite an experience to suddenly wake up one morning to discover you are a playwright. But not wanting to make a fool of myself (odd in a humourist, I know) I decided to plunge deep and dirty into this unique world known as Native theatre. The sudden renaissance of Native theatre (or the Big Red Bang as I like to call it) was only a few years old. Reverberations from the original production of *The Rez Sisters* and its remounts were still being discussed, *Dry Lips Oughta Move to Kapuskasing* was on the horizon, and there I was in the midst of this groundswell of popularity having practically no understanding of where I was and what I was expected to do.

That had never stopped me before.

So I started reading as many Native plays as I could. I believe the word is called research. I also tried to see as many plays as I could. I wanted to understand and know what this new genre called Native theatre was. And I did . . . to a certain extent. It was enlightening and puzzling at the same time; enlightening because I saw what theatre could do. What it could teach.

What it could achieve. And because of that, I was amazed and dazzled. To me, it became apparent that theatre was the next logical progression from oral storytelling; it had the ability to take the audience on a journey using the storyteller's voice, body, and imagination. It was an epiphany for me.

I was also puzzled because most of what I read and saw coming out of the Native community was dark, depressing, bleak, sad, and angry. Almost all the characters I saw on the page and on the stage were oppressed, depressed, and suppressed. This bothered me because that seemed to be the entire range of possibilities being explored. If it was angry it was on the stage, and very little of what I was seeing seemed to reflect my own personal experiences, or that of my mother or immediate family. I remembered laughter as a child, not so much alcoholism and rape. Possibly I was cursed with having had a reasonably happy childhood. Since that childhood, I have been fortunate to have visited about 130 Native communities across North America, and in every one I was usually greeted with a smile and laughter.

One play after another detailed the seemingly dysfunctional aspects of the Aboriginal community, frequently focusing on alcoholism and the sexual abuse of women. In fact, it seemed the dominant metaphor most Native writers used in exploring the First Nations community dramatically was rape. Practically every play dealt with some form of violence against women. If I am exaggerating, it's not by much. And if properly understood, rape may indeed have been the most logical way to dramatize what the largely patriarchal western civilization and religion did to the vast majority of Aboriginal cultures. Overall, it seemed to me to be a form of cathartic writing.

I am also aware that portraying the more problematic or conflict-oriented characteristics of society has a long tradition on the stages of the world. It's called drama for a reason. So is comedy. Art, in whatever form, should reflect as many different aspects of a culture as possible. We are a multi-faceted people with many different stories to tell. That's how I came into exploring the world of humour. After going to depressing play after depressing play, I found myself puzzled, thinking, "Is this all we are?" Wasn't it our sense of humour that somehow allowed us to survive the darker aspects of five hundred years of colonization and its fallout?

As one Native actress once told me during a lunch, she was feeling a little down after coming off one play and starting rehearsal for another. "Sometimes it's very tiring being raped eight times a week. Twice on Wednesdays."

But it was a conversation with an Elder on the Blood Reserve in Alberta that truly put things into perspective for me. Somehow we got into a conversation about this dichotomy and he said to me that, in his opinion, for Native people, "Humour was the WD-40 of healing." Those handful of words said so much to me as a fledgling playwright. It was then and there I decided I was more interested in that healing than in cataloguing Aboriginal suffering.

So from all that I decided to write a comedy, just to test the waters. I wanted to kill the stoic Indian. Back in the early nineties, the term "Aboriginal comedy" was an oxymoron. A lot of people felt, and to a certain extent still do, that Native theatre by definition should ask difficult questions, make the audience squirm, push the social envelope, and so on. I disagreed. It should do more than just make the audience uncomfortable. Even that early in my theatre career, I knew that humour and comedy had the power to educate, entertain, and illuminate: three of the hallmarks of good theatre, at least my theatre. Humour has the ability to inform and shape perception without people being aware of it happening. And making people laugh was a heck of a lot more fun than making them suffer.

Thus was born the aforementioned *The Bootlegger Blues*. It's a play about a fifty-eight-year-old good Christian woman, who through a series of circumstances finds herself in possession of 143 bottles of beer that she has to bootleg to help purchase an organ for the church. This is loosely based on a true story. Produced by De-ba-jeh-mu-jig Theatre Group on Manitoulin Island, this play toured to many Native communities throughout Ontario. When Larry Lewis, Artistic Director at the time, asked me to write something, I came up with this story. To me, it mirrored all the funny stories I had heard over the years that were being told around an array of kitchen tables or bonfires, or on long car rides with friends. It was funny. It was "real." And most importantly, it reflected the Aboriginal sense of humour.

Overall, the play and tour were successful. Audiences really enjoyed seeing the Indigenous funny bone on stage. They knew the characters, the situations, and the repartee. It was like seeing old friends on stage. The only envelopes being pushed were the ones full of money from the box office. Sometime later, when the play was published, I even ended up winning the Canadian Authors Association Award for Best Drama. Needless to say, I was pleasantly surprised. Daniel David Moses commented on my win by wondering whether it was just the least objectionable play published that year. I didn't care. It was recognition from my peers and the cheque cleared.

But it was what happened next that opened my eyes to the power and influence Native humour had on stage. Sometime later, a theatre company located in Port Dover, Ontario, contacted me about that same play. Somehow they had gotten a copy of it and had decided to produce it. I was delighted. This would be one of my first forays outside of the cloistered world of Native theatre companies. If all went well, I was going to make some of that lucrative Caucasian money I'd heard so much about. A director whom I was familiar with and I did auditions and a production was put together. Off we went to Lighthouse Festival Theatre on the shores of Lake Erie to introduce Aboriginal theatre comedy to the non-Native world.

Opening night came and our show opened. I was very nervous. The theatre itself sat about three hundred people, mostly of a tourist and blue-rinse crowd. Still, I was honoured and delighted to be there . . . until the play began. The curtain went up on *The Bootlegger Blues* and my marvellous little comedy began . . . to complete silence. No laughter. In the distance I thought I could hear coyotes howling. I imagined tumbleweeds rolling across the stage. My dreams of collecting pockets full of that fabled Caucasian money soon evaporated.

Something was definitely wrong. People weren't laughing. Maybe, as unbelievable as it may sound, there was some disconnect of some sort or a loss of understanding between the worlds of Native and non-Native humour. Apples and oranges. Apple and Microsoft. One thing I forgot to mention, Port Dover happens to be about twenty minutes from the largest Native community in Canada, a place called Six Nations, which contains well over twenty thousand Iroquois. Two of the cast members were Mohawk, from Six Nations. As a result, at every performance there was a smattering of Iroquois—family and friends—scattered throughout the audience. So on that fateful opening night, though the theatre was essentially silent, somewhere in the back corner, in the balcony, I did hear some laughter coming from about eight or ten Six Nationites. And the most amazing thing took place.

As I watched, I noticed that after about ten minutes or so, the white people seated around the Mohawk party began to laugh. Another few minutes passed, and then the next circle of white people began to laugh. Gradually, that ring of laughter began to expand outwards. It was like throwing a Native comedy stone in a non-Native theatre pond and watching the ripples of laughter grow outwards. It took me a while to realize what was happening. This was during the early era of Political Correctness. These well-educated, middle-class white people had been told that you don't laugh at Native people anymore! "Do you know what these poor people have been through?" And they were responsible!! Add to that, the comedy was about Native people and beer. This was all before Sherman Alexie and Tom King started teaching people the wonders of Native humour and irony.

Essentially, as I understood it, the audience was waiting for permission to laugh. Once they saw the Native people in the audience chuckling and giggling, they realized it was okay for them to laugh too. Halfway through the first act, everybody was laughing. The run of the play beat the box-office projection and I had three other plays produced at that theatre company over the years. I saw hope.

My second comedy, *The Baby Blues*, dealt with an aging fancy dancer who spent all of his summers going from one pow wow to another, dancing, partying, and chasing women—but not necessarily in that order. The man was getting too old to win dancing competitions anymore, but he refused to acknowledge the passing years. The story begins as he arrives at a reserve he hasn't been to in a long time. He's setting up his tent when he sees a beautiful young lady down by the water. He tries to pick her up but both he and we find out it's his long-lost daughter from his last visit there eighteen years ago.

He tries to get away but runs into the mother of the girl, who sabotages his truck and won't let him leave the reserve until, that weekend, he can come up with seventeen years of back child support. One of my more successful comedies, it was produced several times in Canada and the States. One day, out of the blue, I got a phone call from somebody saying they would like to produce the play in Venice, Italy!?! I thought this was amazing . . . a pow-wow play in an Italian teatro. I asked why the interest in a play about an aging lothario with no responsibilities who just wanted to party, chase women, and have a good time. "I think it's something Italians could relate to," I was told.

I was intrigued and we spent some time translating it into Italian. I wasn't there to see the actual production but they sent me a videotape, and it was one of the most surreal things I had ever seen. Picture it: a pow-wow set designed by an Italian who had never been to a Native community, let alone a pow wow. A costume designer who had never met a Native person, let alone been to a pow wow. And Italian actors who had never been to a Native community or a pow wow, and had probably never met a Native person, running around the stage going, "Il Pow wowa!" Native theatre and humour had gone international.

My next comedy was titled *The Buz'gem Blues*, with "buz'gem" being the Anishinaabe word for boyfriend/girlfriend/sweetheart. It was an Elder's love story, with the woman from *Bootlegger* meeting up with a character from *Baby* at an Elder's conference and falling in love. I wanted to explore how Elders would date and fall in love. Not that long ago it was produced by the Trinity Repertory Company in Providence, Rhode Island, possibly the largest single production of a Native play in North America. It was the last play produced at the Trinity Rep by Oskar Eustis, who now runs the Public Theater in New York. Canadian Aboriginal theatre artists were exporting our wares to the world!! On quite a sizable scale.

My next comedy came from personal experience. To date, I have done fifteen lecture tours of Germany and am absolutely amazed at the German preoccupation with Native culture. I have seen teepees, jewellery stores, and a variety of Aboriginal wares and symbols embraced by that country. So I had to write a play about it. Thus was born *The Berlin Blues*, an amusing story concerning a German business conglomerate that comes to a small Ojibway community in central Ontario wanting to build the world's largest Native theme park called OJIBWAYWORLD ("It's Ojibwaytastic!"), with rides such as bumper canoes and a forty-four-metre high dreamcatcher with laser-beam webbing that keeps killing all the birds. But the big draw is a production of *Dances with Wolves—The Musical!* I'm told by theatre critics it's a humorous commentary on globalization. Who knew?

Surprisingly, or maybe not, the published version of this play is one of the most popular texts taught in Canadian or English Drama, or in Aboriginal Studies programs at a plethora of German universities.

It should be noted that I don't just write comedies. Over the years I have written a number of dramas (*In a World Created by a Drunken God, God and the Indian,* and others), which have a lot of humour. For me that is because a mix of drama with comedy reflects true Aboriginal life. Comedy and tragedy. Who said the Greeks had the monopoly on those two masks? I also write theatre for young audiences, and what I call intellectual satires, which incorporate humour in setting up unique and different explorations of contemporary Native or non-Native culture. But there are already so many excellent Native playwrights out there writing stories of a darker nature; I write comedies to help balance the portrayals of our people.

What I find interesting is the different reactions to the concept of Native humour in theatre. On one scale, the reaction has been overwhelming. Otherwise, I would not have been so vigorous in pumping out so many comedies over the years. Places like Magnus Theatre in Thunder Bay, the Gordon Tootoosis Nīkānīwin Theatre in Saskatoon, and the Firehall Arts Centre in Vancouver have repeatedly produced my work with great response. I have had audience members come up to me and say how delightful it is to see Native people on stage and not want to get angry at some social issue or cry for what happens to the characters. Instead, they get to laugh and celebrate the Aboriginal sense of humour. That is why I do what I do.

Yet in some places the response is the opposite. Toronto, for example, is the third-largest English-speaking theatre community in the world, after London and New York. Comedy, especially Native comedy, is seldom embraced. In fact, it's often scorned. I had one artistic director of a multicultural theatre company tell me specifically, "I don't do comedies." How earnest and limited.

The artistic director (A.D.) of a Native theatre company that once asked me to be their playwright-in-residence told me explicitly, "Drew, I know you can be funny; I would rather you write something serious." Another A.D. of that same company subsequently told me, after seeing a rather excellent production of *The Berlin Blues*, how much they "despised" the play. This person's words. I've had bad reviews before but "despise" is pretty strong language.

I know of one European theatre academic who openly dismisses my work, saying "he only writes comedy," which, as I mentioned, I don't. But if that's the worst kind of criticism I get, I suppose I can live with it. The belief that Native theatre should be difficult and uncompromising and not . . . "enjoyable" I guess is the right word . . . still exists. Stories showing Native people laughing at their own misadventures should be avoided.

In my comedies I have explored such serious topics as absentee fatherism, the Scoop-up, the loss of language and culture, fear of approaching death, alcoholism, cultural identity, and a cornucopia of topics not normally seen in comedies.

I am also aware that I am not the only purveyor of Native comedy working the circuit these days. Going back to the beginning, both of Tomson Highway's seminal plays were chock full of humour. Darrell Dennis's *Tales of an Urban Indian* will make you laugh. Margo Kane, Turtle Gals, and other wonderful Native theatre artists have the ability to leave their audience chortling. But those are few and far between.

Where this all leaves things I don't know. I have devoted a good chunk of my career to exploring, celebrating, and sharing the Aboriginal sense of humour, both on stage and off. I have directed a documentary on Native humour for the National Film Board of Canada. I have edited and compiled a book exploring and deconstructing Native humour called *Me Funny*. And I have written over two dozen books of plays, essays, and novels drawing my wonderful, humorous world of my ancestors. So I know the people out there are just as interested in the subject matter as I am.

If given a choice of making people cry, making people angry, or making people laugh, I would choose to make them laugh. They are more open to suggestion that way.

NATIVE EARTH PERFORMING ARTS'S *DEATH OF A CHIEF*: UNEARTHING SHAKESPEARE'S *JULIUS CAESAR*

JASON WOODMAN SIMMONDS

In February 2008 Native Earth Performing Arts (NEPA) claimed the theatre space at the National Arts Centre with a promotional poster that was positioned just outside the Studio Theatre. Along with the requisite dates, times, and ticket prices, the poster has Nina Lee Aquino's head-and-shoulders picture of Monique Mojica as Caesar: Mojica's head and one exposed hand are in black and white; a stark red blanket draped over her shoulders and clutched closed by her hand covers the rest of her. The title "Death of a Chief" marks the top of the poster to the left of her image. Below this, just beneath her left shoulder, the poster declares "Shakespeare's tale of Julius Caesar is unearthed . . . this time on Native ground." The production itself highlighted NEPA as an intertribal performance community, which, drawing on numerous pre-contact performance traditions, claims Shakespeare and, by extension, theatre spaces in Canada as locations for the communal self-fashioning of (urban) Aboriginal identities.[1]

---

1   My reading of *Death of a Chief* comes from Yvette Nolan and Ric Knowles. The idea of "claiming access" to Shakespeare is—implicitly—Nolan's, though Knowles actually uses the phrase in "*The Death of a Chief*: Watching for Adaptation" (64). In the programs for the National Arts Centre (NAC) and Buddies in Bad Times Theatre productions Nolan notes that while the representational world of the play speaks to the effects of colonization, "The very act of making *Death of a Chief* has been the action of our community writ small; a group of diverse people, from different nations, different practices, working together to find a way to coexist, to produce together, to move forward together" ("Director's Note"). Similarly, after seeing a workshop of *Death of a Chief* at the Weesageechak Festival, Ric Knowles observes

ON NATIVE GROUND

"Ground" in this context is enriched by the cross-cultural significances it
takes on when employed by Native Earth Performing Arts. Ground can de-
note physical space: as a general location it can designate, according to the
Oxford English Dictionary (OED), "the surface of the earth" or "the substance of the earth's surface" or an "area or distance on the earth's surface."
With these significances in mind, "Native ground" is NEPA's recognition of,
even a land-claim to, the section of earth, its surface and depth, that is now
called Canada. As physical space, ground can also signify a specific location, "an area of a special kind or designated for special use" or "an area of
[usually] enclosed land attached to a house etc." These more specific meanings suggest that Native Earth Performing Arts designates the stages in the
NAC, and in its immediately subsequent run at Buddies in Bad Times Theatre
in Toronto, as grounds for their performance. The poster not only "claims"
Shakespeare, as Knowles has suggested of the play ("*Death*" 64), but it lays
claim to the theatre space as a land-base from which to stage the reclamation
of Aboriginal performance traditions. By establishing a presence in Canadian
theatres, Aboriginal performance artists claim those specially designated
"theatre grounds" as "Native ground."

Along with physical space, "ground" can also indicate conceptual or intellectual space, as in the phrase "that book covered a lot of ground," or "an area or
basis for consideration, agreement, etc." Western theatrical traditions and western criticisms do not have exclusive rights to Shakespeare's canon and the points
of connection NEPA identifies between *Julius Caesar* and colonial interference
in traditional forms of Aboriginal politics opens Shakespeare conceptually to
Aboriginal performance traditions. In this sense Shakespeare becomes a small

---

that, "Like many First Nations productions in Toronto, this workshop was in part about
building, and negotiating, a kind of pan-Indian, diasporic First Nations community in the
city" (55). Knowles consistently notes that, with this adaptation, "Yvette Nolan doesn't just
claim that Shakespeare is universal, she lays claim, for herself and her community, to that
universality: she claims the right of disenfranchised, colonized people to the authority and
'universality' that 'Shakespeare' represents in contemporary Western culture" ("*Death*" 63).

site, an area or basis for agreement between the members of NEPA. Ground can also be defined as "a foundation, motive or reason." This final denotation resonates in the phrase "Native ground," connecting the physical and conceptual significances of the term. Thus "Native ground" is the conceptual foundation that informs and adapts *Julius Caesar* as *Death of a Chief*. "Native ground" claims theatre institutions in Canada, as well as the conceptual and geographical spaces those institutions occupy. In particular, "The Prologue" to *Death of a Chief* engages these possible significances of ground to establish "Native ground" in the past, present, and future as physical location, as the land and theatre buildings in Canada, as cultural heritage, and as reclaimed traditions.

Although the OED presents loosely related material and abstract definitions of ground, from the perspective of what Marie Battiste and James (Sa'ke'j) Youngblood Henderson call Indigenous knowledge, the significances of "ground" are not loosely related symbols, but formative realities:

> Perhaps the closest one can get to describing unity in Indigenous knowledge is that knowledge is the expression of the vibrant relationships between the people, their ecosystems, and the other living beings and spirits that share their lands. These multilayered relationships are the basis for maintaining social, economic, and diplomatic relationships—through sharing—with other peoples. All aspects of this knowledge are interrelated and cannot be separated from the traditional territories of the people concerned. (42)

In this view, the ground—as both "the earth's surface" and the "substance of the earth's surface"—is the foundation for Aboriginal languages, cultures, and traditions. Without the physical ground, the ground of identity for distinct peoples vanishes. The suggestion of land-claim, then, in NEPA's poster statement is not only about claiming artistic territory in a predominantly non-Native-run theatre industry that has either ignored Aboriginal performers or perpetuated typecast roles, it is also a reminder that Canada was and is on Native ground. On this ground NEPA claims the rights to self-representation in Canada's theatre industry.

Figure 1. Native Earth claims Native ground. Michelle St. John, Michaela Washburn, Keith Barker, Lorne Cardinal, Cheri Maracle, and Falen Johnson in the Native Earth production of *Death of a Chief*. Photo by Nir Bareket.

NEPA performs the reclamation of Native ground at the NAC (see Figure 1). As a conceptual, physical, and foundational theatrical ground in Canada, the NAC is a Crown corporation and has been actively involved in nation-building through the arts since the building opened in 1969 (Jennings 9). It is financially accountable to Parliament through the Minister of Canadian Heritage, to whom it reports directly (Government of Canada, "Chapter 7" 10). In its mission statement the corporation declares that it wants to "develop and promote the performing arts by establishing the National Arts Centre as the pre-eminent showcase, acting as a catalyst for the performing arts nationally, and nurturing and supporting artists and arts organizations in communities across the country."[2] The NAC suggests an artistic federalist

2   The NAC has the financial backing to support such an ambitious artistic and cultural mission. In the 2008–2009 fiscal year, the NAC "had revenues of $30.8 million from box office sales, parking, hall rentals, and the National Arts Centre Foundation as well as parliamentary appropriations of $39.8 million for operating and capital expenses" (Government of Canada, "Chapter 7" 10).

model for Canadian arts whereby, in the interest of creating "Canadian theatre," it presents itself as a unifying centre to provincial artistic expressions.[3]

Through *Death of a Chief*, NEPA presents the claim to NAC as Native
ground through a negotiation of intertribal alliances. Native ground, in this
case, is the active relationships among members of the NEPA community, and
between the actors and several pre-contact performance traditions. Native
ground is also the active relationships between the multiple communities from
which those traditions emerge. NEPA established these multiple expressions
of "Native ground" with a communally authored intertribal creation story
that they performed as "The Prologue" to *Death of a Chief.*

NATIVE GROUND AS PERFORMANCE

At the NAC production that I saw, "The Prologue" to *Death of a Chief* started after the house lights faded to pitch black for a few seconds and the stage
lights then slowly intensified to dimly illuminate a circle of large rocks among
smaller stones and gravel on an otherwise bare stage. In a matter of minutes,
the rocks, which were the performers clothed in earth-toned hoodies and
pants, exploded into gasping breaths and embraced each other as equals.
Simultaneously, "The Song of the Deathless Voice," a Dakota song about a warrior whose voice defied death by singing even after he had been killed, began
to chant in the background. Then, suddenly, four silks from the four colours
of the Medicine Wheel unfurled from the rafters, their bottoms hanging ap-
proximately six feet above the stage floor. The performers broke into a Rabbit
Dance, chanting in unison as the floor they stood on turned to tarmac—a
highway divided by a yellow line. Clasped by the Oracle—a shamanistic figure

---

3   The NAC was created by G. Hamilton Southam, who, as Sarah Jennings notes in *The
History of the National Arts Centre*, wanted the centre to "showcase a cooperative Canada"
(40). Southam saw this cooperative model as "national in character and scope" (40). This
vision seems to me to suggest artistic federalism. By artistic federalism I mean the opera-
tion of a centralized artistic "authority" that produces art as Canadian art.

played by Waawaate Fobister (Ojibwe)[4]—the red silk dropped from the rafters and, cut off from the earth by the road, the performers elected Caesar as
their leader, draping Mojica in the red cloth and shouting uproariously (see
Figure 2). This led into Brutus's famous speech, "What meanes this shouting?" By framing the play with an explicitly Indigenous creation narrative,
"The Prologue" became the embodied, dramatic representation of the statement on the poster.

From one perspec-
tive, "The Prologue,"
like the poster, elides
the Canadian state by
suggesting Indigenous
histories old enough to
contain Shakespeare,
Julius Caesar, and even
Julius Caesar as emblems
of the pre-Christian em-
pire. In a post-contact
world, however, the
sources of Indigenous
cultures—the tradi-
tion(s), the land—have
been buried by coloniza-
tion. Whether the ground
in the phrase "Native
ground" is taken to mean
the earth as the source
of all life or the cultural
ground, the tarmac in the

Figure 2. Waawaate Fobister as the shaman/soothsayer
in the Native Earth production of *Death of a Chief*, surrounded by the company. Photo by Nir Bareket.

---

4   There are variant spellings of Ojibwe, Ojibwa, and Ojibway. While I have been using
the spelling Ojibway throughout this project, I adopt the above Ojibwe because it is the
spelling used by Native Earth Performing Arts in the NAC's and Buddies's programs.

opening scene implies that Native ground is forever changed by contact. At the same time, these conceptual and geographical claims to "Native ground" declare that before anyone else, Native peoples belong in and have rights to the theatre spaces, and to the cities, and, indeed, the country wherein those spaces exist.

In the program for the NAC production, Nolan states what Knowles identifies as the "practical use of Shakespeare for First Nations communities" (Knowles, "*Death*" 63). For Nolan, in both Shakespeare's world and the worlds of First Nations, Métis, and Inuit in Canada, "the people struggle with the idea that power corrupts." Rather than addressing Shakespeare's work as a tool of colonization, *Death of a Chief* engages what Nolan sees as Shakespeare's universalism: "Every community, every cultural group has been able to find their own experience reflected in Shakespeare, even though he wrote in English" (Nolan, "*Death*" 2). In the mouths of representatives from empire, claims to Shakespeare's universalism are highly suspect mystifications of material power imbalances, and thus ways for empire to retain power. When spoken by Nolan, however, this identification challenges those very power imbalances by suggesting that Shakespeare's texts belong to everyone.

Furthermore, NEPA seizes on Brutus's insight that "Th' abuse of Greatnesse, is, when it disjoynes / Remorse from Power" (Nolan and MacKinnon 394) as one of the universal themes in Shakespeare's *Julius Caesar*. For Nolan and NEPA, then, Shakespeare's text interrogates the corruption created when people in positions of power are not stewards of the well-being of those they govern. While Nolan is clear that this problem is not unique to post-contact First Nations governments, she also uses Shakespeare's play to examine the abuse of power within Aboriginal communities in what is now Canada. Nolan remarks on the general political applicability of Shakespeare's text, so that, while "*Julius Caesar* happens to be particularly timely right now because of the war in Iraq, because of the President down there [at the time George W. Bush]," the play also "works on every level in Native communities" (3).

Critics such as Alan Hager note that power struggles plague local communities the world over, and in *Julius Caesar* "Shakespeare examines steps of a process observed in human affairs from the microcosm of disorder in the schoolyard to the macrocosm of international strife" (88). If the play "examines" power politics as "steps of a process," as Hager suggests, Nolan also sees the healing potential in adapting and staging *Julius Caesar* as an examination of that process, a process that, with the intrusion of western models of government, has allowed for "th'abuse of greatness" within the reserve communities. Though "th'abuse of greatness" is a universal feature of human communities, the play's particular representation of it addresses the concerns of the members of NEPA. Nolan's invocation of Shakespeare's universalism challenges any critical manoeuvres that would ghettoize Native Earth Performing Arts's examination of "th'abuse of greatness" as solely a post-contact "Aboriginal issue."

STRUCTURAL COMPARISON OF *JULIUS CAESAR* AND *DEATH OF A CHIEF*

The structure of *Julius Caesar* opens up another cross-cultural contact zone between Shakespeare and Native performance traditions. *Death of a Chief* keeps much of Shakespeare's language and structure intact. The changes come in the rearrangement of scenes so that the running dialogue between Cassius and Brutus in Act 1.2 is interspersed with conversations between Caesar, Calpurnius (not Calpurnia), and Antony. Translated onto the stage, these textual divisions contribute to the building tension between the two factions because Caesar's party and Brutus and Cassius occupy opposite ends of the stage for much of the opening act, as the dramatic action shifts back and forth between the two parties. The most significant changes are "The Prologue," which cuts Caesar's failed coronation scene (as well as the Lupercalean festivities that follow) in favour of an intertribal creation narrative; the interjections of the Plebeians and their interactions with the audience; and the regendering of the play's characters whereby Julius Caesar, Antony, and Cassius are women and Calpurnius is a man. As Knowles has noted of the workshop productions, "There was nothing particularly startling about either the cutting or the intercutting within these scenes—nothing, that is, that might not appear in a fairly heavily cut production at the RSC or at any North American Shakespeare festival" ("*Death*" 60). In fact the production at the NAC was not "heavily cut" because, unlike the workshop productions, it included the final two scenes.

In one of the few alterations of the Folio *Julius Caesar*, the Plebeians in *Death of a Chief* pose the problem of colonial resistance to Native reclamation. During Brutus's and Cassius's opening speeches, in which they expressed their fear that "the People choose Caesar / For their Chief," and just before the Oracle warned Caesar "Beware the Ides of March," the Plebeians took centre stage to pose the problem:

PLEBE 1: How do you un-ring the bell?

PLEBE 2: If we could have back what's been lost and stolen,

PLEBE 3: Could we rebuild what's been lost and stolen?

PLEBE 4: What will we look like in a different light or will the light simply illuminate the emptiness that can never be filled?

PLEBE 5: How does one stand alone? (391)

The Plebeians consistently play a presentational role in both texts. In *Julius Caesar* their role is typified in the opening scene with the exchange between Flavius, Marullus, and the witty Cobbler. As Andrew Hadfield notes, "The disenfranchised citizens of Rome had no stake in their collective destiny and it may have been this aspect of their lives that struck the English audience at the Globe" (183).[5] The affiliation between the Plebeians of Shakespeare's Rome

---

5   In "Is This a Holiday?" Richard Wilson suggests a more complex relationship in the opening scene of *Julius Caesar* between early modern audiences and the actors on stage. In Wilson's reading, "The first scene acted at the Globe can be interpreted [. . .] as a manoeuvre in the campaign to legitimize the Shakespearean stage and dissociate it from the subversiveness of artisanal culture" (33). However, while Wilson's interpretation of this

and the groundlings, comprised mostly of London tradespeople, takes on new significances in the context of *Death of a Chief*. In the above quotation the disenfranchised speak and, just as with Shakespeare's Plebeians, these Plebeians speak not only as characters in the play, but also as actors. Their identities as urban Aboriginals means that they are geographically separated from the reserve politics the play represents, even though they may still maintain their relationships with family and friends on the reserve. But this separation also extends to Canadian politics in the form of legislated disenfranchisement. It is the Canadian government, after all, which legislates disenfranchisement from reserve communities for certain Aboriginals through the Indian Act. The questions are questions of identity. How do we reassemble ourselves as distinct communities in a post-contact world? The questions the Plebeians ask are crucial to the act of reclamation.

Before someone can reclaim tradition, land, and identity they have to ask "How is it possible?" The Plebeians' questions do not elicit simple solutions. They suggest a continual process of asking and attempting to find answers, which—because the answers are incomplete and because colonization has not ended—creates a cyclical return to the same questions. Furthermore, these questions operate in both the tribal and associational modes of theatrical comportment. Intertribal affiliations are marked by the deictic references "we," which in the above address is repeated three times to identify a community of Plebeians who occupy the fringes of the reserve community of Rome. Laying claim to Shakespeare on Native ground in all its senses presents one response to the questions. In this production the members of the theatre community are

---

scene rightly implies, unlike Hadfield, that early modern audiences at the Globe were mixed, and that, in 1599, the theatre was struggling to legitimate its cultural authority by dissociating itself from medieval playing traditions, the scene suggests a much more complex interplay between the representational and presentational, one more in keeping with Robert Weimann's analysis. The authority of Flavius and Marullus is not unambiguously associated with the representational authority of the stage. After all, as Cassius remarks, "Marullus / and Flavius, for pulling scarfs off Caesar's images, / are put to silence" (1.2.281–82).

not "standing alone" but together to portray themselves in "a different light," even if they do so, as Floyd Favel Starr has suggested, as orphans.

At the same time, the Plebeians' questions also remark on the difficulty of eliding the Canadian state in the reclamation of performance traditions. With the intrusion of the Canadian state on the self-governance of Native nations, the address opens the question of reclamation to theatre audiences at the NAC and, in this case, crosses from the tribal to the associational in its performance of a central problematic facing urban Aboriginal (theatre) communities. "How do you un-ring the bell" of colonial interference and intrusion (Nolan and MacKinnon 394)? These questions also indicate audience members' responsibility to Canadian political institutions and colonial legislation such as the Indian Act. Instead of this colonially imposed model of Indian identity, Native Earth presents a self-governing, intertribal theatre community whose leadership works from consensus and whose membership is determined by the community and not the Canadian state.

As I suggested earlier, "The Song of the Deathless Voice" in the opening scene of *Death of a Chief* is an example of declaration and of the resilience of Native voice despite the best efforts of the state. As the program for the NAC production notes of the music in the adaptation, "All songs have been reclaimed and adapted by the company from a variety of sources." "The Song of the Deathless Voice" was reclaimed by NEPA from the Indianists, those early twentieth-century musicians who recorded traditional Indigenous songs and reworked those songs, combining them with classical scores in an effort to develop uniquely American music.[6] Reclaiming this voice is an assertion, like the

---

6   "To label composers such as Edward MacDowell or Arthur Farwell broadly as 'Indianists' is a problematic classification," as Choctaw scholar Tara Browner notes, "considering the bulk of their work does not use American Indian music. At the same time, very few of the Indianist composers wrote only Indian-inspired music: so ultimately the term 'Indianist' is a vague one, used primarily for convenience" (266). As with many of his songs, the score and words for "The Song of the Deathless Voice" were taken by Arthur Farwell from anthropologist Alice Fletcher's *Indian Story and Song from North America*. Fletcher prefaces "The Song of the Deathless Voice" with a story translated by Francis La Flesche from Dakota (Fletcher, *A Study* 39). La Flesche, according to Browner, was "the son of

dramatization of creation, of Native ground as cultural source. Though "The Song of the Deathless Voice" is taken back, it is forever changed by its contact with the Indianists. In 1900, the son of an Omaha chief and an ethnographer, Francis La Flesche, translated the story into English. According to La Flesche's translation, "Death had claimed the body of this warrior and compelled it to return to dust, but had failed to silence the voice of the man who, when living, had often defied death" (Fletcher 41). Reclaiming this voice, then, is a powerful way to represent the persistence of Aboriginal voices in North America. The assertion of a voice that cannot die, a voice that continues forever, also marks the (adapt)ability of Aboriginal cultures to survive despite attempts to assimilate and destroy them. Like "The Song of the Deathless Voice," Native ground is not something that can be easily annihilated because of its existence in a pre-contact past. In fact, it persists because it continues to speak from that past. Thus Native ground encompasses past, present, and future. Its existence in a pre-contact past matters now and for the future because it is past and because it is simultaneously the ground as earth, culture, and ontological foundation, as source. In this case, the past is not a stable, self-defining noun or a distant ideality; it is an ongoing process that gives coherence to right now. The past in *Death of a Chief*, in the history of colonization in Canada, and as historiography, has always just passed. Therefore it is always just with us and therefore re-presented (made present again), like the earth or our traditions.

In *Death of a Chief*, NEPA continually emphasizes the interconnectedness of members of the dramatized reserve community. One of the most effective instances of scene splicing, for example, foregrounds what in *Julius Caesar* is the exchange between Portia and Brutus in the orchard. As in *Julius Caesar* the conspirators meet after Brutus's and Portia's conversation. During the couple's exchange, however, the conspirators' voices intrude with the ominous refrain that insists on Caesar's fate, "It must be by her death" (395). Portia appears

---

an Omaha chief and noted ethnographer" whom Fletcher adopted as an adult (274). An appropriated version of "The Song of the Deathless Voice" can be found on *American Indianists: Volume 2*, compiled by Dario Müller. Arthur Farwell founded Wa-Wan Press, a recording company out of Newton Center, Massachusetts, a company central to the Indianist movement (Pisani 39), and receives credit for the song.

on stage and Brutus questions her: "Portia: What meane you? wherfore rise you now? / It is not for your health, thus to commit / Your weake condition, to the raw cold morning" (394). Caesar and Calpurnius are in bed upstage sleeping under the red silk that is Caesar's imperial robe. When Portia finishes responding to Brutus's question ("Not for yours neither. Y'have ungently Brutus / Stole from my bed . . . " (394)), the conspirators interject, "It must be by her death" (395), while Brutus and Portia continue their conversation. After Portia's final "Is Brutus sicke?" speech, the conspirators state once again more loudly and insistently Caesar's fate: "It must be by her death; it must be by / Her death; it must be by her death; it must" (395). This final insistent refrain seems to wake Caesar and Calpurnius. Caesar gets up and, followed by Calpurnius, "enters the playing space" (395). The world of politics emblematized by the conspirators intrudes upon Brutus and Portia's as well as Caesar and Calpurnius's marriage to betray the colonial myth of separate spheres of existence. According to this colonialist myth the domestic sphere is gendered female and separated, even protected, from the masculine world of politics.

Death of a Chief emphasizes the irrationality of attempting to live in starkly separated domestic and political spheres. As Coppélia Kahn points out regarding this separation, "In Rome and in Shakespeare's England, whatever the actual scope of women's activities, home was held to be the woman's place: the domus, from which word domestic is derived, a private dwelling set in opposition to the public forum of politics" (99). This separation partly explains the lack of female roles, or what Barbara L. Parker has identified as the "monolithic maleness" of *Julius Caesar* (251). In a play about Roman/early modern English politics there is little room for the domestic or private. When Portia confronts Brutus about his conspiracy, her declaration of lineage through the line of her father (not her mother) is also a desire for co-partnership that allows her to participate with Brutus as an equal in marriage and politics:

I graunt I am a Woman; but withal,
A Woman well reputed: Cato's Daughter.
Think you, I am no stronger then my Sex
Being so Father'd, and so Husbanded? (397)

With this speech Portia "changes tack" (Kahn 97). Previously she had pressed Brutus to disclose his conspiratorial plans (Nolan and MacKinnon 396). Furthermore, Kahn rightly argues that "Portia shows, as it were, a fine discernment in this strategy of constructing herself as a man, for [. . .] men mutually confirm their identities as Roman through the bonds with each other. Brutus can trust Portia only as a man" (99). Portia's rhetorical shift from Brutus's wife—and when this fails—to his political equal (in other words a man) through the line of her father illustrates a polytemporal connection between the patriarchal political order of Rome and that of (early modern) England. NEPA's adaptation suggests that patriarchy is also the order for politics in Canada. However, this was not the case for many tribes. As Laguna/ Pueblo/Sioux author Paula Gunn Allen notes in *The Sacred Hoop*, "Traditional tribal lifestyles are more often gynocratic than not, and they are never patriarchal" (2). Though the adaptation avoids oversimplified representations of a battle of the sexes by regendering both the side of the conspirators and those loyal to Caesar, like the struggle for power within Aboriginal communities, the struggle for power in this play is inflected by gender roles.[7] In fact, Calpurnius is subject to the same patriarchal separation of domestic and political spheres as Portia. Regardless of his sex he is forced to occupy a marginal, domestic role that precludes him having any role in the political life of his community. As with Portia's appeal to her partnership with Brutus, Calpurnius's appeal to his partnership fails.

As Caesar is deciding whether to walk to the senate with Decius or stay home listening to the Oracle's warning and Calpurnius's forbidding dream, Calpurnius begs her not to leave, appealing to her not as Caesar, but as his beloved wife: "Alas my Love, / Your wisedome is consum'd in confidence: / Do

---

7   Although in a different context Nolan suggests another, more pragmatic reason for the mixed casting of this production—"I cannot cast six young Aboriginal men. It's impossible. There aren't that many. There aren't that many old ones." Such practical reasons, that there are very few male Aboriginal actors young or old, align with the political reasons for producing an adaptation of *Julius Caesar* that troubles the gender hierarchies of colonial cultures and the effect of these gender hierarchies on post-contact Aboriginal cultures (Nolan, Personal interview).

not go forth to day" (401). To which Caesar, almost convinced and after some deliberation, replies, "How foolish do your feares seeme now Calpurnius? / I am ashamed I did yield to them" (403). She effectively silences her partner and yields to the seduction of the possibility of "a Crowne to mighty Caesar" (402). The domestic is separated from and then trumped by the political sphere. This hierarchy interferes in what could be a harmonious relationship between Brutus and Portia, Caesar and Calpurnius. This hierarchy is exposed next to the alternative of equality suggested at the beginning of the play. The adaptation levels a critique at the principles of emulation and competition informing the hierarchies of colonial polities such as Rome, but also England and present-day Canada.

The separation of domestic and political, private and public is a western colonial construct. Nishnaabeg scholar Leanne Simpson points out that recognizing this colonial interference and figuring out ways to establish traditional models of governance in a contemporary context is an important part of decolonization. Although she writes specifically of Nishnaabeg traditions of governance, Simpson's statement resonates intertribally:

> We must build strong leaders according to our own traditions. This begins with women, the centre of the family, the mothers. Our traditional models of governance flow out from the centre of the family, to clans, communities, and nation, and lastly to our relationship with other nations. Our political systems were non-hierarchical, non-coercive, and non-authoritarian. Our political systems begin with how we mother. ("Nogojiwanong" 209)

In *Death of a Chief* creation is the first and continuing act of mothering, and mothering is the first and continuing act of creation.[8] Portia's assertion of

---

8   In *Seeking Alternatives to Bill C-31* Jo-Anne Fiske and Evelyn George observe the connection between matrilineal ancestors and the land:

> Matrilineal clan membership constitutes identity, which is inseparable from traditional lands. In the past, in each nation the traditional lands were inhabited

her paternal lineage covers over, like the tarmac in "The Prologue," lines of descent that go back to this maternal act. In a family, clan, community, and nation grounded in traditional models of governance, Portia would have been de facto a participating member, a centre even, in the life of her community, and that includes its politics. The questions of the disenfranchised Plebeians speak directly to Portia's own disenfranchisement. Within post-contact models of governance, Portia has to fight, deny, and maim herself in order to gain access, mediated through her husband, to the political life of Rome, Ontario, even as that life intrudes upon her relationship with Brutus. In order to gain a political voice, she continually re-enacts the history of colonization on her body by denying her maternal line, and therefore her lifeline.

Unlike Portia, who has to fight for minimal access to the political sphere, in *Death of a Chief* Caesar is a woman who occupies the highest possible formal political role, that of Chief. Caesar as female Chief suggests a parallel with Queen Elizabeth I, as "the anomalous 'woman on top' in a patriarchal society" (Kahn 93).[9] While early modern England had women leaders in formal political roles, in Canada under the Indian Act, up until 1951, First Nations

---

in an annual cycle of subsistence activities; families and clans were tied to the land through matrilineal ancestors. Family and clan leaders cared for the land and through it provided daily subsistence and wealth for the feast hall. (30)

9   As Kahn notes, emulation was an integral part of the English aristocratic ethos:

In the cultural milieu of Elizabethan England in 1599, Shakespeare had good reason to be interested in the emotional sway that emulation held over men. Quite simply, it was central to the ethos of England's nobility and gentry; rank conferred on them a personal sense of superiority honed by the particular method of their humanistic education. (91)

These agonistic relationships, though encouraged by Elizabeth as a means of neutralizing powerful aristocrats, also found expression in the tyrannicide debate, which culminated in Essex's failed coup against the queen. The political ambivalence of Shakespeare's play can be seen, in this light, as a careful balancing act that refuses to come down on either side of the debate. The concept of emulation violates the creation narrative at the beginning of *Death of a Chief*.

women could not run for band council or become chiefs (Dickason 298).[10] Even after this legal shift, colonial models of governance have so infiltrated First Nations' governments that to this day women face discrimination. As Cora Voyageur concludes in her recent study *Fire Keepers of the Twenty-First Century*, "Many female chiefs felt they had to break into the old boys' club. For the most part, the First Nations community is conservative, male-oriented, and often paternalistic" (95). Prior to contact, in many tribes women could and did occupy the role of chief. But the term chief is problematic in that it glosses over the distinctive political organizations of each tribe and, at least in this contemporary context, often connotes a patriarchal form of leadership. Yet political power in many tribal traditions was not usually centralized in one figure, and, as I have already noted, those in positions of leadership led by consensus as opposed to coercion. In a matriarchy being a woman means occupying a formal political role. In a patriarchal system, occupying a formal political role means denial of the female body, or, in the case of Queen Elizabeth, embodying a masculine ideal of femininity.

---

10   Cora Voyageur describes one of the ways in which First Nations women mobilized to engage politically prior to 1951. The Canadian government had established "Indian Homemaker's Associations" in order to "domesticate" First Nations women. However these associations provided a means to organize on a national scale:

> An opportunity to organize politically inadvertently presented itself to Indian women in the form of the Indian Homemaker's Association. In 1937 the Department of Indian Affairs encouraged Indian women to gather regularly to acquire sound and approved practices for greater home efficiency. The women were also encouraged to form local chapters of the Native Homemaker's Association on reserves across Canada. Little did the department know that these seemingly harmless women's meetings served as a means for Indian women to organize dissent and create strategies for change in their condition both on the reserve and in the wider Canadian society. Thus, Indian women were primed for official political involvement when legislative changes finally came. (10–11)

This political activity meant that the women still had to operate within a patriarchal political system based on competition. In other words, like Portia they had to fight to be heard, and fight they did.

Caesar's apotheosis is, like Portia's, a denial of the ontological ground
presented in "The Prologue." Caesar gradually becomes unable to think of herself apart from her political office, referring to herself continually as "Caesar."
Thus in response to Cassius's request that Cymber be "infranchised," Caesar
declares,

> 'Tis furnish'd well with Men,
> And Men are Flesh and Blood, and apprehensive;
> Yet in the number, I do know but One
> That the unassayleable holds on her Ranke,
> Unshak'd of Motion: and that I am she.
> Let me a little shew it, even in this:
> That I was constant Cymber should be banish'd
> And constant do remaine to keepe him so. (404)

In keeping with the Roman ethos of emulation that Kahn identifies, Caesar
compares herself to other notable Romans. Unlike those Romans she is, in
her view, the "One," the "unassayleable," and the "unshak'd." But the apparent
constancy of Caesar depends on those others whom she has implicitly belit-
tled as assailable, shakable, and therefore, at times, inconstant. The crucial
difference between Caesar and a female chief, as Monique Mojica notes, is
that "there's no such thing as an Aboriginal woman today who has the omnipotence of Caesar in Rome. What's present in our world but not in Caesar's is
the experience of being colonized; his community was the empire, while the
community of our setting has been under the boot" (qtd. in Kaplan). Likewise,
no Aboriginal woman exists today who has the omnipotence of Elizabeth I in
England. Within the strictures of the patriarchal Indian Act, chiefs—female or
otherwise—answer to the Crown.[11] For most of Shakespeare's life, Elizabeth

---

11   Voyageur notes that:

      Chiefs often face divided loyalties between the community and Indian and
      Northern Affairs Canada. They represent the people of the community and
      are responsible for its smooth running. They are also responsible to the federal

was the Crown. While Elizabeth used emulation to maintain, and thereby control, potent aristocratic factions, *Death of a Chief* represents a community infected by emulation as a means of colonial control, whereby Aboriginal leadership is constantly undermined by limited resources despite the promises of the numbered treaties. The politics of emulation are fundamentally opposed to traditional models of First Nations, Métis, and Inuit governance.

Considered in the light of the history of the resurgence of Native political organizations on post-contact Turtle Island, the mixed casting takes on further political significance. Nolan notes:

> I have political problems with what tradition has been reclaimed and by whom, because one of the things that I found as an Aboriginal woman is that the people who are claiming to be empowered to reclaim the traditions, very often are men, and the traditions they reclaim very often exclude women, or put them in subservient positions. (qtd. in Knowles, "*Death*" 57)

Indeed, in order to communicate with the Canadian and American federal governments the early American Indian Movement, the National Indian Brotherhood, and the Assembly of First Nations have had to operate within patriarchal power structures that exclude women from the political process of self-definition and reclamation. For those women who do not want to

---

government, as are provincial governments, because of the transfer payments made to them. They must ensure that the monies are spent according to the terms of the transfer agreements and report compliance to the government agencies that fund them. (19)

With limited resources and communities recovering from the effects of colonization (the residential-school system and the 1960s scoops whereby Social Services were given jurisdiction in reserve communities and as a result "scooped" children from their homes are two devastating examples), chiefs are precariously positioned between the often competing interests of their community and that of the federal government. Add to this mandatory two-year elections, as opposed to hereditary chiefdoms with the requisite checks and balances, and you have an unstable political system to say the least.

or (because of Indian Act legislation) cannot compete for a formal political position in a reserve community or at the national level of the Assembly of First Nations, gaining a political voice has also been a struggle. Like Portia, many First Nations women and some men both prior to and after Bill C-31 have been forced into a position of disclosing their paternal line or, in the case of many women, the paternity of their children, in order that they may claim their family homes and participate in the life of their own communities.

Though *Death of a Chief* primarily tackles the effects of colonization on First Nations reserve communities, it speaks out from the stage to audiences composed of Natives and non-Natives to suggest the import of reclamation of Native ground to the Canadian now. Canada is mentioned only once in the play, but the address speaks to the difficulty of eliding the state in self-representations of aboriginality. After the conspirators leave Antony with Caesar's body, alone Antony declares:

> Over thy wounds, now do I Prophesie,
> A Curse shall light upon the limbes of men; Domesticke Fury,
> And fierce Civill strife,
> Shall cumber all the parts of Canada. (410)

The speech is similar to that in the extant Folio versions of *Julius Caesar*, but for two changes: Nolan cuts two lines, "Which like dumb mouths . . . ," marked in the Arden edition in parenthesis (3.1.260–61), and replaces "Italy" (3.1.264) with "Canada." What in *Julius Caesar* is an ambiguously representational moment, NEPA renders a distinctly presentational address to the largely non-Native theatre audiences of the NAC. When Antony (played by Jani Lauzon) speaks this prophecy, she is speaking the words of Shakespeare, but she is doing so as an Aboriginal woman in Canada whose legal identity is dictated by the Canadian state through the Indian Act. In other words, by addressing the effects of colonization on First Nations' governments in Canada the production inevitably addresses the state, and, more generally, colonial constructions of aboriginality. In my reading, however, a polemical stance need not comport itself solely against the colonial state—in other words it is not a synonym for the post-colonial. Rather, the self-representation of Native agencies inevitably threatens the interests of the Canadian state because that state is a colonizer. As a colonizer it does not recognize or accept Indigenous forms of life outside of its own definitions of indigeneity. In this case the polemical may mean simply standing one's Native ground, as the state or other colonial agents comport themselves against Native peoples and land.

RECEIVING *DEATH OF A CHIEF*

As polemic Antony/Lauzon's prophecy anticipates some of the reviews for *Death of a Chief*. In these reviews the critics seemed to confuse their colonial fantasies of the Indian with aesthetic criteria that they used to judge productions. Their reviews are useful, if for nothing else, as an illustration of the interchange between paratheatrical and intertheatrical scripting against Aboriginal self-representation. In their defence of Shakespeare after the NAC and Buddies productions, many of the critics suddenly became experts and thereby border guards of what constituted a "Shakespeare" performance and also of what constituted a performance of Aboriginality. Thus one theatre reviewer, J. Kelly Nestruck of *The Globe and Mail*, remarked that "the play fails to make any resonant connections to Aboriginal issues." Another reviewer, *The Toronto Star*'s Richard Ouzounian, seemed to think there was a limited selection of Shakespeare plays fit for the "faithful performance" of Aboriginal identity: "There are many Shakespearean plays I could see in a native setting, from *A Midsummer Night's Dream* to *Coriolanus*, but *Julius Caesar* isn't one of them." By an odd though familiar colonial manoeuvre, the theatre critics take their particular experiences in the theatre world as a body of knowledge that extends magically in the form of an opinion about what constitutes authentic Shakespearean performance and impose their opinion onto the experiences of NEPA's self-fashioned community. Their critiques of the aesthetics of a particular production of *Death of a Chief* become the non-Native reviewers' critiques of Native Earth's (mis)understanding of "native setting" and "Aboriginal issues." In their reviews of NEPA's productions they implicitly assert colonial representations of "authentic" Indians in an attempt to silence, invalidate, and cancel self-representations of aboriginality. They attempt to isolate high culture, and by implication the Shakespearean, as a mark of civilization, from the colonial constructions of Aboriginal identity.

In interviews, Nolan's discussions of Shakespeare as a necessary theatrical tool act paratheatrically to demystify Shakespearean acting techniques, neutralizing them as symbols of high culture to be policed by Canadian state-run education systems or theatre establishments in Canada. Discussing the training of *Death of Chief*'s cast, she notes that "I see it happening at workshop after workshop, and of course, they get better, because they've got the tools. And it's not such a big deal. It's just having the same information that everybody else has about how to read Shakespeare" (*"Death"* 3). Her suggestion anticipates colonial paratheatrical scriptings like those of the aforementioned reviewers that suggest Aboriginal bodies and voices cannot occupy some or all Shakespearean roles. Once the text as agent is allowed to interact with the actors as agents these particular colonial constructions of Shakespeare and Aboriginality as discretely bounded identities begin to fall apart. Thus the "issues" of the reviewers are not "Aboriginal issues" but rather their own issues with "aboriginality" in its polytemporal insistence of scriptings and agents that exist before colonial scripting or instead of Shakespeare as colonial script. Their issue is with the power Native Earth has to represent and present itself as Native on its own terms. Native ground remains a defended subject as long as colonial agents, including the Canadian state, attempt to bind and define it in order to own it. Polemic is a strategy for protecting Native ground. Read as polemical stance, then, Antony/Lauzon's speech addresses the western gaze head on. As one of only a few unambiguously presentational moments in *Death of a Chief*, her address calls attention to the activity of theatrical gazing and the colonially scripted expectations of that gaze. If the play dramatizes the effects of colonization on reserve polities in Canada, Antony/Lauzon's address is a paratheatrical indictment of theatre audiences as "actors" gazing at Native Earth.

Death of a Chief moves Antony's address from its place immediately following the conspirator's exit to the funeral oration. As the rest of the cast battle each other, Antony/Lauzon projects the speech over the noise of the battle. Antony/Lauzon's prophecy comments on the polarization of Native and non-Native to suggest that while reserve politics are not immediately accessible to many of the NAC audience members, unacknowledged questions of Native ground signalled at the beginning of the play implicate them in current debates around Aboriginal self-government.

Another review of the play, by Denis Armstrong in the 19 February 2008 *Ottawa Sun*, featured prominently an image of Lorne Cardinal as Calpurnius in the midst of the aforementioned fight scene, above which stood the offensive caption "Shakespeare Goes Native." I mention this review here because of its resonances with familiar non-Native media images of Natives who actively reclaim traditional ground, as with, for example, the Idle No More movement, the Unist'ot'en resistance to pipeline development in their territory, the Mohawk resistance at Oka to the township's attempt to build a golf course on their traditional land, or the resistance at Ipperwash. In mainstream media representations, these disputes are often presented as discrete historical anomalies rather than ongoing, historically grounded resistance movements. The images reinforce the suggestion of an historical anomaly. The *Ottawa Sun*'s presentation of Cardinal's image and the caption is a case in point. While the article itself includes many excerpts from interviews with Mojica, it incorrectly interprets the play in terms of Ipperwash and more specifically Dudley George's murder by the RCMP: "Set on a reservation outside Rome, Ont., a native leader is murdered when she confronts local authorities about the fate of her community. Any resemblance to Dudley George is completely intentional" (18).[12]

12　Dudley George was a member of the Chippewas of the Stoney Point First Nation. The Nation's traditional territory includes Ipperwash. According to *Ipperwash: Tragedy to Reconciliation*, "In 1942, during World War II, the federal government expropriated land belonging to Stoney Point band under the War Measures Act in order to build a military camp—Camp Ipperwash. Stoney Point residents were moved to Kettle Point First Nation—and the Canadian Government unilaterally amalgamated the two First Nations" (5). Members of the Nation waited for decades for the return of their land. "In 1993, families from the original Stoney Point First Nation began moving back on to the land. The military

Yet apart from the re-grounded opening scene, the script and dramatic action are close to *Julius Caesar*. Caesar's assassination is not by the RCMP, but other leaders within her reserve; Brutus, Cassius, and the other conspirators are members of Caesar's community. The reviewer's impulse is to do exactly what Antony/Lauzon's prophecy warns against. He filters the dramatic action through the colonial image, misreading *Death of a Chief* as a polemic that separates Native or Native ground from non-Native Canadians. Antony/Lauzon's speech, however, warns that Native and non-Native ground touch one another, that they are agents existing simultaneously and that, through colonization, their futures are intertwined: "Domesticke Fury, and fierce Civill strife, / Shall cumber all the parts of Canada" (Nolan and MacKinnon 410). What I have suggested is a polemical speech turns out in fact to offer audiences configurations other than the colonial representations of the media attending its post-production. Audience members can choose whether they will unfreeze the colonial "frame" (to borrow theatre scholar Rob Appleford's term) in order to recognize, address, and negotiate with Native agents on Native ground as these agents perform now—"this time"—in the world of the theatre and the world as theatre. As an alternative to the colonial models of interaction signified by the tarmac-covered earth, NEPA demands and enacts interaction based on respect. Like the Plebeians' questions earlier on in the play, this prophecy—and by extension *Death of a Chief*—turns out in fact to also negotiate with audiences calling for their political involvement against Canada's continuing attempts at assimilation.

While the earliest workshop versions end here, the production at the NAC offered another significant change to Shakespeare's tale, developing an ending

---

withdrew in September 1995, when another group of Stoney Point citizens marched onto the base" (5). On 4 September 1995 members of the Stoney Point First Nation, among them Dudley George, occupied the Ipperwash Provincial Park, a park built on their ancestral burial grounds. Ontario's premier at the time, Mike Harris, dispatched the police to the park in full riot gear. On 6 September 2005, police shot Dudley George. He died in hospital. His death sparked an inquiry nearly ten years later. On 20 December 2007 the Government of Ontario returned the park to the Stoney Point First Nation.

deceptively close to the one presented in *Julius Caesar*. Whereas in life Caesar gradually "slips over the brink" until she "disjoins remorse from power," in her death, as a ghost, Caesar remembers her obligations to Native ground in all its significances. This reconciliation makes sense of the "two-peak" structure of the play. Responding to Brutus's demand "Speake to me, what thou art," Caesar's ghost declares "thy evil spirit Brutus?" (419). In *Shakespeare's Political Drama*, Alexander Leggatt anticipates Kahn's reading of emulation to suggest that the pinnacle of interdependence in Shakespeare's play is also the relationship most fraught with rivalry. For Leggatt, "the play's sharpest image of the interdependence of its characters, who find not just the meaning of their actions, but their very identities in the eyes of others," is the moment Caesar's ghost appears to Brutus and, instead of using his own name "Caesar," "borrows one from Brutus" (160). There is, as Kahn notes, a consistent and thoroughgoing need for the characters to affirm their existence "in another man's eyes" (80). However, in *Death of a Chief*, Caesar's status as Brutus's "evil spirit" is a question, a continual negotiation that extends beyond the grave and connects the living with the dead. Whereas in *Julius Caesar* the ghost is somewhat of a surprise to Brutus, in *Death of a Chief* Brutus is still in relationship and accountable to Caesar because Caesar, even after death, is not gone. As in *Julius Caesar*, Caesar's ghost appears to Brutus and brings news of Portia's and the senators' deaths, but, unlike

Figure 3. Monique Mojica (Caesar) and Keith Barker in the Native Earth production of *Death of a Chief*. Photo by Nir Bareket.

in *Julius Caesar*, Caesar's ghost also speaks in concert with the Plebeians. Together they remind Brutus of the very obligations that in life Caesar forgot, and that in his pursuit of power Brutus, too, is forgetting:

PLEBIANS: Be stewards of our traditional lands

CAESAR: On this side the Tyber, we have left them you,

PLEBIANS: streams and rivers, fresh and tidal waters,

CAESAR: And to your heyres for ever: common pleasures

PLEBIANS: the singing firs, the dusk, and—you, and—you

CAESAR: To walke abroad, and recreate your selves. (419)

Despite this reminder of traditional lands and the relationships to living things that flow from these lands, Brutus, like Caesar, does not heed the warnings, but instead pursues a course of action within the competitive political structure. The possibilities for change are hinted at, offered up, but not, within the world of the play, ultimately embraced. In the pursuit of political power, Brutus forgets traditional teachings and the principle of stewardship that acknowledges the first act of creation. But as with the Plebeians' earlier questions, the repetition of "you, and—you" resonates out from the stage to include the audience, Native and non-Native alike. As Taiaiake Alfred notes more generally:

Challenging mainstream society to question its own structure, its acquisitive, individualistic values system, and the false premises of colonialism is essential if we are to move beyond the problems plaguing all our societies, Native and white, and rebuild relations between our peoples. A deep reading of tradition points to a moral universe in which all of humanity is accountable to the same standard. Our goal should be to convince others of the wisdom of the indigenous perspective. (45)

The Plebeians' imperative "be stewards of our traditional lands" is also the collective voice of Native Earth Performing Arts reminding audiences that what is now Canada is still Native ground. That ground, as the foundation of the earth's surface, is also the foundation of existence for Natives and non-Natives alike.

Intertribally, *Death of a Chief* offers a hopeful moment at what could be considered one of the tragic peaks—the point when Brutus's vision of a new republic fails in his military loss and death. Shortly after Caesar's ghost appears to Brutus prior to the battle at Philippi, bearing news of Portia's death, the rest of the cast sings "Brutus's 49er": [13]

Oh my darling
Caesar's ghost is calling me
As I hug my sword so closely
I am thinking of you hih yanh
I slew my best lover for the good of Rome, hih yanh
Wenh yanh hanh, wenh yanh hanh yonh. (423–24)

After Brutus impales himself, Caesar's ghost emerges, catching him as he begins to fall, and looks him in his dying face. The embrace offers a moment of hope, anticipated by the "49er," when the abuses of power, gendered and political, are forgiven and the abusers reconciled. The hope of forgiveness, reconciliation, and healing, however, is only short-lived as Caesar drops Brutus's

---

13   According to "Cultural Revitalization and Mi'kmaq Music Making," "A 49er is a song, often with romantic and/or humourous text or undertone, which features a combination of vocables and English language, and is sung to a round dance beat (dotted rhythm in long-short pattern)" (Tulk). In the footnote to the published version of *Death of a Chief*, Knowles provides the following explanation for a 49er: "A 49 is a social song often sung at powwow gatherings outside of the arbour. 49's often tell the stories of everyday life" (Nolan and MacKinnon 423).

body and walks off the stage. But the hope is there nonetheless and unmistakable. If, as Hadfield suggests, *Julius Caesar* is "a form of English history writing, which seeks to contextualize English history in terms of a foreign past and potential future" (115), *Death of a Chief* is a form of history writing that seeks to contextualize Aboriginal histories by interpreting the politics of foreign states from the perspective of reclaimed traditions for the sake of future generations.

While the play world offers mere glimpses of hope that reclamation of Native ground can triumph over destructive political ideologies, the workshop history of the play, along with the productions, performs the possibility. For Native Earth Performing Arts, the process of adapting Shakespeare's tale is a continual process of answering the questions posed by the Plebeians. The problems portrayed in the adaptation and created by the imposition of colonial power structures onto First Nations communities continue to this day. In *Death of a Chief*, the combination of mythic ground, the now of performance, and the location of the dramatic action "20 minutes from now in an urban Aboriginal community" (Kaplan 67) engages performers and audience members in a complex negotiation of an intertribal community. As Nolan points out, "The very act of making *Death of a Chief* has been the action of our community writ small; a group of diverse people, from different nations, different practices, working together to find a way to coexist, to produce together, to move forward together" ("Director's Note"). The process of adaptation provides a complex hermeneutics of communal self-fashioning for NEPA as an urban Aboriginal organization.[14]

Theatre spaces, along with other urban spaces, offer alternative locations to those set aside and bounded by the Canadian government with the reserve system. In these spaces, Aboriginal identities are not subject to the criteria set out in the Indian Act. As Susan Lobo points out:

---

14   As Nolan notes, "We're all urban Aboriginals; we're all choosing not to live in those communities but to live in the city. Everyone who is involved in this project, they're all urban Aboriginals" (*"Death"* 2).

In some respects urban Indian communities reflect pre-reservation/
pre-European contact, or more traditional structural characteristics. . . . In urban areas social and political boundaries are less rigid
and more fluid than on reservations because for example, membership is not tied exclusively to a charter of blood-quantum or
genealogical criteria. (7)

Furthermore, Lobo notes, urban Aboriginal communities are able to organize apart from band or, in the United States, tribal councils: "Nor is there
a formal over-arching political structure, equivalent to a tribal council that
governs the entire urban community" (7). Without this direct, legally regu-
lated colonial interference, urban Aboriginal communities are in a position
of choosing, to some degree, how they organize. Thus communities such as
NEPA may be comprised of members connected to a number of different
tribes, but because of these connections, they are able to find meaningful
intertribal points of contact between their own tribal traditions and those
of others. As urban Aboriginal communities explore these points of contact,
intertribalism is becoming a powerful means of reconnecting and re-estab-
lishing lines of affiliation between Indigenous communities on Turtle Island
that existed before colonialism.

There is an affinity between Shakespeare and Native identities, though he
is from another place. As with Native peoples in Canada, the Canadian state
(through its education system) has attempted to control where he can and
cannot travel, where he is and is not authentically Shakespeare. This perhaps
explains why, after *Death of a Chief*, reviewers rushed to protect their beloved
version of the bard from Native self-representations. Shakespeare is inextricably linked to Canadian national identity. As Knowles notes:

At the middle of the 20th century . . . Shakespeare helped, perhaps
belatedly, to constitute Canada as a Nation state, while Canada in turn
constituted Shakespeare as its National Bard, its sign of high cultural
maturity and value, and its great Canadian Playwright. (*Shakespeare
and Canada* 13)

Indeed, at least as far back as the Royal Commission on National Development in the Arts, Letters, and Sciences, 1949–1951 (Government of Canada, *Royal*), Shakespeare has been acknowledged as a central figure in Canadian theatre and a standard of cultural maturity. Shakespeare was used, in other words, to help establish a cultural identity within a nation-state that in the 1950s excluded Aboriginal peoples from participating in federal elections.

Julius Caesar, however, suggests the possibility that Shakespeare foresaw that his work was not limited or bound to one nation, or one people. Cassius famously remarks on the presentational possibilities of the theatre, its ability to move beyond its place and time: "How many ages hence / Shall this our lofty scene be acted over / In states unborn and accents yet unknown!" (3.1.111–13). While "states" in this phrase is not a firm reference to the modern nation-state, because in 1599 it was just beginning to be realized in England, the statement indicates a sense or perhaps a hope that the play would travel well beyond the walls of the Globe.

In *Death of a Chief* the Oracle fulfills those prophetic words, only to prophesy again in Ojibwe, "Aaniin minik dasing awiyga ge-ichigewaad / owe ge-ini-izhiwebag, / bebakaan miziwe gaye, bebakaan ezhi-giigidong?" (389). These words can be taken up again in the future in Cree, in Iroquois, or Maliseet, or in any of the other Indigenous languages of Turtle Island; for like the traditions NEPA reclaims in its self-fashioning of an intertribal community, they are vital points of (re)connection to Native ground in all its variety. They are also, consequently, a reminder that any version of Shakespeare used to establish Canadian identity will have to realize that those identities are and always will be articulated on Native ground, no matter the determination of the Canadian state to ignore or eradicate this fact.

"THAT'S WHO THE STORIES ARE ABOUT": CREE WAYS OF KNOWING IN KENT MONKMAN'S *MISS CHIEF: JUSTICE OF THE PIECE*

JUNE SCUDELER

Miss Chief Eagle Testickle, clad in a pink headdress and beadwork-bedecked high heels, saucily declares, "I am up against some very large problems, which require a very large personality" (Testickle 109). Miss Chief is the alter ego of Kent Monkman, a Swampy Cree visual/performance artist and filmmaker. The problems she is up against include racism, homophobia, and the erasure of Two-Spirit peoples from dominant history.[1] Monkman insists that Miss Chief is not a drag persona, but is based on an Indigenous Two-Spirit sensibility. Speaking of his performances as Miss Chief, Monkman emphatically states that "there's this perception that it's 'just drag.' I don't think of it as drag. I see Miss Chief as being . . . two-spirit . . . So it's not about trying to be a female impersonator. I really like to distinguish what I'm doing from what is more commonly known as drag; I really am very careful about crossing that line" ("Q&A"). For Monkman, drag is a non-Indigenous practice. Instead, he combats homophobia and racism by grounding his work in Indigenous ways

---

1 Two-Spirit Swampy Cree scholar Alex Wilson defines Two-Spirit as a "self-descriptor increasingly used by Aboriginal gay, lesbian, bisexual and transgendered Canadians who live within a traditional Aboriginal worldview. It asserts that all aspects of identity (including sexuality, race, gender and spirituality) are interconnected and that one's experience of sexuality is inseparable from experiences of culture and community" ("N'tacimowin inna nah" iv).

of knowing, which encompass epistemologies, histories, stories, language, spirituality, legal systems, and artistic practices. His art is a Swampy Cree response to colonization, especially sexual colonization. Monkman, like other Indigenous performance artists, uses Indigenous ways of knowing to create new artistic traditions, particularly in urban settings. These new traditions are integral to the continuing resurgency of Indigenous peoples and cultures in spite of the devastating effects of colonization.

As a Métis scholar I believe it is essential to centre Indigenous ways of knowing in my scholarship.[2] Two-Spirit writers and performers dare "to imagine land, self, and family in the wake of attempted genocide" (Tatonetti ix). I use the Cree concepts miyotôtakêwin—being hospitable or "happy to welcome guests" (LeClaire, Cardinal, Hunter, and Waugh 330)—and miyo-wîcêhtowin—the principle of getting along well with others, good relations, expanding the circle (Cardinal and Hildebrandt 14)—to explore how Monkman invites viewers to learn more about historical and contemporary issues faced by Two-Spirit people. Although Monkman strives to communicate with non-Indigenous audiences, he stresses that his primary audience is "Aboriginal, they are my community. That's who the stories are about. An Aboriginal audience will be the first to understand what I'm doing, but the work will be open enough so that others can enter it" ("Kent Monkman: Miss Chief" 53). He emphasizes the importance of his Swampy Cree ancestry to his art: "It's just part of who I am and deeply informs my work" (qtd. in McCord).

In this essay I explore how Monkman uses Miss Chief to enact miyo-wîcêhtowin in his 2012 performance *Miss Chief: Justice of the Piece* at Washington, DC's National Museum of the American Indian. Miss Chief creates a Nation of Mischief that rejects the strictures imposed by the Canadian Indian Act and related blood-quantum restrictions in the US. Monkman's performance takes place at the centre of colonial power, but Miss Chief

---

2   My Métis ancestry includes Plains Cree, who are relatives to some Métis, with many of the same ways of knowing. I audited two Plains Cree classes at the University of British Columbia, which is the "y" dialect of Cree, which I use in this article. Some of Monkman's family, although not including Monkman, speak Swampy Cree, or the "n" dialect.

counteracts that power through her exhaustive knowledge of colonial (art) history, which she uses against colonial restrictions of Indigenous identity. Monkman stresses that he "play[s] with sexuality and gender to discuss power" (qtd. in Morris) and to counteract the erasure of Two-Spirit people in dominant art discourses. Queer historian Jonathan Katz describes Monkman as "part Cree, part European, a gay man who was raised straight, a highly political dissident who has had major one-person shows in major museums, [which] highlights his contradictory interpellation" (22). But, as Monkman's art demonstrates, the idea of contradictory interpellation can be reframed into Cree ways of knowing.

Monkman's work also affirms Indigenous sovereignty: "I feel that my work in many ways is very much about drawing from these experiences and looking at history to really understand how, not just my family, but Aboriginal people overall have been treated through this colonial process" (qtd. in "Artist Profile: Kent Monkman"). Monkman's mission is to highlight the importance of Two-Spirit people in some Indigenous societies, especially before contact.[3] Monkman explains "there's been a lot of repression about sexuality" in Indigenous communities, for which he firmly blames the Catholic and Anglican churches (qtd. in National Gallery). By creating his own Nation in *Miss Chief: Justice of the Piece*, Monkman challenges what Mark Rifkin calls the straightening of Indigenous peoples, the "coordinated assault on native social formations that has characterized U.S. [and Canadian] policy since its inception" in order to make heterosexuality compulsory as a way of "breaking up indigenous landholdings [and] 'detribalizing' native peoples" (*When Did* 5–6). Government policies that undermined the power of women and Two-Spirit people in many Indigenous societies allowed settlers to take over Indigenous lands, a process that impacted Monkman's family.

---

3   It is important to note that not every Nation has a Two-Spirit tradition. While there is a Plains Cree word and tradition for a man accepted / living as a woman (ayahkwêw), I am unsure if there is a Swampy Cree equivalent (âpihtawikosisân).

According to Miss Chief, "the genocidal blood quantum policies of the Canadian and US governments were indeed designed to shrink our First Nations" (Monkman, *Miss Chief* 85). Instead Monkman's cultural productions imagine "alternative kinds of Indigenous being" that exist outside the "bureaucratic apparatus of self-determination" (Rifkin, *The Erotics* 39). Status cards and constitutional acts can provide official identities but in *Miss Chief* Monkman creates a space where Indigenous people can explode the idea that a status card or enrolment is all one needs to be Indigenous. Instead, Monkman moves beyond white settler and state recognition by using Indigenous ways of knowing.

Monkman, while a status Indian and mixed-blood himself, clearly disagrees with US blood-quantum regulations and with the Canadian Indian Act, governmental apparatuses that determine who is an Indian for legislative and governance purposes. Instead of relying on government legislation, Miss Chief states:

> I have decided, contrary to the colonial policies and laws of discrimination, racism and genocide perpetrated by the governments of the United States and Canada—which are designed to shrink the numbers of First Nation, Native American, and Aboriginal people—that I will begin to build a great nation, unbounded by geopolitical borders and blood-quantum laws. (Monkman, *Miss Chief* 76)

Rather than Miss Chief's welcoming notion of nationhood, tribal/band governments in the US and Canada were prompted by the need to allocate resources into adopting mainstream notions of what could constitute legitimate membership, including blood quantum. Although this move by Indigenous reserve and reservation communities can be understood as an assertion of sovereignty, it violates traditional notions of hospitality and long-standing practices of adopting people into the community. Indigenous conceptions of membership are in conflict with Canadian-government-imposed membership criteria: "The government's legal definition of Indian and the level of assistance that it afforded [to Indians] changed over time" in clear efforts to reduce expenditures (Innes 141). Miss Chief asserts, "Why don't WE absorb people into our nations and expand our populations instead—the way we used to do it?" (Monkman, *Miss Chief* 81).

Although Monkman doesn't use Cree terms like miyo-wîcêhtowin to describe his work, he repeatedly uses the word "communicate" in a CBC interview ("Kent Monkman on Reimagining"). Expanding the circle involves sharing stories, which is an important mode of communication. Miyo-wîcêhtowin can also be translated as "living in harmony together" ("miyo-wîcêhtowin"), which involves communicating with others to strengthen bonds and reduce conflict. Monkman clearly wants to share the story of Two-Spirit people with both Indigenous and non-Indigenous peoples. He explains, "I think art functions to communicate ideas. I want my art to speak to people and I have a lot of things I want to communicate" ("Kent Monkman on Reimagining"). This accessibility is "an entry point for people to absorb a different version of history" ("Kent Monkman on Reimagining"), particularly a Two-Spirit version of history. Alex Wilson (Swampy Cree) explains, "traditionally, two-spirit people were simply a part of the entire community; as we reclaim our identity with this name, we are returning to our communities" ("How We Find" 305). Monkman is helping to bring Two-Spirit people back into the circle. He foregrounds Two-Spirit people, demonstrating that a way "to assert our self-determination, to assert our presence in the face of erasure, is to free ourselves from the ghost-making rhetorics of colonization" (Justice, "Go Away" 150). Monkman stresses that he is "presenting . . . an empowered perspective and an empowered way of life, looking at our own sexuality" (qtd. in Gonick 24), by using his performances to foreground hidden histories.

Emphasizing that communication is also a way of building kinship with both Indigenous and non-Indigenous peoples, an act of miyotôtakêwin, Monkman affirms communication as a way of bringing people into the circle; however, while the circle seems inclusive, Monkman and Miss Chief ensure Indigenous people are the most welcomed. Because Monkman also invites non-Indigenous viewers into his paintings, films, and performances, his work consists of what Métis artist David Garneau calls Aboriginal sovereign display territories, which he compares to a "keeping house located on reserve land (including urban reserves) that is managed by Aboriginal people of that territory," a safe space that "would encourage Aboriginal people to make work that not only spoke to their own people but also to visitors" ("Imaginary," *West Coast* 37). Garneau is quick to point out that the "non-Aboriginal viewer who seeks conciliation ought to enter Aboriginal sovereign display territories as guests" (37), a protocol Monkman enacts in *Miss Chief: Justice of the Piece* by, for example, lecturing the audience about the Indian Act, a sexist piece of legislation in which status Indian women lost their status if they married a non-status man.[4]

There is danger to this emphasis on hospitality, as "it was through miyotôtakêwin and the desire to do good by visitors that Indigenous communities were also exposed to the violence of settler colonialism. Indeed, the settler is perhaps the example par excellence of the bad houseguest" (Gaertner). This is a risk that Miss Chief illustrates by lecturing non-Indigenous people about their complicity with colonial history.

Although Miss Chief allows everyone into her Nation, she undermines the non-Indigenous applicants' desire to be Indigenous by lecturing them on colonial history. She uses humour in her lectures, but it is a biting humour that shows applicants' romanticized ideas of Indigeneity that relegates Indigenous

---

4   Legislation stated that a status Indian woman who married a non-Indian man would cease to be an Indian. She would lose her status, and with it, she would lose treaty benefits, health benefits, the right to live on her reserve, the right to inherit her family property, and even the right to be buried on the reserve with her ancestors. However, if an Indian man married a non-Native woman, he would keep all his rights. His wife would in fact gain Indian status. Even if an Indian woman married another Indian man, she would cease to be a member of her own band, and would become a member of his. If a woman was widowed, or abandoned by her husband, she would become enfranchised and lose status and her rights altogether. (Hanson, "Marginalization")

This legislation was revoked in 1985 in Bill C-31, which restored status to those who had lost it through "marrying out" and through the "double mother" provision, while also terminating status for people who only had it through marriage and problematically introducing a "second-generation cutoff" of status.

people to the past. Miss Chief rolls her eyes and sighs audibly when a German
Indian hobbyist and a New Age enthusiast who was an Indian princess in
a past life petition to join the Nation of Miss Chief. And as I will discuss
shortly, Miss Chief makes acerbic comments to the German hobbyist that
signals a willingness to adopt people while offering a critique of stereotypes
of Indigenous people.

In an interview, Miss Chief remembers how nineteenth-century settlers were changed by contact with her. While she is very happy to welcome
guests—she readily reveals that European men were submissive by nature—
she stresses that "European males . . . were becoming more sophisticated, and
more cultured" because of their interaction with Indigenous people, Miss
Chief in particular (107). Miss Chief sees settlers as the uncivilized savages,
who are civilized by having artistic and, as she proudly emphasizes, sexual
contact with Miss Chief.

Monkman uses his art to critique settler accounts of Two-Spirit people.
For example, he subverts American painter George Catlin's (1796–1872) den-
igrating comments about the Sauk/Fox dance to the Berdache,[5] by turning
Catlin's words into a celebration. Monkman makes Miss Chief an Indigenous
rebuttal to the anthropological idea of the Berdache. Miss Chief explains:

> Our nations had names for us in our own languages, Winkte, Illhama,
> Agokwe, and so on [. . .]. The French called us the Berdache, which
> stems from an Arabic word—Bardaj—meaning male concubine.
> It shows how little they understood of us; we were men who from

---

5   Catlin writes,

> Dance to the Berdache is a very funny and amusing scene, when a feast is given
> to the "Berdache" as he is called in French . . . Who is a man dressed in a wom-
> an's clothes, as he is known to be all his life, and for extraordinary privileges
> which he is known to possess, he is driven to the most servile and degrading
> duties, which he is not allowed to escape; and he being the only one of the tribe
> submitting to this disgraceful degradation, is looked upon as medicine and sa-
> cred, and a feast is given to him annually. (qtd. in Ace 11)

childhood were blessed by the creator with the role of the opposite gender. (Monkman, *Miss Chief* 87)

Catlin, who painted staged portraits of Indigenous people, in Monkman's re-inscription felt Miss Chief was inauthentic because she borrowed from Eurowestern culture. But Catlin still desires Miss Chief, showing that she has sexual and artistic power (Testickle 109).

Monkman is very successful in the mainstream art market, even as he critiques colonization. Dubbed the "rock star" of Indigenous art in Canada by art historian Elizabeth Kalbfleisch (qtd. in Yogaretnam), Monkman has produced, starred in, and/or directed fourteen films and has had numerous solo and group exhibits. Monkman calls his performance pieces "Colonial Art Space Interventions," which he has staged at mainstream art institutions like the Royal Ontario Museum, the McMichael Canadian Art Collection (home to the iconic modernist Ontario-based Group of Seven) and the Denver Art Museum. Miss Chief's "Colonial Art Space Interventions," which include *Miss Chief: Justice of the Piece*, are a response to the "obliteration of our cultures through this canon of art history . . . We have the strength of our own voice to balance their perspectives on our cultures" (Monkman, *Miss Chief* 109). Monkman disrupts this obliteration with Miss Chief's colourful presence, especially in historical contexts. Inspired by Cher's costume for her 1973 hit song "Halfbreed," Miss Chief's regalia includes black and pink headdresses, (very) red high heels emboldened with beadwork, and Hudson's Bay blanket loincloths.[6] Miss Chief appeals to viewers with her colourful regalia, but very much on her own (Indigenous) terms: Monkman uses Miss Chief to create new traditions. Indigenous cultures are not ossified and stuck in the past, but continue to grow and to change to reflect the contemporary realities of Indigenous people. While their ancestors' stories, protocols, and culture in-spire Indigenous people, Indigenous people build upon these traditions to create new ones.

---

6   It takes two hours and a crew of people to ready Monkman for his Miss Chief appear-ances, which perhaps explains why Miss Chief appears so rarely.

Monkman's artwork has entered "the auction market—a privilege re-
served for the safely dead or famous" (Hannon, "The Pink Indian" 56).
Although Monkman is in some ways part of the art world, being a Two-
Spirit Swampy Cree man also makes him an outsider. Woods Cree playwright
Tomson Highway explains that what he appreciates about his sexuality is "that
it gives me the status of outsider in a double sense. That gives you a wider vision, a more in-depth vision into the ways of human behaviour, into the way
the world works" (Hannon, "Tomson" 36). The Nation of Mischief is queer
because, in the words of Cree curator Richard William Hill, Monkman is "one
of the first [Indigenous artists] to explicitly recognize, respond to, and ma-
nipulate the operations of desire at work in those representations" of colonial
ideology ("Spirits of Mischief" 38). Miss Chief's Nation is very much about
her own desires as a Two-Spirit person, who both lusts after and critiques the
non-Indigenous men who petition to join her Nation. By lusting after non-Indigenous men, Miss Chief reverses the power of the "deep links between
desire and colonial politics through the process of ideological fantasy" (*ibid.*).
Monkman's performances not only tackle colonization and the mainstream
art world, but also reflect his own desires as a Swampy Cree Two-Spirit man.
Monkman seduces people into his paintings, films, and performances and
disrupts colonial history by inserting queer Indigenous sexuality into a narrative that still dominates Canadian and American discourses of Indigeneity.
Yet, Monkman's success places him in the paradoxical position of being a
highly successful Two-Spirit artist in an overwhelmingly white art market.
However, Monkman uses his visibility to help Two-Spirit communities and
Indigenous artists by enacting wâhkôtowin, or interrelatedness, especially in
his connections to his communities.

Monkman treats, in the words of Cherokee scholar Daniel Heath Justice,
"kinship as a verb, rather than a noun" ("Go Away" 150). Monkman uses his
talent to support Two-Spirit communities and the urban Indigenous communities of which he is a part. He points out, "I think my strongest support
has always come out of the aboriginal community" ("Laughing"), a kinship
reflected in his subject matter, his donation of artworks to AIDS organizations and his mentoring of Indigenous youth. While most of Monkman's work

addresses historical injustices, he also embodies wâhkôtowin in more explicitly contemporary and activist ways. Referring to Maria Campbell's *Halfbreed*, Deanna Reder (Cree-Métis) notes, "The autonomy Maria regains is not individualistic but rather one in community and kinship, in relationships based on reciprocity and respect" (134). Monkman follows this reciprocity by donating twenty-five prints as a fundraiser for Casey House, the first free-standing HIV/AIDS facility in Canada. Monkman's poster for AIDS Action Now!, a Toronto AIDS activist organization, features his painting *Kiss the Sky* (2010), a homoerotic depiction of the Icarus story, emblazoned with the caption "The Creator is Watching You Harper!"

Monkman's work for his communities has not gone unnoticed. In 2012 he was a recipient of the EGALE Leadership Award, from Canada's national lesbian, gay, bisexual, and trans human rights organization. He was also the 2014 Indspire Indigenous Achievement Arts recipient. While he refers to himself as a "gay man, a queer man" for non-Indigenous people, he quickly asserts that "it is important to identify myself as a Two-Spirited person within Aboriginal culture because our cultures were accepting of homosexuality, of bisexuality, of other sexualities the Europeans could not comprehend and could not find a place for in their own culture" ("2012 EGALE Leadership"). It is important to note that not all Indigenous cultures have a Two-Spirit tradition like the Plains Cree âyahkwêw, a distinction that would make Monkman's statement seem, perhaps, overly hopeful and a bit romantic.

One of Miss Chief's earliest appearances was in Monkman's 2002 painting *Portrait of the Artist as a Hunter*. At first glance, the painting appears to be a standard Western scene; two Indians and a cowboy ride alongside a stampeding herd of buffalo, with one lucky buffalo running away toward the lower right side of the painting. But closer inspection reveals that the cowboy seems to have forgotten his pants and is clad in buttless chaps, which is a fortunate oversight for Miss Chief, who aims her arrow at the seemingly oblivious cowboy. Miss Chief is wearing a pink headdress, a gauzy pink loincloth, and her familiar pink high heels, but the cowboy is seemingly unaware of Miss Chief's presence. Why is he wearing buttless chaps? Was he secretly hoping for just such an encounter with the fabulous Miss Chief? Monkman then decided to do performance art dressed as Miss Chief. As curator David Liss says, "Witnessing Monkman in performance, confident in his charismatic presence and good looks, flamboyant in costume, carrying himself with pride, it is obvious he relishes the role-playing and the attention" ("Wild West" 103), a pride he shares with his audiences.

Miss Chief is also performing in and repopulating settlers' ideas of an empty landscape or terra nullius, but with Two-Spirit people. For example, Indigenous peoples are spectral absences in the work of the nineteenth-century American Hudson River School of painters, who produced bucolic landscapes void of Indigenous presence. But Indigenous peoples haunt these landscapes, even if colonial versions of history try to erase their presence. Monkman reinserts Indigenous people, particularly Two-Spirit people, as an act of erotic sovereignty. Situating Indigeneity as an erotics "offers an alternative vision of Native politics, and an attendant account of the effects of settler imperialism, by foregrounding embodiment as the entry point for representing Indigenous political ontologies" (Rifkin, *The Erotics* 39). Monkman's incarnation of Miss Chief in performance, films, and paintings is not merely an assertion of self as a contemporary, Two-Spirit Swampy Cree man. Miss Chief's larger-than-life persona counteracts the erasure of Two-Spirit people from colonial history. Moreover, she plays up male settler desire for the "Indian" as she refers to George Catlin as her "first employer, nemesis, and lover" (Monkman, *Miss Chief* 75–76).

Although Monkman's family has lived off-reserve for several generations, he firmly blames his lack of connection to the Swampy Cree language particularly on the assimilationist policies of the Canadian government and their agents, the Christian churches. Both Monkman's Swampy Cree father and artistically inclined Anglo-Irish mother were Christian missionaries.[7] Monkman's initial exposure to the Cree language came through Christian hymns and prayers when as a young boy he visited northern Cree communities

---

7   Monkman was born in 1965 in the small town of St. Mary's, Ontario, his English-Irish mother's hometown, and then moved to the northern Manitoba Cree community of Shamattawa until his family's move to Winnipeg when Monkman was two. He is a member of the Fisher River First Nation in southern Manitoba, which signed Treaty 5 in 1875.

where his preacher father delivered sermons in Cree. Monkman's family's relationship with Christianity and with his Swampy Cree ancestors is inextricably
intertwined. Curator Gerald McMaster (Cree) sees Miss Chief as a time-trav-
eller, "moving in and out of history as a self-inserting corrective, defying the
written and painted narratives espoused by the so-called victors, which have
become naturalized with each succeeding generation" (100). Monkman realized that art is an effective tool for showing the impact of Christianity on
Indigenous people.

Monkman grasped the power of performance during his internship
as a set and costume designer in 1993–1994 for Native Earth Performing
Arts when Tomson Highway was Artistic Director. He was drawn to his
role in the theatre because he noticed "they had Native actors onstage,
they had Native writers and Native directors, but there wasn't yet anyone
from the Native community who was designing for the stage" (Liss, "Kent
Monkman" 80). Liss believes that Monkman's theatricality may have also
been inspired by his father's work as a travelling preacher (*ibid.* 81). Miss
Chief's theatricality is in the interstices between theatre and religiosity.
Miss Chief preaches, but in *Justice of the Piece*, she champions Indigenous
and Two-Spirit rights.

MISS CHIEF: JUSTICE OF THE PIECE

Miss Chief: Justice of the Piece enacts miyotôtakêwin to affirm Indigenous
rights. Miss Chief acts as the multi-roled arbiter of the Nation of Mischief:
"chief magistrate, clan mother, CEO, president, chairman of the board, secretary, publicist, spokesmodel, minister of finance, minister of immigration
and citizenship, queen, princess and all around boss lady" (Monkman, *Miss
Chief* 76). Clearly, Miss Chief lives up to her reputation of being eagletestickle
(or egotistical), deciding who should enter her inclusive Nation of Mischief.
Justice argues that Indigenous nationhood is not simply predicated upon political independence or cultural identity, but rather on "an understanding of
a common social interdependence within the community . . . the tribal web

of kinship rights and responsibilities that link the People, the land, and the cosmos together in an ongoing and dynamic system of mutually affecting relationships" ("Go Away" 151). By establishing her own Nation of Mischief, Miss Chief creates a space for those who are negatively impacted by state apparatuses; she enacts sovereignty in the absence of a communal land base.

By opening her Nation to everyone, moreover, Miss Chief uses miyo-wîcêh-towin as an act of radical hospitality. Miss Chief may not have her own military, but she has her own citizenship papers and treaty money.[8] The citizenship certificate, emblazoned with a seal featuring a stylized pink-and-black eagle with Miss Chief's face in its torso, mimics the language of Canadian citizenship certificates, legalized by Monkman's signature as Miss Chief:

> I, the undersigned, Secretary of State of Mischief Nation, do hereby certify and declare that (Name of Applicant), whose particulars are endorsed hereon, is a Mischief Nation citizen and that he/she is enti-tled to all rights, powers and privileges and subject to all obligations, duties and liabilities to which a natural-born Mischief Nation citizen is entitled or subject. In testimony whereof I have hereunto subscribed my name and affixed the seal of the Department of the Secretary of State of Miss Chief Nation. ("Certificate of Miss Chief Nation")

Miss Chief skewers the absurdity of nationhood even as she creates her own Nation. By inviting everyone into her Nation, moreover, Miss Chief shows the ridiculousness of colonial governments ruling on who is or is not Indigenous. But Miss Chief also critiques contemporary Indigenous notions of nationhood. She insists on an Indigenous nationhood based on inclusiveness, art, play, and eroticism, a recognition that "Indigenous nationhood is more than simple political independence or the exercise of a distinctive cultural

---

8   "Treaty annuity payments are paid annually on a national basis to registered Indians who are entitled to treaty annuities through membership to bands that have signed historic treaties with the Crown" ("Treaty Annuity Payments"). The annual handing out of treaty money is a symbol of the sacred ties between treaty First Nations and the Crown. Because the money was not tied to inflation, treaty First Nations peoples still receive five dollars.

identity" (Justice, "Go Away" 151). Hill believes that *Justice of the Piece* "sat-
irizes the essentialism and simplistic identity politics that have emerged in
certain strains of Indigenous nationalism" ("Spirits of Mischief" 39). Miss
Chief is pointing out how some members of Indigenous communities, whether urban, rural, or academic, decide who is Indigenous based on skin colour,
community collection, and status or Métis cards. Miss Chief asks, "Isn't culture
a more realistic way to define ourselves?" (Monkman, *Miss Chief* 81). However,
by using culture as a benchmark for acceptance, Miss Chief is asking how
far connection to culture can stretch. She doesn't state that petitioners who
are accepted into her Nation will magically become Indigenous, especially
as the Mischief Nation "doesn't oppose taking a little creative licence" (79).

Instead, Miss Chief playfully turns the National Museum of the
American Indian into a
courtroom in which she
decides who is admitted
into her Nation. Actors,
who are scattered around
the audience, petition Miss
Chief to join the Miss Chief
Nation. Escorted to her ju-
dicial podium by her bailiff,
Miss Chief models a black
headdress, thigh-high black
stiletto boots, her bare torso
covered by a train of black
gauze, and the pièce de ré-
sistance, a raccoon jockstrap.
She leisurely settles herself in
her seat behind her judge's
desk and reapplies her lip-
stick, making sure she always
looks her best (see Figure 1).

Figure 1. Kent Monkman as Miss Chief Eagle
Testickle in *Miss Chief: Justice of the Piece*. Photo by
Kent Monkman.

The Nation of Miss Chief, as mentioned previously, is also decidedly queer. Ron and his Cherokee husband, whose marriage is not recognized by the Cherokee Nation, petition Miss Chief for citizenship so they can adopt Cherokee children. He explains, "His family accepts me . . . It's heterosexist that same-sex partners cannot be recognized by their tribes" (Monkman, *Miss Chief* 86–87). Miss Chief welcomes Ron and his family into her Nation: "It's sad that our own nations, who once embraced and revered two-spirited people, have become so conservative. I think the most dangerous and insidious part of colonisation is the self-hatred within our own communities" (87). She goes on, with a certain amount of hyperbole, to explain how every Indigenous Nation had a Two-Spirit tradition: "We were keepers of culture, mediators between the sexes, shamans, or medicine people" (87).[9]

Although Miss Chief accepts non-Indigenous people into her Nation, there are boundaries to Indigenous hospitality, and she treats people who have only an imagined connection to Indigeneity very differently than people like Ron, whose husband is Cherokee, and whom she treats with compassion. She makes pointed jokes about the non-Indigenous applicants, and her body language reflects her exasperation as she sighs audibly and fidgets, much to the audience's amusement.

Indeed, Monkman plays up the mischievousness of the new Nation by making fun of the idea that anyone can claim an Indigenous identity. Hans Neumann, who makes himself into a "new man" when he pretends to be an Indian, is a German "Indian" hobbyist who applied to join many

---

9   While it is understandable that Miss Chief (and Monkman) want to celebrate Two-Spirit people, Justice cautions that "while many communities . . . have well-documented examples in both oral and written texts of gender-variant people who might also be considered sexually variant in today's vocabulary, comparative evidence for hundreds of other tribes is scant" (Justice, "Notes" 215). Members of Nations that do not have a Two-Spirit tradition, or those that have one that has been buried because of Christianity are creating new traditions. For example, Saylesh Wesley (Stó:lō) chronicles the difficulty of connecting with her Christianized grandmother after Wesley transitioned to a woman. While Wesley has trouble finding a Two-Spirit tradition in Stó:lō culture, she connects with her grandmother through cedar weaving.

nations—"Cheyenne [. . .] Cree, Plains Cree, Swampy Cree . . . even the Metis[10]—but they do not want me" (78). Like Garneau's keeping house that welcomes guests as long as they are respectful, Miss Chief enacts miy-otôtakêwin, or being hospitable, but only up to a point. Neumann, or "Sings With Sparrow," his weekend Indian name, explains that German hobbyists have pow wows and "sing and dress and live like traditional Native Indian people" because "when we are living as Indians, we feel more ourselves . . . We ARE Native!" (77). The hobbyists believe performing Indianness is a way to be in tune with nature. Neumann's conception of the "Indian" allows a freedom that Europeans lack because Europeans live in a world that is "so busy, so full of technology, so dirty and polluted" (78). By adopting a German, Miss Chief is following the tradition in some Indigenous Nations of "aggressive assimilation" (Monkman, *Miss Chief* 86)—the absorption of neighbouring and enemy tribes or white settlers (85–86)—but what is modern is that she is using bureaucratic forms, rather than initiation rites. Miss Chief's use of citizenship papers mocks the use of such documents and governmental bureaucracy to decide who is Indigenous.

Miss Chief is also very conscious that Neumann's interest is also sexual. Neumann makes a point of telling Miss Chief that the hobbyists gather "to live and dress, or rather undress—a bit like you do—part time. We like to be completely naked under our loincloths, so we feel natural and authentic like real Indians" (77). Monkman recognizes the "deep links between desire and colonial politics through the process of ideological fantasy" (qtd. in Hill, "Spirits of Mischief" 38) by showing the desire Neumann has for the stereotypical "Indian" men. Miss Chief draws attention to the intersections between desire and colonization as she replies that in the Mischief Nation "it is true that we rarely wear underwear, or encourage anyone else to do so, with the exception of the occasional raccoon jockstrap, buckskin thong, or lo-rise Calvin briefs" (79). But she accepts Neumann into her Mischief Nation with a numbered certificate of membership, which, instead of lower on-reserve

10   Monkman is pointing out how Métis is seen as a catch-all category for non-Indigenous people, who don't qualify for Indian status or think they may have some Indian ancestry.

gas prices, entitles the bearer to discounts at "leading retailers: Louis Vuitton, Hermès, Chanel, and various other luxury brands with which I have lucrative contracts" (79). Miss Chief knows how to take care of herself and, perhaps to a lesser extent, her people, because she knows colonial governments can't be trusted.

Monkman "continues to do what has been done since time immemorial: to speak a language through [his] work that is capable of communicating beyond the moment of interaction, creating an experience that posits a memory that forever alters the bearer of that memory and imposes a responsibility to its remembrance and recalling" (Hill, "Kent Monkman's" 54). Miss Chief uses rights-based language to counteract the invisibility of Two-Spirit people and, in the words of Jean O'Hara, to "ultimately support Indigenous sovereignty and World views" (xxii). Likewise, Cindy Holmes and Sarah Hunt (Kwak'waka'wakw) remind us that

> colonial policies imposed sociolegal categories that were defined and managed in ways that were intended to lead to fewer and fewer Native people over time. Inherent in this project of erasure was the imposition of a binary system of gender which simultaneously imposed Indigenous rights and status along heterosexual lines and suppressed Indigenous systems of gender that went far beyond the gender binary. (159)

Monkman uses Miss Chief to make a Swampy Cree response to colonization, including sexual colonization. Using Indigenous ways of knowing, especially miyotôtakêwin, Monkman is asking all of us to remember Two-Spirit histories and to join his Nation as respectful guests.

(RE)ANIMATING THE (UN)DEAD
MICHELLE LA FLAMME

Living in Canada requires certain attentiveness to the political reality of murdered and missing Aboriginal women. In the absence of the actual bodies and the many missing narratives of how women came to be disappeared in Canada, various artistic imaginations have called these absent bodies into spaces for witnesses to engage with. These engagements are uniquely and inherently politicized in the context of the murdered and missing women in Canada. First of all, at the semantic level there is a strategic essentialism implied by pairing missing with murdered women in Canada. How do we grieve the missing and is it appropriate to grieve the missing along with the murdered women? Besides my interest in this conflation of different women into one singular category (MMIW), I am much more interested in making sense of the performative and symbolic elements used in Canadian gatherings, installations, and theatre productions, and specifically in how these spaces and artists imaginatively animate a sense of the disappeared and the deceased. I explore a few of these contemporary events such as the annual February 14th march, *The REDress Project*, and the *Walking With Our Sisters* installation with an eye to how corporeality, ceremony, and spectral elements are invoked in order to create the context for my primary examination, which is Marie Clements's use of theatrical devices to stage the absent-present Aboriginal woman's body in her play *The Unnatural and Accidental Women*.

At these performative site-specific locations, ceremonial elements, and props are utilized to (re)animate the dead through the creation of a dynamic between the dead, the missing, and the living bodies of the witnesses/audience. Consequently, these performative spaces have the potential to offer a complex synaesthetic relationship between bodies—the bodies of the audience members or witnesses, performers, and finally of the absent bodies of missing Aboriginal women and the abject bodies of murdered Aboriginal women. In particular I argue that these installations, gatherings, and performances are: 1) using both material objects and abstraction in unique ways, 2) conflating the abject murdered body with the absent missing Aboriginal woman's body in complex ways, and 3) creating intimacy with these disappeared and deceased bodies by kinesthetic and synaesthetic means.

SPACES THICK WITH MURDER

The performative gestures/ceremonies that I examine here have particular inherent and instrumental value. Thoughts and feelings about the lives of these absent women are perpetually re-ignited in commemorative gestures that require participant engagement. The overt purpose of the annual Canadian gathering that occurs in urban spaces on February 14th is to remember murdered and missing Aboriginal women. In Vancouver, crowds gather at actual sites where women have fallen victim to violence. By visiting these sites, we stand in compassionate empathy with the families whose relatives have been murdered and we console those whose relatives are still missing. As women drum and sing an honour song and the smudge spirals to the heavens, many weep. I realize we are there not just to recall the names, lives, and deaths of missing and murdered Aboriginal women, we are also there to imagine the unknown and untold stories that led to their demise. We are there to think deeply about these absent and murdered bodies. We are at these specific sites to vicariously feel the violent encounters that they experienced. And we are there to imagine and feel their spirits while we collectively grieve. These are just some of the inherent values associated with the February 14th gatherings in Canada.

An important instrumental value of these marches, speeches, and candle-lighting events is to suggest that these moments of collective remembering energize family, friends of the victims, Aboriginal peoples worldwide, and allies

by providing collective grief rituals and animating hope. The less overt purpose of the February 14th commemorative gatherings is to offer a politicized
performative act that doubles as a critique of the nation-state by recreating
through the abstract and empty spaces a symbolic link to the bodies and lives of
murdered and missing Aboriginal women in Canada. The February 14th commemorative activities reanimate the absent-presence of missing and murdered
Aboriginal women in Canada, ironically and strategically organized on the day
associated with romantic love. These gatherings provide an important forum
for social justice advocates pressing the government to be accountable and to
investigate the emerging patterns that indicate racialized and gendered violence
against Aboriginal women in Canada. The Stolen Sisters Report by Amnesty
International (2004); the Missing Women Commission of Inquiry (2012); and
the recent police report on the serial-killer Robert Pickton, *Missing Women:
Investigation Review* (2010), are three recent examples of contemporary inves-
tigations into the missing and murdered Aboriginal women. The recent Truth
and Reconciliation Commission recommends a national inquiry into the absence and deaths of these women. Many social-justice advocates agree. Others
place government inaction within the enduring legacy of apathy and systemic
violence toward Aboriginal peoples. Still others argue that we have had enough
reports on this topic and the focus of our energy should be to collectively grieve
and simultaneously press the government to *act* on the recommendations in
the reports compiled to date. Despite the previous government's inaction, the
Minister of Justice and Attorney General of Canada as I write, the Honourable
Jody Wilson-Raybould, has started her tenure with a public announcement
of the first phase of the national inquiry (December 2015). We can only hope
that the very public demonstrations on February 14th have indeed affected this
recent federal government response and their stated commitment to action to-
wards justice and accountability.

  The Canadian cultural landscape is full of complex responses to murdered
and missing women, causing me challenging thoughts about my own mortali-
ty, my own body, my own safety, their murdered and missing bodies, and their
(lack of) safety. As a woman of Aboriginal descent I am necessarily implicated
in and moved by this disturbing Canadian reality. In many of the performative

and ceremonial spaces I am discussing I am forced to contemplate unknown stories and absent and abject bodies; the locations of the corpses, the places where the missing women might be, murder scenes, women who might be stuck and waiting to be discovered; and the very real possibility of becoming a victim of targeted gendered and racialized violence. Symbolically, I am forced to consider both absent and deceased bodies in light of my own living body as I imagine their narratives. I cannot help but imagine what happened to them. It is an excruciating contemplation and it is Aboriginal women artists and activists who make that process somewhat manageable. I will turn now to an examination of a few of these culturally specific performative and ceremonial events in order to suggest a context within which we might read Marie Clements's play *The Unnatural and Accidental Women.*

In addition to the February 14th event and the numerous reports on the topic, the Canadian cultural landscape keeps murdered and missing Aboriginal women's bodies in the frame by way of documentaries, testimonials, and heart-wrenching public speeches by family members begging for redress. We have seen photos of missing and murdered women and we have heard testimonials from survivors and family members at community events. We have seen television shows and films regarding murdered and missing women, and we have listened to plaintive commemorative songs for these women. In each instance we are invited as audience members and witnesses to think deeply about who these murdered and missing women were. Such forums offer methods for mourning and political action, and the Canadian arts scene has increasingly become a place to examine this loss. Clearly the topic of the missing and murdered Aboriginal women is continually resurfacing in Canada as we struggle with personal, communal, and national grief and confusion. An analysis of the diversity of these depictions and an examination of the different mediums for mourning is beyond the scope of this essay, but I do want to note an array of genres and methods of cultural production that exist. The missing and deceased bodies are often presented through the arts because of the dearth of evidence about what happened to many of these murdered and missing women. The unknown stories and missing bodies are inspiring the need for us symbolically to imagine these narratives. In many artistic productions we are asked imaginatively to visualize the missing and it is this aspect that I find complex, unnerving, and fascinating.

RED DRESS REDRESS

How do Aboriginal women's bodies get reimagined in contemporary Canadian arts praxis that uses public spaces, galleries, streets, installations and theatre stages? What happens to the viewers in such performative spaces? The intimate process of identification with, and distancing from, the corporeality of the murdered and missing women is central to the power of the Canadian installation named *The REDress Project* (see Figure 1).

Artist Jaime Black is an emerging Métis multidisciplinary artist who is based in Winnipeg. In an interview about the project the artist says that it is an "installation art project based on an aesthetic response to this critical national issue" ("About"). It seeks to collect six hundred red dresses by way of community donation for the purposes of a touring installation. She says, "I imagine the dresses taking over public spaces, streets and parks and trees covered in empty red dresses, until the whole city is mourning the loss of these women, until something is

Figure 1.

done" ("About"). Through the installation process, each individual dress is made to stand in for any and all missing and murdered Aboriginal women. The process itself takes something personal and renders it symbolic, impersonal, and public in service of a political agenda.

What does this red dress in a public space do to the viewer? For some of us it brings to mind tobacco ties and fabric left in the trees after ceremony. For others, these dresses represent the sacred energy of women symbolized by the red fabric. Menstruation, violence, "ladies of the night" will come to mind when others see these red dresses. At the core, these dresses are always-already about (dis)embodiment. Missing and murdered Aboriginal women's bodies are both absent and evoked in this installation. Black suggests that the installation "evoke[s] a presence through marking of absence" (Black). She hopes that the use of red dresses in the installation will "allow viewers to access a pressing and difficult social issue on an emotional and visceral level" ("About"). I want to explore just how this works, and to consider the use of the red dresses as signifiers that evoke a synaesthetic response.

Black notes that during the experience of the installation people "are attracted to the dresses and often connect to them before learning what the project is about, what the dresses represent," and subsequently they often feel "overwhelmed" ("About"). Photos of the red dresses are being made and there is also a film called *Dispatch: REDress Project* that documents various installations of *The REDress Project*. In each genre, the viewer is asked to shift from the visual element to experience an absented female body: that of one of the missing and murdered Aboriginal women in Canada. In each instance the *abject* corpses of murdered women and the *absent* bodies of missing women are conflated to form a single entity, ostensibly invoked as the witness imagines the dresses embodied. Some of the missing women may still be alive but the installation conflates the murdered with the missing in this symbolic gesture of hanging these red dresses. It is this imagined embodiment and the nostalgia and melancholia that the red dress (as prop) performs. Simply seeing these red dresses installed in public spaces, Black hopes, will cause the viewer to both grieve for these women and become inspired to seek some form of political "redress" for these imagined victims. This intent is evident in the duality of the title.

This installation has moved many people in its evocative ghostly presence. It is as if the red dresses themselves are demanding recognition by causing the viewer to experience a kind of cognitive dissonance as we see them out of context and contemplate the possible narratives that would have led to these dresses being placed in such public locations. In this respect the absenting of the owner or woman who might have worn the dress is simultaneously evoked and denied. Thus, the absent-presence of the missing and murdered Aboriginal women's bodies is signified by these red dresses animating the barren "set" of the public installation site. According to *The REDress Project* website, the installation is "an aesthetic response to the more than 1000 missing and murdered Aboriginal women in Canada" (Black). In this installation we are asked to bear witness to a gendered space that calls into question the disappearance of the Aboriginal women who, as the installation implies, might have worn the dresses. This sacred colour red communicates Aboriginal women's power in a way that is understood by many Aboriginal viewers and others to be representative of the collective community of Aboriginal women who have been murdered or missing in Canada.

What are we to experience when we place a red dress in a tree as other women do the same? How does the wind animate the ghostly presence of the murdered and missing body? Why red and why a dress? These questions haunt me. I believe the scale of the horror of murdered and missing women in Canada necessitates symbolic means for addressing it. Often such creative means require the evocation of corpses and missing bodies. It is this evocation of these bodies in service of empathy, hope, and action that will continue to mark this epoch in creative production in Canada.

ARE YOU NEXT?

I would like briefly to examine two more Canadian examples of the contemporary artistic practice of evoking/invoking Aboriginal women's bodies before I delve into the play itself. In trying to place murder and gendered violence within one cohesive framework, I had to be selective and attentive to my own visceral reaction(s) in order not to become overwhelmed by this topic. As a brown-skinned woman with Aboriginal ancestry I often ask myself, "Am I next?" Others are asking themselves the same question. I want to examine one such response that has been prevalent in cyberspace. An online activist campaign was started by Holly Jarrett of Hamilton, Ontario, that involved Aboriginal women posting selfies while holding handmade signs with the text: "Am I Next? #MMIW." Other women were disturbed by this activism and began to counter this by taking selfies and holding up signs that said "I'm Not Next," offering a more empowered reframing of the original question.

I want to investigate another online movement that used abstraction rather than selfies. This second "Am I Next?" Facebook movement has involved Aboriginal women *removing* their profile photos and replacing them with an abstract graphic silhouette of a head framed by the question "Am I next?" This activist movement has indicated in a literal way the pervasive fear faced by this demographic. In a symbolic way the action to replace one's profile image was a method to suggest the link between the *real* women (understood here as murdered and/or missing but nonetheless "disappeared") and the living women who used their agency to "disappear" their image (and self) in a symbolic and simultaneously commemorative gesture. Thinking about corporeality and spectatorship here, two salient points come to mind: 1) the issue of the missing, murdered, and decidedly absent Aboriginal woman's body is manifest by way of the abstract representation of the "body" that stands in for all murdered and missing women; and 2) the performative act of replacing one's profile picture suggests an agency that was not afforded to the deceased. Lastly, "Am I Next?" online activism also offers a visual link between the demographic of dead and living Aboriginal women in Canada while creating a community of women visually identified by their "Am I Next?" profile image.

The action of absenting one's real image from one's profile and the use of the text "Am I Next?" have offered means for Aboriginal woman who are also Facebook users to acknowledge the subtext of fear that we all live with. This is just one of many recent gestures to align living women with the deceased and "disappeared" through symbolic commemorative acts. What is unusual is that the "Am I Next?" movement occurred in cyberspace. Perhaps because of this it managed to create community. It was using living women's agency to "disappear" themselves from the "frame." Consequently, if we are to understand the disappearing of the profile image as a death of sorts, it symbolically expanded the demographic of the "missing" and murdered to include those of us still living. What I find most fascinating about this commemorative Facebook activism is that 1) it creates community, while 2) it conflates the past *real* deceased women's bodies as the silhouette with our present body (the "I" posting the image), and 3) it posits a fearfully imagined and inherently disempowering future victimization all at once.

WALKING WITH SPIRITS

The notion of the interrupted lives of the murdered and missing Aboriginal women in Canada and the difficult questions involved in respectfully representing their bodies is at the core of the touring installation in Canada entitled *Walking With Our Sisters* (see Figure 2). In this exhibition, a collection of 1,763 moccasin vamps (uppers) plus 188 children's vamps are set up in a circle in gallery spaces for people to remember those who are missing and murdered (see Christi Belcourt, qtd. in Sandals). As in the case of "Am I Next?" very real, living Aboriginal women are entwined with the deceased both symbolically and literally in several fascinating ways. And as in the "Am I Next?" movement and the *REDress* installation, missing and murdered Aboriginal women are conflated into a single category. Also as in those other performative events, community is implied and created. Beyond these shared features, however, this installation develops a deeper synaesthetic response as it also engages the participants in a kinaesthetic experience.

Figure 2. Moccasin vamps assembled for Christi Belcourt's *Walking With Our Sisters*.

The *Walking With Our Sisters* installation suggests the agency and embodiment of the living people whose hands sewed and beaded the uppers. The creation of this installation brought together many Aboriginal women to engage in this very traditional and performative act to honour these missing women. In this sense it had an inherent value for the creators of the uppers, as they were connecting and creating community by sharing tradition that was tied to a larger artistic and social justice goal. One can imagine them applying their hands to such simple elements as beads and leather while perhaps praying into the beads sewn onto the hide for these women. Of course, the matriarchal and indigenized vitality of the creators is ironically juxtaposed with the absent corporeality of the missing and the abject corporeality of the deceased. What I want to point out here is the relationship between bodies and the way in which the exhibition may be read symbolically.

Secondly, the community that re-creates these installations is honouring "the energy of [then] 1,372 different artists" (Belcourt, qtd. in Sandals). The sheer volume of the installation, the number of artists and community members involved in creating the vamps and touring the installation nationwide, mark it as a very significant public arts event. According to Christi Belcourt, the Métis artist who is lead coordinator of the project, the installation is slated to tour for seven years (Sandals). How does this installation use the physical space and the symbolism of the uppers to evoke a synaesthetic and kinaesthetic response?

Thirdly, at a symbolic level the beaded uppers simultaneously evoke the *absent* corporeality of the missing and the *abject* corporeality of the deceased as they are the "imagined" personal moccasins created by an imagined set of hands who "knew" them. The unfinished aspect of the moccasin suggests the abrupt ending of the lives of many Aboriginal women. The performative gesture to honour the women is incomplete, because the "auntie" making the uppers did not get to finish them or offer them to the imagined, and presumably deceased, women whose lives the exhibition is meant to commemorate. Looking at these uppers, viewers simultaneously imagine the loving traditional hands throughout various communities who are vitally alive and honouring tradition in contrast with the murdered and missing, absent bodies of the deceased. Thus the interruption of the process of completing the moccasins signifies both the interruption of the creators' processes, the interruption of the ceremonial giving of the moccasins, and, most obviously, the interruption of the lives of the women.

A fourth aspect of the performative complexity of this installation is linked to the framing of this exhibition, bringing the absent corporeality of the missing and the abject corporeality of the deceased as they are the "imagined" into the gallery space. The exhibition both constructs a *real* ceremony and re-creates an *imagined* traditional ceremonial honouring of these women ostensibly by the "family" who created the moccasin uppers. According to Belcourt, in addition to these performative enactments, real ceremony is involved in these spaces. The Elders conduct traditional opening ceremonies at each site and incorporate local ceremonial aspects into the installation space as they "come together as a community to honor" (Belcourt, qtd. in Sandal). In absence of a national space for mourning missing and murdered women in Canada, the touring exhibition offers a mobile space that is paradoxically a mausoleum and a ceremonial space. Its power is evident in the ways in which simple objects invite kinesthetic responses for the witness/audiences who participate in this installation-cum-ceremony.

Finally, I want to further examine the kinesthetic aspect of this installation by considering the language that is used to frame the performative experience. In this exhibition people enter the gallery space and are invited to "walk" with the deceased and missing, thus connecting the live bodies of the viewers/walkers with those missing and in the spirit world. The visitor is walking "for" the murdered and missing women and also "with" them, as the title suggests. The title of the exhibition also brings dead and living bodies together in dynamic ways that inscribe a particular cosmology. The title suggests that by entering the exhibition space and considering the interrupted lives of these women one is able to "walk with" the "sisters," implying that there is an active connection to the missing and murdered women within the space.

The title and the installation itself suggest that by witnessing the installation and walking the circle of vamps within ceremonial contexts, the viewer is transported into a connection that pairs their own life with those of the deceased, who become animate and walk "with" us in the space. This active notion of "walking with" rather than "praying for" is a significant aspect of managing grief as it suggests an active and dynamic relationship between the deceased and the living community of women whose bodies are symbolically walking together in the diverse spaces where the installation tours.

At the simplest level, the synaesthetic and kinesthetic aspects of this installation provide diverse communities with an outlet to manage grief and an opportunity for catharsis. Tanya Kappo, among others, suggests that *Walking With Our Sisters* is distinct as an installation and that it "is ceremony, it is art, and it is memories." For Kappo it is "the ceremonial and sacred aspects" of the installation that make *Walking With Our Sisters* a "transformational experience, and not just an art show." I am interested here in the ways in which bodies are pressed into service for these aesthetic, political, and spiritual agendas. As in *The REDress Project* and the February 14th gatherings, the corpses of the murdered women are abject bodies that are conflated with the absent bodies of the missing women. Like *The REDress Project*, these conflated bodies are evoked through physical objects in the space. However, this installation adds another dimension to the experience as we are asked to imagine these vamps reanimated by spirit "sisters" while we walk "with" them in the gallery space. Belcourt references the synaesthetic dimension of the exhibition when she states, "You almost see them standing there wearing their moccasins." Yet, we also are invited to have a kinaesthetic experience because we are not just watching the women standing or walking, but we are invited to walk *with* their disembodied presence in the space.

This imagining of Aboriginal women's abject and absent corporeality is directly aided by the ceremonial aspects of the installation. Traditional songs are played in the space and the sacred medicines of tobacco, cedar, sage, and sweetgrass are utilized by Elders as an integral part of the touring exhibition. There are also eagle staffs in the gallery space, one for missing women and girls and the other for murdered women and girls (Kappo). However, not everyone agrees with the protocols surrounding the installation/ceremony. Anishinaabe performance artist Rebecca Belmore, for example, declined to enter the space; according to David Garneau, she "did not appreciate the gendering of the exhibition space, namely being asked to don a dress and be smudged before entering the space" ("Indigenous"). Cree curator Richard W. Hill was also critical of the installation. According to Garneau, Hill "challenged the use of clichéd and dubious signifiers of Indigeneity" ("Indigenous"). These critiques are relevant to the discourse surrounding such commemorative displays and certainly ask us to think critically about pan-indigeneity and protocols that might not appeal to everyone. An important part of this emerging discourse must include dissent, unpacking of the signifiers, and critical consider-ations of the use of props, ceremonial items, and the imagined corporeality that combine to offer affective encounters in these sites.

My own interest in these performative events/ceremonies is in the way in which the body is evoked. How the evocation of these missing and murdered women's bodies causes witnesses to experience identification through the ab-jection of the murdered and the absence of the missing fascinates me. As I have argued earlier, the floating referent of the absent signifier of the missing Aboriginal women's bodies and the missing narratives of the murdered and missing women's stories create an impulse to make sense of these narratives by other than literal means as one way of managing grief. In a sense, these installations are abstract rituals to replace the referential "real" bodies that are missing and to create a narrative in absence of the "truth" about what happened to these women. How we are led by synaesthetic, theatrical, and kinesthetic means to this engagement is the focus of my analysis here. We are asked to engage in a form of vicarious suffering and trauma through these installations, where our imagined wearing of moccasins intended for the deceased or red dresses used to signify the disappeared and deceased becomes animated by our projections of the deceased and, simultaneously, our projections of our selves. This creates an unsettling aspect to the performance spaces as we simultaneously commemorate the other, mourn the missing, and imaginatively *become* the deceased. The perpetually denied referent of the missing bodies in the *real* world causes a particular set of synaesthetic and, in the case of the "walking" installation, kinesthetic responses evoking melancholia and nostalgia for the missing and murdered Aboriginal women framed here as "our sisters."

The rhetorical, physical, and spiritual complexities of the *Walking With Our Sisters* exhibition and the motive behind the February 14th march and other commemorative gestures bring me to my current space of thinking through my body about the depictions of missing and murdered women's bodies and the ways in which art can evoke a symbiotic spiritual link through the physical. Commemorative events like the February 14th walk, and the *REDress* and *Walking With Our Sisters* installations create complex synaesthetic experiences that are anchored by real Aboriginal women's bodies, whether as active participant/creators, abject corpses, and/or absent bodies. These artistic encounters evoke the absent corporeality of the missing and the abject corporeality of the deceased as they are "imagined" through signifiers such as red dresses in trees, half-finished moccasins in the gallery space, or the locations where women have fallen victim to violence. In each case, the performative act of commemoration involves physical objects and a "calling in" of the body through the imagining of the abject and absent corporeality of the victims. The idea of the absent presence of the deceased Aboriginal women's body is something that I will investigate further as it pertains to Marie Clements's play *The Unnatural and Accidental Women*. I will now begin a close reading of her play and connect Clements's use of corporeality, absent-presence, and violence to represent murdered and missing women in terms of embodiment and spirituality.

THE UNNATURAL AND ACCIDENTAL WOMEN

Clements's play *The Unnatural and Accidental Women* offers a sensitive depiction of the lives and deaths of some of the murdered Aboriginal women in the Downtown Eastside of Vancouver. The play was written in 1997 and a staged reading was given at the Vancouver East Cultural Centre in the same year. The play premiered in 2000 at the Firehall Arts Centre in Vancouver and was first published in 2001. *The Unnatural and Accidental Women* offers a vision of corporeality and the spirit world that suggests that murdered women have an influence on the present in ways that extend beyond the point of their murder. Clements has managed to write beyond the death of these women by employing a specific set of narrative techniques. In *The Unnatural and Accidental Women*, the tragedy of the women's deaths is transformed by Clements's use of a fictional revenge plot in which the murdered Aboriginal women, who appear as ghosts, execute the man who has murdered them. Karen Bamford has brilliantly examined the revenge plot in the play so I will not be repeating her insights. However, I want to outline the ways in which issues of corporeality, witness trauma, and spectatorship are foundational elements to Clements's play by way of a close reading of the scenes in which dead and living women's bodies are connected.

Although the basis of this play is factual, Clements takes creative licence to extend the power of these murdered Aboriginal women to affect change beyond the grave by giving them an embodied and active presence as ghost accomplices to the play's final killing. The "truth" about these murdered women is that the killer, Gilbert Robert Jordan, was only sentenced for one of the eleven murders, served six years, and was released. However, by choosing to construct a play in which the murderer is killed on stage, Clements effectively rewrites the events in a way that empowers the Aboriginal women who were murdered, despite their agency coming posthumously. I have drawn on some of the insights I offered in an earlier essay on this topic, published in a special issue of *Theatre Research in Canada* on Marie Clements (see La Flamme).

The first of several innovative choices that Clements has made to represent murdered and missing women is related to the basic plot structure. Clements consciously avoids representing the murder of the women on stage. Instead, she chooses to focus on their vitality and frames their stories around the last few hours in their lives before they were killed. The indication that the women have been murdered is represented by way of slides that document the "official" versions of the coroners' reports:

SLIDE: Mavis Gertrude Jones, 42. Died November 30, 1980 with a 0.34 blood-alcohol reading. An inquiry concluded Jones' death was "unnatural and accidental." (57)

Though Clements has constructed fictional characters, she uses real data about the real victims and real data about the coroners' reports to create this series of slides. In this respect, Clements refuses to simply end the play with the horrific murders of the Aboriginal women while simultaneously finding a way to foreground the murders in the performance.

A second consequence of Clements not representing the murders of the women on stage is related to how their stories are presented. In this play we see the women in the last few moments of their lives before they were killed, and the small hotel rooms in which we see them offer a number of different dynamics for the audience. Most obviously, we gain insight into their backstories, which are filled with personal moments, hopes, and dreams. This in turn brings the audience into a deeper empathetic relationship to the characters and (ideally) the original victims. By staging their stories this way, Clements presents the women as more than corpses or statistics and emphasizes their individuality and humanity.

But there are other, more insidious implications that are the inevitable consequence of the audience being virtually brought into the room with the victims before their murders. I want now to examine how Clements uses narrative and theatrical means to bring the deceased characters into contact with

Rebecca, the play's protagonist, in her search for her missing mother, Aunt Shadie. In particular I am interested in the distinct ways in which Clements slowly and almost imperceptibly conflates the abject deceased body with the live body. How exactly do the ghost characters of the play's second act engage with the live characters on stage? What impact does witnessing this interaction have on the audience? What cosmological implications are there inherent in such a production?

First I want to consider how Clements uses setting and props in service of imagining a horror that is never depicted directly. In the play two characters are represented as being in intimate and violent relationships with the objects in their hotel rooms. By staging these scenes in this way Clements foreshadows the tragic and violent encounters that she does not show on stage—the murders themselves. She brings us into the location of the murders, reveals the feelings of the women, foreshadows dialogue between the murderer and the murdered transposed through the dialogue between the objects in the room and the characters, but she does *not* offer the spectacle of the murders. The corporeality of the murdered is strategically absent.

By choosing to close each woman's vignette in the space where her body was found Clements implicates the audience in a profound way. First of all, we see these women in the places where they were killed. We see the women just as they would have been discovered by the killer. On stage, in their hotel rooms, the women are clearly alone, far from home, and longing for family and connection. Secondly, this is also presumably where the bodies of these murdered women were discovered, so the spectatorial role is doubled. The "domestic" space of the single room occupancy is transformed into a crime scene; a murder has occurred that we do not witness on stage but are asked to imagine. The space is also transformed into the imagined forensic space where the body would have been discovered. In both cases there is an imagined person acting upon the body and those two actions (murder and forensic examination) are strategically occluded from the narrative. The absence of the murder itself on stage is re-created in our imaginations through Clements's choice to bring us to the precipice of their murders then deftly end a scene with the slide announcing the cause of death as "unnatural and accidental."

The slides are a fascinating physical and literal means by which to bring the abject deceased bodies into the narrative without placing them on the stage as objects of spectatorial voyeurism.

I want to now consider how the body is positioned in Clements's use of slides to end each of these vignettes. In the play, slide projections of the coroners' reports indicate to the audience that the last scene in each vignette was indeed the last moment of the woman's life before she encountered the killer. For the audience, the assumption is that the deaths are indeed "unnatural and accidental." The playwright strategically replicates this error by utilizing the slides to offer the official narrative of each woman's death after engaging the viewers in an empathetic relationship with them by sketching aspects of their human stories. Each slide chillingly announces that the character we have begun to feel for is now dead. As the pattern emerges the audience begins to realize that we may have been the last to witness each woman alive—and this has profound implications for the audience.

Most obviously the use of these slides offers an ironic comment on the play's title. While this official paperwork is how we come to know that the women are deceased, we do not get to know that the actual lives were taken by murder until the end of the play when it becomes clear that these "official" documents stating the cause of death as "unnatural and accidental" were not accurate. The official rendering of the cause of death on a slide asks the audience not to transform the domestic space into a crime scene but rather to understand it as a place of potential suicide. Clements's use of this slide projection is more than a static official accounting that is reversed when it is revealed in the last third of the play that the deaths were neither "unnatural" nor accidental.

In addition, each slide stands in for two performative acts that implicate the audience as spectators. As the audience we realize we have been witness to each woman's life before the murderer arrived. In a sense we have been at the scene of the death. The slides stand in for the staged act of murder: we see the slide instead of the murder. The second performative act suggested by the slide is that of examining the body of the deceased. The playwright uses the slide to occlude both the murder of the women and the intimate and performative act of examining the murdered bodies. Each woman's murdered body is missing from the stage but present in the narrative; the coroner is only *imagined* as the author of the report shown on the slide. We know that the person who has signed the death certificate has been in close proximity to the deceased and yet the coroner is absent as a character, just as the murderer is signified by the violent furniture and not by his actual presence or the staging of the murder itself.

The fourth complicated issue of corporeality that affects spectatorship is of course the dramatic climax of the play in which the murderer is killed on stage by his intended victim. We, as spectators, are also part of the spectral chorus that is "present" in the barber shop as he sits in his chair and gets his throat cut. Before I examine this scene in detail I would like to outline some of the theatrical means by which Clements aligns the deceased and the living women's bodies in the play in order to create this powerful synaesthetic relationship between bodies: the abject murdered Aboriginal women's bodies, the absent body of the missing mother, and the character Rebecca who represents the living Aboriginal woman's body.

SLIPPAGE INTO SPIRIT AND SPIRIT INTO FLESH

Clements first draws attention to the absent-presence of the women/ghost/victims whom we have seen in the first act in another domestic space. Here Rebecca, as the daughter of a missing (and, as we discover, murdered) mother, is alone with Ron, who is a police officer with whom she has had a one-night stand. The ghosts of the women murdered in the first act, present in the room, show a sexual interest in Ron's body parts. So too, are they represented as having other human needs. This is a complex and interesting choice the playwright has made to align dead and living Aboriginal women's bodies on stage.

VIOLET: Why are you mad?

VERNA: Because I am dead, and I am still thirsty.

VIOLET: Thirsty?

Verna leans over and screams at her silently.

VERNA: THIRSTY, you fuckin' parrot. I'm thirsty . . . for . . . my kids, my man. I'm thirsty, thirsty, thirsty, THIR-sty, THIRSTY, dehydrated, dry, parched, thirsty. Get IT? (92)

As Rebecca's very much alive and young body moves toward becoming a spirit, the spirit bodies become increasingly humanized, animate, and present. This parallelism has profound implications at the climax of the play, as it foreshadows the slippage between spirit and flesh, dead and living, mother and daughter, and eventually victim and perpetrator.

The spirit women are made more "real" as the play progresses. The sexual interest in Ron's parts underscores their very physical human needs. Additionally, they are shown "touching and using Rebecca's things" in this moment of the play:

VALERIE is going through REBECCA's laundry that's lying in a basket. She's pulling out different pieces of underwear and trying them on. MAVIS is sitting at REBECCA's desk playing with the phone. VIOLET has been in REBECCA's bedroom swinging on her swing and playing with REBECCA's pretty things. Gradually, THE WOMEN pick what they want out of REBECCA's clothing and make-up and put them on. (100)

While their ghost bodies exist in an imagined and invisible spirit world (Rebecca and Ron cannot see them), they become increasingly linked to

Rebecca's body. The women don Rebecca's clothes and symbolically "become" her as they go in search of her. This is a clear example of that slippage from dead to living, corporeal to ghostly and back. Once the audience has accepted the connections between this community of dead women and the living Rebecca, the playwright adds complexity to this dynamic by slowly shifting Rebecca into contact with the ghost characters and then shifting her once again into the symbolic body of the murderer by way of role-play.

The ghost women enact the start of the kill by tormenting Gilbert in his shop as Rebecca arrives for her wallet. She has inadvertently left her wallet in the bar where she went in search of her mother (see Figure 3). The murderer, Gilbert, has found Rebecca's wallet and confirms that he has seen her missing mother when he tells Rebecca that the photo she is carrying looks like Aunt Shadie. This moment of recognition is critical as it confirms that her mother was indeed in this area and had interacted with this man. Once in the barbershop with Gilbert, the "missing" mother figure slowly transforms into a murdered woman just as Rebecca shifts from prey to predator.

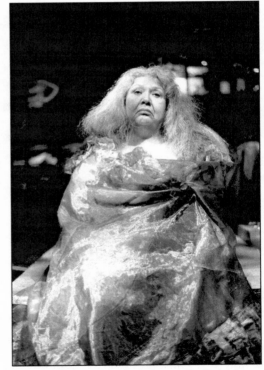

Figure 3. Muriel Miguel as Aunt Shadie in the Native Earth production of Marie Clements's *The Unnatural and Accidental Women*. Photo by Nir Bareket.

THE DANCE OF PREDATOR AND PREY

The absent missing mother is now becoming recognized by the audience as a murdered woman as we witness Rebecca discovering the truth. At this scene, Rebecca's body begins to become a symbolic replacement for that of her murdered mother as the barber begins to fixate on Rebecca's hair:

GILBERT: Can I braid it? I like women in braids.

REBECCA: No, it's alright. Thanks . . .

He grabs her hair from behind.

She grabs her hair back.

Enough.

GILBERT: (*he turns. To himself*) You fuckin' uppity bitch. (121)

Clearly the mention of the mother, the hair, and the braids has incited the killer's thirst again. However, just as he is moving toward victimizing Rebecca, she is simultaneously becoming empowered by proximity to her mother's ghost body. The conflation of the bodies of mother and daughter is necessary before the role-play/transformation between Gilbert and Rebecca can occur. Rebecca must become both deceased mother and alive self before she can "play" the role of Gilbert and transform from potential prey to hunter.

A specific prop is used to link the ghost women characters to Rebecca, the one living Aboriginal woman character. The reference to Gilbert's interest in the braid, women's braids, and his desire to braid Rebecca's hair work together to provide a clue to the backstory of the murders. Gilbert's reaction also foreshadows the significance of the "trophies" that Rebecca will discover. Rebecca's discovery of the items he has kept for "safekeeping" (117) provides a pivotal moment in the play. The barber's light is hiding the murdered women's braids. In this grisly scene, the absent presence of the murdered bodies and the missing body of Rebecca's mother all become condensed in this single prop, linking the dead bodies and the living intended victim together. Just as the ghost women wearing her clothes suggested their link to Rebecca's body and fate, so too does the discovery of the hair link Rebecca's real body in danger with her mother's murder and murderer:

> *She goes to pull out a drawer and then stops and looks at the red-and-white barber light. She stops for a long moment and breathes. She walks directly towards it, taking the bottom off the light. A handful of long black braids fall to the floor. She gasps and touches each one until she gets to her mother's. She picks her mother's braid up and buries her face in it and sobs. REBECCA hears GILBERT approaching. Shaken, she takes her jacket off and covers the braids and tries to get herself together again.* (121) (see Figure 4)

Clearly, the barber's fixation on Rebecca's hair and his abrasive language are understood as his moment of "marking her" as prey. Finding the braids is both *her* moment of recognition as she begins to channel her mother's ghostly essence and the marking of *him* as her prey. Once she discovers the braids, she takes full control of the scene by seducing him and claiming power over the barber shop and the tools of his trade, effectively and symbolically becoming him through role play.

Following the moment when her mother's body is referenced through the braid, the question of

Figure 4. Rebecca (Lisa C. Ravensbergen) finds the braids of the murdered women. Photo by Nir Bareket.

her disappearance becomes transformed into Rebecca's knowledge of her mother's murder. After discovering this crucial prop and the story that it implies, Rebecca embodies the murderer and the murdered becomes the prey. By donning his position as "barber" and using seduction and violence as he had, she forces *his* body to conform to his own sadism, ironically and fittingly in the chair where his previous victims may have sat. Rebecca even "becomes" Gilbert in terms of assuming his phallic power in that he becomes the disoriented and needy victim while she transforms into the aggressor. She is the one who determines the pace, uses alcohol to entice him, and offers to meet his needs just as he had done to the victims. This transformation of power is most evident when she parrots his line, "Can I buy you a drink? Can I get you a drink?" (122), in a symbolic re-enactment of the serial killer's modus operandi. This replacement and substitution between killer and victim is precisely what the audience needs at this point in the play as the identification with Rebecca's plight as potential victim requires a new turn of events (see Figure 5). However, Rebecca's transformation requires something more than the simple reversal of victim/murderer. In order for us to

Figure 5. Rebecca (Lisa C. Ravensbergen) turns the tables on "the demon barber" (Gene Pyrz). Photo by Nir Bareket.

approve of her actions a third element is required: the ghostly presence of her mother's traditional self.

At this point in the play the essence (spirit) of the mother's dead body becomes animated by being transplanted into the live body of the daughter. The slippage between this world and the next, mother and daughter, ghost women and living woman, is all made profoundly manifest. This is reinforced through their diction and through imagery that is connected to corporeality and tradition. This poignant moment connects mother and daughter through a shared recollection of things their bodies have done. These lines are fitting-ly delivered in overlapping dialogue to reinforce the slippage between the murdered Aunt Shadie as spirit and the living Rebecca as potential prey trans-forming into hunter.

> AUNT SHADIE: I used to be a real good trapper when I was young. You wouldn't believe it, now that I am such a city girl. But before, when my legs and body were muscular, I could go forever. Walking those traplines with snowshoes. The sun coming down, sprinkling everything with crystals, some floating down and dusting that white comforter with magic. I would walk that trapline . . .
>
> REBECCA: I would walk that trapline . . .
>
> AUNT SHADIE: . . . like a map, my body knowing every turn, every tree, every curve the land uses to confuse us.
>
> REBECCA: . . . like a map, my body knowing every turn, every lie, every curve they use to kill us.
>
> REBECCA/AUNT SHADIE: I felt like I was part of the magic that wasn't confused. (124–25)

This is the moment in the play in which the past and the present coalesce and Rebecca's body is transformed into the empowered body of her mother as a young woman walking the trapline and using traditional knowledge to survive. Both characters reference this traditional aspect as the time before the "magic" was confused. Thus, Clements posits that traditional knowledge of survival, framed here as hunting skills, transcends the "confusion" of the urban space and even transcends the "real" world of the living.

This play is saturated with transformations. We witness Rebecca transform from living character to role-playing murderer to becoming a conflation of mother/spirit/self. This last transformation occurs just before Rebecca becomes hunter and transforms out of the role of victim. I want to look closely at how this transformation occurs on stage. Rebecca is physically aided first by Aunt Shadie's hand and secondly by her advice:

AUNT SHADIE: If it squirmed, I would put it out of its misery as fast as I could. (125)

Ironically, Rebecca is getting advice on hunting and tradition as a final gift of knowledge from her deceased mother, but it is offered to her in the context of what might otherwise be Rebecca's imminent demise. Thus, the advice is practical as it allows the daughter to "become" the emboldened hunter like her mother had been, despite the slippage in time. The context of the hunt is also entirely different, signifying the shift from a rural space and a woman hunting for food to the urban space and the need to hunt the human killer for survival. Because Rebecca was about to be "taken" by the predator Gilbert, her mother's advice is literally life-saving. It is the very skill she will require to at once defy the murderer, save her own life (and we assume the lives of future potential victims), and become the matriarchal hunter.

RESTORED EMBODIMENT

The slippage between the bodies of the deceased and the single body of the living character of Rebecca is fascinating and offers a particular cosmology. Even after a climax where the slippage is vitally imperative for Rebecca's very existence, the denouement also continues to intertwine dead and living Aboriginal women's bodies. The conclusion to the murder scene uses the absent-presence of the women's bodies signified by their braids to release them back to the spirit world.

> THE TRAPPERS *follow through, as* REBECCA *and her mother stare at each other.* THE TRAPPERS *take the razor, wash it and replace it.* REBECCA *hands each woman their braids.* THE WOMEN *leave in a line. Her mother remains standing.* REBECCA *reaches in her pocket and hands her mother her braid of hair.*
>
> AUNT SHADIE: Re-becca.
>
> *AUNT SHADIE raises a hand and touches her face.*
>
> REBECCA: Meegweetch and thank you. (125)

Bamford refers to this moment as one of "mutual recognition, a kind of blessing" that is "regenerative and liberating for both" (155). Bamford suggests that the replacing of the razor is the women "symbolically restoring order" (154). However, I would like to suggest that the act of replacing the razor is invoking chaos and disorder because their physical manipulation of that important element—"the smoking gun"—is done so that the "real world" crime scene will not implicate Rebecca. This is a trickster move in that it creates disorder for the police in the investigation and enables the murderess, framed here as the perpetrator of justice, to walk free.

This prop of the women's braids is loaded as a signifier. The braided hair becomes much more than a trophy for the serial killer or a clue for Rebecca

about what happened to her mother, or a sign that she will be the next victim. It also connects the dead characters to the one lone surviving woman
character. Erin Wunker has offered profound insight into our reading of this
powerful moment on stage and the use of this prop. Wunker refers to the "stolen braid" as an "effigy" (175). This is certainly an apt adjective to use given
how the return of the braid functions in the narrative of the play. However,
the return of the braids restores more than identity to the women because it
also restores the ghost women's capacity to move from a spiritual limbo to the
spirit world proper. This resolution is clearly indicated in the final scene where
the women rejoice in completeness in the final ceremonial "supper" scene.
Thus while on the surface the braid signifies the dead women's Aboriginal
identity, its role is also clearly linked to agency and movement for the spirit
figures to re-emerge more fully into the spirit world with hair intact.

In addition, Rebecca's act of handing out the braids is also an act of the
one living woman using the trophy evidence of the serial killer to engage bodily with the women who have been haunting her. This is very important for
my own analysis of the relationship that is established and developed in the
play between dead and living bodies. The braid makes the women, who have
been invisible to Rebecca up to this point in the play, visible. So this scene is
also deeply about bodies and absent-presence: the signifier of their succes-
sive murders (the braids) being handed back in such a way that the deceased
become manifest bodily to Rebecca. Rebecca's gesture here instills the power
back into the thing that was taken in a wrong way and yet, in addition, the
handing back of these braids doubles as the means by which Rebecca gains
her agency and saves her life. The braids are also the catalyst that releases the
women from their spiritual limbo.

This hair performs its last role in the final scene of the play where the wom-
en are eating a beautiful banquet with "their long, long hair spilling everywhere"
(126) (see Figure 6). The mystery of the missing women and the reality of their
murders have been unveiled. Also, the mystery of the missing mother has been
solved and both of these accomplishments have come by way of the Aboriginal
women's dead bodies and one Aboriginal woman's live body interacting. Thus,
the mother-daughter unity magically restores order in the play.

Figure 6. The banquet: Gloria May Eshkibok, Michelle Latimer, Sarah Podemski, Deborah Allison, Lena Recollet, Gail Maurice, Valerie Buhagiar, Michaela Washburn, J. Patricia Collins, and Muriel Miguel in the Native Earth production of *The Unnatural and Accidental Women*. Photo by Nir Bareket.

The loving gesture of being named and hugged by her mother eases Rebecca back into the corporeal world as her mother fades to the spirit world with the other women. As Bamford rightly argues, the horrific killing of the barber on stage is "immediately subordinate to the romance structure, for as soon as the barber is dead, Aunt Shadie and Rebecca look at each other for the first time" (154). Many critics focus their analysis on this climactic scene. Bamford argues that "Rebecca does not become monstrous in taking revenge on the barber," in part because "the killing is not a premeditated act: it is spontaneous" (153). Because Clements has the discovery of the mother's braid occur right before Rebecca's sudden desire to shave the barber and moments before her complete transformation into the aggressor it is difficult to support the claim that it is not premeditated. Clements has Rebecca implicitly plan the revenge murder in the moments between the discovery of the braids and the murderous act itself.

Clements forces us to make sense of the symbolism of the deceased women's braids as they relate to Rebecca's intentions, the spirit world, and the

murder itself. Interestingly, Bamford argues that because Rebecca is "seeking her mother, rather than her mother's killer," and that she is acting in
"self-defense," the structure of the revenge defies "the artfulness of the revenge, in classical and Renaissance drama" which is usually "a source of
self-conscious pride for the revenger" (153). I agree with Bamford's statement that the "design of the revenge is providential" (153). Yet the gradually
increasing power that the women show over the "real" world of the play is
Clements's way of ensuring that we understand this final murder as an act
which was enhanced by the presence of the spirit women.

While I agree with Bamford that the play suggests a divinely orchestrat-
ed event, I am focusing on the role of the deceased women and their bodies
in this play and I am arguing that the "divine order" is also framed here as
residing in the bodies of the ghost women characters. Clements's play offers
the audience one example of the power of the ghost bodies to have a defini-
tive role in the present because it demonstrates the ghost women's increasing
ability to affect the real world. Their role, as a collective, matriarchal spectral
chorus offers a particular cosmology that links the living with the deceased.

The conflation of dead and living bodies is given extra weight through
the Biblical allusion that concludes the play. The final scene evokes the idea
of transubstantiation through the body and blood of Christ. The Last Supper
in the biblical narrative is the last day of Jesus Christ's life on earth, while in
Clements's play this final scene is the deceased women's "first supper," in that
they are free, by way of the murder of the serial killer, from the limbo they
were in. Their celebratory moment in the spirit world is a consequence of
Rebecca's brave actions to kill the murderer. Bamford suggests that "in contrast
to most romances in the Western tradition, it is also particularly and specifically a world created by a mother's desire" (155). To me, what is interesting
in the final scenes of the play is how the transformation/transmogrification,
indeed even the allusion to transubstantiation, slips seamlessly from the mur-
derer/intended victim to the mother's (dis)embodied power and is conflated
with Rebecca's body. This synthesis of living and dead bodies fittingly concludes the play as Clements (re)animates the (un)dead. Rebecca is assisted
from the spirit world to protect herself and, like a good hunter, puts an end

to the killer's life with one clean incision. Clearly Clements wants audiences to consider the notion that redress for the missing and murdered Aboriginal women in Canada may be assisted by traditional knowledge, the power of matriarchal community, and perhaps even the spirit world.

TRANSCENDING HORROR

It is with trepidation, regret, and fascination that I have tried to tease out some of the complexities involved in this one Canadian theatrical representation of murder. I set it within a contemporary context by locating and examining performative events that remind us of the missing and murdered Aboriginal women in Canada. Morbid thoughts of my own potential victimization prompt the urgency with which I turn my attention to these issues. We are surrounded by the hypervisibility of murder in social media and on the news. This fixation is evident also in the popularization of murder-themed television shows. In addition, the prevalence of school shootings and evidence of extreme police brutality in America reveal and remind us how common and insidious murder is in North America. However, this Canadian play, like the February 14th gatherings, the REDress installation, and the Walking With Our Sisters ceremony/installation, offers nuanced and politicized ways of revising such victim narratives. In addition, by staging what might have been going on in the lives of the women and bringing the audience into the murder scene without offering the spectacle of their murders, the missing and murdered women are given a crude form of redress through fiction.

Clements's play and these commemorative events and exhibitions offer a cosmology that inextricably connects the bodies of living and dead Aboriginal women. Clements and other Aboriginal artists are seeking to offer deeply nuanced representations of the gendered and racialized aspects of murder in Canada by using key props, ceremonial elements, ritualized spaces, naming, and other commemorative gestures. These diverse creative responses fill the void left by the missing bodies, occluded narratives of what happened to the murdered and missing women, and the absence of a national response to the recommendations written for and about missing and murdered women in Canada. I am asking readers to consider the conflation of the terms murdered and missing and how we commemorate or mourn these lives. I am asking readers to consider the agency involved in the Facebook "Am I Next?" movement, to appreciate the kinesthetic and participatory act of ceremonial marches to the sites where women have fallen victims, to notice how hanging red dresses in public spaces engages the gaze and asks participants to imagine the murdered and missing women's bodies, to understand the complex synaesthetic elements of the installation that includes engaging in the kinesthetic experience of "walking with our sisters," and finally to look at how we witness a play where spectral characters, slides representing actual coroners' reports, and a prop ask us to bring missing and murdered women to life. Such plays, marches, and installations contribute to social justice, empowerment, and resistance, as they ultimately offer a celebration of our agency, despite the prevalence of Aboriginal women being murdered in Canada. It is through witnessing such performative events that the synaesthetic and kinesthetic links between these abject murdered Aboriginal women's bodies, the absent bodies of missing women, and our own visceral existence are made manifest.

TRICKSTERS AND CREATURES AND GHOSTS, HO-LEE! INTIMATIONS/IMITATIONS OF THE SACRED

DANIEL DAVID MOSES

I: AN APOLOGIA, SORTA

I was going to begin by digging into one particular pun, but since I know most folks don't normally waste time with wordplay, puns being "the lowest form of humour," I'll have to instead go into why I often look their way. Why aren't they a waste of my life's short time?

Perhaps it's because as a "playwright" I've found it useful for my craft to take the first of the two words joined in my job description—and in the second syllable of the word "wordplay" itself—as a suggestion or direction or instruction. Is that weird? "Wordplay" might well be a suggestive description of just what we get up to when we wright plays, as long as we don't forget about the performers.

The word "wright," as a contrast, with that "w" that looks almost antique in this age of information, has, as a verb, implications of "making" and "building," of connection to the work human hands did do to, among other things, create this place, this space and time in history where we, at least in the cities of Canada, are more safe than ever before and where the challenges of the rest of nature are, at least for the moment, distant.

(Yes, most of us do know of but haven't yet allowed ourselves to really believe in the dilemma of climate change, or how else did Stephen Harper and his old-time economic-religion—same as it always was, though it's sometimes been fashioned as free-trade capitalism—ever get a hold of the reins of power for nigh on a decade?)

The word "wright," even snuggled into the word "playwright," does feels a bit, well, *outré*, old-fashioned, especially if you've hitched your wagon to time's trusty (but somehow rusty) arrow and are being pulled ecstatically into the future. (Is that particular "arrow" image, like the also old-fashioned but useful defining categories of "Comedy" and "Drama," Greek in origin? I neglected to see the movie *300*.)

Time's arrow just doesn't seem connected to our North American cultural versions of the image/tool . . .

On the other hand, if you're like me, who believes without reason in what he doesn't understand, instinct or reflex or unanalyzed experience, particularly when, surprisingly, for one instance, physicists say that, at least in the understanding of the mathematics they use to describe reality, time doesn't exist. I do find that it takes me a conscious effort to be aware of time, to ask and then to, say, remember, what day it is. More and more so, as I get older, yes, we will all lose our wits, but the perception's always been there. I have to check my watch and/or my calendar when the flow of the reality I'm trying to come to grips with is just so present and tense. No time like the present, indeed.

So what meaning then does the word "history" get, if time doesn't exist? Traditional First Nations cultures, some of them at least, the ones who have found the English phrase "from time immemorial" useful to keep in their quiver, with their understandings formed from the circles and the repeated cycling of nature, night and day, the seasons, the rhythms of their own bodies, with their cultural ordering of it into four or more directions, other sorts of arrows—is it the mathematicians and physicists who call them "vectors"?— also see time as mostly circular and history, that exercise in memory, as a sort of spiralling path. The past isn't distant, isn't forgettable for them in their traditional mindset as it is for those folks riding on the mainstream with their eyes on the future, that unseen set of events over the also distant horizon, the one that just goes on forever, infinitely.

(If this is making your head hurt, consider that one traditional people in central Asia, the Tuva, the *National Geographic* reports, believe quite reasonably that because they can't see the future, that it must be behind them. It is a lack, not having eyes in the back of our heads. Which puts the past for these folks in front because it seems, at least through memory, to be quite visible. It all makes sense if you're connected to your body. Which brings to mind the image I believe Marshall McLuhan, the media pundit back in the 1970s, used to describe western culture, the image of driving a car with a blacked-out windshield, navigating fiercely forward all the while looking for guidance in a rear-view mirror. Am I right in recalling that he found the situation alarming?)

But perhaps the past isn't quite present either for those of us with minds that turn with the circles. The past has already happened, after all. It's more like it's just a step to the side, events you make out in the periphery of your mind, which is perhaps another way of thinking about remembering. It's a reality that is always there for consideration, though as the spirals of the years you live extend and bend back, it does develop some layers, some foldings, the details are harder to remember, more eternal than infinite. The pentimento of one's life?

(I'm remembering the way Monique Mojica described the technique she used in composing or compiling her show, *Chocolate Woman Dreams the Milky Way*, as inspired by the creation of molas, the textiles Guna women wear and the way they are layered and related to stories. Perhaps it's a cultural object as the tangible embodiment of the conception of time folding?)

Now that I am considering it, this circular sort of thinking is an inclination I first was aware of after sampling the published works by the aforementioned Professor Marshall McLuhan that were inexplicably included in the library of my high school in Caledonia, Ontario. None of the classes we took in English made use of the books, but perhaps it was the influence of Mr. Peter Hill, the one teacher in that school who was also from my reserve community. But I know I found the way McLuhan had of using language in a punny way to succinctly compress his big ideas—for instance, it's said he didn't mind the typo that turned his phrase "the medium is the message" into the image "the medium is the massage" because it was a poetic way of saying it's the physical or experiential characteristics of a medium in communicating that can influence society—was something I found to my taste or understanding.

The pun, then, may well often appear to be a low form of humour. It's a medium of the body, the mouth, tongue, and breath, and a bit of the slippage of the mind inside the slop of the brain, so how could you get more basic than the body, lower down than that? But that also means, punningly, that being closer to the ground, it's more grounded, more real, more feet planted on the soil. That is how we dance in traditional cultures, feet on the dirt, shifting around a circle, none of that unnatural or at least immodest leaping toward the stars for us. (My friend Lib Spry tells me the Royal Winnipeg Ballet's *Going Home Star*, which just passed through Kingston on its cross-country tour, mistakenly uses the north star not to find the direction home but as a destination in itself.) So perhaps it's even closer to the roots of things, more rooted and even more radical in the sense of truthful.

Which might explain the value of humour itself. The surprise of it, the something out of joint, the nonsense, darkness, or delight, irony, as just a way to restate in a non-ponderous tone the shifty nature of truth or reality. Maybe.

II: A PRELIMINARY INVESTIGATION

Here's the pun where all this questioning began. It's one that perhaps only I perceive, a pun that I'd be surprised if the author intended, but one that he'd likely like, if I know him at all, and I think, as it is evidence of his talent or instinct, should be credited to the man.

Mr. Tomson Highway's play *Dry Lips Oughta Move to Kapuskasing* includes a character named Creature Nataways. (The word "creature" is rich, indicating something created, usually an animal, not a human being, often something scary or somehow "other." Who makes such creations?) I started remembering the character Creature lately, played by the actor Erroll Kinistino in the play's first production at Theatre Passe Muraille, all those years ago, always surprised or astonished or offended, always having to exclaim or otherwise say:

Ho-lee! Ho-lee. Ho-lee? Ho-lee . . .

In the repetition, the meaning of the word shifts in my hearing from the mere exclamation of astonishment "ho-lee" to the physical description "hole-y" to the metaphysical "holy." The "not understood" becomes the "imperfect" becomes the "sacred" and the character Creature almost a prophet in the play's wilderness. And we all by this time know in our collective retrospection of that distant but still resonant theatrical event, such a creature or archetype might have been taking on the guise or at least the spirit of a trickster, Weesageechak or Nanabozo or Raven or . . .

I've been hearing this "holy" meaning of the word persistently, ever since I started thinking about the question of what we might be up to as First Nations writers as we try to wright plays, try to make sense of our places in the world, try to insist on our human locations even here where our folks had been pushed to the eddies or the dead zones of what those in the mainstream imagine as the current of the culture or history.

This hearing, this thinking is occurring to me in the context of another persistent idea I once read—I'm one of those who as a kid searched in books for ideas and experience—by some Elder, whose identity I didn't note, something that has become one of my mottos. That Elder advised something along the lines of *Right where you are, kiddo—that's the centre of the world.* The centre of anyone's own world, certainly, is the place one can be and act and act out and perform with integrity.

That Elder's advice came back to me a few years later, years ago when I encountered a fellow student artist, the now late J.S., a son of New York City, who invited me to come and see, even to try to live there in what he knew was "the center of the world!" (Or as we spell it "centre.") I knew even then that it might be true for him, but I think I was puzzled by the metaphor or image. A lover of scientific descriptions of reality, I wondered, if the world is round in three dimensions (not worrying at that moment about time as the fourth dimension, see physicists mentioned above), isn't the world's measureable centre miles beneath our feet, full of heat and ponderous pressure, a place no creature like us might be able to survive? In my imagination, young poet J.S. quotes the Kander and Ebb song, the one Frank Sinatra sang. In my mind's eye, he sings, though I know in reality he could not hold a note. The phrase

"If I can make it there, I'm gonna make it anywhere" sounds in his rendition not like a celebration but a dare. Can you play by these rules? (He ended up not a poet but the editor of *Arts and Antiques* magazine, bringing the "Helga" paintings of Andrew Wyeth to broader attention.) I did try to rise to his challenge for a summer but NYC, in that period a struggling city, covered with graffiti, in the summer sweltering under a piss-yellow sky, wasn't the centre of the world for me, though I did discover and delight there, despite the humidity, in the works of Elizabeth Bishop and Joe Orton and Preston Sturges . . .

Holy. It could be the word only comes to my mind because I grew up in the Anglican Church, was a good Christian kid, had all that language of ceremony and story washed over me in my formative years. It may be my particular reflex or instinct, not necessarily something other First Nations writers might experience, though I know a lot of us have had similarly the benefits and oftentimes the deficits of that particular offering of colonization.

This iteration of "ho-lee," coming to me as it did from a Tomson Highway play, plays noted for their combination of humour and earthiness, of course might also just be a theatrical short form of a more down-to-earth, less literary exclamation. I'm suggesting the phrase "holy shit" (I think of that phrase as a coinage of the sixties, something a flower child might say), but even that expression, with its contrasting combination of the sublime and the base, teases us, reminds us of puns between the multisyllabic categories of the eschatological and the scatological. Which one is it that's the study of death, judgment, and the final destiny of the soul and mankind and which the study of obscene literature, particularly that focused on excrement? I want to be sure which is which before I take many more steps, although perhaps it's just the contrast that is telling. All of which is to say, we still seem to be in the territory, ever so glancingly, of the sacred.

Holy. You repeat a word enough times and its meaning starts to come loose, to drift and shift. Finally, eventually this "holy" word moves to the state in your mind of the h-o-l-e-y holy, something full of holes, that fractured thing, but even there the obsessive yearning toward the sacred still holds. Oh, it comforts you, it comforts me, that Leonard Cohen has the words in his song "Anthem," "There is a crack in everything / That's how the light gets in."

How else might we access the light? There are conventions in art and life, protocols inherited within and with our cultures, those of us who have more than one inheritance, that point us in the bright direction, evocative words or sets of gestures that can help us call the illumination forth. Ceremonies of various sorts.

(One of the most important books for me when I was just out of school and struggling to begin as a poet and could only afford to buy and read used books was an already yellowing paperback I found in a bin in a store on Bloor Street West beyond Runnymede: *Masked Gods, Navaho and Pueblo Ceremonialism* by Frank Waters. I perceived it and remember it as being one half anthropological introduction to those southwest cultures and, more importantly for me, one half a description of how their great ceremonies were evocations and embodiments of their creation stories. The reason for taking days of seasonal time from one's life to perform such events suddenly made a sort of sense to me that my own weekly hour or so experience in an Anglican church as a child hadn't made clear. What would I learn from it now if I had the time to go back and read it again at my more advanced age?)

But of course it's my playwright's light mind that for the moment is reconsidering something dark hiding there in plain sight in my own quotidian culture as well: that theatre world joke or superstition or taboo, the one against ever wishing someone "good luck" before an opening performance. (As if we needed luck, really, having been so well rehearsed—but that's a different issue.) "Break a leg!" we say instead, claiming, I've heard as one explanation, it's short for "break a legend and make room for a new one." (And I love the dark historical joke version that's come along in First Nations theatre circles: "Wound a knee!") Or the even more persistent, more uncanny custom of never speaking aloud, perhaps even never consciously putting into print the proper name of the Scottish Play.

Clearly we still feel or believe words have power and that power might include, perhaps, tempting powers even greater, the fates, the gods, one particular jealous entity. We're so aware of being individual selves we project that state of existence onto the world and believe other selves are there—a more comforting assumption than the one that the world isn't so particular or particulated, so singular, that its physics and flow, its movement toward entropy, lacks any awareness. That habit or faith or belief hangs on though none of it makes sense to the rational part of us, that trusted but limited understanding. But it feels entirely necessary in the living present moment.

A weird moment. I'm watching a program on the Public Television Network about the development of monotheism among the Jews. Mention is made of the word or name of their god, usually rendered all in the capital letters Y-H-W-H, four consonants. I remember that I've heard some of this before, that even without vowels, without their breath and/or spirit, the name might be pronounced "Yahweh." But of course it's not a word you would casually say out loud. It reminds me of the still existing convention in English of writing the word "God," at least when referring to the idea of the Christian one, with a capital. The capital letters and the mysteriously missing vowels and the unheard living voices they usually provide move it in the direction of the sacred. Them being missing is a sort of cultural vacuum, perhaps, that our human nature or imagination abhors.

Consider one of my own unexamined habits in my playwright's workaday, a habit that might and usually does appear as simply being attentive to the format for scripts, the "copyscripts" I was given by the Playwrights Guild. I know that I'm almost ready to begin to write, to create something new, when I start putting the format onto a page, typing the names of the characters, all in caps, capital letters, centring them in a column on a description page, a page that's an introduction to the as-yet unwritten play. It is, perhaps, my intent in having those front pages of the manuscript written out with the characters' names, with the play's title, with the setting description as well, with my name and address and maybe even my copyright noted, only the number of pages not yet defined, that all that apparent business-y materialistic clarity might call the play more easily out of non-existence, out of some other dimension into this one.

In that moment, watching that documentary, those character names in capital letters in my manuscripts, like the name of the Jewish god also written in capitals, seemed to me to be numinous.

III: RUNNING OFF IN ALL FOUR OR MORE DIRECTIONS

Now that I think of it, the laughter that long ago night in the Epicure marked a still important difference.

I had been to see a performance of *Jessica*, the play that Linda Griffiths and Maria Campbell had created at Paul Thompson's suggestion, adapting Campbell's autobiographical book *Halfbreed*, the women's co-authorship a cross-cultural and personal struggle they later documented in *The Book of Jessica*. Does that make it an evening in the late 1980s? I was probably in the company of other artists connected with Native Earth Performing Arts. We were sitting with one of the actors from *Jessica*, having a post-performance drink.

Was it Graham Greene or Tom Jackson? Probably Greene, who told us with some puzzlement and definitely humour about an issue that had come up in rehearsals. The story of the play is embodied, enacted by characters both human and supernatural, including mythic animal spirits, Bear, Coyote, Crow, and, if I'm remembering right, even a Unicorn. So it definitely braids different spiritual traditions together with action from the contemporary material world. The trouble for the rehearsals had been to get the white actors to commit to being those beasts, even though, as theatrical characters, they weren't in any way bestial. Or maybe it was the spiritual quality they weren't connecting with? The Native actors had not been able to understand why the white guys couldn't quite make that imaginative leap, suspend their disbelief. Hey, there are ghosts in Shakespeare. It's an art form at its best all about make-believe. Hey, at least with these animal spirits you didn't have to play dead. Why would ghosts have been easier for them? We probably had at least one more beer.

But then around that time, I too was probably dealing with a similar failure of artistic courage. I was hesitating to write *Coyote City*, my first produced play, the piece that introduced me to the Toronto theatre scene as more than a Native Earth board member. I was hesitating because I had realized it was a ghost story. Was I still too much under the influence of my university education, my graduate school creative-writing program, still crediting our materialist scientific culture? I didn't believe in ghosts, never had, even before grad school. I had attended church regularly as a kid—my folks thought it would be good for me—and was regularly presented there with the idea of at least a Holy Ghost or Spirit. But it seems now it all went right in one ear to disappear, as a lot of ideas did.

And then, after all that further education, including at least one physics course (I found the language of that branch of science had a sort of poetry), I knew there was no objective proof that ghosts existed and I was comforted that I myself had never encountered one.

But I needed to work with this Nez Percé story, *Coyote and the Shadow People*, this story about the limits of the power of love that my friend Lenore Keeshig-Tobias had brought into our Indian writers' circle. The story had got to me. "Can love conquer death?" it asked hopefully. I felt the story was true, or at least as true as, say, Orpheus and Eurydice, the ancient story other educated folks would later keep telling me it reminded them of. Ghosts, it seemed, only existed in the distant past, but I wanted to tell the story for now or at least, as it turned out, "just yesterday," and it seemed to me that I would need a ghost character to bring the story to life. And then, beside the cash register in the Occult Book Store—you don't need to know why I was there—I found a stack of small paperback copies of a volume entitled *Phone Calls from the Dead*. I picked it up. The book contained something like a hundred anecdotes about folks who'd received that ultimate long-distance call. All these people had had encounters with spirits and had had them via that foundation of the information age, Alexander Graham Bell's baby, the telephone. (I remembered McLuhan again, his suggestion that the experience the phone allowed, even though we're now so accustomed to it, the hearing of a disembodied voice, was for those first telephoners in essence as spooky as a seance.) I took the book as the evidence I needed, the proof of the social if not the physical existence of ghosts, and was able to write.

Once the play was up and running, friends and acquaintances and folks who just knew I was the playwright started to come forward and confess—often in hushed voices, yes—but they came out of the ghost closet and told me their own experiences of the supernatural. My own lack of experience, I decided, couldn't be a measure of the wider world's truth. Clearly, I was just not tuned in to that dimension of social reality, so I had to take my solace from the stories my fellow travellers told and from metaphor.

How else do you find or define the holy, the sacred, the morally true? In plays being written in the midst of what's largely a secular culture, it seems we've lost what the Greeks used their plays for, that shared ceremony, that acting out of the values and contradictions of their social world. We all have our glowing screens in our separate bed- and living rooms without much sense of our fellows unless there's a laugh track, and we have to be suspicious of just how real that canned reaction can be. But I am always looking for it, I realize, by instinct or training, and with more than my usual expectations as I hunt and gather through the broader culture, especially in the work of my fellow First Nations theatre colleagues. I look out for more ghosts, more spirits, even tricksters. I looked for other old stories that might need to be told to this modern world, and it seemed the trickster sort of spirits, as spotted and defined by anthropologists, were the easiest of these conventions to concoct theatrically for the mainstream audiences' delectation. They in their demo-cratic freedom tend to be uncertain about what they're allowed to believe in and even the most innocent expressions can give them doubts.

Maybe that's why, for instance, when my friend Lenore Keeshig (as she is named now) early on contributed a staging of a Nanabozo story, a section of the Ojibwe creation story that became the children's play *Quest For Fire: How The Trickster Brought Fire To The People*, that despite its focus on a trickster, it got only one short tour. But kids' plays mostly get ignored by adults any-way, so perhaps the piece, not being an introduction to some social issue with its trickster and animal characters and its—at least as I remember it—deft delight, has never been remounted. Lenore, respected poet and storyteller, coulda been a theatrical contender . . .

Of course, a lot of trickster stories still have to be bowdlerized when pre-sented for mainstream audiences. The earthy truths of human life get removed or reinterpreted. In Lenore's storytelling circles, they tell of a trickster story that told, among other things, why the anus is wrinkled, that it was revised for mainstream consumption to explain the thick skin of the elbow: Lenore wondered if this was the origin of the oft-heard phrase about the fellow who couldn't tell his ass from his elbow.

But that prejudice didn't stop Billy Merasty as he developed his play *Fireweed*, the early versions lifting a story about a two-spirited street kid in Winnipeg into realms where spirits, not social workers, are looking out for him on his journey home to deal with a church and abuse, tragedy and a lost love. Did the last version of the piece I remember reading ever get produced? It included the central character re-enacting, in spiritual contrast to the desperate Christianity of the kid's mother, a Weesageechak story. The hero defeats a Weetigo with the help of a weasel who ambushes the monster by invading its body via its asshole, travelling through the monster's intestines to cut the creature's throat, a comic embodiment of the hero travelling to the underworld meme (the same sort of venture I had been engaged by with *Coyote City*). Perhaps that intestinal design challenge is why we haven't seen Billy's play again?

If we allow ourselves to admit such traditional narratives into our shared consciousness, the leftover ghosts that haunt a few mainstream stages suddenly seem quotidian.

In Floyd Favel Starr's *Lady of Silences*, he found another way to think of the ghostly. His street Indian characters—a man, his three sometime girlfriends, and a master of ceremonies—all seem to be dead Indians (the kind General Sheridan preferred) and at times they are even somehow conscious of it. The action they perform, their haunting, takes place not in the real world but in the sacred space of the stage, or maybe the place myth creates in the imagination. For Favel Starr's Indians, the stage has become a limbo where they have to re-enact their characters and the performance we have come to witness as if attending a ceremony. Perhaps they are not exactly "ghosts." Does the phrase "lost souls" work? By repeatedly performing the story of a murder of a white woman, represented only by a white dress (no white actors were forced to leap imaginatively in the production of this play), by repeating their anger and racist resentment and sexual jealousy, these Indians articulate their self-hatred, their internalized racism. Are they also performing a penance, if only for having been at some past point living Indians?

Part of the deep mystery of the cycling action of the play: did the murder even happen? The only proof is that white dress—despite the knife, no blood is in evidence—which seems to perhaps represent whiteness more than any real woman victim. One almost expects that white dress to be worn by the Virgin herself at some point and she, of course, is no Indian. Our Native women can only look sideways at it as they retell their shared stories of the murder. They also look with a longing for what they are no longer, though a monologue by one of the women in the invented persona of Watatoosis evokes an ideal or earlier age of heroic women warriors, reminding us of a cultural vitality that has been lost.

(The play that made most clear for me the theatrical and philosophical possibilities of non-linear time was Ben Cardinal's *Generic Warriors and No-Name Indians*. Look elsewhere for my discoveries in the essay "A Bridge Across Time.")

The supernatural has a hard time appearing on stage in those stories that seem to take place on or nearer our more contemporary material streets. Like time's arrow, those streets run through downtown history and only in the bad or sad parts of that urban construction is there space for the spiritual.

Though Yvette Nolan's *Annie Mae's Movement* explores the real-life story and death of committed Aboriginal community activist Anna Mae Aquash, a Micmac woman who worked with the American Indian Movement (AIM) in the early 1970s, a piece of recent American history, the play presents us with a stage as spare and otherworldly as the one Favel Starr used to suggest limbo. The play's narrative momentum feels filmic, shifting through a montage of two-hander, he-and-she scenes, suggesting both the thriller conventions through which the mystery of Aquash's murder might likely be explored as well as the research and facts we expect from documentary cinema, that ideally objective mode that might give some sort of justice to the murdered woman.

However, the play has moments when these braided strands of materialist genre separate and a dark spirit, an apparition, almost enters the contemporary narrative through the break. Perhaps it is the rugaru, that North American version of the werewolf, an omen of chaos, mentioned early in the play by a secondary character? In Nolan's version, the creature seems almost the embodiment of western culture's misogyny that Aquash faced coming from both American government institutions and the warriors of AIM. At this distance the apparitions of that Aboriginal spirit and the final evocation of the names of women artists and culture warriors force one to wonder just what was Indian about the Movement if the women weren't welcome into and necessary to it?

Ian Ross's *fareWel* tells a story at first clearly material in its dilemma. A small group of Manitoba Indians relies on their reserve's social assistance made unreliable because of an apparently corrupt and definitely absent chief. The sad situation, though, is presented as a social comedy and despite scenes taking place on the forlorn steps of a church, the presence of a credible spiritual dimension to the play's world seems unlikely.

But then among the play's Indians appears the character Sheldon, nicknamed "Nigger," probably because of his dark skin, though as the play progresses, the moniker may also be appropriate because of his social standing. I regularly need to suggest to my predominantly white middle-class students that they get past their reflexive fear of the "N"-word and consider the playwright's choice of the powerful name as more than a slip or "bad taste." The character Sheldon is always the beggar, making do, creating smokes from cigarette butts (tobacco no longer a sacred medicine), the poorest of the poor Indians the play presents.

For all that sad struggle, he's funny and sweet, almost a clown, and so accident-prone it seems inevitable in the play's action that the news arrives, a horrible punchline to his rising action, that's he's been killed. But then he comes back, resurrects I would suggest like Jesus, and becomes in that reappearance the embodiment of a sort of holiness. Is this what's called a "Holy Fool"? It's played as a trickster-ish joke but perhaps that *coup de théâtre* is a cunning strategy to make the eruption of the miraculous palatable for our times? The play did win the Governor General's Literary Award.

As did Kevin Loring's *Where the Blood Mixes*, a meditation on the aftermath of residential schools focused through the friendship of two men who are survivors. Most of the play's action derives from a local bar, but that material location is presented surreally as if it's at the bottom of a river, under the currents, an otherworldly, under-worldly staging most of the audience might just accept at first as a designer whim rather than a spiritual context, until the holy place of the stream in the landscape and drama of the play gradually becomes clear. The men's relationship is written to be played for more of that sort of sad comedy—poverty, generosity, fatigue—we encountered in *fareWel*. One of the men is even nicknamed "Mooch," if the teasing presentation of a materially dysfunctional Indian residential-school graduate weren't clear enough. It's the revelation that his real name is "Edgar" near the end of the play that brings into focus the social reality beyond the cunning, clichéd presentation.

Yes, our First Nations plays find strategies to evoke freeing spirits or ghosts despite the material world that's come to surround us. Consider for yourself the feminist ghosts of Marie Clements's *The Unnatural and Accidental Women*, or the mystery of revised pop-culture Indians in Drew Hayden Taylor's *Dead White Writer on the Floor*, or the clown-like, tricksterish Wooden Indians of Joseph Dandurand's *Please Do Not Touch the Indians*, or the unquiet child spirit of Tara Beagan's *In Spirit*, or how Keith Barker's *The Hours That Remain* turns a mystery genre sort of disappearance into a situation that's both the spiritually mysterious and politically personal. I could go on, but—

IV: "Z" IS FOR ZOMBIE

I hunt and gather stories and writing-craft technique along the margins, that liminal cultural wilderness, that place in need of negotiation and creativity that exists between my assumptions about what makes up human, humane, sacred life, and what the broader culture offers up, sometimes on sale but too often at inflated prices. I try to make clear choices as someone who was brought up on the Six Nations lands in southern Ontario, with its mix of Iroquoian practicality and old-fashioned Christian charity.

At moments lately I have realized that the effort of finding things of human value in that confusing, undefined territory, the free market, tries my patience. All that talk about creativity and innovation (sometimes innovation that even escapes story, falling into a sort of cultural coma) and then we're asked to buy into the surfaces of the exotic or the chaotic or, yes, another remake.

Me, I don't mind convention or tradition. I take comfort in and strength from it; the old stories are where we've been, all the while recognizing that there do have to be new stories, not just seven or twenty-three, as the literary version of an urban legend has it, because we're moving into, as the proverbial Chinese curse would have it, interesting times. Our various visions of the world are being forced by our growing scientific knowledge, our technology, and what passes for a world's economy into something singular, a clear kaleidoscope, a world that's as poly-ocular as good art or a mystic and we don't quite yet know how to take it and not be terrified or lost.

Or maybe I'm just getting old and don't have the energy to engage with the latest trends. Is it being grumpy to have gotten to the point where I only really want to engage with the work of my fellow First Nations artists fulfilling Riel's vision? (And some few others, too. Guillermo del Toro has more than repaid my attention this last decade.) Is it being a grump to want to engage only with those using an aesthetic I might learn something from? There's only so much time left—

But I realize, looking sideways, that I've been spending a lot of psychic energy over the last decade, at least, resisting the pop-culture imagery of, for one instance, zombies. (I could also complain about smart serial killers or the super-hero spawn of Stan Lee or any and all of the unlikely, unconnected memes taking up cultural time and space.) Zombies have become so omnipresent and so drained of any meaningful cultural impact that a character muttering "Brains!" is a *Simpsons* satirical punchline.

This fantasy embodiment of the unconquerable reality of death, the territory Mary Shelley's mad scientist Victor Frankenstein explored almost two hundred years ago, that early science fiction, is still a strange land in which we're the doomed strangers, despite all our growing knowledge, so we try to force zombies into other genres as probes. Will those other scenarios help us make more sense of our puzzlement? (As I punctuated the above sentence, *Pride and Prejudice and Zombies* was about to open in cinemas . . .)

I admit I was witness to the first apparition of the contemporary version of the zombie, was a student when George A. Romero's B picture, *Night of the Living Dead*, got screened in a Curtis Lecture Hall at York University. I do remember being thrilled by the way the film shocked and awed our adolescent audience with images both grotesque and darkly comic and by the way the film ended up, having the hero and survivor of the zombies' stumbling attack, a black man, mistakenly and glibly killed off as if he was part of the film's problem of the unquiet dead. Suddenly the cheap-looking black-and-white images made political as well as aesthetic sense and the movie itself shifted from a dark entertainment to become an inarticulate but political allegory, Black versus White, not just concerned with life and death but America's history of slavery. Now that's something we living couldn't just rest in peace about.

"But Daniel," asks my friend Lib Spry, "what about *Brébeuf's Ghost*?" We've both just seen different performances of Yvette Nolan's mounting of my monster play, not only for the size of the cast, back at York University, my alma mater. "A Wendigo's not the same as a zombie." "Okay, okay," she says encouragingly. My cannibal priest, I try to explain, thanks to the communion ceremony, is not only hungry for flesh. Like the fur trade he was one harbinger for, like a strange creature in service to the economy instead of to his fellows and their lives, he's also there to consume the local culture and its meanings, its future and its soul.

Pride and Prejudice and Zombies? Maybe it'll be fun, maybe it will surprise or provide some memorable images, but I won't hold my breath. Doesn't it feel like the mainstream culture is stuck in the muck, spinning its tires, staring with fascination into the rear-view mirror? If we think the zombies are chasing us, shouldn't we be putting it into park and getting out and getting ready for flight or fight?

There's got to be a better way out of this story.

#MYRECONCILIATIONINCLUDES . . . JUST DANCE!

DAVID GEARY

1. TWO LEFT FEET—DANCING IN THE STREET— SAGE AGAINST THE MACHINE

I thought this article was finished. I thought that it would be about how I'd found in Indigenous dance-theatre some of the most compelling performances I'd witnessed, and I thought I knew why.

But there was something missing. Something I couldn't put my finger on. The irritation that the oyster was trying to turn into a pearl. And let me say now in the interests of full disclosure that I have two left feet, sweat profusely on the dance floor, flailing around like a tranquilized giraffe, and that writing about dancing makes me sweat even more. It's not my thing. I love the story of the dancer who, asked what her dance meant, replied, "If I could tell you, why would I bother dancing it?" So I should've just left it at that, and not taken on this commission, but . . . but . . . Why was it so much fun to be invited to our neighbours' on New Year's Eve to embrace their Wii and *Just Dance*, so that my wife, boys, and I could get hysterical trying to dance along with (Creator, forgive me) Rihanna, Taylor Swift, and the Tetris dance?

But back to the missing link, the missing dance step. I found it in the foyer of our local Parkgate, BC, library when I was confronted by a "#myreconciliationincludes" booth with an invitation to pin up my pledge beside a copy of the Truth and Reconciliation Report. There were also Indigenous books. I flicked through *The Winter We Danced*, published by the Kino-nda-niimi Collective. How could I have forgotten the dancing in the streets for Idle No More? The revival of performance and ceremony as protest and celebration, the chance to bring a community together in action, dancing and singing in rituals the colonizers had, once upon a time, banned. The book's dedication is:

> . . . For those who danced . . .
> and are still dancing (5).

In this spirit, I'd like to dedicate this article to all those who danced and sang during the Idle No More movement, woke up a Nation, and continue to do so. Also, to the tipuna/ancestors who danced before me, who dance with me, and encourage me to dance on . . . to revel in the joy of the body in motion, moving to the music, keeping spirits up, light on two left feet . . . set to dance on to . . .

2. WHAT'S LEFT OF US

> 14th Annual Full Circle Talking Stick Festival, produced by Margo Kane, February 2014: *What's Left of Us* by Justin Many Fingers (Blackfoot) and Brian Solomon (Métis-Anishinaabe).

A WHOOP, a CRY, two men try and ride one bike on stage but the scarf of one has wound around the spokes. The Trickster is in the house. This dance could end before it starts. Ambulances, X-Rays, Fractures, Plaster, Splints, Slings . . . broken legs, necks . . . the scarf still won't come free . . . This could be a tragedy! . . . They abandon the bike . . . make a joke of it . . . It's a comedy! . . . The dance goes on . . . to the soundtrack of a mother speaking of her love for her son . . . It's a love story . . . But these men are different . . . "Look, just look, you know you want to, look at my hand, SEE ME, see that I'm different from you, see my hand with no fingers, just the beginnings, or the ends, or stumps . . . " Disabled? Differently-abled? . . . How will I describe you? The fumble to find a word . . . "SEE ME! Be filled with fear, of the . . . the freak . . . the freakish . . . " What if we have to shake hands afterwards? Will it be awkward? I know, I'll just nod and smile.

The men dance on . . . Another mother's voice speaks of her love for her son . . . The men tell jokes. Dark jokes. One was convinced by his classmates to squirt ketchup on his hand in shop class so the substitute teacher would think he'd sawn his fingers off. She freaked out. Everyone cracked up. The other wore a baggy hoodie down over his hands so the bus driver asked, "What, you got no fingers?" And then the boy showed him exactly that. The bus driver was mortified, was so apologetic . . . "Sorry, sorry, sorry . . . " And we laugh with the boys, the men. "See me, look at me, see all of me, see what's left of us." And they dance, over their mothers' voices talking about how much they love their sons, and we love them too . . .

. . . and we love how in the post-show discussion Brian Solomon tells us that the bike, the offending Trickster bike, is the same one that almost ended his career in a previous life. And Justin Many Fingers laughs about his name, which is beyond irony, as he tells us how he rang Brian up to ask him to make the show—two-spirited First Nations dancers and makers with the same hands.

In the post-show discussion, an older Aboriginal woman wants the dancers to take the show North—every young person must see it. If only . . . if only it could dance on . . . dance back to the mothers, the mothers who the sons rang up and recorded their interviews for research. The mothers who have never met each other but seem to meld into one Mighty Mother of Love, and so the sons decide not to compose a score for the show but let their mothers' voices be the soundtrack to their lives.

"See me, feel me, don't look away and make me invisible . . . dance with me a little . . . here . . . in this moment." It's a universal plea for others to really see us, whoever we are. Otherwise . . . we don't exist.

But I believe all performers also need to really see, and engage with, their audiences, so all shows should have an audience discussion afterwards. Why? Because being talked at, or performed to, or danced in the general direction of, in the dark, for an hour or two, without a right of reply at the end, just isn't right. I like how on our Māori marae—our traditional meeting grounds—there's always a chance to respond, and not just clap politely, turn our mobiles back on, and hope the parking hasn't expired.

Okay, so maybe not after every show, but please can we have more post-show discussions, and/or chances to respond? It can be as simple as: "Please send us an email or post on our Facebook pages. We'd love to hear your responses to our show." After all, aren't we trying to start a conversation with our work, asking others to join our dance?

Similarly, pre-show, all the sponsors are acknowledged, so let's honour the Nations whose territories we are lucky enough to share. Aren't they, the First Peoples, the major sponsor of all of us? And let's not rattle them off like the health warnings for some snake oil sold by infomercials. Let's pause, and breathe, and pronounce their names right, and then take the opportunity for these Nations to say something about how they feel to have this show performed on their land. They may not want to turn up every night, but at least offer them free tickets and the opportunity. Start a conversation. Maybe they have people in their Nation who are interested in the performing arts, would like to learn more, would like to teach us about their songs, stories, and dances. At least ask what they'd like to say in the program about their home, the one we've moved into. It's common courtesy.

These days if I'm introducing a performance or panel, I acknowledge the Tsleil-Waututh, Squamish, and Musqueam peoples and their generosity for allowing us to share their lands; but I also ask that people take the time to read the Truth and Reconciliation Report. Or, at the very least, the first paragraph that ends with " . . . cultural genocide." Better still, have it all read to you by all those people who thought it important enough to record the entire report on YouTube: #ReadTheTRCReport.

3. TRANSMIGRATION

The Cultch (Vancouver East Cultural Centre), March 2015: Santee Smith and Kaha:wi.

On dances Norval Morrisseau—painter, shaman, drinker, dancer—POP! go the paparazzi cameras as he wheels and stumbles—POP!—not just another drunk Indian—POP!—drowning the spirits within him . . . POP! . . . as he finds feathers and flies . . . lets the paint fly and dances across the canvas floor . . . with Santee Smith (Kahnyen'kehàka—Mohawk Nation) and her Kaha:wi (Ga-HA-Wee) Dance Theatre.

Kaha:wi means "to carry" in the Mohawk language, and we are carried away by the dance and the design and the drama and the dream . . . not bogged down in naturalism, not trying to *talk* about our problems . . . but set free . . . so it's more about the spirit, and spiritual. The dance frees us to feel rather than think, 'cause who wants a lecture, right? If you got a message, send it by Western Union. The dance frees us to take giant leaps of faith to . . .

4. THE UBC POW-WOW, MARCH 2015

The first ever UBC First Nations Studies Student Association Pow-wow in the old Memorial gym, which the organizers were sweating bullets about. What if nobody comes? But the downstairs is packed so the floorboards shake beneath our feet, and the earth moves, and the dance and party goes on into the jingle-jangle morning. Who cares if it's not traditional to the west coast, that the pow-wow was a Plains thing? It's the new tradition . . . as old as . . .

5. BINGO!

I'm a winner! I finally get to see Tomson Highway's classic play, *The Rez Sisters*, at the Belfry in Victoria, October 2014, and I am moved by the power of his words; but what sticks with me most is the delightful dance of Waawaate Fobister as Nanabush, the Trickster as Bingomaster, who calls that someone's number is really up then dances on their grave. And then I jump a year forward to September 2015, and BINGO!, Tomson Highway—the man himself—sashays on stage at UBC to giggle as he addresses us as "Second Nations" for his "A Musical Lecture: Native Literature in Canada Today: Eechee-pooti-it Kimaamaa" (Cree translation: "Your Mother Has a Pointy Ass").

Tomson is the Trickster, mixing up moving stories from his life with the naughtiest jokes no white folks would get away with. One moment it's a dick joke, the next he's Mozart with delicate fingers dancing across the piano. Later, signing CDs, we joke about how once upon a time, in a past life, I interviewed him in New Zealand. He says he remembers me, but he's just being kind. He'd love to go back . . . if I can find the money . . . he recalls the haka . . .

6. KA MATE KA MATE

Ka mate, ka mate! (I die, I die!)
Ka ora, ka ora! (I live, I live!)
—Te Rauparaha

So begins the haka/dance that many identify with Māori and New Zealand. It was composed by Te Rauparaha, a rangatira/chief of the Ngāti Toa iwi/tribe, circa 1820, and later adopted by our national rugby team, the All Blacks: https://youtu.be/GkKfM70t7uE. They took it to the world, and now it's probably the most recognizable cultural product we have. I say product because it's in recent years been controversial, as Adidas, the sponsors of the All Blacks, have used it to promote their brand: https://youtu.be/JUiGF4TGI9w.

Is that cultural appropriation? Or should we be proud that it's out there, a sign that Māori didn't die out but dance on? Can it be both at the same time?

I find it's a great way to start a kōrero/conversation, which is why I perform it, teach around it, and encourage others to do it with me whenever I can. It's my small contribution to Indigenous performance in Canada. I taught it to the staff at my sons' elementary school. A teacher asked me, "Is this sacrilegious?" Good question. No, not if I tell them what it means, give some context, and acknowledge Te Rauparaha. I also clear up the misapprehension that all haka are "war dances," when there are many forms of haka for many different occasions. Here's one performed recently to honour the passing of a Māori teacher from my old high school: https://youtu.be/M6Qtc_zlGhc. And another that went "viral," featuring haka at a wedding and including the bride joining in: https://youtu.be/lhhedH6wK6I.

In Te Rauparaha's haka he celebrates beating death, as a war party set on killing him has been sent away by another chief (possibly a hairy/brave one). Te Rauparaha climbs up out of the darkness of the kumara/sweet potato pit he was hiding in, up into the light, composing and performing his haka as he goes. I see this as a powerful symbol for how Māori were almost wiped out but survived and are now on the rise. Surely, that's something worth dancing about. And here's your chance for a lesson from my distant cousin, Rico Gear: https://youtu.be/XPgB0CvNtoQ.

> Ka mate, ka mate! ka ora! ka ora! (I die! I die! I live! I live!)
> Ka mate, ka mate! ka ora! ka ora! (I die! I die! I live! I live!)
> Tēnei te tangata pūhuruhuru (This is the hairy/brave man)
> Nāna nei i tiki mai whakawhiti te rā (Who brought the sun and caused it to shine)
> Ā, upane! ka upane! (A step upward, another step upward!)
> Ā, upane, ka upane, whiti te rā! (A step upward, another . . . the Sun shines!)

7. JOIN THE ROUND DANCE

So what are we waiting for? An invitation to the dance, right? That's where it gets tricky. I'm an outsider. I don't want to join the dance and tread on someone's toes. Yeah, I'm Indigenous, but from another land. I'm still one of Tomson Highway's "Second Nations." So thank the Creator for Wab Kinew's round-dance flash-mob on George Stroumboulopoulos's CBC show, where Kinew invited not just George but all Canadians to be Idle No More and dance together: https://youtu.be/-bzO1YB0Cpw.

Let's all celebrate that Indigenous dance is thriving in various forms across the globe: in the streets and the sports fields, in theatres and studios, pow-wow grounds and Memorial gyms. But more than that, we're all peoples from different places, bringing our own unique steps and moves, songs and grooves (*cue lighters and glow sticks, drums and talking sticks, haka and pow wow, Trickster and treaties*), so roll off the couch, escape death by desk, turn the amp up to eleven, invite the neighbours before they call noise control, get your groove on, and let's learn to dance together.

8. *GOING HOME STAR—TRUTH AND RECONCILIATION*

Royal Winnipeg Ballet at Queen Elizabeth Theatre. Choreography
by Mark Godden, story by Joseph Boyden (Anishinaabe).

Sorry, it happened again . . . I thought I was finished . . . but since I started this
article there was an election in October 2015. The next night an Elder opened
the Vancouver Writers Festival with this: "I'd like to sing a traditional song,
join in if you know it, it's for a man called Stephen . . . Nah Nah Nah, Nah
Nah Nah Nah, Hey Hey Hey, Goodbye!" Trickster in the house! And then new
prime minister Justin Trudeau said he intended to honour all ninety-four calls
to action in the Truth and Reconciliation report, the National Arts Centre announced a new Department of Indigenous Theatre, and the Royal Winnipeg
Ballet brought *Going Home Star—Truth and Reconciliation* to Vancouver.

Before *Going Home Star*, a Musqueam drum group performs and welcomes us to the territory, at half time there is smudging by Elders—sage
against the machine. I ask an Elder what he thinks of the show. He confesses he
walked out after ten minutes . . . "I just couldn't get into it . . . but I heard from
the others that it got better and I wished I'd stayed." It's a shame—there's so
much to love, so much to chew on. Ballet is certainly a new language for many
of us to learn, but how heartening to see one that isn't about a dying swan or
a nutcracker, but instead sweeps us from the frivolous life of a hairdresser to
burning a residential school down—a scene met with cheers and applause.

I applaud the ambition; the design, the international troupe who throw
themselves into the work; the music of Christos Hatzis, Tanya Tagaq, Steve
Wood and the Northern Cree Singers . . . sure, there's some minor missteps
and confusion . . . but I didn't read the synopsis in the program so . . . maybe
it's just me . . . and most of all it's serious and provocative. It makes me want
to find other people who've seen it so I can argue for hours about what it all
means . . . It means the delicate dance of reconciliation has already begun.

SHE BEGINS TO MOVE
MICHELLE OLSON

So much of the past century has resulted in the disconnection to our sense of claimed space. Yet it has been all of the work that has come out of this hardship that has defined us.
—Margaret Grenier, "Carrying my Lineage Through Dance" 15

The theatre is a space/place where two entities meet. The audience comes into the space to sit and observe; the artist comes into the space to share and perform. It can seem like a simple enough exchange but the complexity of power, agency, gaze, and transformation always sits just below the surface. Each time those curtains come up it is unknown how it will all play out.

So let me set the scene:

The stage is black.

An Aboriginal woman steps out onto centre stage and faces the audience.

Light slowly fades up on the woman. The audience sees her. She can barely see them but senses their presence.

A beat for breath.

She begins to move.

This essay is about these brief moments. When the theatre goes black and the stage lights reveal the performer to audience, audience to performer. Whole histories inform this moment, the memories in our blood and bones sit with the audience and stand with the performer. The possibilities to be transformed are within reach for both the performer and audience. The option of staying entrenched in beliefs and retracing the lines of the status quo are there too. A performer or an audience can see these moments as a chance to build community or tear it apart.

BURDENS WE CARRY

I start this essay with a quote by Margaret Grenier for many reasons. She is a choreographer, performer, colleague, and friend, and she has inspired me in the rehearsal room and through her performances. Her insight and perspectives have helped shape my own inquiry into Indigenous performance and the proscenium stage.

Margaret is of Gitxsan and Cree ancestry and she is Executive and Artistic Director for the Dancers of Damelahamid, a company dedicated to reviving Gitxsan dance traditions and bringing this work to the stage. Her late father, Chief Ken Harris, deeply instilled in her the importance of these dances and the value of what they offer each of us individually and collectively. I have seen her, with these values as her foundation, face many challenges with grace and dignity.

Raven Spirit Dance (RSD) hosted an Aboriginal choreographer's workshop in September of 2013. In the circle of choreographers were Margaret Grenier, Starr Muranko (choreographer and Artistic Associate of RSD), and myself, the company's artistic director. Choreographer and Artistic Director of Battery Opera Lee Su-Feh was our outside eye. The purpose of the workshop was to address the proscenium stage in relationship to Indigenous work. This inquiry into why we choose to make work for the western-theatre space brought up tears, laughter, and many questions. Grenier spoke about the weight she sometimes feels walking out on stage and facing an audience in her regalia and her mask. When she steps out onto the stage, she has to meet the gaze of the audience, and this almost immobilizes her. The weight of her responsibility at that moment feels unbearable. Yet she takes up the challenge and pushes through but feels worse for wear after the fact. We ruminated as a collective during this workshop about what this kinetically felt pressure and force is. Why does it exist? What are the implicit power structures and notions that create it?

I have mulled over these questions in my mind over the years. And at this moment my response is in image, in metaphor. The palace. And Dead Indians.

THE PALACE

Our society sees most of its theatre and dance through the frame of a prosce-nium. The rules of power are deeply embedded in its structure and informed by the historical context it was birthed from. It is a space constructed on unspoken assumptions and unseen but imposing power structures. When one steps into this space as a performer or views it as an audience member, one has entered the arena of consumption and the ruling aesthetic. Su-Feh made the proposition that the proscenium stage is a palace on her website *folkandpalace.com*. This website captures three days of conversations at the Scotiabank Dance Centre in May 2008 about dance, the body, folk practice, and the palace. She proposes that the idea of performance seen in this way was birthed in "European courts of Italy, France or Russia or the courts of South-East Asia." She further explains: "Implicit in my definition of the palace is the notion that the dance is being seen and paid for by a party that holds political and economic power. The nobility, the landed gentry, the bourgeoisie."

The physical architecture of the proscenium stage sets up this dynam-ic between performer and audience. The audience sits in opposition to the performer, in a place of power and in a place of judgment. It is the job of the performer to maintain status quo, to essentially become a puppet to the ideas and fantasies that keep this power structure in place. This is something that we can all unconsciously slip into today, because the space reverberates

from its origins in the palace. Out of this complete inequity in this audience/
performer relationship in the palace a gaze arises. The gaze of the oppressor.
The gaze of one in power. And all they want to see is their own supremacy.

Art can be transformative and the artist can be the diviner of spirit yet
this notion of the artist cannot exist within the realm of the oppressor's gaze.
Dance as ritual embraces transformation and divination. A statement that
Cree theatre artist Floyd Favel would say over and over again that resonates
with me is that "theatre is the younger brother of ritual and theatre has much
to learn." The roots of traditional First Nations dance are also in ritual. The
dance connects the dancer to land and to spirit, and the images and sensations
that result from this connection are an offering to the individual as well as the
collective. Audience members are witnesses and it is because of their presence that the event can happen, the dancer can dance. A circle is completed.
Deeply embedded in our human psyche and in our instinct is the need and
desire for the circle. If we are drawn to the theatre by these deeper impulses
for ritual and the circle, we will most likely find ourselves constrained and
contained within the palace.

Before following this thread of thought, I would like to look closer at the
oppressor's gaze. What occurred when Rudolf Laban was asked to choreo-
graph a work for the opening ceremonies for the Berlin Olympics provides
an example of the power and function of the oppressor's gaze. The heart of
Laban's work is about human liberation and the intentional creation of community through movement. He was a major influence in early modern dance
in Germany and in Europe and was a pioneer in movement studies. His work
contains the seeds that grew into our present-day dance therapy, movement
analysis, somatic movement education, and theatre and dance training. His
production *Vom Tauwind und der Neuen Freude* (*Spring Wind and the New
Joy*) was to be the new piece he would premiere at the Berlin Olympic games.
He trained a thousand dancers who were divided into twenty-two groups.
This piece would have been the pinnacle of his career, a culmination of his
knowledge shared on the world stage.

His greatest moment never happened. On June 20th, after the final dress
rehearsal in front of twenty thousand invited guests, Dr. Joseph Goebbels,

Reich Minister of Propaganda, "dismissed Laban's work as a poorly-choreo-graphed piece, one that was intellectual, and had nothing whatever to do with Germans. . . . Obviously, Laban's dance philosophy was not in keeping with the view of the National Socialists" (Hanley 135). Human liberation and the beauty of life did not sit well with the Third Reich. Shortly after the piece was cancelled, Laban was under "town arrest" and fled to Paris in 1937.

Dancing the divine, divining the dance has no room in the palace or at the opening ceremony of the Nazi Berlin Olympics. If we broaden our lens beyond the performative, we can find the oppressor's gaze in many shapes and forms. All we have to do is google "Paris Colonial Exhibition" or "human zoos." Amazing how quickly the information comes up. And Google has no shame, if you ask to see the underbelly it is all the more accommodating.

Human beings were on display for amusement and fascination in hu-man zoos in the late 1700s and early 1800s. These zoos were scattered across Europe. A sad story that encapsulates this whole period in history is the story of the South African Saartjie Baartman, later to be known as the Hottentot Venus. She was born around 1780 and was brought to London in 1810 and put on display. She had the genetic characteristic known as steatopygia—ex-tremely protuberant buttocks and elongated labia—which delighted onlookers and made a visit to the human zoo extra titillating. Later she was brought to Paris and was analyzed by racial anthropologists. She died in poverty, yet her skeleton was cleaned of her flesh and put on display, remaining on show in the Museum of Man in Paris until 1974. Just in 2002, a mere thirteen years from the day I write this, her remains were repatriated and buried in South Africa. The analysis of her body and displaying of her bones mark "the start of the period of description, measurement and classification, which soon leads us to hierarchisation—the idea that there are lesser and greater races" (Schofield).

The Paris Colonial Exhibition (or "Exposition coloniale internationale"), held in Paris, France, in 1931, "displayed the diverse cultures and immense resources of France's colonial possessions," according to Wikipedia. Many First Nations people from North America participated and were displayed as "exotic fruits of the empire"; they were consumed by the masses. In a span of six months over thirty-three million tickets were sold to this exhibition of "other" (a.k.a. brown) people in makeshift replica villages. Different exhibitions like this were scattered across time and space in Europe, dehumanizing the "others" as objects of fascination and titillation.

Our Indigenous bodies have been the site for the colonizer's gaze, the site where the west was won and conquered, over and over again. Buffalo Bill's Wild West Show was founded in 1883 by William Frederick "Buffalo Bill" Cody. This show was first created in Nebraska and toured throughout the United States and Europe. The shows were about entrenching the power of the colonial gaze, asserting the power that the settlers had over the First Nations of North America. Great leaders and warriors of the Native American tribes came into these arenas as entertainment, and their true power as leaders was reduced to a side-show act. Sitting Bull, the leader of the Lakota people, did his rounds with the Wild West shows, not as a career choice, but a decision based on survival and hunger. And the Wild West shows were not just an American phenomenon; Canada also became a stage for these shows. My own community, Tr'ondëk Hwëch'in, Dawson City, Yukon, has a show house. The Palace Grand was built in 1899 by Arizona Charlie. Arizona Charlie was in Buffalo Bill's Wild West Show so he brought with him the flair of vaudeville and the wild west with his tag line "the greatest Indian killer of America!"

The Buffalo Bill Wild West Show still lives on in Paris. It is a bit flashier, and Mickey Mouse and Goofy are the sidekicks alongside some real live Indians riding bareback with Sitting Bull. For a few Euros you are given a cowboy hat, a real Texan meal, and while you enjoy your meal you can see how the west was won. Every night, seven days a week, 365 days a year. This show inscribes deep into our collective consciousness that First Nations are conquered people, puppets for the palace, the losers in the game of power, yet so noble, yet so savage. It is inscribed so deep that it draws blood.

COST OF THE GAZE

In 2010 I saw the Native Earth Performing Arts production of *Almighty Voice and His Wife* by Daniel David Moses in Edmonton, directed by Michael Greyeyes and performed by PJ Prudat and Derek Garza. The play tells the story of a Cree man arrested for killing a cow without a licence in order to feed his hungry family. The authorities threaten to hang him, and there is a year-long manhunt to find Almighty Voice.

The piece is not really about what it is, more about what it does. The first act has a linear storyline. The second act flips the story on its head. It becomes a parodic whiteface minstrel show, selling a bit of snake oil on the side. The play almost becomes a farce, but doesn't. The twists and turns, abrupt impulses and directions, the shifting characters leave one in a whirlwind; it is hard to know how to land. A topsy-turvy version of Gilbert and Sullivan but with a cruel colonial twist. In the end, I was left ragged and worn to the bone, left in such a state of confusion that in my reorientation—my heart being in my feet, my breath in my stomach—I was starting to realign to what I was seeing and feeling. The piece hit me hard. And on reflection, I now understand that in that moment I saw the human zoo. The pieces of me that were wrapped up in those characters, raging within the cages, were locked in those images and being torn apart.

We all have our reasons for going to theatre. Some go for escape, some for the intellectual stimulation, and some to be wowed by spectacle. I go because I want to see the living metaphors that shape my life, my world view, and by seeing them in the space, in the performers' bodies, I can maybe get a glimpse of what it is like outside of these cages and outside of these walls that colonialism built.

DEAD INDIANS

Since contact, the colonial gaze upon the Indigenous body has been our in-herited collective self-perception. As a society we have collectively ingested this perception, and whether we like it or not, it has knit itself into how we see ourselves and how others see us. It was birthed out of the conquering, birthed out of the zoos, and birthed out of the Wild West shows. Thomas King has given this perception a lovely name: Dead Indians. "The Dead Indians I'm talking about are not the deceased sort. They are the stereotypes and clichés that North America has conjured up out of experience and out of its collec-tive imaginings and fears" (*Inconvenient* 53).

If we extend the palace as a metaphor to the larger society, the only real Indian is a dead one. Many North Americans are unable to reconcile their idea of "the Indian" with real, living First Nations people. Here is a personal example. A friend of mine and I were performing in the Yukon as a part of an Indigenous performing showcase. We were explaining to the man at the front desk of our hotel what we were doing. He was floored. We were First Nations? No way. Not possible. He even stated that my friend REALLY didn't even look it; my friend who is full-blood Nakoda and who speaks to her grandmother on the phone in her traditional language every night. Then he asked us if we needed a wake-up call.

King states that the notion of Dead Indian is a simulacrum, "something that represents something that never existed. Or, in other words, the only truth of the thing is the lie itself" (*Inconvenient* 54).

So how do we find the real truths in the rehearsal room, sifting through this colonial mess? And when we lock onto our real truths, what do we do when we leave that room? We have no control over how we are seen or over whether what we have to share will be taken for what it is worth . . . our truth. What a colonial conundrum it is.

When I was working on *Death of a Chief*, Native Earth Performing Arts's 2008 adaptation of Shakespeare's *Julius Caesar*, we found many truths in the room. Hard truths they were, but collectively we carried them forward the best we could out of the rehearsal room and onto the stage at the National

Arts Centre. The image of the rocks that were strewn about the stage was a strong one. Rocks connect us to the earth, and within the context of the play the characters grew out of the earth from these rocks. It was the medicine we carry forward and the power that we all individually hold. The killing scene was done with these stones; Caesar was stoned to death. Metaphorically and literally, this scene was devastating to create as it was a glimpse of what happens in our own community, how the medicine, the gifts we are given, turn into weapons. This was finding a truth that is not a lie. After opening night, a partner of one of the cast members overhead an audience member say, "I do not know why they did not just kill Caesar with tomahawks." This is when the fourth wall of the theatre stage can feel like the bars of the cages at the human zoo.

To be fair there were many, many in the audience that did not think this way, but it is important to acknowledge that such assumptions about "Indianness" are embedded in our collective consciousness as a society, and the power structure inscribed in the mechanics of the proscenium stage can support this. But there are so many of us—performers and audience alike— who are a part of the huge force that is surging through these structures, shaking the foundations and realigning the place of the palace into the place of something bigger . . . into a circle.

So let's start unpacking, shall we? Rules for unpacking: trust instinct, piss on all the corners, and question love.

DESTABILIZING THE GAZE

Socialization is the adoption of the behaviour patterns of the surrounding culture. Part of this process is the individual understanding what is acceptable and what is not: in crude but honest terms, what behaviour will get love and what will not. Socialization happens within the walls of the palace or in the human zoo, and love becomes very complicated in the play of power. Again, it is the work of trying to extract our true selves from this web that we are all caught in. To find the beating heart in the Dead Indian.

Zab Maboungou is Artistic Director of Compagnie Danse Nyata Nyata, a contemporary African dance company in Montreal. She is a choreographer, performer, musician, author, and teacher of philosophy and dance. Maboungou was a part of the Scotiabank Dance Centre conversations about folk and palace and addressed the notion of socialization.

> The first thing you have to learn is to de-socialize yourself from basically these representations that you are supposed to carry in you. You cannot stop people from putting what they want, but you're working at de-stabilizing the gaze. And look(ing) at the expectations of the beloved one. You have to learn to not count on that love anymore. You have to question . . . the very idea of love.

This requires the individual to break everything down to the basic fundamentals and question everything. To question impulse and action and how this may be linked to receiving love, receiving acceptance, or how impulse and action are connected to something much deeper, something much wiser. For me as an artist, this is the point of everything. This is the work.

CIRCLE

I interviewed Paula Ross, an iconic Canadian choreographer, for this article. I shared with her how I am examining the challenges of an Indigenous artist working within the proscenium stage structure. Paula did not miss a beat. "Of course it is problematic. The proscenium stage cuts the circle right in half." Ross is a choreographer and dancer born Pauline Cecilia Isobel Teresa Campbell in Vancouver on the 29th of April, 1941. She is part Scots and part First Nations. She launched her own modern dance company in the mid-sixties, incorporated in 1973 as the Paula Ross Dance Company, and explored her choreographic language that she called "visual poetry" and "universal tribal metaphor" ("Paula Ross"). She won the Jean A. Chalmers Choreographic Award in 1977. Paula described her work to me and what it meant to her to be on stage. She described her work as not reading well on the stage at the National Arts Centre, saying that her work was the most powerful when it was performed in her Vancouver studio performance space, "where you can hear the dancers breathe and [the] movement of the dancers' bodies and [the] fabric of the costumes" (Ross). In moving the work out of this intimate setting to the proscenium stage something was lost.

I was recently brought into a project on the east coast because I am an Indigenous choreographer and the company wanted my guidance in some aspects of their production. My presence in the room was brief and what I offered felt minimal, but I shared my knowledge on how to avoid having "Dead Indians" in the work. On the last day, I proposed a new staging for a scene that the company was working on. The staging was in the thrust, a configuration that existed centuries ago and sits under the umbrella of "the palace." I placed the performers in a formation that created part of a circle, the audience creating the other part. The director shut this down very quickly. There is no way you can make a circle, he stated, and started describing the "rules" of a thrust stage, the angles of the stage, and a theory of classical theatre. After his rant, I continued to stage the piece the way I felt it should be staged, acknowledging the circle. I am sure the moment I left the room he applied the rules and changed it all.

But it really is simple. Colonialism built this theatre house on top of a circle. North American society is built upon circles that are present just a few layers below the concrete. My proposal is that we enter the theatre space to find our humanness, not that we blindly seek love by maintaining the status quo. It is important that we challenge the power structures of the proscenium stage. "Make sure you piss on the the corners" was Su-Feh's advice to me. Being Wolf Clan, this is very appealing.

SOFT ANIMAL BODY

How do we uncover the truth in the lies that can be so deeply embedded in how we see ourselves? How do we untangle the weight of this from our daily actions? How do we even begin to dismantle this? Rosy Simas (Seneca), a Minneapolis-based contemporary-dance choreographer, has a lovely solution. "I like the term atrophy: In order to unlearn the colonized cultural and physical patterns in my body, I have had to allow parts of myself to atrophy (not weaken, but soften) in order to forget, grow and re-build back in a more organic and indigenous dancing body" (qtd. in Tollon). As we soften, we create space between these hard-wired patterns, and in these found breaths and moments there is an opportunity to remember deeply. "Walking," says Linda Hogan, "I am listening to a deeper way. Suddenly all my ancestors are behind me. Be still they say. Watch and listen. You are the result of the love of thousands" (*Dwellings* 155). In this softening and breathing, we expose ourselves to vulnerability. As we dismantle from the inside, we shift in our core knowing. And from this core springs desire, and how we manifest this desire through action shifts space. And this is what extends beyond our bodies into space to hit the edges of the proscenium stage and confront the colonial gaze. This is how we push through the implicit power structures to assert who we are as the Indigenous body in space.

THE RIVER

Journeying back to Margaret Grenier's story at the top of this essay, I would like to share how we collectively addressed her concern about the proscenium stage. We collectively proposed that she perform her mask dance with the audience encircling the space. We staggered the chairs so Grenier could move through the audience like a river moves in and around rocks and islands. With this adjustment of gaze, we became her landscape. Our instincts heightened and our perception refocused; we were given the privilege of being on her territory. Rather than having to stake her claim on the territory of the palace and the colonizer, Grenier could welcome us to hers. She spoke about how she could feel the weight lift off of her and how she could inhabit her mask and her dancing body in a freer way. It is through this softening and this opening that we can find a way forward.

> It is through our work that we redefine and reconstruct our sense of society. It is from this foundation that we work towards a transformed relationship.
>
> [...]
>
> It is most difficult to be in those places of dissonance where we tend to lose hope.
>
> [...]
>
> Yet the integrity of the work also immerses us in the healing which breathes through song and dance. (Grenier 15)

The stage is black.

An Aboriginal woman steps out onto centre stage and faces the audience.

Light slowly fades up on the woman. The audience sees her. She can barely see them but senses their presence.

A beat for breath.

She begins to move.

WORKS CITED

"2012 EGALE Leadership Award: Kent Monkman." *Egale*. Egale Canada Human Rights Trust, 20 Sept. 2012. Web. 7 Sept. 2015.

"About the REDress Project." *Indigenous Foundations*. University of British Columbia, n.d. Web. 15 Oct. 2015.

Ace, Barry. "E-Racing Aboriginal Mythologies: The Manufactured and the Real." *Dance to the Berdashe*. Winnipeg: Urban Shaman Gallery, 2009: 8–16. Print.

Ahmed, Sara. *The Promise of Happiness*. Durham, NC: Duke UP, 2010. Print.

Al Arabiya News. " 'What is Love?' in Top 3 Google Search Questions in 2014." *Al Arabiya English*. Al Arabiya Network, 17 Dec. 2014. Web. 26 Aug. 2015.

Alfred, Taiaiake. *Peace, Power, and Righteousness: An Indigenous Manifesto*. Oxford: Oxford UP, 1999. Print.

Allen, Paula Gunn. *Off the Reservation: Reflections on Boundary-Busting, Border-Crossing, Loose Cannons*. Boston: Beacon, 1998. Print.

---. *The Sacred Hoop: Recovering the Feminine in American Indian Traditions*. Boston: Beacon, 1986. Print.

âpihtawikosisân. "Language, Culture, and Two-Spirit Identity." *Law, Language, Life: A Plains Cree Speaking Métis Woman In Montreal*. âpihtawikosisân, 29 March 2012. Web. 29 April 2015.

Appleford, Rob. "Seeing the Full Frame." Introduction. *Aboriginal Drama and Theatre*. Ed. Appleford. Toronto: Playwrights Canada, 2006. i–xiii. Print.

Aquino, Nina Lee. *Death of a Chief*. February 2008. Production poster. National Arts Centre, Ottawa.

Armstrong, Denis. "Shakespeare Goes Native." *Ottawa Sun* 19 Feb. 2008: 18. Print.

"Artist Profile: Kent Monkman." *ARTSask.* ARTSask, n.d. Web. 17 Jan. 2016.

Bamford, Karen. "Romance, Recognition and Revenge in Marie Clements's *The Unnatural and Accidental Women.*" *Theatre Research in Canada* 31.2 (2010): 143–63. Print.

Battiste, Marie, and James (Sa'ke'j) Youngblood Henderson. *Protecting Indigenous Knowledge and Heritage: A Global Challenge.* Saskatoon: Purich P, 2000. Print.

BC Hydro. "First Nations." *BC Hydro.* BC Hydro, n.d. Web. 28 Jan. 2016.

---. "Traditional unveiling ceremony highlights First Nations artistry." *BC Hydro.* BC Hydro, 11 Feb. 2010. Web. 15 Jan. 2016.

Ben-Ari, Raikin. "Stanislavsky in the Habima." *Habima.* Trans. A.H. Gross and I. Soref. New York: Thomas Yoseloff, 1957. 72–79. Print.

Black, Jaime. "Artist Statement." *The REDress Project.* Jaime Black, 2014. Web. 14 Oct. 2015.

Borrows, John. "With or Without You: First Nations Law (in Canada)." *McGill Law Journal* 41 (1996): 629–65. Print.

Braidotti, Rosi. "The Ethics of Becoming-Imperceptible." *Deleuze and Philosophy.* Ed. Constantin Boundas. Edinburgh: Edinburgh UP, 2006. 133–59. Print.

Browner, Tara. " 'Breathing the Indian Spirit': Thoughts on Musical Borrowing and the 'Indianist' Movement in American Music." *American Music* 15.3 (1997): 265–84. Print.

Bruchac, Joseph. *Roots of Survival: Native American Storytelling and the Sacred.* Golden, CO: Fulcrum, 1996. Print.

Camporesi, Piero. *Bread of Dreams: Food and Fantasy in Early Modern Europe.* Trans. David Gentilcore. Chicago: U of Chicago P, 1996. Print.

Cardinal, Douglas, and Jeannette Armstrong. *The Native Creative Process: A Collaborative Discourse between Douglas Cardinal and Jeannette Armstrong.* Penticton, BC: Theytus, 1991. Print.

Cardinal, Harold, and Walter Hildebrandt. *Treaty Elders of Saskatchewan: Our Dream Is That Our Peoples Will One Day Be Clearly Recognized As Nations.* Calgary: U of Calgary P, 2000. Print.

Cardinal, Richard S. *Native American Testimony: An Anthology of Indian and White Relations: First Encounter to Dispossession.* Rev. ed. Ed. Peter Nabokov. New York: Penguin, Putnam, 1981. 417. Print.

Carnovsky, Morris, with Peter Sander. *The Actor's Eye.* New York: PAJ, 1984. Print.

Ceci, Lynn. "Shell Midden Deposits as Coastal Resources." *World Archaeology* 16.1: *Coastal Archaeology* (1984): 62–74. Print.

Chacaby, Maya. *Kippmoojikewin: Articulating Anishinaabe Pedagogy Through Anishinaabemowin Revitalization*. M.A. thesis. U of Toronto, 2011. Web. 24 Nov. 2015.

"CIT at Artscape Youngplace." *Indigenous Performing Arts Alliance*. Indigenous Performing Arts Alliance, 18 Nov. 2013. Web. 15 Oct. 2015.

City of Vancouver. *First Peoples: A Guide for Newcomers*. Vancouver: City of Vancouver, 2014. PDF file.

---. "Vancouver Takes Next Steps on Truth and Reconciliation Report." *CivicInfo BC*. CivicInfo BC, 21 Jan. 2016. Web. 21 March 2016.

Clements, Marie. *The Unnatural and Accidental Women*. Vancouver: TalonBooks, 2005. Print.

Coates, Ken. *#IDLENOMORE and the Remaking of Canada*. Regina: U of Regina P, 2015. Print.

Coyote, Fred. *Native American Testimony: An Anthology of Indian and White Relations: First Encounter to Dispossession*. Rev. ed. Ed. Peter Nabokov. New York: Penguin, Putnam, 1981. 392–93. Print.

Crean, Susan. "Riel's Prophecy." *The Walrus*. The Walrus Foundation, March 2008. Web. 20 Jan. 2016.

Cusick, Suzanne. "On a Lesbian Relation with Music: A Serious Effort Not to Think Straight." *Queering the Pitch: The New Gay and Lesbian Musicology*. Ed. Philip Brett, Elizabeth Wood, and Gary C. Thomas. New York: Routledge, 1994. 67–84. Print.

Dickason, Olive Patricia. *Canada's First Nations: A History of Founding Peoples from Earliest Times*. 3rd ed. Oxford: Oxford UP, 2003. Print.

Dispatch: REDress Project. Camera by Ray Bourier. Interviews by Jennifer Clibbon. Edited by Janelle Wookey. Web. 14 Oct. 2015.

Dolan, Jill. *Utopia in Performance: Finding Hope at the Theater*. Ann Arbor, MI: U of Michigan P, 2005. Print.

Dumont-Smith, Claudette. "Aboriginal Elder Abuse in Canada." *Aboriginal Healing Foundation*. Aboriginal Healing Foundation, 2002. Web. 20 Nov. 2015.

Dylan, Bob. "Shelter from the Storm." *Blood on the Tracks*. Columbia Records, 1975. CD.

Fanon, Frantz. *The Wretched of the Earth*. Trans. Constance Farrington. New York: Grove, 1963. Print.

Farwell, Arthur. "American Indian Melodies, Op. 11: Song of the Deathless Voice." *The American Indianists*. Vol. 2. Ed. Dario Müller. Marco Polo, 1996. CD.

---. "The Song of the Deathless Voice." *Three Indian Songs*. New York: G. Schirmer, 1912. 32. Print.

Fiske, Jo-Anne, and Evelyn George. *Seeking Alternatives to Bill C-31: From Cultural Trauma to Cultural Revitalization through Customary Law*. Ottawa: Status of Women Canada, 2006. Print.

Fletcher, Alice. *Indian Story and Song from North America*. 1900. Lincoln, NE: U of Nebraska P, 1995. Print.

---. *A Study of Omaha Indian Music*. 1920. Lincoln, NE: U of Nebraska P, 1994. Print.

Foster, Mary Ann. "Changing Neuromuscular Patterns: Active Techniques." *Associated Bodywork and Massage Professionals* (Mar./Apr. 2014): n. pag. Web. 11 Aug. 2015.

Fraleigh, Sondra. "*Das Warten*: A Life in Dance and War." *EastWest Somatics*. EastWest Somatics, 1997. Web. 1 March 2016.

Gaertner, Dave. "Indigenous Protocol in Cyberspace: Hospitality and Kevin Lee Burton's God's Lake Narrows." *Novel Alliance*. Novel Alliance, 20 July 2014. Web. 13 Aug. 2015.

Garneau, David. "Imaginary Spaces of Conciliation and Reconciliation: Art, Curation, and Healing." *Arts of Engagement: Taking Aesthetic Action in and Beyond the Truth and Reconciliation Commission of Canada*. Ed. Dylan Robinson and Keavy Martin. Waterloo, ON: Wilfrid Laurier UP, 2016. 21–39. Print.

---. "Imaginary Spaces of Conciliation and Reconciliation." *West Coast Line* 74 (2012): 28–38. Print.

---. "Indigenous Criticism: On Not Walking With Our Sisters." *Border Crossing* 134 (2015): n. pag. Web. 15 Oct. 2015.

Gonick, Noam. "Contempo Abo: Two-Spirit in Aboriginal Culture." *Canadian Dimension* July/August 2009: 22–27. Print.

Government of Canada. "Chapter 7: Special Examinations of Crown Corporations—2010." *2011 June Status Report of the Auditor General of Canada. Office of the Auditor General.* Government of Canada, 2011. Web. 9 Nov. 2015.

Government of Canada. *Royal Commission on National Development in the Arts, Letters and Sciences, 1949–1951*. Ottawa: King's Printer, 1951. Print.

Grenier, Margaret. "Carrying my Lineage Through Dance." *Claiming Space*. Indigenous Performing Arts Alliance (2012): 14–16. Web. 5 Nov. 2015.

"Ground." *Oxford English Dictionary*. Oxford University Press, n.d. Web. 3 March 2016.

Hadfield, Andrew. *Shakespeare and Republicanism*. Cambridge: Cambridge UP, 2005. Print.

Hager, Alan. *Shakespeare's Political Animal: Schema and Schemata in the Canon*. Newark, NJ: U of Delaware P, 1990. Print.

Hanley, Elizabeth A. "The Role of Dance in the 1936 Olympics Games: Why Competition Became Festival and Art Became Political." *Cultural Relations Old and New: The Transitory Olympic Ethic. Proceedings of the Seventh International Symposium for Olympic Research*. Ed. K.B. Wamsley, R.K. Barney, and S.G. Martyn. International Centre for Olympic Studies (2004): 133–40. Web. 9 Nov. 2015.

Hannon, Gerald. "The Pink Indian." *Toronto Life* 45.9 (2011): 54–62. Print.

---. "Tomson and the Trickster: Stories From the Life of Playwright Tomson Highway." *Toronto Life* 25.4 (1991): 28, 30–31, 35–38, 41–42, 81–82, 85. Print.

Hanson, Erin. "The Indian Act." *Indigenous Foundations*. University of British Columbia, 2009. Web. 9 Oct. 2015.

---. "Marginalization of Aboriginal Women." *Indigenous Foundations*. University of British Columbia, 2009. Web. 24 Sept. 2015.

Harjo, Joy, and Gloria Bird. Introduction. *Reinventing the Enemy's Language: Contemporary Native Women's Writings of North America*. Ed. Harjo and Bird. New York: W.W. Norton, 1997. 19–31. Print.

Highway, Tomson. *Aria: A One-Woman Play in One Act. Staging Coyote's Dream: An Anthology of First Nations Drama in English Volume 1*. Ed. Monique Mojica and Ric Knowles. Toronto: Playwrights Canada, 2003. 75–96. Print.

---. "Author's note." *The Rez Sisters*. Edinburgh: Mainstage, Edinburgh International Theatre Festival, 14–19 Aug. 1988. Print.

---. *Comparing Mythologies*. Ottawa: U of Ottawa P, 2002. Print.

---. *Dry Lips Oughta Move to Kapuskasing*. Calgary: Fifth House, 1989. Print.

---. *The Rez Sisters*. Calgary: Fifth House, 1988. Print.

Hill, Richard William. "Kent Monkman's Constitutional Amendments: Time and Uncanny Objects." *Interpellations: Three Essays on Kent Monkman*. Ed. Michelle Thériault. Montréal: Galerie Leonard & Bina Ellen Art Gallery, 2012. 50–58. Print.

---. "Spirits of Mischief and Self-Invention: Kent Monkman's Performances." *Two-Spirit Acts: Queer Indigenous Performance*. Ed. Jean O'Hara. Toronto: Playwrights Canada, 2013. 37–43. Print.

Hogan, Linda. "A Different Yield." *Reclaiming Indigenous Voice and Vision.* Ed. Marie Battiste. Vancouver: U of British Columbia P, 2002. 115–23. Print.

---. *Dwellings: A Spiritual History of the Living World.* New York: Touchstone, 1996. Print.

Holmes, Cindy, and Sarah Hunt. "Everyday Decolonization: Living a Decolonizing Queer Politics." *Journal of Lesbian Studies* 19.2 (2015): 154–72. Print.

"Home." *Reconciliation Canada.* Reconciliation Canada, n.d. Web. 28 Jan. 2016.

"Indigenous in the City." *8th Fire.* CBC TV. 31 Jan. 2012. Television.

Innes, Robert Alexander. *Elder Brother and the Law of the People: Contemporary Kinship and the Cowessess First Nation.* Winnipeg: U of Manitoba P, 2013. Print.

Ipperwash: Tragedy to Reconciliation. Union of Ontario Indians, 2006. Print.

Jennings, Sarah. *Art and Politics: The History of the National Arts Centre.* Toronto: Dundurn P, 2009. Print.

Johnson, James Weldon, and J. Rosamond Johnson. *The Book of American Negro Spirituals.* Vol. 2. London: Chapman & Hall, 1926. Print.

Justice, Daniel Heath. " 'Go Away, Water!': Kinship Criticism and the Decolonization Imperative." *Reasoning Together: The Native Critics Collective.* Ed. Janice Acoose et al. Norman, OK: U of Oklahoma P: 2008. 147–68. Print.

Justice, Daniel Heath. "Notes Toward A Theory of Anomaly." *GLQ* 16:1–2 (2010): 207–42. Print.

Kahn, Coppélia. *Roman Shakespeare: Warriors, Wounds and Women.* London: Routledge, 1997. Print.

Kaplan, Jon. "All Hail the Chief." *NOW Magazine* March 6–12 (2008): 67. Print.

Kappo, Tanya. "1700 Unfinished Pairs of Moccasins to Memorialize the Missing and Murdered: *Walking With Our Sisters* A Transformative Experience for the Keeper of the Vamps." *CBC News.* CBC/Radio Canada, 14 Feb. 2014. Web. 15 Oct. 2015.

Katz, Jonathan D. " 'Miss Chief Is Always Interested in the Latest European Fashions.'" *Interpellations: Three Essays on Kent Monkman.* Ed. Michèle Thériault. Montréal: Galerie Leonard & Bina Ellen Art Gallery, 2012. 16–24. Print.

Keeshig-Tobias, Lenore. "The Magic of Others." *Language in Her Eye: Views on Writing and Gender by Canadian Women Writing in English.* Ed. Libby Scheier, Sarah Sheard, and Eleanor Wachtel. Toronto: Coach House, 1990. 173–77. Print.

Kidd, Ross. "Reclaiming Culture: Indigenous Performers Take Back Their Show." *Theaterwork Magazine* 3.1 (1982): 32–53. Print.

Kidder, Tristram R. "Making the City Inevitable: Native Americans and the Geography of New Orleans." *Transforming New Orleans and Its Environs: Centuries of Change.* Ed. Craig E. Colten. Pittsburgh: U of Pittsburgh P, 2001. 10–21. Print.

Kimmerer, Robin Wall. *Braiding Sweetgrass: Indigenous Wisdom, Scientific Knowledge, and the Teachings of Plants.* Minneapolis: Milkweed, 2013. Print.

King, Thomas. *The Inconvenient Indian: A Curious Account of Native People in North America.* Toronto: Anchor Canada, 2013. Print.

---. *The Truth About Stories: A Native Narrative.* Minneapolis: U of Minnesota P, 2005. Print.

Kino-nda-niimi Collective. *The Winter We Danced: Voices from the Past, Future, and the Idle No More Movement.* Winnipeg: Arbeiter Ring, 2014. Print.

Knowles, Ric. "*The Death of a Chief*: Watching for Adaptation; or How I Learned to Stop Worrying and Love the Bard." *Shakespeare Bulletin* 25.3 (2007): 53–65. Print.

---. *Shakespeare and Canada: Essays on Production, Translation, and Adaptation.* Brussels: Peter Lang, 2004. Print.

L'Hirondelle, Cheryl. Personal communication with Dylan Robinson. 28 Jan. 2016. Email.

---. *Why the Caged Bird Sings: Radical Inclusivity, Sonic Survivance and the Collective Ownership of Freedom Songs.* MDes Thesis. Ontario College of Art and Design University, 2015. Print.

La Flamme, Michelle. "Theatrical Medicine: Aboriginal Performance, Ritual and Commemoration." *Theatre Research in Canada* 31.2 (2010): 107–17. Print.

Lauzon, Jani. "Indigenous Theatre Working Group ASTR." Message to Jill Carter. 27 Aug. 2015. Email.

---. *A Side of Dreams.* 2015. MS.

Lawrenchuk, Michael. Talking circle. Saskatoon, 20 July 2015.

LeClaire, Nancy, George Cardinal, Emily Hunter, and Earle H. Waugh. *Alberta Elders' Cree Dictionary = alperta ohci kehtehayak nehiyaw otwestamâkewasinahikan.* Edmonton: U of Alberta P, 1998. Print.

Leggatt, Alexander. *Shakespeare's Political Drama: The History Plays and the Roman Plays.* London: Routledge, 1988. Print.

Life and Times of Tomson Highway: Thank You for the Love You Gave. Dir. Donald Winkler. CBC Documentary, 1997. Film.

Liss, David. "Kent Monkman: Miss Chief's Return." *Canadian Art* 22.5 (2005): 78–82. Print.

---. "The Wild West." *The Triumph of Miss Chief.* Ed. Liss and Shirley J. Madill. Hamilton, ON: Art Gallery of Hamilton, 2008. 103–06. Print.

Lobo, Susan. "Urban Clan Mothers: Key Households in Cities." *Keeping the Campfires Going: Native Women's Activism in Urban Communities.* Ed. Susan Applegate Krouse and Heather Howard. Lincoln, NE: U of Nebraska P, 2009. 1–20. Print.

Maboungo, Zab. "The Conversation: May 24th Afternoon." *Folk and Palace.* Lee Su-Feh, 2008. Web. 5 Nov. 2015.

The Magic Flute audience member. Group interview. Vancouver. 12 March 2013.

Manossa, Geraldine. "The Roots of Cree Drama." Diss. U of Lethbridge, 2002. Print.

Manuel, Vera. "Letting Go of Trauma: On and Off Stage." *Redwire Magazine* 7.1 (Oct. 2004): 39–41. Print.

Matthews, J.S. *Early Vancouver: Narratives of Pioneers of Vancouver, BC.* 1933. Vancouver: City of Vancouver, 2011. Print.

Matthews, Pamela. *Native Theatre in Canada: A Report Presented to the Royal Commission on Aboriginal Peoples.* Toronto: Native Earth Performing Arts, 1993. Print.

McCord Museum. "Welcome to the Studio." *Youtube.* Google, 9 Feb. 2014. Web. 2 Aug. 2015.

McMaster, Gerald. "The Geography of Hope." *Kent Monkman: The Triumph of Mischief.* Ed. David Liss and Shirley J. Madill. Hamilton, ON: Art Gallery of Hamilton, 2008. 95–101. Print.

McQueen, Robert. Interview by Dylan Robinson, with responses by Cathi Charles Wherry and Tracy Herbert, Lorna Williams, and Marion Newman. "West Coast First Peoples and *The Magic Flute*: Tracing a Journey of Cross-Cultural Collaboration." *Opera Indigene: Re/presenting First Nations and Indigenous Cultures.* Ed. Pamela Karantonis and Dylan Robinson. Farnham, UK: Ashgate, 2011. 309–24. Print.

Miguel, Gloria. *Something Old, Something New, Something Borrowed, Something Blue.* Native Earth Performing Arts, Weesageechak Begins to Dance Festival. Toronto. 12–22 November 2014. Performance.

"miyo-wîcêhtowin." *Online Cree Dictionary.* Cree Language Resource Project, n.d. Web. 23 Aug. 2015.

Momaday, N. Scott. "The Man Made of Words." *Literature of the American Indians: Views and Interpretations.* Ed. by Abraham Chapman. New York: New American Library, 1975. 96–110. Print.

Monkman, Kent. "Certificate of Miss Chief." *Kent Monkman.* Kent Monkman, n.d. Web. 20 Nov. 2015.

---. "Kent Monkman: Miss Chief." *Practical Dreamers: Conversations With Movie Artists.* By Michael Hoolboom. Toronto: Coach House, 2008. 46–54. Print.

---. "Kent Monkman on Reimagining Canada's Visual History." *Q.* CBC Radio 2, 23 April 2014. Radio.

---. "Laughing 'Irregardless': Multimedia Aboriginal Humour." Fletcher Challenge Theatre, Simon Fraser University, Vancouver. 14 Mar. 2013. Lecture.

---. *Miss Chief: Justice of the Piece. Two-Spirit Acts: Queer Indigenous Performance.* Ed. Jean O'Hara. Toronto: Playwrights Canada, 2013. 71–89. Print.

---. "Q&A: Kent Monkman on the Calgary Stampede, Castors and More." Interview by Leah Sandals. *Canadian Art.* Canadian Art Foundation, 12 Aug. 2013. Web. 24 Aug. 2015.

Moreno, Edgardo. *Spine of the Mother.* 15 Sept. 2015. Print.

Morris, Kate. "Making Miss Chief: Kent Monkman Takes on the West." *American Indian Magazine* (Spring 2011): n. pag. Web. 17 Sept. 2013.

Moses, Daniel David. "A Bridge Across Time: About Ben Cardinal's *Generic Warriors and No-Name Indians.*" *Aboriginal Drama and Theatre.* Ed. Rob Appleford. Toronto: Playwrights Canada, 2005. 140–43. Print.

Muñoz, José Esteban. *Cruising Utopia: The Then and There of Queer Futurity.* New York: New York UP, 2009. Print.

Nabokov, Peter, ed. *Native American Testimony: An Anthology of Indian and White Relations: First Encounter to Dispossession.* Rev. ed. New York: Penguin, Putnam, 1981. Print.

National Arts Centre. *Death of a Chief.* Ottawa: National Arts Centre, spring 2009. Print.

National Gallery of Canada. "The Impact of Sexuality on Aboriginal Sexuality." *Meet the Artist: Kent Monkman.* National Gallery of Canada, n.d. Web. 13 Aug. 2015.

Nestruck, J. Kelly. "Shakespeare Done Right and Wrong." *Globe and Mail* 8 March 2008: R6. Print.

Nolan, Yvette. "Aboriginal Theatre in Canada: An Overview." *National Arts Centre.* National Arts Centre, Sept. 2010. Web. 7 Dec. 2015.

---. "*Death of a Chief*: An Interview with Yvette Nolan." Interview by Sorouja Moll. *Canadian Shakespeares*. Canadian Adaptations of Shakespeare Project, 7 Dec. 2009. Web. 3 March 2016.

---. "Director's Note." *Death of a Chief*. Ottawa: National Arts Centre, spring 2008. Print.

---. Personal interview by Ric Knowles. Toronto. 29 June 2006.

Nolan, Yvette, and Kennedy C. MacKinnon. *Death of a Chief*. *The Shakespeare's Mine: Adapting Shakespeare in Anglophone Canada*. Ed. Ric Knowles. Toronto: Playwrights Canada, 2009: 379–427. Print.

Nye, Joseph S. *Soft Power: The Means to Success in World Politics*. New York: PublicAffairs, 2004. Print.

O'Hara, Jean. Introduction. *Two-Spirit Acts: Queer Indigenous Performance*. Ed. O'Hara. Toronto: Playwrights Canada, 2013. xix–xxii. Print.

Ouzounian, Richard. "*Julius Caesar* Doesn't Work in Indian Setting." *The Toronto Star*. Star Media Group, 7 March 2008. Web. 3 March 2016.

Overmyer, Eric, and Seth Fisher. *Saints and Strangers*. Trans. Jesse Bowman Bruchac. 2016. Unpublished screenplay.

"Paris Colonial Exposition." *Wikipedia*. Wikimedia Foundation, n.d. Web. 6 Feb. 2016.

Parker, Barbara L. "The Whore of Babylon and Shakespeare's *Julius Caesar*." *Studies in English Literature, 1500–1900* 35. 2 (1995): 251–69. Print.

Pastor, Monica. "Review of *The Book of Jessica*." *Performing Arts in Canada* 26:1 (1990): 36–38. Print.

"Paula Ross." *The Canadian Encyclopedia*. Historica Canada, 25 Feb. 2015. Web. 13 Nov. 2015.

Pisani, Michael V. "From Hiawatha to Wa-Wan: Musical Boston and the Uses of Native American Lore." *American Music* 19.1 (2001): 39–50. Print.

Preston, Jennifer. "Weesageechak Begins to Dance: Native Earth Performing Arts Inc." *Native Life, Native Theatre, Native Earth*. Toronto: Native Earth Performing Arts, 2008. 4–23. Print.

Rath, Richard. "Hearing Wampum: The Senses, Mediation, and the Limits of Analogy." *Colonial Mediascapes: Sensory Worlds of the Early Americas*. Ed. Matt Cohen and Jeffrey Glover. Lincoln, NE: U of Nebraska P, 2014. 290–321. Print.

Reder, Deanna. "Âcimisowin as Theoretical Practice: Autobiography as Indigenous Intellectual Tradition." Diss. University of British Columbia, 2007. Print.

Rifkin, Mark. *The Erotics of Sovereignty: Queer Native Writing in the Era of Self-Determination*. Minneapolis: U of Minnesota P, 2012. Print.

---. *When Did Indians Become Straight: Kinship, the History of Sexuality, and Native Sovereignty*. Oxford: Oxford UP, 2011. Print.

Roberts, Diane. "Creation of Aboriginal Work." Talking Stick Festival, Vancouver. 20 Feb. 2014. Panel.

Robinson, Dylan. "Enchantment's Irreconcilable Connection: Listening to Anger, Being Idle No More." *Performance Studies in Canada*. McGill-Queen's UP, 2016. Forthcoming. Print.

Ross, Paula. Telephone interview with Michelle Olson. 20 Sept. 2015.

Roy, Susan. "A History of the Site: The Kitsilano Indian Reserve." *Digital Natives*. Catalogue. Vancouver: Other Sights for Artists' Projects Association, 2011. Print.

Saints and Strangers. Screenplay by Eric Overmyer and Seth Fisher. Trans. Jesse Bowman Bruchac. Dir. Paul A. Edwards. National Geographic Channel, 2015. Television.

Sandals, Leah. "Christi Belcourt Q & A: On *Walking With Our Sisters*." *Canadian Art*. Canadian Art Foundation, 7 July 2014. Web. 15 Oct. 2015.

Schofield, Hugh. "Human Zoos: When Real People Eere Exhibits." *BBC News Magazine*. British Broadcasting Corporation, 27 Dec. 2011.Web. 13 Nov. 2015.

Sedgewick, Eve. "Paranoid Reading and Reparative Reading, Or, You're So Paranoid, You Probably Think This Essay is About You." *Touching Feeling: Affect, Performativity, Pedagogy*. Durham, NC: Duke UP, 2003. 123–51. Print.

Shakespeare, William. *Julius Caesar*. Folio 1, 1623. *Internet Shakespeare Editions*. Internet Shakespeare Editions, n.d. Web. 3 March 2016.

Simpson, Audra, and Andrea Smith. Introduction. *Theorizing Native Studies*. Ed. Simpson and Smith. Durham, NC: Duke UP, 2014. 10–39. Print.

Simpson, Leanne. " 'Bubbling Like a Beating Heart': Reflections on Nishnaabeg Poetic and Narrative Consciousness." *Indigenous Poetics in Canada*. Ed. Neal McLeod. Waterloo, ON: Wilfred Laurier UP, 2014. 107–19. Print.

---. "Circles Upon Circles Upon Circles." *The Arthur* 2 Sep. 2011: 3. Print.

---. *Dancing On Our Turtle's Back: Stories of Nishnaabeg Re-Creation, Resurgence and a New Emergence*. Winnipeg: Arbeiter Ring, 2011. Print.

---. *The Gift is in the Making: Anishinaabeg Stories*. Winnipeg: HighWater Press, 2013. Print.

---. "Nogojiwanong: The Place at the Foot of the Rapids." *Lighting the Eighth Fire: The Liberation, Resurgence, and Protection of Indigenous Nations.* Ed. Simpson. Winnipeg: Arbeiter Ring, 2008. 205–12. Print.

Simpson, Leanne Betasamosake, with Edna Manitowabi. "Theorizing Resurgence from Within Nishnaabeg Thought." *Centering Anishinaabeg Studies: Understanding the World through Stories.* Ed. Jill Doerfler, Niigaanwewidam James Sinclair, and Heidi Kiiwetnepinesiik Stark. East Lansing, MI, and Winnipeg: Michigan State UP and U of Winnipeg P, 2013. 279–93. Print.

Singhal, Amit. "Zeitgeist 2012: What Piqued your Curiosity this Year?" *Google Official Blog.* Google, 12 Dec. 2012. Web. 26 Aug. 2015.

Sluman, Norma. *Poundmaker.* Toronto: Ryerson Press, 1967. Print.

Starr, Floyd Favel. "The Theatre of Orphans." *Aboriginal Drama and Theatre.* Ed. Rob Appleford. Toronto: Playwrights Canada, 2005. 32–36. Print.

Su-Feh, Lee. *Folk and Palace.* Su-Feh, 2008. Web. 5 Nov. 2015.

Tatonetti, Lisa. *The Queerness of Native American Literature.* Minneapolis: U of Minnesota P, 2014. Print.

Taylor, Drew Hayden. "Alive and Well: Native Theatre in Canada." *American Indian Theater in Performance: A Reader.* Ed. Hanay Geiogamah and Jaye T. Darby. Los Angeles: UCLA American Indian Studies Center, 2000. 256–64. Print.

Testickle, Miss Chief Eagle. "Interview with Miss Chief." Interview by Cathy Mattes. *The Triumph of Miss Chief.* Ed. David Liss and Shirley J. Madill. Hamilton, ON: Art Gallery of Hamilton, 2008. 107–10. Print.

Titley, Brian. *A Narrow Vision: Duncan Campbell Scott and the Administration of Indian Affairs in Canada.* Vancouver: U of British Columbia P, 2011. Print.

Tollon, Marie. "Accessing and Healing One's Lineage Through Dance: A Conversation with Rosy Simas." *Triple Dog Dare.* ODC Theater, 29 Sept. 2015. Web. 24 Nov. 2015.

"Treaty Annuity Payments." *Aboriginal Affairs and Northern Development Canada.* Government of Canada, 15 Sept. 2010. Web. 27 April 2015.

Tulk, Janice Esther. "Cultural Revitalization and Mi'kmaq Music-Making: Three Newfoundland Drum Groups." *Newfoundland and Labrador Studies* 22.1 (2007): n. pag. Web. 9 Nov. 2015.

Turtle Gals Performance Ensemble. *The Scrubbing Project. Staging Coyote's Dream: An Anthology of First Nations Drama in English Volume II.* Ed. Monique Mojica and Ric Knowles. Toronto: Playwrights Canada, 2008. 323–66. Print.

United Nations. *United Nations Declaration on the Rights of Indigenous Peoples. United Nations*. United Nations, March 2008. Web. 25 Oct. 2015.

Vancouver Opera. "Synopsis." *The Magic Flute*. Vancouver: Vancouver Opera, 2007. Print.

Vancouver Opera. "Synopsis." *The Magic Flute*. Vancouver: Vancouver Opera, 2013. Print.

Voyageur, Cora. *Fire-Keepers of the Twenty-First Century: First Nations Women Chiefs*. Montréal: McGill-Queens UP, 2008. Print.

Weaver, Jace. Public address. First Nations House, University of Toronto, 11 Nov. 2004.

---. *That the People Might Live: Native American Literatures and Native American Community*. New York: Oxford UP, 1997. Print.

Weimann, Robert. *Author's Pen and Actor's Voice: Playing and Writing in Shakespeare's Theatre*. Cambridge: Cambridge UP, 2000. Print.

" 'Welcome figure' goes up on seawall as sign of ownership." *CBC News*. CBC-Radio Canada, 30 Aug. 2006. Web. 15 Jan. 2016.

Wesley, Saylesh. "Twin-Spirited Woman: Sts'iyóye smestíyexw slhá:li." *Transgender Studies Quarterly* 1.3 (2014): 338–51. Print.

Wilson, Alex. "How We Find Ourselves: Identity Development and Two-Spirit People." *Harvard Educational Review* 66.2 (1996): 303–17. Print.

---. "N'tacimowin inna nah': Coming Into Two-Spirit Identities." Diss. Harvard, 2007. Print.

Wilson, Richard. " 'Is This a Holiday?' Shakespeare's Roman Carnival." *English Literary History* 54.1 (1987): 31–44. Print.

Wunker, Erin. "The. Women. The Subject(s) of *The Unnatural and Accidental Women* and *Unnatural and Accidental*." *Theatre Research in Canada* 31.2 (2010): 164–81. Print.

Yogaretnam, Shaamini. "Portrait of John Ralston Saul Unveiled at Rideau Hall by Artist Kent Monkman." *The Ottawa Citizen*. Postmedia, 17 Dec. 2012. Web. 15 June 2015.

Young, Biloine W., and Melvin Leo Fowler. *Cahokia, the Great Native American Metropolis*. Champaign, IL: U of Illinois P, 2000. Print.

NOTES ON CONTRIBUTORS

Tara Beagan writes, directs, produces, and acts in theatre. She grew up in a story-loving home. Her Ntlaka'pamux mom has always been an avid reader, and her Irish Canadian dad took her to the library weekly. Her older sister Rebecca (now a teacher) taught her the alphabet after learning it in kindergarten, and her younger brother Patrick (lighting designer/theatre administrator) created worlds and characters with her, sharing an interest in enacting stories. She is a proud auntie to Diana and Owen. Tara is now happy in work with her love, Andy Moro, co-helming Indigenous arts activist company ARTICLE 11. More work credits can be found at tarabeagan.com.

Jill Carter (Anishinaabe/Ashkenazi) is a Toronto-based theatre practitioner and Assistant Professor with the Centre for Drama, Theatre and Performance Studies; the Transitional Year Programme; and the Aboriginal Studies Program at the University of Toronto. Jill's research and praxis base themselves in the mechanics of story creation (devising and dramaturgy), the processes of delivery (performance on the stage and on the page), and the mechanics of affect. To complement her scholarly work and artistic praxis, Jill currently serves on the editorial board of *alt.theatre: cultural diversity and the stage*, the executive board of the Indigenous Performing Arts Alliance (IPAA), the executive board of the Canadian Association for Theatre Research (CATR), and the committee of First Story Toronto at Native Canadian Centre of Toronto. She still performs when she can, studies clown and bouffant, eats fire for fun, and enjoys guiding Indigenous history tours in the greater Toronto area.

David Geary is of Māori (Taranaki iwi) and European blood, originally from New Zealand, and now a citizen of Canada. He is a writer, director, dramaturg, filmmaker, and educator. He teaches at Capilano University, North Vancouver, in the Indigenous Independent Digital Filmmaking, Documentary, and Communications programs. He also teaches playwriting at the Playwrights Theatre Centre and tweets haiku @gearsgeary.

Carol Greyeyes is a member of the Muskeg Lake Cree Nation in Saskatchewan. She is the former artistic director of the Centre for Indigenous Theatre (CIT) and the founding principal of the Indigenous Theatre School in Toronto, Canada. Carol holds a BFA and B.Ed. from the University of Saskatchewan and an M.F.A. from York University. Carol was on the faculty of the Aboriginal Screenwriters at The Banff Centre and has taught theatre for First Nations University of Canada, the University of Regina, and the University of Saskatchewan, where she is now an Assistant Professor in the Department of Drama and the coordinator of the new Certificate of Proficiency *wîchêhtowin*: Aboriginal Theatre Program in addition to maintaining her professional acting career.

Michael Greyeyes (Plains Cree) is an actor, director, and educator. Selected directing credits include *A Soldier's Tale* (Signal), *Pimooteewin* (Soundstreams Canada), *Almighty Voice and His Wife* (Native Earth Performing Arts), *The River* (Nakai Theatre), and *Seven Seconds* (imagineNATIVE). In 2010 he founded Signal Theatre to create trans-disciplinary work pushing the boundaries of contemporary Indigenous performance.

Falen Johnson is Mohawk and Tuscarora from Six Nations (Bear Clan). She is a writer, dramaturge, and actor. Her first play, *Salt Baby*, has been staged with Native Earth Performing Arts, Planet IndigenUS, the Next Stage Festival, and the Globe Theatre. Selected theatre acting credits include *The Only Good Indian . . .* (Turtle Gals Performance Ensemble), *Triple Truth, A Very Polite Genocide* (Native Earth), *Death of a Chief* (Native Earth/National Arts Centre), *Tombs of the Vanishing Indian* (Native Earth/red diva), *The Ecstasy of Rita Joe*

(Western Canada Theatre/National Arts Centre), *The River* (Nakai Theatre), *Tout Comme Elle* (Necessary Angel/Luminato), and *Where the Blood Mixes* (Saskatchewan Native Theatre Company). Falen is a graduate of the George Brown Theatre School. She is the former playwright-in-residence at Native Earth Performing Arts and the Blyth Festival Theatre. She is the 2015 recipient of the OAC Emerging Aboriginal Artist Award.

Michelle La Flamme is Métis on her mom's side and Creek on her dad's side and comes from a long line of storytellers. She grew up in the unceded Coast Salish territory known as Vancouver. She has been involved in social justice and teaching in post-secondary institutions for over two decades. She is passionate about performance and storytelling. Her research areas are contemporary Canadian literature and Indigenous performance. In 2006 she completed her doctoral degree at UBC and was awarded the department prize for her dissertation. In addition to having taught at SFU and UBC, she has been fortunate to have been a guest lecturer in Germany, the Netherlands, and Poland. She is excited about the book she is publishing with Wilfrid Laurier University Press: *Living, Writing and Staging Racial Hybridity.* She is equally thrilled to have recently become a grandmother.

Jani Lauzon (Métis) is a three-time Dora Mavor Moore Award–nominated actress, a three-time Juno-nominated singer/songwriter, and a Gemini Award–winning puppeteer. Jani has countless theatre, film, and radio credits to her name. Memorable theatre appearances include Cordelia/Fool in *King Lear* and Yvette in *Mother Courage* (NAC English Theatre), Shylock in *The Merchant of Venice* (SITR), and the Servant in *Blood Wedding* (Modern Times). Television guest appearances include *Hard Rock Medical*, *Destiny Ridge*, and *Conspiracy of Silence*.

She is a former artistic director of the Centre for Indigenous Theatre, was on the artistic directorate of Native Earth Performing Arts, and was the co-managing artistic director for Turtle Gals Performance Ensemble for ten years. Her company Paper Canoe Projects supports the creation and production of her original work.

Andréa Ledding was born and raised in Treaty 6 territory and counts Batoche survivors and kinship to Pauline Johnson amidst the branches of her family tree, but considers her identity complex and has currently settled on the term "northern hemisphere" since she is equally proud of all her relations. She is a photojournalist, poet, playwright, writer, editor, freelancer, and arts practitioner based out of Saskatoon, Saskatchewan, where she has raised her numerous offspring. She recently received her M.F.A. in Writing and her M.A. in English at the University of Saskatchewan, during which time her play *Dominion* opened the twenty-fifth annual Weesageechak Begins to Dance Festival in Toronto; a version of which went on to be excerpted into a ten-minute piece for Watermark Theatre's *Canada 300* cross-country tour. She was also awarded the Dick and Mary Edney Masters Scholarship for International Understanding through the Humanities & Fine Arts for her creative thesis, *Flett*, which explored first contact in three languages, including what remains of the Beothuk language. Her poetry, fiction, and creative non-fiction have won awards and honours including the John V. Hicks Long Manuscript Award and the Lush Triumphant Prize from *subTerrain*.

Daniel David Moses is a Delaware from the Six Nations Reserve in southern Ontario. His plays include *Coyote City*, a nominee for the 1991 Governor General's Literary Award for Drama; his most travelled, *Almighty Voice and His Wife*; and the James Buller Award–winner *The Indian Medicine Shows*. His newest books are *A Small Essay on the Largeness of Light and Other Poems* (2012) and Oxford University Press's *An Anthology of Canadian Native Literature in English*, of which he is a founding co-editor (2013). In 2015 he was awarded the Ontario Arts Council's Aboriginal Arts Award. He teaches as an associate professor and a Queen's National Scholar in the Dan School of Drama and Music, Queen's University, Kingston, Ontario.

Marrie Mumford (Métis-Chippewa Cree) has been the Canada Research Chair in Aboriginal Arts and Literature at Trent University since January 2004, where she is an associate professor and the director of a two-year Indigenous Performance Studies program that she initiated at Trent in 2005, the first such program at a Canadian university. In addition, she is the artistic director of Nozhem First Peoples Performance Space, also the first theatre dedicated to Indigenous performance at a Canadian university. From 1995–2003, Mumford was the first artistic director of the Aboriginal Arts Program at The Banff Centre, negotiated as a partnership by the Aboriginal Film and Video Art Alliance, guided by artists such as Jeanette Armstrong, Maria Campbell, and Alanis Obomsawin to name a few.

Marrie received her M.F.A. in Theatre at Brandeis University, working with Morris Carnovsky, a founding member of the Group Theater and a first-generation Stanislavsky teacher in the United States. During her professional theatre career that spanned over forty years as an actor, director, producer, and teacher, Marrie performed the role of Ersilia in Pirandello's *To Clothe the Naked* at Hart House and Marguerite Riel in Jean Gascon's production of *Riel* at the NAC. She studied in New York acting studios and was invited by Herbert Berghof to audit the playwrights' program that was held in the theatre of the HB Playwrights Foundation. She worked with Native Earth and Debajehmujig Theatre, collaborating with artists such as Tomson Highway, Larry Lewis, Daniel David Moses, and Beatrice Culleton-Mosionier.

Starr Muranko is a dancer/choreographer and Artistic Associate with Raven Spirit Dance. Her featured choreographic work includes *Spine of the Mother* and *before7after*, which have been presented at the Dance Centre, Dancing on the Edge, Talking Stick Festival, Crimson Coast Dance Society, and the Weesageechak Begins to Dance Festival. She is a proud member of the Dancers of Damelahamid and has toured internationally with this group to New Zealand, Peru, Ecuador, and participated in several of the 2010 Winter Olympic Games performances.

Starr holds a B.F.A. in Dance/Cultural Studies from Simon Fraser University's School for the Contemporary Arts and has trained and performed internationally at the School of Performing Arts at the University of Ghana, as well as presented her dance research at the World Indigenous Peoples Conference in Education (WIPCE) and the Dance Alliance-Americas

Conference. As a dance educator she has taught dance classes and workshops through the Native Education College, Roundhouse Community Arts & Recreation Centre, and ArtStarts in BC schools. Starr was a key member of the Roots Research and Creation Collective project *Exploring the Rights of the First Nations Child through the Arts: Our Dreams Matter Too* in Attawapiskat, Ontario, and was choreographer for the production *Guardians of the Muskeg* at the opening of Kattawapiskak Elementary School in 2014.

Starr honours and celebrates her mixed ancestry of Cree/Métis and German in all of her work and is the founding artistic director of Starrwind Dance Projects. For more information, visit www.starrwind.com.

Michelle Olson is a member of the Tr'ondëk Hwëch'in First Nation (Yukon) and Artistic Director of Raven Spirit Dance. She studied dance at the University of New Mexico with Bill Evans (contemporary) and Andrew Garcia (Pueblo Social Dances), The Banff Centre for the Arts in Aboriginal Dance under the direction of Marrie Mumford and Alejandro Ronceria, and furthered her performance training with Full Circle: First Nations Performance as an ensemble member under the direction of David MacMurray Smith and Margo Kane. Through her studies with the Laban/Bartenieff & Somatic Studies International, she received her certification in movement analysis.

Michelle works in areas of dance, theatre, and opera as a choreographer, performer, and movement coach and her work has been seen on stages across Canada. Selected choreographic credits include *Northern Journey* (Raven Spirit Dance), *Gathering Light* (Raven Spirit Dance), Mozart's *The Magic Flute* (Vancouver Opera), *The Ecstasy of Rita Joe* (Western Canada Theatre/National Arts Centre), *Death of a Chief* (Native Earth Performing Arts/National Arts Centre), *Ashes on the Water* (Neworld Theatre/Raven Spirit Dance), and *Evening in Paris* (Raven Spirit Dance). She is the recipient of the inaugural Vancouver International Dance Festival Choreographic Award. Her current projects are taking her overseas to New Zealand and Australia.

Dylan Robinson is a Stó:lō scholar who holds the Canada Research Chair in Indigenous Arts at Queen's University, located on the traditional lands of the Haudenosaunee and Anishinaabe peoples. His research focuses upon the sensory politics of Indigenous activism and the arts, and questions how Indigenous sovereignty and settler colonialism are embodied and spatialized in public space. éystexwes shxwelméxwelh sxelá:ls. His current research documents the history of contemporary Indigenous public art (including sound art and social arts practices) across North America. He is the co-editor of *Opera Indigene: Re/presenting First Nations and Indigenous Cultures* (Ashgate Press, 2011) and *Arts of Engagement: Taking Aesthetic Action in and beyond the Truth and Reconciliation Commission of Canada* (Wilfrid Laurier University Press, 2016).

June Scudeler (Métis) received her Ph.D. in English from the University of British Columbia. She used Cree methodologies to analyze how Tomson and René Highway and Kent Monkman use their art not only to combat racism and homophobia, but more importantly to show the survivance and vibrancy of Indigenous ways of knowing. Her work has been published in *Queer Indigenous Studies: Critical Interventions in Theory, Politics, and Literature* (University of Arizona Press), *Studies in Canadian Literature, Native American and Indigenous Studies*, and *American Indian Culture and Research Journal*.

Jason Woodman Simmonds is Métis. He lives in Salmon Arm, British Columbia, with his wife, Barbara, and his two sons, Jakob and Luke. Since completing his doctorate at the University of New Brunswick in 2011, he has focused on the development of community-based solutions to complex, interconnected issues in Aboriginal governance, economy, policy, land use, health, and education. He is the owner and director of Simmonds Research Consulting.

Drew Hayden Taylor is an award-winning playwright, novelist, journalist, filmmaker, and storyteller. He has done practically everything from performing stand-up comedy at the Kennedy Centre in Washington, DC, to serving as Artistic Director of Canada's premiere Native theatre company, Native Earth Performing Arts. 2016 saw the publication of his twenty-eighth book, *The Best of "Funny, You Don't Look Like One,"* and he is currently enjoying a stint at Wilfrid Laurier University as their writer-in-residence. Taylor lives in the community where he was born, Curve Lake First Nation.

Ric Knowles is a settler dramaturge, director, editor, and scholar, as well as Professor of Theatre Studies at the University of Guelph, co-editor (with Monique Mojica) of the two volumes *of Staging Coyote's Dream: An Anthology of First Nations Drama in English,* and member of the Chocolate Woman Collective.

Yvette Nolan is a playwright, director, and dramaturg. Her plays include *The Unplugging, Annie Mae's Movement, Job's Wife,* and *BLADE.* She is the editor of *Beyond the Pale: Dramatic Writing from First Nations Writers and Writers of Colour,* and of *Refractions: Solo,* with Donna-Michelle St Bernard. From 2003–2011, she served as Artistic Director of Native Earth Performing Arts. Her book *Medicine Shows,* about Indigenous theatre in Canada, was published in 2015 by Playwrights Canada Press. She is Artistic Associate with Signal Theatre.

INDEX

25th Street Theatre 101, 141

A

Abenaki 119–21
Aboriginal
  ancestry 221
  comedy 161
  communities 173, 180, 194–95
  self-government 189
  self-representation 187
  voices 178
  wares and symbols 164
  worldview, traditional 197
aboriginality 13–14, 17, 186–88
abundance 9, 24
abuses 48, 65, 173, 193, 257
  alcohol 107
  elder 48
  sexual 160
activism 221
Act IV Theatre 75, 82
adaptation 8, 16, 167–68, 177, 180, 194, 278
adultery 53, 59
AIDS Action Now! 206
alcoholism 53, 160, 166
Allen, Paula Gunn 55
alliances, intertribal 171

Almighty Voice and His Wife (Moses)
  118, 277
Alvarez-Acosta, Jhaimy 148–49, 151, 157
American Indian Movement 185, 258
"Am I Next?" movement 221–22, 245
amnesia, civic 23
Amnesty International 216
ancestors 8, 19, 34, 36, 40–41, 43, 51–52,
  80, 84–85, 94, 166
Anishinaabe 34, 37, 45, 53, 66–68, 74, 77,
  79, 80, 81, 86, 127, 164, 226, 264, 270
Annex Theatre 54, 75
Annie Mae's Movement (Nolan) 258
apathy 53, 216
apparitions *See* ghosts
Aquash, Anna Mae 258–59
Aria (Highway) 54
art, contemporary Indigenous 24
ARTICLE 11 116, 126–30
artifacts 14, 18, 127
Arts and Antiques magazine 251
Assembly of First Nations 185–86
assimilation 34, 190, 212
Association for Native Development in the
  Performing and Visual Arts (ANDPVA)
  71–73, 77
audience, implicated 143, 145, 161, 192,
  214, 224, 229–31, 244, 272, 274, 281–82

authority
  cultural 176
  local 189
  representational 176
Awasikan Theatre 72
*Ayum-ee-aawach Oomama-mowan: Speaking
  to Their Mother* (Belmore) 13

B

The Baby Blues (Taylor) 163
Banff Centre 85
Battery Opera 272
BC Hydro 12, 28–29
Beagan, Tara 3, 126, 128–30, 260
Berdache 203
The Berlin Blues (Taylor) 164, 166
Berlin Olympics 274–75
Bill C-31 181, 186, 202
birds 165
bisexuality 197, 206
Black, Jaime 218
blood quantum 195, 198, 200
bones 4, 63, 150, 272
The Book of Jessica (Griffiths and
  Campbell) 254
The Bootlegger Blues (Taylor) 158, 161–62
boundaries 20, 22, 24, 32, 211
  ethnic 116
  international 21
  political 195
  provincial 136
boundary identification 23
Boyden, Joseph 270
braids 235–36, 240–42, 254
Brandeis University 2, 69–71, 75, 80
Brebeuf's Ghost (Moses) 262
Brenna, Dwayne 112
Brook, Peter 74

Bruchac, Jesse Bowman 120–21
Buddies in Bad Times Theatre 167–68,
  172, 187
Buffalo Bill's Wild West Show 276
Buried Child (Shepard) 118
Bush, George W. 173
The Buz'gem Blues (Taylor) 164

C

Caesar's ghost 191–93
Campbell, Maria 3, 104–5, 254
Canada's National Ballet School 115
Canadian Indian Act 198, 200
Canadian state 21, 172, 177, 186–88,
  195–96
capitalism, free-trade 246
Cardinal, Douglas 35
Carnovsky, Morris 2, 69–70, 78
Casey House 206
Catalyst Theatre 79, 106
Catholicism 87, 199
Catlin, George 203, 207
celebration 13, 73, 203, 245, 251, 263
Centre for Indigenous Theatre 3, 72, 108
ceremony 66–68, 79–80, 133–35, 137, 151,
  154–55, 157, 214, 219, 224–26, 244, 251,
  256–57, 262, 263
  eternal 157
  performative 134
  religious 9
Chaikin, Joseph 74, 90
Chan, Marjorie 94
Charlie, Arizona 276
Chien, Sammy 155
Chocolate Woman Dreams the Milky Way
  (Mojica) 248
choreography 9, 155
Christianity 55, 208, 211

church 87, 161, 255, 257, 259
circles 3, 39, 55, 66–67, 163, 171, 198, 201,
    222, 225, 247–49, 252, 255, 274, 279–81
clans 66, 181–82
cleansing 47, 144
Clements, Marie 4, 217, 227–30, 232, 234,
    239, 242–44, 260
climate change 246
clowns 89, 110
Cody, William Frederick 276
Cohen, Leonard 251
collaboration 4, 8, 19, 130, 147, 155
colonialism 36, 39, 93, 119, 177, 192, 195,
    199, 276–78, 281–82
colonization 86, 91, 148, 167, 172–73, 176,
    178, 182, 185–86, 188, 190, 198, 201, 205,
    211–13
  sexual 198, 213
commemoration 216, 224, 227, 245
commodification 41
communication 151–52, 201
communion 52, 262
communities
  collective 220
  intertribal 194, 196
  isolated 100
Compagnie Danse Nyata Nyata 280
compassion 46, 51, 63, 211
conflation 29, 214, 235, 239, 245
conflict 43, 124, 126, 137, 200–201
conquest 41, 55
consciousness, collective 102, 276, 279
consecration 143
contact, colonial 91, 173, 178, 183, 195,
    199, 203, 278
corporeality 214, 218, 221, 227–28, 230,
    232, 238
  abject 223–24, 227
  absent 223–24, 226–27

imagined 226
Cortés, Hernán 55
cosmology 147, 244
Covent Garden (Tahn) 102
Coyote and the Shadow People (Percé) 255
Coyote City (Moses) 254, 257
creation stories 33–36, 61, 64, 252
Cree 1, 2, 19, 68, 71, 77, 81, 82, 99, 101,
    102, 106, 108, 111–13, 115, 126, 136, 141,
    196, 197–99, 200, 205–08, 212, 213, 226,
    267, 270, 272, 274, 277
critics 143, 173, 187
Croce, Cesare Giulio 47
cultural appropriation 268
cultural milieu 182
cultural vacuum 253
cultural vitality 25, 258
curriculum 72, 114, 118, 140
Cusick, Suzanne 14
Cypress Hills 68–69

D

dance 52–53, 80, 85, 99, 102, 108, 118–19,
    155, 203, 263–70, 272–75, 280, 283
  traditional 100
  war 268
Dancers of Damelahamid 272
Dancing Sky Theatre 141
"Dead Indians" 273, 278–79, 281
Dead White Writer on the Floor (Taylor) 260
death 61, 94, 166, 178, 193, 215–16, 228,
    230–31, 251, 258, 261
Death of a Chief (Nolan and MacKinnon)
    93, 167, 169–79, 181–83, 185–91, 193–
    96, 278
Debajehmujig Creation Centre 115
Debajehmujig Storytellers 3, 75, 91, 161
decolonization 15, 17, 33, 38, 181

degradation 203

denial 183–84

Department of Indian Affairs 183

dependency, abject 41

desire 205, 212, 274, 282

  colonial 18

destruction 41, 47–48, 53, 55, 59

detribalization 199

dialogue 94, 99, 138–39, 230

  intercultural 17

Dispatch: REDress Project (film) 219

disability 264

discrimination 183, 200

disease 42, 53

disempowerment 222

disenfranchisement 176, 182

dissonance 220, 283

diversity 73, 113, 137–38, 217

DNA 117, 149

dolls, cornhusk 131–32

Dominion (Ledding) 139

Dora Mavor Moore Award 85, 91, 93

dreamcatchers 40, 44, 165

The Dress (Benedict) 102

drums 80, 270

Dry Lips Oughta Move to Kapuskasing
  (Highway) 53–54, 59, 159, 249

Dry Streak (Minogue) 139

Dumont, Gabriel 68

dysfunction 53–55, 59

E

earth 41, 53, 57–58, 152, 168, 172, 178, 279

effigy 241

EGALE Leadership Award 206

Elder James Buller 3, 72–74, 108

elders 8, 47–48, 60, 62–63, 66–67, 79, 84–
  85, 145, 148, 152, 157, 161, 164, 226, 250

Elder Sam Osawamick 92

Electra (Euripides) 75–76

Elizabeth I 183–84

embodiment 61, 149, 207, 219, 223, 228,
  240, 248, 252, 257, 259, 261

empathy 17, 215, 220

empowerment 245

endurance 29, 34, 61, 65, 198

energy

  psychic 261

  sacred 219

  unseen 57

entertainment 143, 262, 276

epiphany 87, 160

epistemology 14, 198

erotics 200, 207

essentialism, strategic 210, 214

Eurocentrism 99

Eurydice 255

eu•tha•na•sia (Lauzon) 95

Evans, Tasha Faye 150–53

exclusion 14, 16, 20, 196

experience

  kinaesthetic 222, 226, 245

  transformational 225

Expo 86 28–29

F

Factory Theatre 38, 82, 125

faith 36, 80, 83, 107, 253, 267

famine 33, 47

fareWel (Ross) 259–60

Farm Show, The (Theatre Passe Muraille) 101

Farwell, Arthur 177–78

feasts 66, 77, 79, 135, 203

femininity 47–48, 54–56, 58, 65, 183

Fences (Wilson) 118

Fetal Alcohol Syndrome (FAS) 53

Firehall Arts Centre 165, 228
Fireweed (Merasty) 257
First Peoples' Cultural Council 8
Fisher, Seth 122
Fobister, Waawaate 172, 267
forgiveness 193
Four Winds Theatre 72
fragility 63
fur trade 262

G

Gabe (Bolt) 137
Gabriel Dumont's Wild West Show (National Arts Centre French Theatre) 137
gathering, spaces of 5, 7–8, 77, 100, 133, 214
Gear, Rico 4, 269
gender 180, 197, 199, 213
Generic Warriors and No-Name Indians (Cardinal) 258
generosity 4, 24, 61, 260, 266
genocide 126, 134, 198, 200
cultural 266
survived 70
gentrification 26, 30
George, Dudley 189–90
gestures
unwelcome 5, 15, 17–18, 20, 24–25
welcome 3, 7, 15–18, 20–23, 32, 73, 76, 140, 145, 198, 201, 203, 211–12
ghosts 44, 104, 191, 228, 232, 246–47, 249, 251, 253–61
gift economy 40–41
Gitxsan dance 272
globalization 165
Globe Theatre 141
God and the Indian (Taylor) 165
Godden, Mark 270

gods 50, 112, 165, 252–53
Going Home Star (Godden and Boyden) 270
Gordon Tootoosis Nīkānīwin Theatre (GTNT) 141, 165
Gordon Winter (Williams) 141
governance 43, 48, 181–83
government 9, 40, 84, 88, 174, 185, 190, 200, 216
Canadian 170, 176, 183, 189, 194, 196, 207
colonial 213
provincial 83, 185
Governor General's Literary Award 259
grace 43, 272
grammar of animacy 40, 56
grandmothers 44–45, 54–55, 59, 62, 68, 79–81, 122, 137, 211, 278
gratitude 23, 57, 65
Great Mysteries 80, 144
grief 62–63, 217, 225
Griffiths, Linda 103
Grotowski, Jerzy 74, 90
ground 52, 55, 129, 168–69, 172, 178, 193, 249
Native 167–73, 176, 178, 187–91, 196
Group of Seven 204
Gudirr Gudirr (Marrugeku Theatre) 116–17
guests 11, 14, 16, 28–30, 32, 203, 212–13, 274
Guna 60–62, 130, 248

H

Haida 31,
haka 267–69
halfbreed 124, 126
Halfbreed (Campbell) 71, 85, 104–5, 124, 206, 254

Halfe, Louise 79

hard power 35–36, 40–42, 46–48, 50, 52, 55, 58–59, 62

Harper, Stephen 246, 270

Harris, Mike 190

Haudenosaunee 2, 133, 134, 136

healing 92, 161, 174, 193, 283

Heap of Birds, Edgar 23–24

Heather, Jane 107

Hemeon, George 28–29

heterosexuality 199

hierarchy 181

high theory 35

Highway, René 3, 77

Highway, Tomson 2–3, 53, 71, 75, 83, 85, 102, 159, 166, 205, 208, 249, 251, 267, 269

historiography 178

history
  colonial 202, 205, 207
  oral 72, 80, 85, 148

HIV/AIDS 81, 131, 205–6, 235–36, 240–42, 254

home 16, 18, 43, 45–46, 62, 65, 69, 71, 74, 77, 81, 130, 133–34, 147, 151

homophobia 197

homosexuality 197, 206, 211

hope 4, 7, 12–13, 15, 34, 45–46, 68, 124, 126, 130, 143–44, 193–94, 196, 216, 219–20

hospitality 24, 200, 202, 209

humility 39, 57, 65

humour 2, 78, 158, 160–61, 164–66, 202, 249, 251

hunger 41, 48, 59, 276

Hyland, Frances 104

hymns 207

hypervisibility 31, 244

I

I Call myself Princess (Lauzon) 95–96

iconography 32

identity 6, 10, 21–22, 103–4, 136, 138, 169, 176, 180–81, 191, 196–97, 201, 210, 241, 250
  cultural 2, 101, 108, 166, 196, 208
  legal 186
  national 195

ideology, colonial 205

Idle No More movement 13, 51, 189, 263–64, 269

Île-à-La-Crosse 105–6

imagination 36, 47, 103, 149, 160, 214, 230, 250, 257

immigration 208

impotence 48

imprisonment 94

In a World Created by a Drunken God (Taylor) 165

inclusion 5, 8, 12, 18–20, 28, 30–32, 127

Indian Act 84–85, 176–77, 182, 186, 194, 202

Indianist movement 178

"Indianness" 212, 279

Indigenization 13, 17, 20

Indigenous People's Theatre Association (IPTA) 73

Indigenous rights 3, 208, 213

Indigenous Theatre School (ITS) 109

individuality 229

Indspire Indigenous Achievement Arts Award 206

information age 255

inheritance 42, 252

injustice 37, 48–49
  historical 206

interdependence 191, 208

interpellation, contradictory 199
intertribalism 33, 176, 195
inuksuit 6, 24
irony 163, 249, 265

J

Jarrett, Holly 221
Jean A. Chalmers Choreographic Award 280
Jessica (Griffiths and Campbell) 3, 85, 254
Johnson, Falen 2, 132, 134, 170
Jordan, Gilbert Robert 228
joy 45, 126, 130, 264
judgment 251, 273
Julius Caesar (Shakespeare) 3, 93, 167–69, 172–75, 178–80, 186–87, 190–92, 194, 196, 278

K

Kaha:wi Dance Theatre 266–67
Kalbfleisch, Elizabeth 204
Kane, Margo 115, 166, 264
Keeshig-Tobias, Lenore 255
Kehewin Native Performance 72
Kidd, Gladys 79
Kimbercote Farm 108
Kinew, Wab 270
King, Thomas 6, 163, 278
King Lear (Shakespeare) 94
Kino-nda-niimi Collective 263
kinship 13, 40, 81, 205–6
kippmoojikewin 66
kiyânaw 19
KKK 136
knowledge
   ancestral 56
   cultural 122, 132
   Indigenous (IK) 20, 33, 68, 80, 169

traditional 148, 152, 239, 244
Knowles, Ric 167
Kwak'waka'wakw 9, 16, 213

L

Laban, Rudolf 274–75
Lady of Silences (Starr) 105, 257
La Flamme, Michelle 3
Lafond, Harry J. 110–11, 113
land 31–34, 40, 43, 46, 48, 84, 140, 147, 151–53, 169, 181–82, 187, 189–90, 192, 266
   claims 48, 102, 168–69
language 14, 17, 33–36, 40, 43, 53, 56, 80, 102, 105, 119–21, 123, 136, 138, 140
laughter 76, 99, 158, 160, 162–63, 254, 272
leadership 72, 79, 126, 183
Lee, Stan 261
Lewis, Larry 3, 77, 82, 161
L'Hirondelle, Cheryl 19–20
Lil'wat7úl 29,
longhouses 6, 16, 132
loss 78, 85, 88, 94, 217
Louis Riel (Somers) 137
love 33, 35, 37, 45, 52–53, 64–65, 279–80

M

Macdonald, John A. 81
MacDowell, Edward 177
magic 44, 90, 94, 238–39
The Magic Flute (Mozart) 5, 8–11, 16
Magnus Theatre 165
Maliseet 196
Manitoulin Island 75–76, 115, 161
Māori 4, 265, 268
marionettes 51
marriage 70, 78, 136, 179, 202, 211
Marrugeku Theatre 116

Martin, Vera 79
masculinity 179, 183
masks 9, 91, 99, 165, 273, 283
matriarchy 55, 145, 223, 243
Mayflower 117
McArthur, Sera-Lys 129
McLuhan, Marshall 248, 255
McMichael Canadian Art Collection 204
medicine 49, 53, 62, 68, 80, 92, 148, 203, 279
  sacred 226, 259
  western 92
Medicine Line 68, 81
Medicine Wheel 171
Me Funny (Taylor) 166
melancholia 219, 227
memory 34, 41–42, 44–45, 47, 50, 52, 54,
  62–63, 133, 138, 149, 151, 158, 213, 247–48
  ancestral 42, 51
The Merchant of Venice (Shakespeare) 93
mêskanaw 98, 102–3, 111, 113
metaphor 250, 256, 273, 278
Métis 1, 2, 13, 17, 19, 35, 38–40, 42, 87,
  89, 102, 105, 128, 136, 139, 173, 185, 198,
  201, 206, 210, 212, 218, 223, 264
  ancestry 198
  heritage 40
A Midsummer Night's Dream
  (Shakespeare) 187
Miguel, Muriel 90, 102, 234, 242
Mi'kmaq 124, 193, 258
miscarriage 59
Miss Chief Eagle Testickle *See*
  Monkman, Kent
Missing and Murdered Indigenous Women
  (MMIW) 55, 145, 214–30, 235–36, 241,
  244–45
Missing Women Commission of Inquiry
  (2004) 216

Missing Women: Investigation Review
  (2012) 216
mixed-blood 38–39, 76, 200
miyotôtakêwin 201–2, 208, 212–13
miyo-wîcêhtowin 198, 201, 209
moccasins 133, 224, 226–27
Mohawk 2, 77, 102, 133–34, 136, 162, 163,
  189, 266–67,
Mojica, Monique 55, 62, 90, 167, 248
Monkman, Kent 3, 197–213
Moreno, Edgardo 153, 155
Moro, Andy 126, 130
Moscow Art Theatre 69
Mother Courage (National Arts Centre) 94
Mother Earth 147–48, 150, 153–54
mourning 217–18, 224
Mozart, Amadeus 5, 8, 267
multiculturalism 17
Museum of Man 275
music 63, 108, 110, 113, 138, 177, 264
Musqueam 13–14, 24–26, 266, 270,
myth 44, 55, 117, 179, 194, 254, 257

N

Nahwegahbow, Barbra 79
Nakota 129
Nanabozo *See* trickster
Narragansett 120
National Arts Centre (NAC) 3, 94, 115,
  130, 167–68, 170–73, 175, 177, 186, 190,,
  270, 279, 281
National Indian Brotherhood 185
National Museum of the American
  Indian 198
National Theatre School 116
Native Canadian Centre 76, 79–80, 85
Native Earth Performing Arts (NEPA) 2–3,
  73, 76, 82–85, 105, 108, 118, 125–26, 134,

167–68, 170–73, 177–78, 186–88, 193–95, 254

Native Homemaker's Association   183

Native Survival School   104–6, 110

Native Theatre School (NTS)   72, 90, 107–8, 110–12

Nehiyaw   2, 99, 136

Neutral   21

neutrality   91, 93

Night of the Living Dead (Romero)   262

Noh theatre   90

Nolan, Yvette   115, 124, 140, 168, 262

North West Mounted Police   68

nostalgia   219, 227

Nozhem First Peoples Performance Space   2, 66–67, 74

Ntlakapamux   1

Nuu-chah-nulth   28, 29

O

Odawa   2, 80, 90, 92

Oïda, Yoshi   90

Ojibwe   66, 77, 127, 164, 172–73, 196, 256

omnipotence   184

oppression   52, 93

oppressor's gaze   14–15, 19, 188, 245, 271, 274–76, 280, 282

orality   6, 15, 92

  textual   7

Orpheus   255

Ortner, Ines   155

Overmyer, Eric   122–23

P

palace   273–76, 278–81, 283

pan-Indigeneity   168, 226

Paper Wheat (25th Street Theatre)   101, 103

patriarchy   180

Paula Ross Dance Company   280

payment   185, 209

pedagogy   89–90, 116, 123

Pedagogy of the Oppressed (Freire)   72

performative act   221, 223, 227, 231–32

Persephone Theatre   104, 141

pestilence   36, 47

Petun   21

Pickton, Robert   216

Playwrights Guild of Canada   253

Pocahontas   55

Point, Susan   24

politics   84, 179–80, 182

  Canadian   176

Popular Theatre Boot Camp   107

Portrait of the Artist as a Hunter (Monkman)   206

post-colonialism   187

Potawatomi   40, 57, 80

poverty   260, 275

power

  abuses of   92, 173, 193, 199, 274, 276

  artistic   204

  economic   273

  phallic   237

  political   183, 192

pow-wows   164, 193, 212, 267

prayer   92, 94, 207

prejudice   257, 261–62

pride   9, 40, 98, 137, 207, 261–62

Pride and Prejudice and Zombies (film)   261

priests   87, 90

prophecy   85

Prophecy Fog (Lauzon)   95

proscenium   272–73, 279–82

purification   16

Q

Quechua 147, 149
queer 205–6, 211

R

racism 62, 197, 200
  internalized 257
rape 55, 160
Rappahannock 60, 130
Raven Spirit Dance (RSD) 9, 116, 272
reappropriation 64
reciprocity 41, 206
reclamation 33, 36–37, 168, 176–77, 185
reconciliation 5, 12, 17, 189, 191, 193, 270
  spaces of 18
re-connection 148, 153, 195
re-creation 35, 54, 64
redress 24, 43, 217, 220, 244
The REDress Project 214, 218–20, 222,
  225, 244
re-education 56
re-enactment 137, 237
regalia 9, 273
regendering 174, 180
religion 137, 160
religious practices 41
remembrance 213
renaissance 85, 159
  cultural 101
reorientation 277
repetition 90, 94, 192, 250
representation 31, 127, 172, 176, 186,
  205, 280
Reserve-response 18
residential schools 48, 56, 83, 87, 259
resistance 14, 36–37, 42–43, 68–70, 81,
  140, 189, 245

restoration 40, 55, 67
resurgence 38, 43, 66–67, 86, 185
revenge 228, 242–43
reverence 53, 154
The Rez Sisters (Highway) 3, 53, 76–78,
  82–85, 102, 159, 267
Riel, Louis 68, 81, 85, 136–37, 142, 261
ritual 89–90, 151–52, 274
Robert Gill Theatre 62
Robertson, Gregor 17
Robin Hood (Disney) 137
Ross, Paula 280
Round Dance Revolution 51
Royal Canadian Mounted Police (RCMP)
  189–90
Royal Commission on Aboriginal Peoples
  (RCAP) 84
Royal Ontario Museum (ROM) 127–28, 204
Royal Shakespeare Company (RSC) 175
Royal Winnipeg Ballet 249, 270

S

The Sacred Hoop (Gunn) 180
sacrifice 43–45, 59, 61
Saints and Strangers (Overmyer and Fisher)
  117, 120, 122–23
Saskatchewan Native Theatre Company
  (SNTC) *See* Gordon Tootoosis Nīkānīwin
  Theatre
Saskatchewan Playwrights Centre's Spring
  Festival of New Plays 139
savage 122, 203, 276
scatology 251
Schellenberg, August 94, 115
scopophilia 13, 18–19
Scotiabank Dance Centre 273, 280
The Scrubbing Project (Turtle Gals) 38–39, 90
"Second Nations" 267, 269

Secwepemc 36

segregation 18

self-defense 243

self-discovery 101

self-fashioning 167, 194, 196

self-governance 177

Səlílwət 10–11, 17, 25, 29–32

Seven Fires Prophecy 79, 85

Seven Stages of Life Teachings 74, 80

sexuality 197, 199, 201, 205–6

Shaffer, Olivia 156

Shakespeare, William 3, 89, 93, 139–40, 167–68, 172–73, 176, 182, 186–88, 190–91, 195–96, 254

shame 39, 41–43, 48, 137, 139, 275

Shelley, Mary 261

A Side of Dreams (Lauzon) 38–39, 45, 49, 64, 95

Signal Theatre 116, 128

silence 39, 42–45, 50, 66, 88, 95, 105, 143, 145, 176, 178, 181, 188, 257

collective 42

silencing 144–45

Simpson, Leanne 3, 6, 37, 42, 64, 86

Sinatra, Frank 250

Site C Dam 28

Skwxwú7mesh 10–11, 17, 25, 29–32

slavery 55, 262

Smith, Santee 115, 266

smudge, ceremonial 52, 64, 132, 134–35, 144, 215, 226, 270

social justice 69, 216, 245

soft power 4, 35–36, 40, 43, 45–48, 51, 56, 63–65

Something Old, Something New, Something Borrowed, Something Blue (Miguel) 60, 62–63

Soto, Jock 115

sovereignty 3, 6–7, 11–13, 18, 20, 26, 28, 35, 64, 207, 209

Indigenous 5, 15, 29, 35, 64, 199

spaces

ceremonial 63, 217, 224

claimed 271

decolonized 86

dedicated 144

gendered 220

Indigenous 8, 13, 20

multicultural 18

non-Indigenous 15

performative 146, 214, 218

sacred 94, 144, 146, 257

sovereign 7, 10, 13–14, 18, 32

unsafe 24

spectacle 143, 230, 244, 277

speech acts 34–35, 57

Spiderwoman Theater 2, 61, 90, 102

Spine of the Mother (Raven Spirit Dance) 147

Starr, Floyd Favel 105, 177, 258, 274

status 17, 20, 202, 205, 210, 213

status cards 200

St. Bernard, Donna-Michelle 118

steatopygia 275

stereotypes 70, 203, 278

St. John, Michelle 90, 125

Stolen Sisters Report (2004) 216

Stó:lō 1, 6, 10–11, 14, 25, 30, 211

stories 33–34, 37, 41, 79–80, 83–84, 94, 99–100, 102, 138, 140–41, 144, 149–50, 152–54, 157, 229

ancient 255

epic 157

ghost 254

traditional 133

storytellers 36, 61, 63, 104, 256

storytelling, oral 160

Stratford Festival 101
Strombergs, Vinetta 75
Stroumboulopoulos, George 270
The Study/Repast (NAC) 115
subversiveness 175
suicide, potential 231
suicide rates 107
sun dance 84
superiority 93, 182
supernatural 254, 256, 258
superstition 252
supremacy 274
  illusions of 70
surveyance 18
survival 37, 46, 239, 276
survivance 50, 61, 63, 198
Suzuki, Tadashi 74
symbolism 224, 242
synaesthesia 215, 219, 222, 224–27, 232, 245

T

tales
  fairy 46
  folk 46
Tales of an Urban Indian (Dennis) 166
Talking Stick Festival 128
teachings
  cultural 87, 89
  traditional 147–49, 154–55, 192
technology 127, 151, 212, 261
terra nullius 207
territory
  ancestral 20
  artistic 169
  traditional 40, 169, 189
  undefined 260

theatre
  American 89
  Canadian 101, 103, 171, 196
  classical 281
  community 105–6
  Greek 80
  popular 104, 106
Theatre of the Oppressed (Boal) 72
Theatre Passe Muraille 85, 101, 118, 125, 249
theft 37, 41
Third Reich 275
Three Fires Confederacy 80
Thunderstick (Williams) 141
tobacco 67, 80, 152, 226, 259
Tootoosis, Gordon 141
Toronto Fringe festival 143
tradition 11, 20, 80, 85, 90, 114–15, 169, 171–72, 178, 181, 185, 199, 204, 212, 238–39
traditionalism 132
traditions
  cultural 84, 127
  oral 74, 78
  reclaimed 169, 194
  spiritual 254
  theatrical 99
  tribal 183, 195
  western 99, 243
tragedy 50, 80, 94, 165, 189, 228, 257, 264
trail of tears 34
transcendence 63
transformation 52, 85, 143, 235, 237, 239, 243, 271, 274
translation 13–14, 116, 121, 138
transmogrification 243
transubstantiation 243
trauma 38, 43, 87–88, 94, 227

treason 137

tribes 99, 180, 183, 195, 203, 211, 268

trickster 84, 240, 250, 256–57, 259–60, 264–65, 267–70

Tr'ondëk Hwëch'in 9, 276

trophies 59, 235, 240

Trudeau, Justin 270

trust 60, 94, 107

Truth and Reconciliation Commission 216

Truth and Reconciliation Report 263, 266, 270

Tsleil-Waututh 25, 266

Turtle Gals Performance Ensemble 38–39, 94, 166

Turtle Island 117, 195–96

Turtle Mountain 81

Two-Spirit 197–99, 201, 203, 205–8, 211, 213

U

United Nations 126

United Nations Declaration on the Rights of Indigenous Peoples 3, 127

unity 169

universalism 173–74

University of British Columbia (UBC) 13, 24, 198, 267

University of Calgary 73

University of Ottawa 158

University of Saskatchewan 2, 103, 112–13

University of Toronto 82, 130

University of Winnipeg 39

The Unnatural and Accidental Women (Clements) 4, 214, 217, 227–31, 234, 242, 260

unwelcome figures 32

Upsasik Theatre 102, 105, 110, 113

V

Vancouver 2010 Winter Olympics 29

Vancouver East Cultural Centre (Cultch) 228, 266

A Very Polite Genocide (Murray) 134

victimization 222

victims 48, 78, 215, 217, 227, 229, 232–33, 237, 239, 241

fallen 215, 227, 245

imagined 220

intended 232, 243

potential 237, 239

vindication 49

violation, cultural 41

violence 42, 51, 53, 55, 62, 160, 202, 215, 219, 227–28, 237

gendered 216, 221

racialized 217

systemic 216

Virgin Mary 56–57, 95

visibility 100, 205

vision 36, 57, 67, 72, 84, 86, 107–8, 112, 125, 139, 155, 171, 205, 207, 228

voice 60–61, 72, 88, 101, 109, 157

authentic 15

collective 193

disembodied 255

hushed 255

Indigenous 5, 49, 128

political 182, 186

voicelessness 145

Vom Tauwind und der Neuen Freude [*Spring Wind and the New Joy*] (Laban) 274

voyeurism 231

vulnerability 50, 94, 282

W

Walking With Our Sisters (Belcourt) 214, 223, 225, 227, 244

war 36, 173

War Measures Act 70, 189

Watermark Theatre 139

Wa-Wan Press 178

wealth 4, 182

web, tribal 208

Weesageechak *See* trickster

Weesageechak Begins to Dance Festival 62, 96, 139, 167

welcome figures 5, 10–13, 15, 24–31

Wendat 21

Wendigo 78, 262

Whale (Young People's Theatre) 91

What's Left of Us (Many Fingers) 264–65

Where the Blood Mixes (Loring) 259

White Buffalo Youth Lodge 139

wîchêhtowin: Aboriginal Theatre Program 2, 113

Wilson-Raybould, Jody 216

The Winter We Danced (Kino-nds-niimi Collective) 263

The Witch of Niagara (Moses) 110

words
  last 39
  prophetic 196
  wise 39

World Assembly of First Nations (WAFN) 100–101

World War II 189

X

xʷməθkʷəy̓əm 10–11, 17, 25–26, 29–32

RECYCLED
Paper made from recycled material
FSC
www.fsc.org   FSC® C103567

Printed on Enviro 100% post-consumer EcoLogo certified paper, processed chlorine free and manufactured using biogas energy.